$14.00

JUBILEE'S JOURNEY

The Wyattsville Series – Book Two

BETTE LEE CROSBY

JUBILEE'S JOURNEY

Cover design: Damonza.com
Interior formatting by Author E.M.S.

ISBN-13: 978-0-989128-92-6

BENT PINE PUBLISHING
Port St. Lucie, FL

Published in the United States of America

For The Pence Family

Who showed me the joy that comes

with believing.

Jubilee's Journey

The Wyattsville Series – Book Two

As It Was...

On an icy cold November morning in 1956, Bartholomew Jones died in the Poynter Coal Mine. His death came as no surprise to anyone. He was only one of the countless men forever lost to the mine. They were men loved and mourned by their families, but to the world they were faceless, nameless people, not worthy of mention in the *Charleston Times*.

Morning after morning those men descended into the belly of the mountain, into a world of black dust that clung to their skin with a fierceness that no amount of scrubbing could wash away. In the winter the sky was still black when they climbed into the trolley cart that carried them into the mountain. And when they returned twelve hours later, daylight had already come and gone.

None of the men complained. They were the lucky ones, they told one another. They were the ones who slept easy. Their family had food on the table and coal for the stove when winter blasted its way across the ridge of the mountain.

At one time Bartholomew thought he could beat the odds, break the chain of events that carried itself through generation after generation. His daddy had grown up in the mines, starting when he was barely big enough to carry a bucket of scrap coal from the chute to the hopper. His granddaddy had done the same. It was the way of life, a dirty, lung-polluting job handed down from grandfather to father and ultimately to son.

But Bartholomew had different plans.

In 1932 he left home to join the navy. "Go," his daddy said happily. "Go and don't ever look back." A life built on a hunched back and blackened skin was not something any man wished for his son, and even though it meant he might never see the boy again he was glad.

After two months of basic training Bartholomew was assigned to the Norfolk Navy Yard and for the next six years he loaded and unloaded machine parts on the ships that sailed in and out of the port.

Norfolk was where he met and married Ruth.

It was love at first sight. Ruth was in town visiting her sister, and as fate would have it he happened to be standing in back of them while the girls waited to buy tickets to see "The Big Broadcast" with Bob Hope and Dorothy Lamour. To Bartholomew's eye Ruth was far prettier than Dorothy Lamour, and he said so ten minutes after they'd struck up a conversation.

"Aw, go on," she'd said with a smile.

As they eventually made their way down the aisle of the strand, Bartholomew followed the girls. Before they'd gone nine rows in Ruth pointed to a spot with three empty seats together. "Let's sit here," she said. She looked back at Bartholomew, an invitation in her smile.

After the movie Bartholomew took Ruth and her sister, Anita, for ice cream sodas. Before it came time to pay the check, he was in love. Forever, eternally, and deeply in love. With her soft brown eyes and lips that fairly begged to be kissed, Ruth was as warm as a wool coat on a blustery day.

Anita was the exact opposite. She frowned for the entire two hours they lingered over sodas, and on three different occasions tapped her finger against the face of her wristwatch indicating it was time to go. The glares she gave Bartholomew were so icy they froze in midair.

When Bartholomew asked Ruth if she'd like to go to dinner the next evening, Anita spoke up.

"I'll not hear of it!" she snapped. "The Walker girls are not the type to date total strangers!"

"Oh, Anita," Ruth said with a laugh. "Don't be such a fuddy-duddy. Bartholomew's not a stranger. Why, we've spent the entire day with him." She turned to Bartholomew and told him she would be delighted to join him for dinner. From that day on they were inseparable. Two months later, on the day Bartholomew was discharged from the Navy, they were married. Anita, who was Ruth's maid of honor, never once cracked a smile.

Bartholomew got a job making twenty-eight dollars a week at a warehouse where he and thirty-seven other fellows crated replacement parts for tractors. Confident that good times were here to stay, he and Ruth moved into a two-room walk-up and bought a used bedroom set and a brand new radio.

Nine months later the warehouse closed its doors without paying the men their final week's wages.

"Don't worry," Bartholomew told Ruth. "I'll get a job. A week, two at the most."

But other than strength and a willing heart, he had no skills. A month passed, and he found nothing. First they sold the radio; then the bedroom set. After that they moved to a furnished room so small Ruth had to walk sideways to climb onto her side of the bed.

For three months Bartholomew looked for a job. He left the room early in the morning and returned long after dark. He went from door to door asking for work. "I'll do anything," he said, "wash dishes, mop the floor, scrub toilets." But he always got the same answer. "Nothing right now, try again next week." At night he'd drag himself home, ashamed of returning empty-handed but so weary he could barely manage to slide one foot in front of the other.

Ruth stretched what little money they had and made every penny count. She ate the tiniest scraps of food and used a single tea bag for a week, leaving it to soak in the hot water just seconds before pulling it out and setting it aside for the next day. There were no more movies, no dinners at restaurants, no ice cream sodas. Many nights they shared a half can of Campbell's soup. Ruth would eat two or three spoonfuls, then suggest Bartholomew finish the bowl. By that time she had begun to look pale and hollow-eyed. Several mornings in a row she could not hold down even the weak tea she'd brewed. But when Bartholomew asked what was wrong, she simply smiled and shrugged it off.

When he finally insisted, Ruth told him she was carrying a child. That's when Bartholomew made the fateful decision—the decision he swore he'd never make. It was the one place where he knew he could find work. The same work his daddy and granddaddy had done.

They packed one small bag and walked to the railroad station. Using their last three dollars, Bartholomew bought two tickets to Coal Fork, West Virginia.

That spring Ruth gave birth to a baby boy, and they named him Paul.

"He'll grow to be a man of wisdom," Bartholomew said. "As soon as he's old enough to speak I'll teach him what he needs to know so that one day he'll leave this mountain and never look back."

Before the boy was three Bartholomew's hands had become blackened and his soul weary, so it fell to Ruth to teach the boy and she did.

The second year Ruth planted a garden behind the house. She grew corn, tomatoes, string beans, and summer squash. When the bounty was harvested, she planted turnips and potatoes. She planted more than they could eat in a summer, and when there was plenty she cooked the extra and packed it in mason jars sealed with a layer of wax. She continued to do it year after year, so Paul grew healthy and strong. She nourished the child's body with the food she'd grown and his mind with words and stories from the books she loved.

Then the summer Paul turned nine, Ruth again grew pale and queasy. Most mornings she'd turn away from the strong coffee sitting atop the stove and drink only a cup of weak tea. Even then, she'd start to gag moments after the second swallow.

"Do you think possibly…?" Bartholomew glanced at her stomach.

"After all these years, I doubt it," Ruth answered laughingly. But by November she knew for certain. By then her breasts were swollen and tender. She could not stand the smell of tomatoes, and even the briefest glance of raw meat made her retch. In late December Ruth felt the baby move for the first time. It was different from the way Paul had moved. He'd shifted himself slowly from side to side in movements that were barely perceptible. This baby kicked at Ruth's ribs as if it were anxious to be free.

"This one is certain to be another boy," Ruth said, laughing, "and a feisty one at that."

Pleased with such an idea, Bartholomew began thinking of what he would call the boy.

Bartholomew trusted that choosing a name from the Bible brought special blessings, so each night he sat in the rocking chair and turned page after page looking for the right name. With Paul he had wished for only wisdom, but that was before he spent nine long years hacking bits of coal from the hardened walls of the mine. Nine days later Bartholomew settled on the name Jeremiah. This boy would be named after a man who could look to the future and be wise in the ways of the world. Surely he would be a child not destined to spend his days in the mine as Bartholomew did.

"Such a big name for a little baby," Ruth said, but since it was Bartholomew's will she accepted it. That winter Ruth bought several yards of bunting at the company store and hemmed in into four soft baby blankets. In the center of each one, she embroidered a large "J".

In February, two days after a blizzard passed through West Virginia and left the mountain covered in snow so deep the mine closed down, Ruth's labor pains began. For almost forty hours she was wracked with pain, and by the time the baby passed through the birth canal her eyes had rolled to the back of her head.

"No!" Bartholomew screamed and lifted her into his arms. "Please, Ruth, please don't leave me." He held her for hours as little Paul wiped the baby clean, wrapped her in a warm blanket, and placed her in the same cradle they'd used for him.

Just before dawn, Ruth's eyelids fluttered open and she asked, "Jeremiah—is he okay?"

For the first time in many hours Bartholomew smiled. "Your prediction was wrong. Jeremiah is a girl." He placed the baby in Ruth's arms and sat beside them. "I think maybe we'd best come up with a new name."

Ruth looked up at her husband. He was so strong and yet so gentle. He was a man who asked for little and gave much. She thought back on how this baby had kicked, how she'd struggled to be free. Paul was like Bartholomew, strong but gentle. This child was stronger. She had a lust for life and a fierce determination to live it. She'd waved her tiny arms and legs and celebrated life even before the time had come. The words Ruth spoke were her gift to Bartholomew.

"We'll name her Jubilee," she said, "because this child is a celebration of our love."

Bartholomew smiled and nodded his approval.

And so it was.

Cruel Winter

They called the child Jubie for short. Right from the start she was small, undersized even for a girl. Whereas Paul had been a content child who slept for hours after being nursed, Jubilee was a red-faced, squalling bundle of energy who cried through the night and slept during the day.

Before she was a year old, Ruth could see the girl was the spitting image of Anita.

In the winter of Jubilee's first birthday, a plague of influenza came to Coal Fork. First folks stopped going to church; then children dropped out of school. The company store closed down for a full two weeks, and half the men who worked the mine stopped showing up. The men who did continue to work, the men like Bartholomew, carried heavier loads and worked longer hours.

The week before Christmas Ruth began coughing. "Just a cold," she told herself and continued with her daily chores. After three days she could no longer hold food in her stomach and was weakened to the point where she had to sit and rest after walking across the room. Sitting in the straight-backed kitchen chair, she'd explain to Paul how to make the biscuits and stoke the stove.

When Bartholomew returned from the mine a warm dinner sat atop the stove just as it always did, but Ruth was in bed.

"Mama's not feeling so good," the boy told Bartholomew.

After a long day of hunching over a pick and shovel, Bartholomew was weary to the point where he could barely lift the spoon to his mouth and he had no strength to question the boy.

Day after day Paul cooked the food and tended to his baby sister. "You're such a good boy," Ruth gasped, but even speaking those few words exhausted her and she fell back into her pillow.

Finally one night the boy went against what Ruth had asked of him. When Bartholomew sat down at the table, Paul said, "Mama told me I ain't supposed to worry you with this, but she's real bad sick. She don't get out of bed no more."

Bartholomew looked at the boy quizzically. "Since when?"

"Monday."

"Monday?" Bartholomew repeated. "Why, that's five days back!"

Bartholomew left the food and hurried into the bedroom. Leaning close to Ruth he placed his hand on her forehead. Despite the coal dust still clinging to his fingers, he could feel the heat of her skin.

"Good God!" he shouted. He turned quickly and headed for the door of the cabin. As he passed through the kitchen he gave Paul an angry glare. "You should've told me sooner, boy," he said. "Your mama's got the fever!" With that he slammed out the door.

Bartholomew ran three miles down the mountain, once sliding partway into the creek bed and twice stumbling to his knees. When he reached Doctor Hawkins' house, every light was turned off and it was obvious they'd all gone to bed. Bartholomew pounded on the door with such ferocity that lights popped on in the house next door as well as Doctor Hawkins' bedroom. "You've got to come right now," he said. "Ruth's come down with the fever!"

It seemed the doctor pulled trousers, boots, and a jacket over his pajamas at a pace too slow for even a snail. "Hurry," Bartholomew urged repeatedly.

Riding in a car the return trip up the mountain took nowhere near as long as his journey down. But the moment they entered the house, Bartholomew could hear the wheeze of Ruth's breath.

"Get a pot of water boiling," the doctor ordered. Bartholomew waved a finger at Paul, and minutes later the boy had the coal fire blazing and a full pot of water atop the stove. Bartholomew followed the doctor to the bedroom and remained there, his hand clamped tight around Ruth's. The doctor wiped Ruth's face, arms, and legs with clean diapers dipped in icy cold water, and when the heat coming from her skin lessened he gave her pills to swallow and moved her to a sitting position so she could breathe in wisps of steam from the boiling water.

For three days Bartholomew did not go to the mine. He sat beside his wife repeating prayer after prayer, beseeching God to save her from the fate that had fallen upon so many others. It was Paul who kept a pot of water boiling and brought it to his mama's bedside hour after hour. It was Paul who cooked the food and fed the toddler who had begun to cling to his leg like a koala bear.

On the fourth morning when Ruth could sit up and sip a lukewarm broth and sassafras tea, Bartholomew returned to the mine. Although Ruth's temperature went back to normal and she claimed that she felt almost as good as new, the truth was she had become frail and weak. For the remainder of that winter, Paul stayed home from school. Once Bartholomew had gone off to the mine, Paul did the cooking, cleaning, and tending to Jubilee. Ruth told him how to do each task, and he followed her directions so precisely that Bartholomew never thought to question the change.

When the weather finally turned warm Ruth could sit outside and a hint of color gradually returned to her cheeks, but the weakness never left. Her back ached constantly, and at times taking a breath seemed to require more effort than she could muster. Although she did small bits of cooking there was no garden that year and the care of Jubilee, who was not yet two, was left to Paul.

Jubilee learned to call Paul's name whenever she wanted something. "All," she'd say, holding out a cup that needed to be filled. She hadn't yet learned to say the first letter of his name, and that's when Paul began teaching her.

"Pa..." He said repeatedly. "Pa..." Paul put his lips together, then rounded them open as he pushed the sound out emphasizing the P. "Pha..aul. Now you try it."

Mimicking what her brother had done, Jubilee scrunched her face, squeezed her mouth closed, then spit out, "All."

That summer he worked on getting her to say his name but to no avail. He continued to be All. Paul read the same books Ruth had read to him and the words came quickly to Jubilee, but the sound of a P was never there. "All, leese lay wif me," she'd say.

"You mean, 'Paul, please play with me'?" he'd ask tolerantly. Then he'd stop what he was doing and follow along to see what she had in mind.

On the second Tuesday of September Paul did not return to school when the other children did. The week prior Ruth had collapsed on the kitchen floor as she stood there trying to slice apples for a pie. "Mama!" he'd screamed, then lifted her from the floor and carried her to the bedroom. By that time Ruth was thin as a skeleton, and her bones were lighter than those of a sparrow.

"Please don't tell your daddy," she begged Paul. "He's already got enough worry."

"But, Mama," Paul argued, "maybe Doctor Hawkins can—"

"There's nothing." Ruth grimaced, remembering the blood-stained hankie she had tucked in the pocket of her apron.

That evening Paul told his daddy what had happened.

"Is that the honest truth?" Bartholomew asked. "Because your mama don't look sick."

"It's just pretend, Daddy. That's all. Mama puts pink stuff on her face so you won't know. But when she coughs, blood comes out of her mouth."

"Lord God," Bartholomew said with a moan as he dropped down into a chair. "How long has this—?"

"A long time," Paul answered tearfully. "A real long time."

And Thus It Happened...

Ruth died of tuberculosis in early December. The hard part of winter that crusted the mountain with layers of ice and snow came early that year, and with it came the heartache of reality. On the day Bartholomew returned from work to find Ruth gone, he howled with such heartache that it shook the mountain. It was said that men working the night shift deep in the belly of the mine felt the earth tremble beneath their feet.

Paul was the one who explained the situation to Jubilee. Although the two-year-old girl's eyes often grew teary and saddened, she was too young to accept that gone meant gone forever. For months afterward Jubilee would speak of Ruth as if she'd be back momentarily.

"Where's Mama?" she'd ask, then look around with a puzzled expression.

"Mama died," Paul would explain patiently. "She's gone to heaven."

"Oh. Okay," Jubilee would answer. Then she'd turn back to whatever she'd been doing.

Unfortunately, Paul did understand. And at times the weight of understanding was more than a boy of eleven could carry. The day his mother breathed her last, he stumbled into the woods behind the house, sat on a felled tree, and gave way to all the fear and sorrow he'd held inside. It started with a silent stream of tears, then, feeding upon the ugly truth, it grew into heartbreaking sobs heard a mile away. Lost in a misery that went far beyond words, he sat with his head dropped between his knees and his back hunched. When he heard the small voice it startled him.

"Don't cry, Paul."

He lifted his head and gave a weak smile. "Jubie, you said Paul!"

She nodded and smiled. "Paul," she repeated.

He pulled his baby sister to his chest and held her there for such a long time their heartbeats mingled and bonded them one to the other for the rest of their lives—however long or short that time might be.

With Ruth now gone, Bartholomew became a lost soul. He moved through the days putting one foot in front of the other and thinking about nothing. He rose early in the morning and went off to the mine. When he returned there was always a warm supper atop the stove, but both children were sleeping. On Sundays the mine closed so Bartholomew washed the coal dust from his hands and face, and with his children trailing behind the pitiful threesome trod the dirt road of the mountain and took their seats in the last row of the Pilgrim Faith Church. With the last "Amen" still hanging in the air, Bartholomew took Paul by the hand and started for home.

In the five years that followed he never really came to know his daughter. Some believe he held the child responsible for her mother's death; others think his soul simply died along with Ruth and he no longer had a heart capable of love.

For the next two years, Paul was not in school. In places like Coal Fork, mining families came and went. Children were there one year, gone the next, so no one questioned the boy's absence. It was simply assumed that his family, like so many others, had moved on to a place where there was more work, better pay, or less danger.

In those years Paul became both mother and father to Jubilee. He taught her to read and write, he taught her numbers, and explained how the money Daddy put in the sugar jar each week paid for food and clothes. He showed her how to make biscuits and pull weeds from the garden. Patiently and lovingly he shared with her all the things Ruth had taught him.

When Jubilee turned four, he carried the girl down the mountain on his back and returned to school. Jubilee was smaller than the other children but she was smarter, and in that first year she jumped from a group learning their ABCs to a class adding two-digit numbers.

Paul was not so fortunate. In the two years of being away, his earlier classmates had learned new things and moved on. It shamed him that he now had to sit with a group of children who were both younger and smaller.

One evening when Bartholomew came in from the mine, Paul was at the kitchen table working on long division problems he couldn't seem to grasp. Bartholomew washed his hands, carried his supper plate to the table, and sat alongside Paul.

"Whatcha working on?" he asked.

"Long division," Paul answered. "I just ain't getting this."

"Let's see," Bartholomew said. "Maybe I can help."

Wide-eyed, Paul turned to his father. "You know long division?"

"I sure enough do." A faint trace of fond remembrance twinkled in Bartholomew's eyes. "You might not think it by what I am today, but I got a high school diploma."

That evening father and son sat together and talked long into the night. Bartholomew told Paul how he'd left the mountain with intentions never to come back. "Once you get a speck of coal dust on your hands, you're doomed forever," he said remorsefully. "There's no escape."

For a short while Bartholomew forgot the sadness that was his constant companion and allowed the muscles in his face to relax. With an expression that was the closest he'd come to smiling in more than two years, he shared stories of the life he'd had in Virginia and how he'd met Ruth at a movie show.

"Your mama was with her sister," he said, "and if Anita had her way, they'd have gone on without me. But the minute your mama and I set eyes on each other, we knew."

The mention of an aunt Paul knew nothing about prompted him to ask, "How come Mama never spoke of Aunt Anita?"

"They had a falling out years ago," Bartholomew answered wistfully. "Anita, she was a lot different than your mama." As the memories settled in, he repeated, "A whole lot different."

That was the night Bartholomew elicited an oath from Paul: a promise that Paul would continue to study until he was smart enough to leave the mountain and find work elsewhere.

"Swear," Bartholomew said, "that you'll never step foot inside of a mine."

"I swear," Paul replied, understanding that it was a promise he would have to keep until the day he died.

That night Bartholomew pulled his son into his arms and held him closer than the boy had thought possible. There were no words spoken, but Paul could smell the black dust of the mine mixed with love, regret, and sadness.

Two years later there was a knock on the door late in the evening. It came at just about the time Paul expected his daddy to come home from the mine. It was Harold Brumann standing at the door with Bartholomew's hard hat in his hand.

"I'm real sorry to bring you this bad news," he said. "A trolley cart broke loose, and your daddy was killed along with two other men."

Paul stood there looking expressionlessly into the face of the man who spoke.

"I brung you his hat and pail 'cause I was thinking maybe you'd want to—"

"Daddy's dead?"

Harold Brumann nodded. "It happened quick. The cart broke loose and came at them faster than—"

"Daddy's dead?" Paul repeated.

Brumann nodded again.

Paul reached out and took the hard hat and lunch pail from Brumann's hands. "Thank you for telling me," he said and closed the door.

That night he again sat with seven-year-old Jubilee and explained how Daddy had gone to be with Mama in heaven.

"What about us?" she said tearfully. "Who's going to take care of us?"

"I am," Paul answered.

Jubilee cried for hours on end, and each time she voiced the same fear of who would take care of them. The questions went from a simple unadorned "why" to concerns that stretched far into the future. They circled around and around with each answer generating another question. Was Paul going to work in the mine? If he did work in the mine, would he die also? Did Mama die because she worked in the mine?

"I'm not going to die," Paul said. "I'll always be here to take care of you." His voice was soft but reassuring until at long last Jubilee's tears stopped.

That night after she had gone to sleep, Paul sat at the table and counted up exactly how much money they had. He tried to figure how he could make it last long enough for him to finish his final two years of high school. Maybe if he was lucky and could get some odd jobs, he could stretch it out to six or eight months. But two years?

When Paul spread his money on the table and counted it up, he figured on staying in the cabin they'd been living in ever since he was born. He didn't figure on the fact that the mining company owned the cabin just as they owned everything else in town.

And he sure as hell didn't figure that less than a month later the foreman would come knocking on his door.

"This ain't my doing," the foreman said. "It's company rules. You gotta be working for Poynter Mining, or you gotta move out."

"My daddy worked at that mine for almost seventeen years!" Paul argued, but he could just as well have saved his breath. As far as Poynter Mining was concerned he was nothing more than a squatter...unless he went to work at the mine.

That night responsibility weighed heavily on Paul's shoulders. He had Jubilee to take care of and he had made two promises, both of which he intended to keep. The first was to his mother when he swore he watch over Jubilee no matter what. The second was to his father when he swore never to step foot into the mine.

Two days later Paul and Jubilee walked down off the mountain, never to return again. He carried with him a small bag with a few clothes, three photographs, the family Bible, a remembrance of Bartholomew, and five faded letters he'd found in his mama's keepsake box. They were the last letters she'd received from Anita. No return address, but it was postmarked Wyattsville, Virginia.

Many Miles Away

No one knew where Hurt McAdams got his name. They only knew that he lived up to it. George McAdams, Hurt's daddy, was said to be the meanest man in Pittsburgh and every bit as hard as the iron he welded into grillwork day after day. When Hurt was fourteen his mama had all she could take of George and walked out the door, leaving Hurt and his mean-ass daddy behind. When she disappeared as suddenly as she did, neighbors speculated that George had done something unthinkable to Brenda McAdams. But the simple truth was she'd hitchhiked across nine states and settled in Arizona.

By then Hurt had already developed a pattern of following in his daddy's footsteps. Before he had made it to sixth grade Hurt had been thrown out of school five times, and the last time the principal told his mama not to bother with bringing him back.

It started when he was not quite five. Hurt, small-boned and short like his mama, had come in from playing with his mouth turned down in the sort of pucker that holds a person back from crying.

"What's wrong with you?" George asked.

"Alfred took my scooter and won't give it back," Hurt told his daddy. George flared up like a Fourth-of-July rocket. "And you let him get away with it?"

Five-year-old Hurt let go of the tears he'd been holding back. "He's bigger than me," he said with a moan. "Way bigger."

With a calloused hand as hard as a rock George whacked Hurt across the back of his head.

"You chicken-shit! Get back out there and get what's yours, or I'll give you a beating way worse than what that kid can do!"

"But Daddy—"

"Get going!"

When Hurt went back out the door George followed a few yards behind, still yelling insults. "If you ain't got the guts to clobber him yourself, grab onto a baseball bat and swing it."

Alfred was almost a foot taller than Hurt, but more afraid of his daddy than he was the boy Hurt tore into Alfred with a vengeance. Twenty minutes later Hurt had his scooter back, and his daddy said how proud he was of the boy.

That did it. Hurt, who'd been trying to please his daddy since the day he was born, went from protecting himself to picking a fight with anything that moved. It didn't matter that almost all of the kids were bigger than him; Hurt was meaner. When neighbors began to knock at the door complaining Hurt had beat up their boy, his daddy's smile was wider than ever.

In the early years it was mostly kids and neighborhood animals who felt the sting of Hurt's aggression. Then when his third-grade teacher Missus Kelsey tried to discipline him for fighting in class, she too became a victim. While she had hold of his arm, Hurt kicked her shin so hard she had to let go. He hightailed it out of the classroom and didn't come back. That afternoon when Missus Kelsey went to get her car for the drive home, she found it had four flat tires and a shattered windshield.

For almost three years the teachers tried to ignore Hurt's behavior. Although no one said so, they were silently grateful when he failed to show up for class and never questioned his absence. But things finally came to a head when Hurt threw a rock that missed the math teacher's head by inches. Fearful of the boy, Mister Riffkin threatened to quit.

That's when the principal telephoned Brenda McAdams and told her Hurt was not allowed back in the school.

Whatever meanness Hurt had got worse when he met Butch Muller. Butch was twenty-eight at the time. Now, you might wonder why a twenty-eight-year-old man would have an interest in being pals with a seventeen-year-old kid, but the truth is they were kindred spirits. By that time Hurt was almost as mean as his daddy, and whatever evil-doing he didn't know about Butch taught him. First it was just snatch-and-grab robberies, but before long they'd gotten to a point where either of them could clobber an unsuspecting passerby on the head, take his wallet, and walk off without a look back to see if the man was dead or alive.

After two years of doing what proved to be less profitable than they'd originally thought, they moved up to robbing stores with a fistful of dollars in the cash register. They went in with kerchiefs covering the lower part of their faces. At first they were armed with just a crowbar and the machete Hurt bought second-hand. But when they eyed the jewelry store, Butch said he thought they'd be better off with guns.

"That way we'll know they're taking us seriously," he said, and Hurt agreed.

Butch knew a pawn shop owner on the far side of town who was short on questions but plentiful on what he sold in the back room. As far as Hurt was concerned it was a worthwhile trip, because he came away with a Smith & Wesson .38 special and more confidence than he'd ever known. Just holding the gun in his hand felt good. With the gun Hurt was bigger. He was stronger. He was unstoppable. With the gun, Hurt didn't have to take any guff from anybody—including his daddy.

The jewelry store was a pushover because Eloise Mercer, the woman behind the counter, was well into her sixties and nervous as a cat. "Please, please," she cried. "Take whatever you want, but don't shoot me." They didn't, but it was a decision Hurt later regretted.

The Stop n' Shop was also a breeze. They were in and out in less than a minute and with a whopping three-hundred–and-six dollars from the register. Having a little money made Hurt feel good. Having a lot of money made him feel better. He wanted more. They began to look for bigger stores, the kind of stores that kept a lot of cash on hand.

The 24-hour drugstore promised to be an easy target. If they waited until after midnight, the store would be empty. With no one there but Old Man Hamilton, they could take their time. Rumors were he had a back room safe where he kept a wad of extra cash. Of course, neither Butch nor Hurt knew that more than a year ago Gus Hamilton had installed a silent alarm that was wired directly into the police station two blocks south of the store.

Hurt was the one holding a gun to Gus's head when the police walked in. Butch saw the patrol car pull up, and without shouting a warning to his partner he slipped out the storeroom back door.

It was Hurt who was arrested. He was the one who sat in the holding room for nine hours straight without even a drink of water. He was the one bombarded with questions. And he was the one who refused to say where he'd gotten the gun or who was with him.

"You'll get off a lot easier if you give him up," the arresting officer said. Still Hurt refused. Butch was his friend—so he thought.

Since Hurt's description matched the one Eloise Mercer gave when two men robbed her jewelry store, he was put in a lineup and identified as one of the perpetrators in that robbery also.

With two counts of burglary and not a twinge of cooperation, the judge didn't feel one bit lenient when he handed down the sentence. Hurt spent the next seven years in the Camp Hill Correctional Institution, and every day he was in there he grew meaner. He'd counted on having both his daddy and Butch Muller stand by him, but not once in the whole seven years did he hear from either of them.

When Hurt was released they handed him a bus ticket back to Pittsburgh, thirty-five dollars, and a note with the address of his parole officer.

Before he boarded the bus for Pittsburgh, Hurt wadded the paper in his fist and tossed it in the trash can.

Once he was back in town, Hurt's first stop was the pawn shop. He got what he came for, but it cost him twenty bucks. He then went in search of Butch. Nine stops later Hurt stood face to face with Butch in the alleyway behind the Bluebeard Barbershop.

"I thought you was my friend," Hurt said. Then without so much as a wince, he pulled the gun from his pocket and shot Butch in the head. "You just can't trust nobody," he mumbled as he turned and walked away.

Twenty minutes later Hurt stood in front of the house he'd lived in as a boy. When he started up the walkway the next-door neighbor leaned over the porch rail and called out, "You ain't looking for your pa, are you, boy?"

Hurt looked over. Old Man Kubick had become white-haired and so hunched he was almost unrecognizable. "Yeah, I am," Hurt answered.

"He's gone. He been gone for three, maybe four years."

"Gone where?"

"South. Miami Beach maybe." The old man scratched his head and hesitated a minute, trying to recall where George McAdams had said he was going. "Come to think of it," the old man mused, "I believe it was Myrtle Beach," but before he got the words out, Hurt was gone.

It was late in the afternoon, and the Greyhound station bustled with people. Hurt got in line behind two men and a small woman wearing the same perfume his mother wore. It was the smell of gardenias. Without thinking he leaned forward and sucked in the smell. *If Daddy hadn't driven her away years earlier, Mama would have come to visit.* "He's the cause of everything," Hurt grumbled.

The woman turned. "Excuse me?"

"Wasn't nothing," Hurt answered. Then with barely a breath in between, he asked, "You got a boy, ma'am?"

When she smiled, she bore a strong resemblance to how Hurt

imagined his mama would now look. "I sure do. Four of them. I'm off to spend some time with my boy in Kentucky right now."

"Ain't that nice," Hurt replied; then he looked down at his shoes and quit talking.

When the woman left Hurt moved up to the ticket window. "How much for a one-way to Miami?"

"Miami...let's see..." The clerk ran his finger down the list of fares. "Ah, yes, here it is. Miami, twenty-eight seventy-five. That's with a three-hour stopover in Wyattsville, Virginia."

"You got anything cheaper?"

The clerk ran his finger down the list again. "Afraid not."

"Nothing?"

The clerk shook his head.

Hurt had fifteen dollars and no desire to remain in Pittsburgh. "What was that place in Virginia?"

"Wyattsville?"

"Yeah. How much to Wyattsville?"

The clerk looked at the book again. "Thirteen seventy-five."

"Gimme that," Hurt said. He pulled the three wrinkled five-dollar bills from his pocket and pushed them through the window grill.

Forty-five minutes later Hurt was on his way to Wyattsville. He had a score to settle in Miami, but in order to get there he'd have to stop and pick up some cash along the way. The three-hour layover was plenty of time.

PAUL

Walking down that mountain was the scariest thing I ever done. I was remembering how Mama used to say people ought not burn the bridges behind them, but that's just what it felt like we was doing. It ain't right when a person's gotta choose between keeping a promise and putting food on the table.

We was all the way down to where the creek bed ends when I come within a whisker of turning back. I'd stopped so Jubie could rest and was thinking how she'd be sleeping in her own bed if I'd do what maybe I should do. Then there was this loud crack of thunder, and I heard a voice say, "Keep going!" It sounded the exact same as Daddy. I ain't saying it was Daddy, and I ain't saying it was the Almighty. But I am saying you don't argue with something like that. "Yes, sir," I answered, then picked Jubie up and carried her the rest of the way.

When Jubie said she was scared of going to a place she didn't know, I told her not to worry. I said it was a good thing, 'cause we was going to see an aunt we never knew we had. Then she started smiling. The whole time I was telling her how good everything was gonna be, I was wishing I had someone to tell me the same thing.

Looking for Anita

Paul and Jubilee boarded the Greyhound bus at the Campbell's Creek Depot. He had a ticket; she didn't. When he'd asked the clerk at the window how much for two tickets to Wyattsville, Virginia, she answered, "Eight dollars and fifty cents." While Paul stood there counting out the quarters and dimes, the woman peered over the counter at Jubilee. "Make that four-twenty-five," she said. "There's no charge for kids under five."

"Oh, Jubie just looks small," Paul started to say, "but—"

"Maybe you don't hear so good." The ticket clerk cocked an eyebrow and looked Paul square in the face. "I said we don't charge for kids under five," she repeated. then cranked out a single ticket and handed it to him.

Once they were settled on the bus Jubilee leaned over and whispered in Paul's ear, "I'm hungry." He reached beneath the seat and pulled a jelly sandwich from the bag he'd been carrying. After the sandwich was gone she settled back into her seat, and for a while was content to watch the scenery fly by. When darkness dropped a blanket over the countryside, she scooted closer to Paul and began a barrage of questions.

"Is Aunt Anita nice?"

Paul shrugged. "I don't know. I suppose, like everybody else, she's got some good qualities and some not-so-good ones."

"Oh." Jubilee hesitated a moment then asked, "Did Mama think she was nice?"

Paul shrugged again. "Hard to say. Mama never talked about her, leastwise not to me."

"How come?"

"Judging by the letters I read, Mama and Aunt Anita didn't get along real well."

"What if we get to Virginia and Aunt Anita don't get along with us either?"

"You ask too many questions. Stop worrying. Try to sleep." He wrapped a long arm around her shoulders and nudged her closer. "Tomorrow's gonna be a big day."

Jubilee closed her eyes and before long drifted off to sleep. For Paul, sleep was impossible. He kept asking himself the same questions Jubilee asked. Unfortunately, he knew something she didn't. He knew what Anita had written in those letters. Paul thought back on the last letter, the letter dated just two months after Jubilee was born. The angry words were written in a heavy-handed script, and even after seven years the smell of bitterness still permeated the ink. *If you refuse to listen to reason,* Anita had written, *then I wash my hands of you.*

Since there were only a handful of letters, five to be exact, Paul had no way of knowing what Anita wanted his mama to do. He could only pray that by now her anger had subsided.

The bus pulled into Wyattsville shortly after daybreak. Paul gave Jubilee a gentle shake to wake her. "We're here," he whispered.

The bus station was something Paul could have never before imagined. Four buses stood side by side, each one coming from someplace far away and heading to someplace else. A loudspeaker crackled the last-minute warning for folks headed to Chicago. Men and women moved through the terminal without slowing, each one confident of where they were headed.

Wyattsville apparently was a lot larger than Paul had anticipated. Finding Anita might not be that easy. Holding tight to Jubilee's hand, he made his way toward the front door of the station.

Their first stop was a luncheonette where they sat at the counter. Jubilee whirled herself around on the stool three times; then Paul told her to stop. He looked down the menu prices, then ordered a glass of milk and biscuit for Jubilee and coffee for himself. He was on his second refill when the waitress, a woman with a badge indicating her name was Connie, asked, "Can I get y'all something else?"

"You got a telephone book?"

"Sure do, honey." She waggled a finger toward the rear of the shop. "Right past the restroom."

Jubilee's eyes widened. "You got a special room for resting?"

Connie laughed then leaned across the counter and whispered, "It's a toilet. We just call it a restroom for the sake of politeness."

After warning Jubilee not to budge from the stool, Paul headed toward the back. The phone book, nearly three times the size of Charleston's, had way more names than he was hoping for. He turned the pages to W. He knew two things: Anita was supposedly their aunt, and her last name might be Walker like his mama's once was. None of Anita's letters mentioned a husband, so Paul was hoping she was still a Walker. There was a full page of Walkers. Not one of them was an Anita.

As he made his way back to his seat Paul began rubbing his hand across the back of his neck, the way his daddy did when he was worrying. Sitting at the counter he pulled the remainder of the money from his pocket and counted it again. Twelve dollars and eighty-seven cents.

When Connie poured a third refill, Paul pushed two dimes and a nickel across the counter and said, "Thank you, ma'am." When she came back with another biscuit for Jubilee, he asked if she knew of any rooming houses in the area. "Not too expensive," he added.

"I sure do," Connie answered. "Missus Willoughby has a real nice place, and I think she only charges two dollars a night."

"Two dollars just for sleeping!" Jubilee exclaimed.

Connie leaned closer. "'Course, if you was to mention you were short on cash, I think she'd be willing to let you stay in that upstairs room for a dollar."

Connie then explained how they were to get to Missus Willoughby's boarding house. "You can't miss it," she said. "It's a big three-story house with a yellow sign out front."

Fifteen minutes later Paul and Jubilee started walking north on Rosemont, and when they reached Main Street they turned right. "I think it's less than a mile from here," Paul said, but before they'd gone four blocks a sign in the grocery store window caught his eye.

"Help Wanted" it read. Underneath in smaller print was "Stock Boy—$30 a week."

A few doors down, on the opposite side of the street, Paul spied a park bench. "Come on," he said and took Jubilee by the hand as they crossed.

The Greyhound bus from Pittsburgh pulled in ten minutes after Paul and Jubilee left the station. They were nine blocks from the luncheonette when Hurt McAdams walked in. He looked down the long row of stools, and on the far end he saw the back of what he believed to be a uniformed policeman. "No sense asking for trouble," he mumbled. He turned, walked out the door, and started toward what looked to be the center of town. He strode with long deliberate movements, his eyes fixed straight ahead and his features locked in a look of determination.

In three hours he had to be back on that bus. He had to get back to the station, buy a ticket, and be sitting on the bus when it pulled out for Miami. Hurt glanced down at his wristwatch. Two hours and twenty minutes left. Forty minutes already gone. He had to hurry.

Hurt turned off Rosemont and walked along Washington Street. There were plenty of stores but none of them open. He reached into his pocket and wrapped his hand around the gun. He could feel the energy coming from it. It had power, and with it *he* had power. The butt of the gun could smash a window to smithereens. He considered the thought, then pushed it away. If the store had alarms they'd be all over him before he could get back to the bus. No good. He turned east, walked three blocks, and took a left onto Main Street.

Hurt glanced at his watch again. Two hours. He had to find something soon. He looked down the long street. At the far end he saw a Wonder Bread delivery truck pulling away from the front of what looked to be a small grocery store.

Perfect. No people. He'd grab what he came for and leave no witnesses. Before anyone knew what happened, he'd be back on the bus headed for Miami.

Hurt began walking toward the store.

Paul took the small bag he'd been carrying and sat it on the bench alongside Jubilee. "I want you to stay here. I'm probably gonna be gone a while, but don't worry. I'll be back soon as I can."

"Why can't I come with you?"

"Jubie," he said with a laugh. "Men don't bring their baby sister when they're asking for a job."

Giving him a look that argued the point, she griped, "I ain't no baby!"

"I know you're not. But right now I need you to be a really big girl—a really big girl who can stay here and keep an eye on our things."

"You're trying to trick me."

"Not at all," Paul said, holding up his right hand. "That grocery store's willing to pay thirty dollars a week. If I get a good job like that, we won't need to find Mama's sister. We'll have enough money to get ourselves a nice room to live in and good food to eat."

Finally Jubilee agreed.

Before he turned and crossed the street, Paul shook a warning finger. "Now don't leave this bench, no matter what. And don't talk to strangers."

"Everybody in this town's a stranger," Jubilee grumbled resentfully.

"In time they won't be," Paul answered and turned toward the street.

The bread truck blocked Hurt's view of Paul crossing the street. And the girl, small as she was, sitting on a bench party hidden by an oak tree, was beyond the scope of where he'd fixed his vision.

He moved down the street with long strides. No cars out front: good. No passersby: good. Hurt had to make sure there were no witnesses. Witnesses only meant trouble. He'd gone soft in the jewelry store heist when Eloise Mercer had whimpered and cried, and what did he get in return? She pointed an accusing finger at him, and he spent an extra five years in prison.

"No more," he mumbled. "No more."

Paul was standing in front of the counter asking Sidney Klaussner about the job when the store door opened.

Sidney Klaussner was fifty-eight years old but sharp as a tack. He was also damned and determined that nobody was ever gonna rob his store again. A year earlier three thugs who had jumped off a freight train came in waving a gun and walked off with more than four hundred dollars. For a good six months Sidney berated himself for letting them get away with it; then he went out and bought a Browning 16 gauge shotgun. It was an automatic that could fire off five shots faster than a rabbit could run across the yard.

Whenever the store door swung open, Sidney always looked up and nodded a hello. It was his way of greeting people. When Hurt walked through the door, Sid saw him reach into his jacket pocket and pull the gun out. Before Hurt closed the gap between them Sidney pulled the rifle from beneath the counter, and without taking time to aim he began firing.

Hurt was faster. His bullet tore through Sidney's chest like a cannon ball.

Sidney squeezed off two shots as he fell. The first one hit Paul in the head. The second one went wild and lodged itself in the ceiling.

Hurt stepped over Paul and banged open the cash register. He grabbed all the bills, then turned and walked out of the store like a man who'd just stopped in for a pack of cigarettes.

He never noticed Martha Tillinger. Without her hearing aid she'd been unaware of what was happening until she heard the bang of gunfire and that's when she squatted down behind the cereal boxes.

Martha, afraid for her life, stayed behind those cereal boxes for nearly twenty minutes before she found the courage to venture out. When she finally tiptoed out and saw the bodies in the floor, she screamed so loud that Mario Gomez heard her two doors down. He came running from the barber shop, and that's when they finally called the police.

By time the patrol car pulled up in front of Klaussner's Grocery, Hurt McAdams was five blocks from the bus station.

Angry Faces

The Klaussner's Grocery Store robbery occurred at 8:06 on the first Wednesday of March. By 8:30 there were two ambulances and five patrol cars sitting crosswise on Main Street. Cars were rerouted to Washington, but those on foot could cut through the park and come out on Main. Within twenty minutes there were nearly fifty people who had come from out of nowhere crowded in front of the store.

Ethan Allen left for school at 8:40. It took ten minutes to get there and he had ten minutes to spare, so when he bicycled across Ridge Road and saw the flashing red lights a block down on Main he turned and headed in that direction.

Leaning his bicycle against the lamppost, he edged his way into the crowd and looked for a familiar face. Seth Porter's was the first one he saw.

"Hey, there, Mister Porter," he called out.

Porter turned and scanned the faces in the crowd.

"It's me," Ethan Allen called and pushed past a hefty woman who'd been blocking his view. "What's going on?"

"Ain't you supposed to be in school?"

"Yeah, I'm on my way."

"Then you'd better get moving."

"What's going on?" Ethan Allen repeated.

Porter glanced at his watch and thumbed his finger in the direction of the school. "Get going. It's five 'til nine."

"School don't start 'til ten today," Ethan answered. "So what's going on?"

"A robbery," Porter finally said. "Sidney Klaussner got shot. They're saying he shot one of the bandits, but the other one got away. " He eyed Ethan Allen suspiciously. "You sure school don't start 'til ten?"

"Positive."

Moments later Carmella Klaussner jumped out of Henrietta Banger's car and pushed her way through the crowd screaming, "Sid! Sid!" The poor woman was almost hysterical, and it was all anyone could do to hold her back. She screamed, cried, and pleaded, but still Ed Cunningham refused to allow her past the barricade he'd set up. It was Ed's third day on the job, and he was starting to think that maybe being a policeman wasn't what he was cut out for.

"This is a crime scene," he kept repeating, "and no one except the police and medics are allowed in."

Of course the crowd of onlookers sided with Carmella.

"Let her in!" somebody shouted. "She's got a right to see her husband!"

"Yeah!" several others yelled. "Let her in!"

"Nobody's allowed in," Cunningham repeated, but by then beads of nervous perspiration were building on his forehead. He wanted to explain how the police were trying to collect the sort of evidence they needed to find the perpetrator, but the crowd was obviously not in the mood to listen.

It was after ten-thirty when the medics carried out the first stretcher. Cunningham pushed the crowd back to clear a pathway to the ambulance, then helped Carmella in so she could be with her husband. As the doors slammed shut, the last thing he heard was Carmella's voice crying, "Say something, Sid, say something…"

The second stretcher was carried out minutes later, and when the medics went by an angry rumble rolled through the crowd.

"Murderer!" someone yelled; then others echoed the word. Once the gurney was locked in place, the second ambulance sped off.

"You should've just let the hoodlum die!" somebody shouted. After that a loud and angry discussion ensued about what was right and wrong.

"If someone repents of their sin, the Lord forgives them," Pastor Brian argued.

"An eye for an eye!" Bob Ballard yelled.

"Yeah," several people agreed. "An eye for an eye."

Cunningham started to sweat profusely. "Let's all calm down. There's nothing more to see here. Just go home and let well enough be."

After a lot of arguing and yelling, Pastor Brian left the group and made his way back across the park. Little by little the others began to drift away.

Only then did Seth Porter realize he'd lost track of the time. It was well after eleven when he finally shooed Ethan Allen off to school.

Making his way through the now-thinning crowd, Ethan Allen noticed the girl sitting on the bench. She was a little kid, sitting there all by herself. *She probably should be in school too,* he thought, *but nobody's telling her to scram.* As he pedaled past the bench, a fleeting twinge of resentment caught hold.

"How come *she* gets to stay here?" he grumbled as he turned the corner and headed toward Wyattsville Junior High.

Jubilee remained on the bench throughout the morning. She'd heard the gunshots, but she'd heard gunshots before. In Coal Fork it simply meant the men had gone hunting. Even as she watched the crowds gather she was not alarmed. This was the city. Paul had warned her things were different in the city.

When several hours had passed and he still hadn't returned, she began to search the faces of the stragglers standing in front of the store. The expressions were hard and the voices angry, so Jubilee remained where she was. She thought back on Paul's words.

"You can't go talking to strangers," he'd said. "People in the city ain't like us. They got their ways, and we got ours." So far, Jubilee was none too fond of their ways.

For a brief moment there had been a boy who seemed different—someone she might ask to go in search of her brother. The boy looked at her for a moment, then climbed onto his bicycle and pedaled off. Once he rounded the corner and disappeared, Jubilee knew it was a foolish thought. He was like all the others.

When the last of the cars and people were gone, tears settled in the little girl's eyes. With the crowds she had not been so terribly alone. Yes, they were city people, but she felt if need be she could ask for help. There was always that thin sliver of hope she'd find a friendly face in the crowd. Now there was nothing.

She looked across at the stretches of yellow tape crisscrossed over the doorway of the store where Paul was working and thought back on where she'd seen the same type of thing. It had been an abandoned mine. A place where her daddy said people died. Fear mingled with loneliness and became sorrow.

When the sorrow became unbearable, Jubilee stuck her thumb in her mouth. It was something she hadn't done since she was two. But the thumb was there; it was an old friend that brought comfort. It was something she could count on. After a long while the tears stopped.

Jubilee had no idea how long she'd been sitting there, but the sun was low in the sky when she thought she saw the bicycle boy coming toward her.

Olivia Doyle

When Ethan Allen turned twelve, I thought my troubles were over. Taking in a child of his age is a handful for anybody, never mind a woman who's closing in on her sixtieth birthday. I didn't expect it to be easy, but neither did I expect another problem to come knocking at my door. Of course, Ethan Allen is a boy who can find trouble even when there's none to be found.

I have to laugh at how foolish I sound when I say things like "I never expected." Of course I didn't. Nobody expects the turns their life is going to take, good, bad, or otherwise. When life takes you someplace other than where you had in mind, the only thing you can do is hang on and make the best of whatever happens.

I tried to remind myself of that when Missus Brown called and told me Ethan Allen was going to be late coming home because he had detention for an hour after school. She said he had to stay and do the social studies lesson he'd missed because of getting there two hours late and without an excuse note.

Lord God, *I thought,* what's he up to now?

Girl on a Bench

Normally Ethan Allen didn't travel down Main Street on his way home from school. He went along Cypress and then turned onto Ridge Road. But with the robbery this morning, he thought it might be his only chance to get a look at a real crime scene. Now that he was allowed to stay up and watch "Dragnet" on Thursday nights, he'd discovered how fascinating crime-fighting could be. Of course, this morning had been somewhat of a disappointment. The Wyattsville detectives didn't sound anything like Joe Friday, but then neither did Jack Mahoney.

Ethan Allen braked to a stop when he saw the doorway to Klaussner's covered with a crisscross of yellow tape that read "Crime Scene – Do Not Cross." He climbed off the bike and approached the store. Cupping his hands around his face and pressing his nose to the glass, he peered inside. Too dark; he couldn't see anything other than what he'd expect to see. He stepped over the bottom line of tape and ducked beneath the one above it. Just as he was jiggling the handle to check if maybe the door had been left unlocked, the street lamp snapped on. He let go of the door handle and scooted back under the yellow tape. He was seriously considering trying the back door when he noticed the girl still sitting on the bench, in the exact same spot.

It was the time of year when the temperature fell quickly once the sun had set, and nights were chilly enough for a wool coat. Ethan had already pulled on his sweater, but the girl was wearing just a thin, blue dress. She looked cold. She looked scared too.

Ethan Allen turned away and headed for the back door of the store. Most likely the police had locked that too, but it was worth a shot. He was halfway around the building when he started to remember the night his mama and daddy were killed. He was eleven at the time. An eleven-year-old can handle something like that. An eleven-year-old can drive his mama's car and hitch rides. This girl was just a kid—four, maybe five years old. Ethan turned and headed back.

He crossed the street and sat on the bench alongside the girl. "Hi."

She turned, looked square into his face, and said nothing. She didn't smile or frown. She just looked at him with big eyes peering from beneath a fringe of bangs. Behind those eyes Ethan Allen saw the all-too-familiar landscape of fear.

"Ain't you kinda cold?"

She nodded.

He shrugged his sweater over his head and handed it to her. "Here, put this on. I got a heavy enough shirt."

The girl smiled and took the sweater from him. She stood and pulled the sweater over her head. Her hands disappeared in the sleeves, and the bottom hung longer than her dress.

With more than a year of learning Olivia's rules for proper behavior and mannerly things to do, Ethan prodded, "Ain't you supposed to say something?"

"Thanks," she mumbled.

"Jeez, that's the best you can do?"

"I'm not supposed to talk to strangers."

"I ain't no stranger!" Ethan Allen said. "I'm a kid. Kids can talk to kids, right?"

She shrugged. "You're still a city person, and my brother said don't talk to no—"

"I ain't a city person!" Ethan said indignantly. "I'm off a farm, so you got no cause—"

She broke into a wide grin. "Back home we grew a whole lot of stuff. It wasn't no farm, but the stuff still growed."

"Where's back home?" Ethan asked.

"Coal Fork."

"Coal Fork? I never heard of no place called Coal Fork."

"It's a long ways away. We rode on the bus to get here."

Ethan gave his name, then asked hers.

"Jubilee Jones," she answered. "But everybody calls me Jubie."

"Well, Jubie," he said, "how come you been sitting here all day?"

"I'm supposed to wait for Paul."

"Who's Paul?"

"My brother. He went to get a job."

When Ethan asked where the job was, Jubilee lifted her arm and stretched a finger towards Klaussner's Grocery.

"He ain't in there," Ethan said. "Ain't nobody in there. That store's closed up tighter than..." He was going to say a bull's ass, but remembered how Grandma Olivia had warned him against such language. He settled for saying, "He likely forgot you was waiting."

"He did not!" Jubilee snapped. "He promised he'd be back!"

Ethan remembered the promise his mama made—"Tomorrow morning we're leaving for New York," she'd said. But there was no New York, and there were no more tomorrows. Maybe there was no more Paul either. He reached across and wrapped his arm around the girl.

"It's okay," he said. "I can take you home."

Jubilee's eyes filled with water, and she started to cry. Not the kind of wailing you might expect from a frightened little girl, just a silent cascade of tears falling from her eyes and rolling down her cheeks.

"Jeez, Jubie, you got nothin' to cry about. I said I'd take you home." Ethan fished in his pocket for the hankie Olivia always told him to carry. When he came up empty, he wiped her cheeks with the sleeve of his sweater. For the next fifteen minutes, he tried asking questions that would give him some idea of where the girl lived. In the end he didn't know anything more than he did at the start. If Jubilee had an address she either didn't know what it was or wasn't going to say.

Not knowing what else to do, Ethan Allen suggested Jubilee come home with him. "Grandma Olivia's nice," he assured her. "She helps kids in trouble."

Jubilee eyed him with a suspicious look. "I ain't in trouble."

"Maybe not," Ethan Allen answered. "But if your brother got that job, he might stay working all night."

"Oh."

"If that happens, you don't want to sit here cold and hungry, do you?"

She shook her head. "No, but..."

Ethan grabbed the notebook from his bicycle basket and tore a page out. "We'll leave a note so he'll know where you went. How's that?"

She smiled. "Yeah, that's good."

He wrote the note then showed it to Jubilee, who nodded her approval. Ethan Allen placed the note on the bench and put a rock on top of it so it wouldn't blow away. Once that was done, Jubilee slid her hand into his and allowed him to lift her up onto the crossbar of his bicycle.

After Missus Brown's call Olivia had suffered through a harrowing afternoon of worry about what mischief Ethan Allen was up to. That's when she started cooking. Clara swore it was impossible for a person to cook and worry at the same time, so Olivia decided to make a lemon pound cake. Then it was three dozen oatmeal cookies done from scratch. Once she'd made the stew and set it to simmer, she also made a meatloaf and two pounds of mashed potatoes. When she realized that she'd cooked up more food than they could eat in a week, possibly even two, Olivia portioned the meatloaf and potatoes onto three dinner plates and delivered them to Clara, Barbara Conklin, and Jack McGuffey, who'd been nursing a cold for nearly a week.

Barbara protested, saying she'd decided to become a vegetarian. But Olivia insisted almost all vegetarians also ate meatloaf. "They just don't talk about it," she said. Shoving the overloaded plate into Barbara's hands, she then scurried off in case Ethan Allen was trying to call home.

By the time the clock chimed five, Olivia had grown increasingly worried. She began scrutinizing the movements of the minute hand, and with each tick her apprehension increased. Before another fifteen minutes had passed she was so edgy it was impossible to sit still. That's when she decided to try her hand at homemade potato chips. Ethan banged through the front door moments after she had a skillet of hot grease sizzling.

"It's about time!" Olivia called out angrily. Bounding from the kitchen in a few quick steps, she stopped short when she saw the frightened-faced girl.

"Ethan Allen," she grumbled. "You'd better have a good explanation."

"It ain't my fault, Grandma," Ethan said. "It really ain't." He told how he'd been distracted by the robbery, stopped to see what was going on, and spotted Jubilee sitting on the bench early this morning. After telling how he'd met Seth Porter and a lengthy description of the bodies being carried out, he shrugged and said, "Anyway, she was still sitting there waiting, and since her brother wasn't back yet I asked if she wanted to come home and have dinner with us. That ain't so wrong, is it?"

"Isn't so wrong," Olivia corrected. "And, no, it isn't." Her anger subsided, but a cluster of suspicions still picked at her brain. It wouldn't be the first time Ethan Allen had stretched the truth to the closest edge of a lie.

"Even though you claim to have had good intentions," she said, "you're still in trouble for stopping when you were supposed to be on your way to school."

Olivia looked at the girl who was half the size of Ethan and skinnier than a string bean. She squatted to the girl's height and looked into eyes as blue as Charlie's had been. "Jubilee, dear, how old are you?"

"Seven."

"Do your parents know you came home with Ethan Allen?"

Jubilee shook her head.

"Good gracious!" Olivia exclaimed. "By now they're probably worried sick. You're certainly welcome to stay for dinner, but first let's call and let them know you're here."

"There ain't no need," Jubilee said.

"Of course there is," Olivia replied. "Why, your mama's probably worried crazy—"

Jubilee shook her head. "Mama ain't worried, on account of she's dead."

"Dead?" Olivia blinked. "Your mama is dead?"

Jubilee nodded.

"Well, what about your daddy? Surely he's—"

"My daddy's dead too."

"Your daddy is dead too?" Olivia gasped.

Jubilee nodded again.

Believing the child had to be making up such a horrible story, she repeated the question. "Jubilee, are you telling the honest truth when you say your mama and daddy are both dead?"

The girl tucked her head down and without looking up answered. "Yes, ma'am."

Olivia could see the weight of sadness bending the child's neck and knew Jubilee had spoken the truth. She stammered a few words about how sorrowful such a situation was and then inquired who Jubilee was staying with in Wyattsville.

"Who's taking care of you?"

"Paul," Jubilee answered. "He's my brother."

"Okay, then, we'll call Paul and let him know where you are."

"You can't. He still didn't come back from a job."

"Well, when he does get back he's sure to be worried. Give me your home number, and I'll leave a message."

"I don't got a home number."

Growing a bit less tolerant Olivia said, "Then give me Paul's address, and I'll have Ethan take a note over and leave it in the mailbox."

Jubilee gave Olivia a quizzical look. "I done told you, Paul ain't at no address, he's still at the job."

"Well, I have to notify someone. So give me the address or telephone number of wherever or whomever you are staying with here in Wyattsville."

"We ain't staying nowhere yet. We're gonna get a sleeping room after Paul gets money."

"You're homeless?" Olivia gasped. "A child your age homeless?"

The word had a shameful sound and slammed into Jubilee like an angry fist. "We ain't homeless! We're gonna get our own sleeping room, or go stay with Aunt Anita! We just ain't decided yet."

"Oh," Olivia backed off. "Thank God you have someone." For a brief moment, she'd feared the girl was another Ethan Allen, a child with no one. "Well, then, we can call Aunt Anita."

"Before you start asking me again," Jubilee warned, "I ain't got her address or telephone number either."

"Just tell me her last name. I can look it up in the phone book."

Jubilee struggled to remember Paul's words and after several seconds said, "Walker. She was Mama's sister, I think."

"Anita Walker," Olivia replied. "That should be easy enough to find." She pulled out the telephone book and began flipping through the pages.

Before Olivia even reached W, Jubilee said, "That ain't gonna do no good."

"What isn't going to do any good?"

"Calling Aunt Anita."

"Why not?"

"She don't know Daddy's dead, and she don't know we're coming to stay with her." Jubilee remembered Paul's warning about Aunt Anita possibly not wanting them, and she wasn't anxious to check it out alone.

"Your aunt doesn't know you're coming to stay with her?" Olivia repeated. The reality of the situation became apparent—Jubilee and her brother were not from Wyattsville. They weren't from anywhere around here. The girl was different, her way of speaking, her dress…

"Where did you and your brother come from?" Olivia asked.

"Coal Fork."

"Where is Coal Fork?"

"Up the mountain," Jubilee said. "Past Campbell's Creek."

"In Virginia?"

Jubilee rubbed her nose with the palm of her hand and thought for a moment; then she shook her head. "I don't think so."

Bewildered by this turn of events, Olivia asked. "How on earth did you get here?"

"On the bus," Jubilee said indignantly. "We paid our fares like everybody else."

Olivia's chin dropped. "Does anybody at all, any grownup, know you're here in Wyattsville?"

"Just Paul." Jubilee shrugged.

"And Paul left you on the bench and didn't come back?"

Jubilee folded her arms across her chest and glared at Olivia. "He's gonna come back, soon as he finishes the job."

"So you say." Olivia sighed. Then she lowered herself into the chair and began wondering what to do. After a good half-hour and no other ideas, she remembered Ethan Allen had brought the girl home for dinner. "Jubilee, are you hungry?"

When the girl nodded, Olivia stood and gave a forced smile. "Perhaps a nice bowl of beef stew is what we need." She took Jubilee by the hand and led her into the bathroom. "Wash your hands, sweetheart, and when you're finished we'll have dinner."

The thought of having another belongs-to-nobody child made Olivia cringe. She'd been down this road before, and it wearied her soul to think of it. Although she could hardly fault Ethan Allen for doing the right thing, she kept asking herself, "Why me?" Irritated at such thoughts, she also grew impatient with Ethan Allen for presenting the problem. As she passed through the living room she glared at him and said, "Make sure you wash your hands too."

"They ain't dirty," he answered.

"Yes, they are," she said sharply and continued to the kitchen. Food was never really an answer, but for now it was the only one she had. Olivia began spooning up three bowls of stew—a stew that, like her fears, had simmered for too long.

Olivia set the plates on the table and called the kids to come to dinner. "Ethan Allen, make sure you've washed those hands."

"Okay," he answered, then took the ball he and Dog had been playing with and tossed it across the room. He swiped his hands across the back of his pants and followed Jubilee into the kitchen.

After she poured two glasses of milk, Olivia sat opposite the children and watched Jubilee gobbling up the stew. She couldn't help but notice what a pretty little thing the girl was; tiny but with a sweet smile and blue eyes that would one day have lads swooning. Surely the child was mistaken. Someone knew she was missing. Someone had to be looking for a child like this—a brother, an aunt, an uncle. They were probably out there right now, walking through the streets, calling her name.

Olivia thought back on the night Ethan ran away and felt a stab of pain remembering the anguish that came with the realization he was out there alone. A missing child meant a broken heart for someone. She couldn't let that happen. She had to find the child's family.

Unsure of whether the girl knew something she wasn't telling or was simply telling all she knew, Olivia made up her mind to discover whatever there was to discover. She thought back on the way Ethan Allen had stubbornly refused to tell what he knew until he'd come to trust her. Trust. It was the dividing line between truth and nothing. She had to cross that line.

"So, Jubilee," she said sweetly, "is your Aunt Anita pretty like you are?"

Jubilee gave a bewildered shrug.

"Does she look like you or your mama?"

"I don't know. I never saw her."

"But you talked to her on the telephone, right?"

Jubie crinkled her nose and shook her head. "We didn't have no telephone."

"Didn't have a phone? Everybody has a telephone."

"Not in Coal Fork. Nobody has a telephone."

"Nobody has a phone?"

"The company store has one, but folks ain't supposed to use it."

"How did your mama communicate with her sister?"

"What's com-une-i-cake?"

"It means talk," Olivia said, "or send messages."

"Oh. Okay."

"Well? Did Aunt Anita send your mama letters?"

"I don't know," she replied with an air of exasperation. "I think maybe Aunt Anita didn't like Mama."

"What makes you say that?"

"Paul told me."

"That's too bad." Olivia gave a sympathetic sigh. "When you came to Wyattsville, were you and Paul going to visit your Aunt Anita?"

"Maybe visit," Jubilee clarified. "Paul don't know for sure where she is."

"Did he have her address?"

Jubilee spooned another bite of stew and shook her head. "Unh-unh. We ain't too sure of her name either. It was Walker like Mama's, but if she got married it likely ain't anymore."

"Oh." Olivia felt stymied and wondered where to go from here. She hesitated a moment, then asked, "When Paul told you to wait there, was he going to look for your aunt?"

Jubilee shook her head. "I told you, he was going to do a job."

"What job?"

"In the store." Jubilee scooped one last carrot from the bowl.

"Do you know the name of the store?"

Jubilee looked up like she was thinking, then shook her head again. "I ain't remembering the name. But it had a sign for working."

"Okay, that's something." Olivia gave her a reassuring smile. "I know remembering is hard, but you're doing a very good job."

Ethan Allen, who generally had something to say about everything, was strangely silent as he listened to the exchange. Then when Jubilee said she didn't know the name of the store, he jumped up from the table saying he thought he'd forgotten to wash his hands after all. Olivia was going to say he needn't bother now that he'd finished dinner, but before she could say anything he'd darted off to the bathroom.

"Can I have more?" Jubilee asked and pushed her empty bowl toward Olivia.

"Of course you can." Olivia filled the bowl a second time, handed it to Jubilee, and then went back to her questions. Hoping for even a scrap of information she asked, "Did Paul say anything about where you were going when he came back?"

Jubilee nodded proudly. "He said we was gonna get a nice place to stay and good food."

"Did he say what the name of that nice place was?"

"Unh-unh. He just said if he got money from the job, it wouldn't matter none if we didn't find Aunt Anita."

"Were you going to return home?"

Jubilee thought back on the cabin they'd left behind. "No. We can't live there no more. The mine man said so."

"The mine man?"

Jubilee nodded. "He said only people what work in the mine can have houses, and 'cause Paul promised Daddy he wouldn't work in the mine we had to give back the house."

When Olivia asked how old her brother was, Jubilee wrinkled her nose and gave a shrug. "Sixteen, I think."

After almost an hour, two bowls of stew, a dish of ice cream, a slice of lemon pound cake, and three cookies, Olivia had learned almost nothing. The girl came from a place where people didn't have telephones, her last name was Jones, her brother had brown hair, and they had come to

Wyattsville looking for an aunt who might or might not be named Anita Walker.

When Olivia was satisfied she had gotten all the girl knew, she settled the kids in front of the television with a bowl of popcorn. Disappearing back into the kitchen, she began calling all of the Walkers listed in the Wyattsville telephone directory. There were one hundred and forty-seven, thirteen with the initial A, and not one with the name Anita. When the twenty-eighth Walker slammed the receiver down and said it was too damn late to be bothering people about such nonsense she abandoned the project, at least for the remainder of the evening.

Olivia wondered whether she should call the Wyattsville Police Station when she noticed Jubilee asleep on the sofa. If she notified the police and they couldn't find the missing brother or the questionable aunt, the poor child would be carted off to a foster home or—worse yet—an orphanage. Olivia shuddered at the thought.

Remembering how Ethan Allen had come into her life because he'd gone in search of his grandfather, she could understand why Paul was trying to find their Aunt Anita. "Family is family," she said with a sigh. Convinced there was an Aunt Anita and the only challenge would be finding her, Olivia decided not to call the authorities. If worse came to worst and she became desperate, there was one person she could trust. She hadn't spoken with Jack Mahoney in almost six months, but she knew he'd be there and he'd answer the call.

Olivia removed Jubilee's shoes, carried her into the bedroom, and tucked her into Charlie's side of the bed. She placed the sleepy little head on a fluffy pillow that hadn't been used for two years.

When Olivia returned to the living room, her eyes were watery. "That poor child…" she murmured.

Ethan Allen, who'd been focused on watching a television show, looked up. "You ain't even heard the worst yet."

"The worst?"

"Yeah. You know that robbed place I was at? Well, that's where Jubie said her brother was supposed to be working."

"Klaussner's Grocery Store?" Olivia gasped.

Ethan Allen nodded.

"Dear God," Olivia said. "You don't suppose her brother was involved in that."

"I ain't supposing nothin'—I figured you was gonna take charge of that."

Olivia shooed Ethan Allen off to bed and changed the channel on the television. Maybe there'd be something on the news.

There was.

Ethan Allen

I didn't want to tell Grandma this on account of she's a worrier. Mama never worried about nothin', but Grandma, she worries about everything. The sorry truth is I didn't see no live people come out of that grocery store. Far as I could tell, they was all dead.

With him needing money, I wouldn't be the least bit surprised if Paul was the one robbing Mister Klaussner. Jubie said he was gonna do a job, and that's what crooks call it when they're gonna rob a place. Maybe her brother ain't really a crook, but when you got no place to go and nothin' to eat you gotta do something—even if it's something you ain't none too proud of doing.

Whatever he did, I can say for sure Jubie's got nothin' to do with it. I know what feeling scared looks like, and Jubie was honest-to-God scared. Not the kind of guilty-scared you get from doing something you ain't supposed to do, but the kind of scared that's 'cause you're all alone and you got nobody to turn to.

I ain't no do-gooder like Grandma, but I sure felt bad for Jubie. I think it's 'cause she's so little. She said she was seven, but I'm thinking more like five. If she's really seven, then for sure she's the runt of the litter.

Late News

Olivia sat glued to the television as she listened to reports of the robbery. According to Martha Tillinger who was being interviewed on the ten o'clock news, two men had walked into Klaussner's grocery store in broad daylight, brandished a gun, and started shooting. At that point Martha, who had been on the far side of the store selecting a box of crackers to go with her homemade onion dip, ducked behind a large display of cereal boxes and rolled herself into a ball.

"I couldn't see what was happening, but I know the sound of gunfire when I hear it," she told the reporter. Martha then went on to render the opinion that it would have been far wiser for Sid to just hand over the money instead of trying to shoot it out with two armed bandits.

The reporter nodded solemnly, then turned back to the camera for a close up. "Sidney Klaussner was shot twice in the chest, and his condition is listed as critical. One of the alleged assailants suffered a head wound and is now in surgery."

"Thanks for that update, Ken," the blond anchorwoman at the KWNB news desk said. Then she said they had very few details at this time, and although detectives acknowledged that one of the alleged assailants had escaped, the name of the second young man had not yet been released. "Join us at seven o'clock tomorrow morning when we'll have more details on this event that has rocked our peaceful little community."

Olivia continued to watch as the weatherman came on and explained that a cold front was headed their way. After the weather there was a long shot of the news desk, some jovial banter, and then it was over. A voice said to stay tuned for Jerry Lester's "Broadway Open House."

There was not one word about Paul Jones or a missing child.

"Oh, dear," Olivia said. She snapped off the television and sat silently in the chair. It made no sense. Why would these kids have come to Wyattsville, unless...

The more she mulled it over, the more sense it made. Paul had obviously contacted the aunt and said they were coming. Maybe he sent a letter or a postcard. Reasoning that a seven-year-old child quite possibly did not understand the specifics, she began to imagine the aunt frantic with worry.

The bitter taste of memories about the night Ethan Allen disappeared swelled in Olivia's throat. He'd been gone just a few hours when a search party set out looking for him. People cared. Even though they'd known Ethan Allen only a short while, they cared. In a room so silent you could hear the whisper of wind, Olivia sat and listened. She hoped to hear a voice calling for the girl, but there was nothing. Twice she thought she'd heard the sound of sobbing, but both times it was simply the choke of a motor car miles away.

The clock chimed midnight. Olivia got up and tiptoed into the bedroom to check on the girl. Jubilee was sound asleep, her tiny fingers curled into a fist and a thumb stuck in her mouth. Her dark hair lay scattered across the pillow, in need of a trim perhaps, but clean. Olivia returned to the living room and sat in the same chair, the silk chair that stood where Charlie's club chair once sat.

Most evenings she went to bed shortly after she'd said goodnight to Ethan Allen. She seldom sat in this spot with everything silent as it was now. It brought back memories—good memories, but too many of them, and they always ended with the same thought, the same longing. The clock ticked, a faraway horn blared, Dog rustled around, scratched at his hind leg, then dropped back to sleep again. Familiar sounds all of them. Yes, familiar and comforting, yet tonight the quiet was disconcerting.

The tiny shoes were still where they had fallen when Olivia removed them before carrying the child to bed. From where she sat Olivia could see a small hole in the bottom of one shoe. She lifted the shoe in her hand and turned it over. A piece of grey cardboard had been trimmed to size and stuffed inside to cover the hole. It was obvious that someone cared for this child, but who? And where were they now?

It was after one o'clock when Olivia dialed Seth Porter's number. The telephone rang ten times. No answer. Certain she'd not get an answer on the eleventh ring, Olivia was just about to hang up when someone lifted the receiver. She expected a hello, but all she heard was the loud thump of something falling. "Seth?"

"Yeah, yeah," a hollowed out echo answered back.

"Seth, are you okay?"

"Mostly," he finally answered. "What's wrong?"

"I'm not certain. There's something about the robbery at Klaussner's that's troubling me."

"Good grief, that happened early this morning!"

"Yes, I know, but Ethan Allen mentioned he saw you there, and I was wondering—"

"He was late for school, wasn't he?"

"Well, yes, but that isn't—"

"I knew it! Three times I told him to get going and—"

"Were there other kids there?"

"You mean other kids being late to school?"

"Not school kids, little kids. Girls maybe?"

"There was a sizable crowd of folks, but no babies far as I could tell."

"Not babies, little girls. Maybe sitting on the bench across the street?"

"I can't say who was back there. I was looking to see what happened."

"Oh." The sound of disappointment was obvious in Olivia's voice. "Maybe you ought to come down here. There's something I need to ask you."

"I'm in my pajamas. Does it have to be now?"

"I'm afraid so."

Minutes later the apartment doorbell bing-bonged. Olivia pulled it open and made a shushing gesture. "Be quiet. I don't want to wake the children."

"Children?" Seth said. "There's more than one?"

Olivia nodded. "Ethan Allen brought this little girl home—"

"He's only twelve! Boys ain't supposed to start that stuff 'til—"

"No, it's a *little* girl! Ethan said he found her sitting on the bench across from Klaussner's." Olivia quietly eased open the door to her bedroom and pointed to the sleeping child. "That's her," she whispered. "Did you see her there today?"

Seth tiptoed across the room, looked down at the child, then looked back at Olivia. He shrugged and shook his head.

After they left the room and closed the door behind them, Olivia told Seth the story Ethan Allen had told her.

"So the kid said this Paul guy was inside Klaussner's?"

"Not exactly," Olivia answered. "She just said she was supposed to sit there and wait for him. But when Ethan asked where Paul was, she pointed to the store."

"Maybe she meant the barber shop next door?"

"I doubt it," Olivia said. "If that's where he went, why didn't he come back?"

Seth ran his fingers through his already-rumpled hair. "Hmm, that's a point. This Paul, is he the kid's father?"

"No, her brother," Olivia answered. She explained that the girl's name was Jubilee Jones and apparently her parents were deceased. "When I asked where her parents were, she said dead."

"Maybe the kid's lying," Seth suggested. "Remember how Ethan Allen—"

Olivia shook her head. "I don't think so. This girl is different. She doesn't volunteer anything, but when she does say something you kind of know she's telling the truth."

"Kids are kids," Seth said, thinking back on how Ethan Allen could tell a story longer than a person's arm.

"There was not one word about a missing girl on the news. Not one," Olivia said. "So now I'm in a quandary as to what to do. I thought maybe you'd have some suggestions."

"Me?" Seth gasped. "Why me?"

"Well, you were there."

"I didn't see the girl. I've got nothing to do with this."

"But maybe you could find out whether or not her brother was involved."

They argued for almost twenty minutes with Seth insisting that Olivia was getting mixed up in something that was none of her affair, and Olivia claiming the child was much too young to be turned over to the authorities.

"Ethan Allen never did admit it," Olivia said, "but I knew how frightened he was. This girl is half his age! Imagine being seven years old and all alone."

"But with Ethan Allen you had a right. You were related to him," Seth argued. "You're not related to this kid in any way."

"Maybe not, but somebody is. Once I call in the authorities they're going to take her away, lock her up in a home for orphan children."

"Yeah, well, if they find out you've got a kid what don't belong to you, they'll lock you up!"

"They're not going to find out. All I have to do is find the child's Aunt Anita."

"Have it your way," Seth said angrily, "but when they come and arrest you for kidnapping, don't call me!" With that he turned and stomped out the door.

Olivia did not go to bed that night. She sat in the straight-backed chair until four-thirty; then she napped on the sofa until six. Since she was already awake, she got up, washed her face, and began waiting for the six o'clock news to start.

The Hospital

The last time a shooting took place in Wyattsville was back in 1944, and it was little more than a superficial leg wound. Walter Clemmons had put a bullet through the thigh of his brother-in-law. Although everyone knew the two of them didn't get along, Walter claimed he'd mistaken his wife's brother for a burglar. It was nothing more than a family squabble that got out of control and could hardly be considered a crime. This was an out-and-out crime—armed robbery and, from the look of things, conceivably homicide.

When the first ambulance driver called in his report saying, "Gunshot victim, white male, fifty-eight, chest wound, heavy bleeding, non-responsive," the emergency room supervisor issued a "Code Blue," the crisis management procedure they practiced monthly but had never before used.

Minutes later two interns, two orderlies, and three nurses stood in front of the emergency entrance. Sidney Klaussner was rolled from the van and taken to Exam Room One where Doctor Kellerman waited. Minutes later Sidney was on his way to the operating room.

Paul wasn't quite so lucky. When the second ambulance rolled up no one was waiting. The two ambulance attendants brought the gurney in. The only doctor still on duty in the ER was Alfred Peters, a second-year neurosurgery resident. He would have been in the operating room with Doctor Kellerman were it not for the fact that Alfred was nursing a hangover and hung back when the others rushed to answer the Code Blue.

"You gotta be kidding," he grumbled when the second gunshot victim was brought in. Alfred had the makings of a great surgeon someday, but unfortunately this wasn't the day. His head ached, and his eyeballs felt fuzzy and out of focus. If it were a kid with a broken arm or a woman showing signs of the flu, he could have stumbled through the process with no problem. But the boy on the table had a gunshot to the head.

The kid was eighteen, nineteen at most. Alfred looked down at a face younger than his own. The boy seemed to drift in and out of consciousness, but the fear in his eyes was palpable. Trying to gather his thoughts, Alfred asked, "Can you hear me?"

No answer.

"You're at Mercy General Hospital. You've been shot, but we're going to take care of you." Alfred was trying to sound confident, trying not to let his voice reflect the haze he was stumbling through. "Do you remember what happened?"

Without moving anything but the focus of his eyes, the boy looked up. It was an almost imperceptible movement, but one that pushed through the hangover fog and grabbed hold of Alfred's heart.

"Let's get this kid stabilized!" Alfred shouted. Somehow he forgot the pounding in his head. He was no longer a resident intern with a hangover; he was Doctor Peters. Fifteen minutes later Paul, who by then had lost consciousness, was sliding through a CT scanner. Doctor Peters stood behind the glass watching attentively.

"Okay," he said when he saw where the bullet had cut a swath across the right side of the boy's skull. If he used the kind of skill he was capable of the kid had a decent chance, but given the swelling and external trauma anything could happen.

When Alfred Peters walked into the operating room, he felt a responsibility greater than any he'd ever before known. Life or death. A functioning human being or a forever comatose boy. It was up to him.

Although the bullet had not penetrated the brain, the boy's head was already starting to swell.

When Paul was brought in, he had twelve dollars and a handful of change in his pocket. No driver's license, no voter registration, no "in case of emergency contact" information, not even a wallet. He was listed as John Doe.

Sidney Klaussner had been in surgery for five hours, but to Carmella it seemed a lifetime. She paced back and forth across the waiting room, first sobbing softly, then wailing so loudly it could be heard at the far end of the fourth floor hallway. Twice nurses came in and suggested she go home and try to get some rest.

"We'll call you the minute your husband is out of surgery," they said, but Carmella would have none of it.

"Go home?!" she screeched. "Go home when my poor Sidney is in there fighting for his life?" Not only did she refuse to consider the idea, she also refused the sedative they offered. At that point there was little anyone could do other than sit beside Carmella and comfort her.

After what she could have sworn was a week of waiting, Doctor Kellerman walked into the waiting room looking worn and weary. He sat on the sofa alongside Carmella.

"Your husband's out of surgery and doing as well as can be expected."

"As well as can be expected?" Carmella repeated. Her left eye blinked furiously, and a look of panic grabbed hold of her face.

"There was quite a bit of damage," Doctor Kellerman said. "One of the shots went clear through Sidney's upper left lung. The other hit his colon and stomach. There was a lot of trauma and swelling, but I expect…"

Threaded throughout the words he spoke was the sound of Carmella's sobbing. "Dear God," she repeated over and over.

"Sidney will be out of the recovery room in two or three hours," Kellerman said. "You'll be able to spend a few minutes with him once he's settled in intensive care." At that point Carmella no longer acknowledged his words; she just sat there praying for divine intervention. After he'd told all he could tell, Kellerman sat there for several minutes saying nothing but nervously rubbing his hands together as Carmella rattled off three Hail Marys.

It was almost ten o'clock that evening before Carmella was ushered into Sidney's room. In a husky whisper the nurse informed her that it would be best if she didn't stay more than ten minutes. "Right now what your husband needs is rest," she explained.

Carmella knew better. After thirty years of marriage, she knew what Sidney needed was her by his side. She quietly slipped to the far side of the room and sat in the darkest corner, the corner behind the ventilator. She remained there for a long while listening to the machine whoosh air into her husband's injured lung. At first she counted the breaths, wondering how many it would take before Sidney again opened his eyes. And when she lost count of the breaths she counted heartbeats as they bleeped across the monitor. In between the heartbeats and breaths she prayed, sometimes silently, sometimes in a whisper so small only an angel hovering overhead could have heard.

No one noticed Carmella was there until well after midnight; then she was told to leave. "I know my Sidney," she argued feebly. "He'd want me here."

When the nurse flatly stated, "Rules are rules," Carmella leaned over and kissed Sidney's cheek. "I'll be back first thing in the morning," she said. Then she turned and walked down the long hallway that led to a bank of elevators. Tears rolled down her face, and the sound of her own heartbeat thundered in her ears.

Although Carmella, a woman who insisted she grew faint if she skipped a meal, hadn't eaten all day she had wanted to stay. At least until Sidney opened his eyes.

Blinded by concern for her husband, Carmella walked past the room two doors down, the room where a uniformed policeman stood guard at the door. She left for home not knowing that inside that room was a teenage boy with a shaved head swaddled in bandages. The same sounds of breath and heartbeats could be heard in the boy's room, but nobody cried. Nobody prayed. The policeman standing outside the door yawned and checked his watch. *Four more hours 'til my shift is over,* he thought.

The Next Day

A half-hour before the early morning news started, Olivia was fully dressed. By five-forty-five she'd downed three large cups of coffee. She sat on the sofa and snapped the television on. The test pattern flickered across the screen. For what seemed like a very long minute, she waited. Her right leg crossed over the left, and her right foot jiggled up and down. Three times she moved, crossing and uncrossing her legs, scooting an inch to the right and then to the left. Finally she clicked the television off, reached for the phone, and dialed Clara's number.

A sleepy voice answered. "Who is this?" It was more of an accusation than question.

"I'm sorry," Olivia said. "I know it's early, but—"

"Olivia?"

"You know it's me," she answered. "I realize you don't usually get up this early, but—"

"Early?" Clara thundered. "Why, it's the middle of the night!"

"It's almost six. Besides, this is sort of an emergency. Ethan Allen—"

"Oh, no. Please don't tell me the boy is in trouble again."

"He's not in trouble, but this girl he brought home—"

"He's way too young for that. You've got to tell Ethan Allen—"

"She's not that kind of girl."

"Unh-huh," Clara muttered dubiously. "That's what they all say."

Olivia started to explain the situation, but before she could get to where she was going the clock chimed six. "I've got to go. The news is coming on." With that she hung up the phone and snapped on the television.

The weatherman was only partway through his forecast when the doorbell bonged. "Wait a minute," Olivia called out, her eyes focused on the screen. When he finally said, "Now stay tuned for a word from our sponsor," Olivia rose from the chair and opened the door.

"What's going on here?" a puffed-up Clara asked.

"I'm trying to see if I can find out something about the girl." Olivia motioned Clara toward the living room. "Hopefully it'll be on the news. Watch."

"Watch what?" Clara asked as she lowered herself onto the sofa.

"About the robbery," Olivia said. Her voice turned to a whisper. "I think the girl's brother may have been involved. At least that's what Ethan Allen—"

"I knew it!" Clara exclaimed. "He's in trouble, isn't he?"

"No." Olivia turned back toward Sara Jean Plott who was finishing up a traffic report. "It'll be on now, so pay attention."

Tom Horsham started with the local news.

"Well, folks, it seems that big-city crime is no longer content to plague the metropolitan areas. It has now shown its ugly face right here in Wyattsville." As he spoke a camera panned across the large crowd gathered outside of Klaussner's, then zoomed in on the flashing lights of police cars and ambulances. When the film ended the camera blinked back to Horsham, who shook his head sadly.

"This was the scene yesterday at Klaussner's Grocery on West Main shortly after two armed gunmen held up the store. Store owner Sidney Klaussner was shot twice, once in the chest and again in the abdomen. Now in critical condition at Mercy General Hospital, Klaussner has been unable to identify either of the assailants. According to Sheriff's Deputy Bob Willis, it is believed that before Klaussner was shot he wounded one of the alleged robbers. That suspect is also in critical condition and has not yet been identified."

A sketchy rendering of a mature man flashed on the screen and Horsham continued. "If you know or can identify this man, please contact the sheriff's office. A five-hundred-dollar reward has been offered by the Wyattsville Merchants Association for information leading to an arrest of the suspects." After several other local stories, Sara Jean was back with a reminder for traffic headed south on Main Street to watch for the detour. When Sara Jean disappeared, an announcer said to stay tuned for the "Dave Garroway Morning Show."

Olivia clicked off the television and turned to Clara with a worried expression. "There was no mention of a girl."

"What were you expecting?"

"I'm not exactly certain," Olivia replied. "I thought maybe they'd give the name of the man they caught or say if there was a missing girl. Wouldn't you think a policeman or somebody would have noticed a kid all by herself? Did you see the crowd?"

"Well, of course, I did." Clara answered. "I was sitting right here."

"No, I mean did you really *see* the crowd? Ethan Allen was smack in the middle of it."

"I didn't see Ethan. I did see someone who could've been Seth Porter, but Seth usually wears a baseball cap and this man didn't have—"

"It was Seth. Ethan saw him there."

"I don't understand what they've got to do with—"

"It's not them. I'm worried about the girl," Olivia said. "Ethan Allen told me she was there, but I didn't see her in any of the pictures."

"So?"

"We-ell," Olivia stretched the word out, making it seem a dalliance. "The girl Ethan Allen brought home told him she was there waiting for her brother. When Ethan asked where the brother was, the girl pointed to Klaussner's!"

Clara's sleepy eyes opened so wide you could see the white all around. "No!"

"Yes." She went on to relate all that Ethan Allen had told her. But before she got to the part about the mysterious Aunt Anita, a sleepy-faced Jubilee appeared in the doorway.

The little girl rubbed her eyes and asked, "Did Paul come back?"

"Not yet, Jubilee, but Ethan Allen is going to stop by the store this afternoon and check to see if he's there."

"Oh." The little girl looked down at her feet with a visible sadness. It was a sadness Olivia knew only too well: the sadness of being alone in the world.

"Don't worry," Olivia said. "Maybe the store was extra busy and needed Paul to work for a longer time." Her words were not what she would have considered a lie. They were simply a measure of comfort for a frightened child. But when she looked up Clara's jaw was hanging open, and she wore a look of disbelief.

"Olivia Doyle! You know—"

"My goodness," Olivia interrupted, "look at the time! Ethan Allen has got to get up and start getting ready for school."

"But," Clara stammered, "you told me—"

"Clara, you'd best be getting along now." Olivia nudged her friend toward the door, cutting off the opportunity for more conversation and things that were better off unsaid. "I'll give you a buzz after Ethan leaves for school." Without a moment's delay, she hustled the bewildered Clara out the door.

"Don't you think—" Clara started to say, but by then the door was closed.

For the next hour, Olivia tried to make everything appear as normal as possible. Although she had more than a dozen questions about the truth of the robbery, she brushed them aside and tried to focus on the business of the day. On Saturday mornings Ethan Allen was up at the crack of dawn and on his way to the playground before the clock struck eight. School-day mornings were a different story. Ethan had been awake for more than a half-hour, but he was still in his pajamas. Olivia poked her head into his room.

"Get dressed," she told him for the third time. "You'll be late again if you don't get a move on."

"I got plenty of time," he answered and continued wrestling with Dog.

Olivia thumped her hands on her hips and glared across the room. "Five minutes," she said. "Breakfast will be ready in five minutes, and you'd better be sitting at the table."

"Okay." Ethan Allen reached for the socks on the floor.

"Those are yesterday's," Olivia said. "Get a clean pair." She turned and headed back to the kitchen. The daily routine of getting Ethan off to school was so hectic that she'd momentarily forgotten about their visitor. Maybe not forgotten, but simply set aside thoughts of the homeless girl, the missing brother and the mysterious aunt. When she passed through the living room she was pushed back into the reality of those things by the sight of Jubilee huddled in the corner of the sofa with her thumb stuck in her mouth.

Olivia stopped and watched the girl for a moment. Curled into a ball as she was, Jubilee had the look of a throw pillow—smaller maybe, but equally zipped up. The two children were so different, and yet in some ways they were alike. Olivia thought back on how Ethan Allen had slammed into her life with an anger that stuck out like the quills of a porcupine. He'd clattered through the apartment, banging into things, filling the emptiness of her days with ball bouncing and boisterousness. Ethan Allen was a boy with a huge chip on his shoulder and the sorrow of life written across his face. Jubilee was a blank chalkboard.

"Jubilee, dear," Olivia said, "I'm getting ready to make breakfast. Is there something particular you'd like to have?" It had taken almost a year to get Ethan settled into eating things like cereal and eggs, so she was hoping the girl wouldn't say potato chips.

She didn't. In fact, she didn't say anything, just shrugged her shoulders without ever removing her thumb from her mouth.

"Isn't there some special breakfast you'd enjoy?" Olivia urged. "Cereal maybe? Or waffles with maple syrup?"

There was an almost imperceptible shake of Jubilee's head.

"Bacon? French toast?"

This time there was not even a head shake.

Olivia tried another approach. "At home what do you have for breakfast?"

Jubilee pulled her thumb from her mouth and said, "Biscuits and gravy."

"Oh, dear," Olivia said. "I'm afraid that's the one thing I don't have." She took Jubilee by the hand and tugged her into the kitchen. "Let's see if we don't have something almost as good."

Promising that pancakes were every bit as good as biscuits and gravy, Olivia began mixing the batter. She wished the girl would talk, even if it was to argue or complain as Ethan had, but instead Jubilee sat there without saying a word. When an uncomfortable silence began to settle into the room, Olivia padded it with the sound of her own words. She began by describing the step-by-step process of pancake making, then moved on to the fact that it promised to be another cloudy day as opposed to the sunshine she'd been wishing for. For almost ten minutes she rattled on about anything and everything except was at the forefront of her mind: the child's missing brother. After she'd set three plates of pancakes on the table, she called Ethan.

"Hurry up," she said, "or you'll be late for school."

Jubilee's eyes brightened. "We're going to school?"

Olivia turned and smiled. "Ethan has to go to school today, but you can stay here with me."

"I don't want to stay here. I want to go to school with Ethan."

Before Olivia could answer Ethan Allen slid into his seat and said, "You can't. My school's just for big kids."

"I go to school with Paul, and he's big."

Ethan shoved a chunk of pancake into his mouth and didn't answer.

Although Olivia tried to avoid thinking about Paul, he had come to breakfast. He was in the room, a ghost, as real as a person waiting to be served up an order of pancakes. The missing brother was as Charlie had been in the early months, not here and not quite gone. How strange it seemed that a woman with so many years of living behind her and a child with a like number of years in front of her should experience the same empty-hearted longing.

"Well, Jubilee," she said, "I have a lot of baking to do today, and I was hoping you'd be able to help me. You do like to bake cookies, don't you?"

Jubilee gave a half-hearted shrug. "I never made cookies."

"Well, wouldn't you like to learn?"

Before Jubilee could answer Ethan volunteered to stay home and help.

"Absolutely not," Olivia replied. "You're going to school."

"Grandma, I gotta tell you, making me go to school ain't such a good idea."

"Isn't such a good idea," Olivia corrected. "And why isn't it?"

"We got a history test today, and I studied but I ain't nowhere near ready. Gimme a few more days and—"

"You're going to school." The finality of Olivia's words ended the discussion. Fifteen minutes later Ethan Allen begrudgingly picked up his books and headed for the door.

Jubilee followed him through the living room and stopped when he opened the door. "Bye, Ethan" she said sadly.

"Bye," he answered, then was gone.

Once Olivia was alone with the child, the uncomfortable silence was back. Olivia pulled the flour and sugar from the cabinet.

"Cooking and baking always helps me to feel better when I'm worried about something," she told Jubilee. "I bet it will help you too."

There was no answer.

Olivia continued on. Just as she'd given the step-by-step of pancake making, she now went into cookie baking. Once she'd mixed in the melted butter and eggs, she fluffed a covering of flour on the counter and plopped the ball of dough in the middle. She pulled a rolling pin from the drawer, and for the first time since Ethan left the girl spoke.

"I can do that," she said and reached for the rolling pin.

Olivia smiled. "I thought you said you never made cookies."

Jubilee looked up with a sly smile. "This's same as making biscuits," she countered and began rolling out the dough.

Once Olivia busied Jubilee with the second batch, she slipped into the living room and called Clara. "I apologize for hustling you out the door," she said, "but I was afraid you'd say something to upset the child."

"I hardly think that excuses—"

"I know," Olivia replied, "but under the circumstances..."

She went on to say that she didn't want to burden the girl with such bad news until she had a bit of good news. She explained how there was an aunt who hopefully lived in Wyattsville and hopefully had the last name of Walker. "I'm hoping to find this woman, so Jubilee can at least be with family."

"That sounds like a whole lot of hoping without much to go on."

"I know." Olivia sighed. "But I was thinking maybe you'd be able to help."

"Me? Why me?"

"Because you're my friend."

Clara was wordless for a few moments. Then she said, "I suppose I could lend a hand, but I'm not gonna stand around and listen to you telling the kid those bare-faced lies."

"Fair enough."

"Okay then , if we're really gonna try and find the kid's aunt we need more information," Clara said. "When Ethan brought the girl home, did she have anything with her? A bag or suitcase maybe?"

"Yes, a travel bag."

"Go through it. If the brother was planning to go to the aunt's house, maybe her address is in there. You might also find out something more about him."

"Good idea," Olivia answered. She glanced over and saw the small bag that had arrived with Jubilee. It was still sitting in the far corner of the living room.

After Clara promised to check out the remaining Walkers listed in the telephone book and call Seth Porter to get more information, they hung up.

Olivia returned to the kitchen and pulled a second cookie cutter from the drawer. "Do you want the circle or the tree?"

Jubilee laughed. "That's a Christmas tree! It's not Christmas."

"I know," Olivia said, "but Christmas tree cookies taste good any time of year."

Jubilee scrunched her nose as if she doubted such a thing was true. "I'm gonna do the round ones," she said and kept a tight grip on the cookie cutter she already had.

As they worked, Olivia talked. She peppered the girl with questions but learned nothing more. Every answer was a yes, no, or obscure statement that gave no hint of where the brother was headed or what their plans had been.

When the last tray of cookies was pulled from the oven, Olivia said, "Well, now that that's done, let's get you cleaned up." She retrieved Jubilee's bag and carried it into the bedroom. "First we'll get you a clean dress, then a bath." She unzipped the bag and right on the top were three slightly faded pictures.

"That's me," Jubilee said, pointing to a baby the woman held in her arms.

"And is this Paul?" Olivia pointed to the young boy in the picture.

Jubilee nodded, then went on to say the other two were her mama and daddy. "That's when I was bab-sized," she said proudly.

Olivia turned the picture over and on the back was a hand-written date—July 17, 1949. She was hoping for something more recent, something that would let her know if the missing Paul resembled the man in the television sketch. In this picture he was just a boy, so it was impossible to tell.

The second picture was a studio portrait of a young woman. The logo of Milburn Photography was gold stamped in the lower right hand corner.

"That's Mama," Jubilee said.

On the back of the photograph was written "Ruthie Jean Walker, 1931."

The third picture was a group of coal miners, but it was so faded that the faces were almost impossible to make out. Olivia checked the back. Nothing. "Who's this?"

Jubilee pointed to the man third from the right. "That's my grandpa," she said, "but I never knowed him."

Beneath the pictures she found a handful of threadbare underwear, a coal miner's hat, a music box with a picture of a rose on the top of it, a worn Bible, and a book of Grimm's Fairy Tales. Olivia pulled these things from the bag, then asked, "Did your brother have another suitcase?"

Jubilee shook her head, "No, ma'am."

"You didn't bring any clothes?"

"We just brought what was important."

Olivia looked at the hard hat. It was greyed with coal dust. In the front just below the lantern light were black letters reading B. Jones.

Olivia

I can understand holding on to things that were part of someone you've lost. God knows I did it for way longer than I should have. If it wasn't for Clara and the girls, Charlie's toothbrush would probably still be hanging in the bathroom. What I don't understand is children leaving home with stuff like that and not a stitch of clothes. If Jubilee's brother is old enough to work, then he ought to know the girl would need something to wear.

While Jubilee was taking her bath, I started putting the stuff back in the bag. That's when I discovered the letters folded inside the Bible. Maybe it's wrong to go prying through someone else's personal belongings, but since the envelopes were postmarked Wyattsville I thought they'd give information enough to find the aunt.

The letters were from Anita all right, but there was not one word about her last name or where she lived. There was plenty of criticizing her sister. Downright scorn for Bartholomew, who I'm assuming was Jubilee's daddy, and one mention of a baby. Right off Anita struck me as a person who was heavy handed on advice and short on tolerance.

Her mean-spirited words had me riled, until I thought back on how I used to squabble with my sister. We'd get to fussing over some silly nonsense and say the awfulest things to one another. Then before a week went by we'd make up and go right back to being friends. Sisters don't weigh their words with each other; that's just how it is. When you've got a gripe on your chest you say what you're thinking, whether it's hurtful or not. You never stop to consider there might not be a tomorrow when you can take it back.

I can't imagine what a terrible burden it must be for Anita, carrying around a guilt such as that.

Thinking It Through

Olivia put the letters back into the bag, zipped it shut, and set it in the floor of the living room closet.

But putting the bag away didn't erase thoughts of the letters. Anita's words remained in her head, and the more she mulled them over she more convinced she became that not only did Jubie need her aunt but Anita needed her sister's child.

Olivia thought back on all the times she'd argued with her own sister. In the heat of anger she once told Geraldine she detested the sight of her face and never again wanted to lay eyes on it. The name-calling and angry glares lasted for almost two days and disrupted the entire household. It finally ended when their mother said she'd disown both of the girls if they didn't stop that infernal arguing.

When Olivia remembered the hatefulness that had passed between them, she felt a stabbing pain shoot through her heart. Her hand flew up to her chest, and she fell back into the chair. "Lord God, what if Geraldine had died in the midst of all that?"

It was a question, but Olivia already knew the answer. She would gather all five of Geraldine's children to her bosom and treasure them as if they were her own. Anita would surely feel the same. Olivia could almost see the joy in the sister's eyes when she met the delightful little girl she had never known. A sense of excitement began to surge through Olivia. It was the thrill of bringing such happiness to someone who, for now, was a stranger.

After Jubilee dried herself and climbed back into the wrinkled dress, Olivia suggested they go downtown and pick up something for her to wear.

"You'll want to look your best when you meet your Aunt Anita." She then went on to describe the wonders that awaited. "Aunt Anita will want to take you everywhere: to the circus, to the zoo, out to lunch..."

Jubilee looked up with the right side of her face twisted in an expression of doubt. Her eyebrows were slanted and her mouth pulled up. "That don't sound right to me."

"Doesn't sound right," Olivia corrected. "And what doesn't sound right?"

"All of it."

"Why? What's wrong?"

"This Aunt Anita don't even know me. Why's she gonna do all that stuff?"

"Because you're her niece, her sister's child. Aunties always love their little nieces."

The crinkled map of doubt spread across Jubilee's face. "That ain't what Paul said."

"Isn't what Paul said," Olivia corrected. After a year with Ethan Allen she'd developed a habit of doing it without thinking. "Why? What did Paul say?"

"He don't know if Aunt Anita is gonna like us."

"Nonsense," Olivia poo-pooed the words. "She's your aunt, your mother's sister!"

"Yeah, and that's why she ain't gonna like us."

"No," Olivia said emphatically. "That's the reason why she'll not just like you, she'll absolutely love you!"

Jubie shrugged, but she still wore that crinkled look of doubt.

It was a twenty-minute drive to Kline's Department Store. On the way Olivia questioned Jubilee about what type of clothes she would like. "Dresses," Olivia suggested. "Pink, maybe, or pale maize."

"Whatever they got is fine with me," Jubilee answered.

"You'll also need undies and some pajamas." For almost a full five minutes Olivia counted up the things Jubilee would need. She even added a new suitcase to carry the clothes to Auntie's house, once they'd found her.

Jubilee listened wide-eyed, and when it seemed Olivia was done with listing all the necessities, she asked, "What about Paul? What's he gonna wear?"

A jolt of reality shot through Olivia. After Charlie died she'd learned to set aside bothersome problems, relegate them to a spot in her mind that served as a storage closet, a place to put things that were not being used but impossible to get rid of. For a brief while she'd locked the missing brother in that closet, but now he was hammering to get free. "Ah, yes, Paul," she said. "Well, first we've got to find him—"

"He don't need finding!" Jubilee said with an air of exasperation. "He ain't lost! He's working! He's coming back to where I'm supposed to wait!"

"Well, perhaps Paul had to go somewhere else," Olivia said softly. "Maybe he wants to come back but can't."

"He's not somewhere else! He's coming back!"

Jubilee turned an angry face to the window, and in the reflection Olivia saw a solitary tear slide down her cheek.

They rode in silence for several minutes. Then Olivia said, "How about this? We'll get you some nice new clothes today, and when Paul gets back we'll buy him some new clothes too."

Jubilee turned to Olivia with a smile. "Really?"

"Yes, really."

Kline's was having their first-Thursday-of-the-month sale, and just inside the door were several rows of colorful dresses. "What size are you?" Olivia asked.

Accustomed to shopping at the company store and settling for anything that looked big enough to last two or three years, Jubilee shrugged. "I dunno. What size they got?"

Olivia eyed the girl, then pulled a size five from the rack. "This looks about right."

"Ain't it kind of small?"

Olivia looked at the dress again, then looked at Jubilee. "Turn around," she said. She measured the dress against Jubilee's back. "No, I think a size five is just right."

"I'm still growing," Jubilee warned.

Olivia chuckled. "I know that but by the time you've outgrown the size five, you'll need new dresses anyway."

They left Kline's with six dresses, ten pairs of lace-trimmed socks, embroidered panties for each day of the week, two pink nighties, and a pair of black patent leather Mary Janes. Jubilee was wearing a red-and-white check pinafore and the Thursday panties. After stopping at Woolworth's for lunch, they started home.

Perhaps it was because she was busy thinking of the time and wanting to get back before Ethan Allen came from school, or maybe it was because she had drifted into remembering her own nieces and nephews who were now grown with families of their own. Regardless of the reason, Olivia drove home without considering what route she should take. They were traveling west on Main Street when Jubilee let out an ear-piercing yelp.

"Stop!"

As she slammed her foot down on the brake, Olivia realized why. They were in front of Klaussner's. She eased the car to the side of the street and turned off the motor.

With a petrified look on her face, Jubilee pointed to the bench. "It's gone."

"What's gone?"

"The note of where I am."

"Maybe the wind blew it over by the grass."

"No." Jubilee sniffed. "Ethan put a rock on it."

"Let's go have a look." Olivia climbed out of the car, circled around, and opened Jubilee's door. "Come on," she said, extending her hand.

With tears already overflowing her eyes, Jubilee looked at the empty bench and shook her head sorrowfully. "It's gone."

The sadness in her voice made her words seem old, like those of a woman who had lived too many years and lost too many loved ones.

"We'll write a new note," Olivia suggested. "And we'll tape it to the bench so it can't blow away or get lost."

Jubilee shook her head again. "Unh-unh, I gotta stay here." She scooted onto the bench and sat with her feet dangling above the ground.

Olivia sat down beside her. "Well, if you stay here, then I'll just have to stay here with you, because I can't leave you here alone."

"Don't worry. You can leave me alone. I'm big enough."

Olivia was looking down at a miniature-sized version of herself. She remembered the lonely times when she was too independent to allow someone else into her life. If she had it to do over, would she do it the same way? Probably not. Being brave on the outside was a lot easier than being lonely on the inside.

"I know you're big enough," she said. "But friends don't run off and leave each other."

There was no response.

After two full minutes had passed, Olivia asked, "We *are* friends, aren't we?"

"I suppose so."

Without another word they sat side by side on the bench for almost two hours. When Jubilee began to fidget—scratch one leg and then the other, lean forward, lean back, puff the skirt of her dress, then smooth it out—Olivia figured it was time.

"I really do think taping a note to the bench would work fine," she said.

"If it rains, the writing will wash away."

"I'll write it in pencil. Pencil doesn't wash away."

"It don't?"

"Doesn't," Olivia corrected.

"What if Paul don't see the note?"

"I'll make it big. If he comes back, he'll have to see it."

Jubilee shook her head doubtfully. "I don't know."

"Why don't we try it?" Olivia suggested. "I'll get some paper and tape. We'll make a new note and tape it to the bench. Then if you don't think it will work, we'll stay here and wait."

"If I don't think the note's big enough, you're gonna stay here with me?"

"Yes."

"Okay then."

"Do you want to stay here and wait while I get paper and tape?"

Jubilee nodded.

When Olivia started walking toward the stationary store a block down, Jubilee called after her, "You're coming back, aren't you?"

Olivia stopped and looked over her shoulder. "Of course I am," she said, then turned and kept walking. She couldn't see the smile on the girl's face, but she knew it was there.

When Olivia returned, she had a yellow legal-sized pad and a fat pencil. "Okay now, what do you think we should say?"

Jubilee tilted her head, thought for a few moments, then answered. "Dear Paul," she began. "You gotta say dear, 'cause then he'll know I ain't mad at him for being gone so long."

"Okay." Olivia printed in large bold letters.

Jubilee went on to say that she'd waited just as she'd been told, but when it got cold and dark she went home with Ethan Allen. She paused a moment then asked, "You think we ought to tell Paul that Ethan's a kid like me and he's off a farm?"

"I suppose so," Olivia answered. Her words had the sound of sincerity, but inside her heart she suspected the missing brother was not going to show up. Why, she wasn't sure. But something was telling her Anita and only Anita had the answer.

Three times Jubilee changed her mind about what was best to say, and three times Olivia tore off the page and started a new note. Once it was finished, Jubilee suggested they add stars to the four corners of the paper. "Paul puts stars on my papers when I do good, and this way he'll know I'm doing good."

Once the stars were added, Olivia wrapped tape twice around the bench to make sure the note would hold. Jubilee nodded her approval, and they started for home.

Olivia wondered if somewhere deep inside Jubilee suspected the same thing she did. Before they reached the corner, Olivia bounced back to talking about the delights that would come with Aunt Anita. "I just know she'll have a dollhouse for you..."

As Olivia made a right onto Park Street, she saw Jubilee turn back for one last look.

JUBILEE JONES

I ain't never had six dresses at one time. And I sure ain't never had underpants with the day of the week spelled out so you don't get mixed up and wear Tuesday's pants on Wednesday. Much as I like having all this stuff, I gotta say it seems a bit wasteful. Ain't one of them dresses gonna fit me, come next year.

Watching Miss Olivia spend money like she had a bucket of it got me thinking about what Paul said. He's right, city people is a whole lot different. Not bad different, but sure enough different.

Miss Olivia is doing her best to make me feel better, and I was having a nice enough time 'til I saw my note gone from the bench. That's when I got scared; real scared. What if Paul came back when I wasn't there? What if he got mad on account of I didn't wait like he said? All this while, I been thinking he's coming back. But what if he's done been here and gone?

I don't care if I have to give back all the dresses and everything. Stuff like going to the circus or having a dollhouse is real nice, but I'd a lot rather have Paul carrying me home on his back. I'm bigger now and maybe I'm too big for carrying; maybe that's why Paul ain't coming back. It could be he's tired of having a kid sister bothering him all the time. I pray that ain't it.

While Miss Olivia and me was sitting on the bench, I got to studying the store Paul's supposed to be working in, and I got a real bad memory in my head. A long time ago, when Daddy was alive, he showed me a place with that same yellow tape. "Keep out" it said. When I asked

Daddy why we had to keep out, he said it was because the roof caved in and killed a whole bunch of people. "Don't you ever go in a place closed off like that," he said. And I didn't.

Miss Olivia said I shouldn't worry about Paul. She said we'll get to finding him, soon as we find Aunt Anita.

I'm thinking we ought to be looking for Paul and just forget about Aunt Anita.

THE BAD PLACE

When Olivia and Jubilee arrived home, Ethan Allen was lying on the living room floor with his head resting on Dog and his nose buried in a Captain Marvel comic book. "Is your homework done?" Olivia asked.

"Sort of."

Knowing this was Ethan's way of circumventing a no, Olivia told him he could play with Jubilee for a little while but to plan on doing homework after dinner. She crossed to her bedroom, hung Jubilee's dresses in the closet, then closed the door and dialed Clara's number.

"Did you find out anything?" she asked.

"No. I called all the Walkers, even the ones you'd already called. Not one of them knows an Anita. That Hiram, he's a nasty old buzzard. Claims if we keep bothering him about Anita, he's gonna call the police."

"I think Hiram's the one who hung up on me last night," Olivia said. Then she asked about Seth Porter. "Did he tell you anything more than what he told me?"

"Nope. But he did say if somebody reports the girl kidnapped, you're gonna be in for a lot of trouble and he wants no part of it."

"Oh, dear," Olivia said. "Why would he think—"

"You know how Seth is," Clara snorted. "But he's right, you do have to find this kid's aunt and give her back. Once you do that, you've got nothing to worry about. Are you sure the aunt's name is Walker?"

Olivia started to say yes, but then she stopped and thought. Jubilee was only seven. What if she mistook her mama's sister-in-law for sister? If such was the case, Anita would then be related to Jubilee's dad.

"The name might be Jones," Olivia said.

After nearly twenty minutes of discussion she and Clara agreed they had to check out all the Joneses in Wyattsville. It was a list four times as long as that of the Walkers, so they were going to need some help.

"Maybe we could ask Barbara Conklin," Olivia suggested. "I brought over a lovely chocolate cake when her daughter came to visit, so she should be willing to help."

"Of course she will," Clara said. "Fred will too."

Caught up in the moment, Olivia said, "If we ask all the neighbors to help out, I'll bet we could find this Aunt Anita in no time."

"I wouldn't go asking everybody," Clara warned. "Jim Turner's on the Rules Committee, and he's still complaining about Ethan Allen running through the hallways. If Jim finds out you've got another kid in here..." She didn't have to finish the sentence.

"I see what you mean. We'd best keep it quiet."

Once it was decided who would be asked to help, Olivia said she would take Jones A through F and Clara agreed to divvy up the remainder.

Olivia looked at the clock. Six-fifteen already. The A through F Joneses were longer than a page, so it would have to be a quick dinner. Then she'd start calling.

As she hurried through the living room, she heard Ethan Allen and Jubilee talking.

"Three tens beats your kings and queens 'cause they ain't matching," Ethan said.

"You sure?" Jubilee then asked how much she owed him.

Before he could answer, Olivia interrupted the game. "Ethan Allen, are you and Jubilee playing poker?"

He shrugged and gave a sly grin.

Jubilee looked up with smile. "Ethan's learning me how."

"I bet he is!" Olivia began gathering the cards from the table. "Ethan, get that set of checkers. Poker is no game for little girls!" Olivia could already imagine Aunt Anita tsk-tsking the thought of her niece learning to gamble. She made a mental note to pick up something more appropriate. If they wanted to play cards, it would have to be Old Maid.

"Jeez, Grandma," Ethan complained, "it ain't like we was playing for real money."

Once supper was over, Ethan settled down with his homework and a tired little Jubilee slipped her new nightie over her head and climbed into the spot where Charlie once slept. That's when Olivia started telephoning Joneses. She was only halfway through B when the clock struck ten and she shooed Ethan off to bed.

By eleven-thirty two people hung up the receiver before she could ask about Anita and the F.L. Jones on Oak Street said there ought to be a law against ringing the telephone late at night and scaring people to death.

"I thought for sure somebody died," F.L. said, and then he slammed the receiver down like an exclamation point.

It was eleven-thirty-five when Olivia dialed the number for F. M Jones; by then she'd already decided this was to be her last call of the evening. The rest of F could wait until tomorrow morning. A woman answered with a hello somewhat like the croaking of a frog.

"Is this F. M. Jones?" Olivia asked.

"Yeah. Who's this?"

"My name is Olivia Westerly Doyle, and I'm trying to find—"

"Olivia Westerly? You used to work for Southern Atlantic Telephone?"

"Why, yes, I did, but that's not why I'm calling."

"Well, I'll be," F.M. said. "Frances Margaret here. Accounting, remember?"

"Yes, I remember," Olivia replied, even though she really didn't. She simply thought it would help to move the conversation along. "What I'm actually looking for—"

"You still live in Richmond?" Frances Margaret asked.

"No, when I married Charlie, I moved here to Wyattsville—"

"So you got married, huh? I never would've thought it. I figured for sure—"

"I'm calling because I'm trying to locate a woman named Anita Jones," Olivia interrupted. "Do you know anyone by that name?"

"Is this for a company reunion?"

"No, it's not," Olivia replied impatiently. "I'm trying to help a little girl who's looking for her aunt, a woman named Anita Jones or maybe Anita Walker."

"I can't recall anybody named Anita working for Southern Atlantic."

"Not just at the company," Olivia said, "anywhere. Do you know an Anita Jones?"

"Can't say as I do. I used to know a Bartholomew, but he didn't work at Southern Atlantic. Him and his wife rented the upstairs flat in my sister's house."

Growing desperate for even the smallest clue, Olivia asked, "Did Bartholomew or his wife have a sister named Anita?"

"I don't think he did, but his missus might've. There was a bossy sort who visited every so often. That one was nothing like Bartholomew's missus. She was a sweet little thing."

"What was Bartholomew's wife's name?"

"Can't say that I recall," Frances Margaret said. "Shoot, that was nearly twenty years ago, when I lived in Norfolk."

"Did Bartholomew and his wife come from Norfolk?"

"Hmm, not to my recollection. He was a Navy man, but I think she came from someplace a ways off. I recall her talking about how, as a kid, she loved swimming in the bay."

Olivia's heart jumped. "Do you know what bay?"

"Surely you're kidding me!" Frances Margaret cackled. "What makes you think I'd know a thing like that?'

"Well, I just thought maybe..." Olivia's hope fell as rapidly as it had soared.

"You sure there ain't no Southern Atlantic reunion?" Frances Margaret asked again.

Olivia assured her there wasn't. "If you think of anything else, can you give me a call back?" She rattled off her telephone number.

"Yeah, okay," Frances Margaret said and hung up, obviously disappointed about the fact that there was no reunion.

Once it was too late to continue calling, Olivia sat in the silk chair and began thinking back through the conversations of the evening. Of all the calls she'd made, only Frances Margaret Jones offered even the slightest bit of information, and even that was pitiful little. Anita was not going to be as easy to find as she'd originally thought. Wyattsville was not a sprawling metropolis and given enough time a person could find something as small as a lost earring, but now there was not only the chance that Anita's last name was neither Jones or Walker there was also a chance that she didn't come from or live in Wyattsville.

Frances Margaret said Bartholomew's wife had swam in the bay, but there were dozens of bays dotting the east coast shoreline and hundreds of towns—maybe even thousands—along the way. Then there was also the possibility that the bay she swam in wasn't on the east coast. When Olivia began to consider the number of bays in California alone, the count soared to unimaginable heights.

Without glancing at the grandfather clock that had hours earlier chimed twelve, Olivia picked up the telephone and dialed Clara's number.

The telephone rang seven times before a sleepy voice asked, "What now?"

"I think Anita may not be from around here!"

"It's two o'clock in the morning! Can't this wait until tomorrow?"

"It's two o'clock?" Olivia echoed.

"Yeah," Clara replied grumpily, "and I'm trying to get some sleep."

"Oh. Well, this seemed important, so I figured you'd want to know right away."

"It can wait until tomorrow," Clara repeated. Then she hung up.

But once you're awake and thinking about a problem, sleep is not easy to come by. After almost twenty minutes of tossing and turning, Clara called back.

"We're gonna need a new plan," she said. "Tomorrow morning, ten o'clock. I'll get Fred and Barbara to meet us at your place; we'll figure out what to do." She then suggested Olivia get some sleep and stop bothering people in the middle of the night.

After Clara hung up Olivia tried to sleep. She slipped into her coziest nightgown, plumped a pillow beneath her head, and stretched out on the sofa. Sleep was impossible. First she tossed and turned, thinking about the number of bays stretched across the country. Then she came to the conclusion that even if Anita had lived near a bay as a child, she could be living anywhere now. It was a transient world. People grew dissatisfied with one spot and moved on to the next place. All she really knew was that Anita mailed five letters from Wyattsville almost seven years ago. Although Olivia couldn't imagine someone being unhappy in Wyattsville, the truth was Anita could have moved on. She could be anywhere now. Texas, Arizona, even Paris.

Olivia was trying to imagine the look of Anita when she heard the soft sobbing. At first it was so faint, she imagined it to be coming from someplace else—blocks away, perhaps even miles. She stilled her thoughts and listened carefully. The sound became more distinct. It was a child crying. Olivia followed the sound, and when she snapped on the bedroom light Jubilee was sitting there with a stream of tears rolling down her face. In four long strides Olivia crossed the room and took the girl in her arms.

"What's the matter, sweetheart?" she said softly.

Jubilee slumped into the embrace. "I had a scary dream."

"Oh, sweetie, I'm so sorry. But it was just a dream. That's all."

Jubilee continued to sob, her tiny shoulders quivering and breath coming in short gasps. For several minutes Olivia held her and whispered comforting words of how a dream was nothing to be afraid of, it was just scary things picking at your imagination. "Don't worry. There's nothing here that can hurt you."

When the sobbing slowed, Jubilee spoke in a small thin voice, "He's not coming back, is he?"

"No, sweetheart, the monster isn't coming back."

Jubie pulled back and looked up quizzically. "What monster?"

"The monster in your dream."

"There wasn't no monster."

Now it was Olivia's turn to look baffled. "If there was no monster, what was so scary?"

"The bad place."

"What bad place?"

"The keep-out place with yellow ribbon."

"Oh." Olivia's voice was weighted with apprehension. "You mean the store where your brother was working?"

Jubilee nodded. "People who go in keep-out places get dead."

Fumbling for words, Olivia said, "Why would you think such a thing?"

"Daddy told me so. He showed me a mine with the keep-out ribbon and said stay away from there because the roof fell down and killed a whole bunch of people."

"But that happened at a mine. It didn't happen at Klaussner's Grocery Store."

"Daddy said it would happen to anybody what goes past the keep-out ribbon!"

"That's nonsense."

"No, it ain't!" Jubilee replied indignantly. "Daddy don't tell me nonsense!"

"I didn't mean what your daddy said about the mine was nonsense," Olivia clarified. "I meant, it's nonsense to think the roof of the store would fall down and kill somebody."

"If Paul ain't dead, then why didn't he come back?"

"That's something I don't know," Olivia answered sadly. Then she hugged the girl tighter.

After a considerable amount of time, Jubilee slipped back into sleep. Olivia never did. By morning she was bone tired and bleary-eyed. With more than a half-hour before she had to get Ethan up for school, Olivia snapped on the television and leaned back into the sofa. Her intention was to watch the news for some information on a missing girl or the unidentified holdup man, but her eyelids slowly drifted down and closed.

At ten-ten the doorbell rang and woke Olivia from a dead sleep. She stumbled to the door, still in her nightgown.

"Why aren't you dressed?" Clara asked, but without waiting for an answer she tromped into the living room followed by seven of their neighbors.

With her flannel nightgown fluttering in the breeze as they passed by, Olivia made a feeble attempt at an apology. "I didn't sleep well," she mumbled, but before she could say anything more the clock chimed for the quarter hour.

"Ethan!" she shouted and darted toward his bedroom. The bed was partially made, and he was gone.

For a moment Olivia breathed a sigh of relief thinking he'd gone off to school, but then she realized Jubilee was also missing. She turned and walked back to the living room still wearing her nightgown, but now she'd added a look of puzzlement.

"I thought you were gonna get dressed," Clara said somewhat impatiently.

"I was," Olivia mumbled, "but I just discovered Ethan and Jubilee are both gone." The expression on her face was a map of confusion.

"Ethan probably took the girl to school with him," Jeanne Elizalde suggested.

"Oh, I don't think he'd—"

Seth Porter interrupted. "See," he said, jabbing a finger through the air, "I told you this was gonna mean trouble! Now he's taken the kid to school, and everybody in town—"

Looking at a sheet of notebook paper he'd lifted from the end table, George Walther said, "Simmer down, Seth, Ethan Allen ain't in school. This note says—"

"What note?" several voices replied in unison.

"This note." George waved the sheet of paper in the air. "It was right here on the end table, and it says—"

Before he could read the note aloud, Olivia snatched it from his hands. For a few moments she stood there reading to herself and mumbling, "Oh, dear."

When Clara insisted they'd come to help and couldn't be of much help unless they knew what was happening, Olivia read the note aloud.

"Dear Grandma. I saw you was real tired so I figured I'd skip school and take care of Jubie so you could catch up on some sleep."

Olivia didn't bother to read the P.S. at the bottom saying he was gonna need an absence excuse for school.

Two to Go

They left the apartment together, Ethan Allen peddling his bicycle, Jubilee perched on the cross bar. He took the route he'd taken to school two days earlier, and just as he'd done that day he turned left onto Main Street. Halfway down the block Ethan came to a stop. They climbed off and he leaned his bicycle against the tree in back of Jubilee's bench—the bench with a large yellow note taped to the back slats.

"Okay," he said. "You know what to do, right?"

She nodded.

They crossed the street together, then walked five doors down to Klaussner's Grocery. The front windows and glass door were covered with plywood boards. The only visible opening was the glass transom above the door. Bright yellow strips of crime scene tape still zigzagged across the entrance.

For a few moments Ethan stood there looking up and down the street, trying to appear nonchalant. When it seemed the coast was clear with no one coming or going along the street, he looked down at Jubilee. "Now," he said and lifted the bottom stretch of yellow tape, motioning for her to duck under. She moved without saying a word because he'd warned against making noise.

Once they were as close as a person could be to the boarded-up door, Ethan hunched down and whispered, "Climb on."

Jubilee threw her left leg over Ethan's back and scooted up until she was sitting square on his shoulders. He braced himself against the rim of tile alongside the door and stood. He took a single step to the left then leaned in.

"Can you reach it?"

"I'm too far away."

He edged half a step closer. "Now can you?"

"Almost."

"Push on the glass."

"I can't reach."

"You gotta lean forward."

Jubilee loosened her grip on Ethan's head and moved ever so slightly.

"You gotta let go and lean way in."

"I'm afraid."

"You're not gonna fall," Ethan assured her. "I've got hold of you."

A terrified Jubilee lifted her left hand and reached toward the glass transom. Her legs were locked around Ethan's neck, and her right hand still glued to his head. "I almost got it," she whispered.

"Use both hands, and you can push it open."

One by one the fingers of her right hand loosened their grip; then for a moment there was no further movement.

"Go ahead, I've got you."

With her knobby little knees pressed hard against the side of Ethan's head, Jubilee thrust herself toward the transom and pushed hard. "I see it," she said gleefully. One glance was all she needed to see the ceiling still intact. She grabbed hold of Ethan again.

"Okay to get down now?" he asked.

"Okay."

When Ethan squatted, she let go of his head and shimmied down his back. He stood, looked down, and said, "Now you believe me?"

She nodded, then reached up and slid her hand into his. He didn't pull away as you might expect a boy of his age to do. Although it was not Ethan's way to be soft about such feelings, the truth was he had a certain pride in taking care of the girl. Maybe it was because she was so small, but more likely it was because she was afraid and alone.

Ethan crept toward the taped entranceway and again looked up and down the street. Several doors down a woman pushing a baby carriage walked in their direction. "Get back," he whispered and shoved Jubilee to the darkness of the far corner. He squeezed in beside her.

The woman passed by without so much as a sideways glance. Ethan breathed a sigh of relief and waited. As soon as the street was clear of passersby, he again pulled the tape up and motioned Jubilee through. They crossed the street and sat on Jubilee's bench. She looked back at the store with lines of sadness pulling at her face.

"Jeez, I figured you'd be happier."

Without any change of expression, Jubilee said, "I'm happy enough."

Ethan knew how it felt to hang on to the thoughts inside your head. You let go of the words to answer a question, but there was always more. There was the ugly stuff, the stuff that's too painful to say.

"You got something else bothering you?" he asked.

She shrugged. "I suppose."

He waited and said nothing.

Minutes passed before she spoke again. "If Paul ain't dead, how come he don't come back?"

Ethan had hoped she wouldn't ask this question. He'd hoped she was young enough and gullible enough to simply accept that if the roof of the store was intact her brother would sooner or later reappear. She wasn't.

"Maybe Paul had to run off, so he wouldn't get caught," he finally said.

Jubilee's expression was one of bewilderment. "Get caught for what?"

Ethan turned to her. "Look, Jubie, I know you didn't have nothing to do with it, but you gotta know there was a robbery in that store."

She gave a reluctant nod.

"I'm betting your brother was in on it."

"He was not!"

"Look, you said he went into Klaussner's, and you ain't seen him since. Well, two men went in there and robbed the store. They shot poor Mister Klaussner, and he shot one of them. The other one got away."

"Paul ain't no robber!"

"I ain't saying for sure he is. But two men was in the store, and two men came out. One ran away; the other one got took to the hospital."

"Paul ain't no robber," she repeated. This time her voice quivered, and tears had begun to well in her eyes.

Ethan scooted closer and put his arm around the girl. "It ain't easy knowing your own kin did something bad. My daddy did way worse than Paul, but Grandma Olivia said that ain't no reflection on me. So Paul being a robber ain't no reflection on you."

"He ain't no robber!"

Moving on Ethan said, "You still got Aunt Anita, just like I got Grandma Olivia. Not knowing a person beforehand don't matter, they love you 'cause you're kin." Ethan remembered Grandma Olivia was not actually blood kin and added, "Sometimes they love you even if you're just kin to their kin."

Jubilee listened but kept her eyes to the ground as Ethan spoke. When he finished, she turned to him. "I don't want to find Aunt Anita. Paul's gonna take care of me, and I gotta find him."

"Jeez, Jubie, if Paul ran off I got no idea where he'd go."

"What if he got shot?"

"He'd be in the hospital."

"Let's go see in the hospital." There was a steely-eyed look of determination in Jubilee's eyes, one Ethan Allen recognized right off.

He rolled his eyes. "The hospital's way on the other side of town, and I ain't supposed to cross Mercer Street."

But when she said, "You gotta help me," he knew he would.

After a considerable amount of back and forth, he elicited her promise that if the man in the hospital wasn't Paul she'd try to help find Aunt Anita. They climbed back on the bicycle and headed crosstown. The plan was to say they were friends of the man who was shot and ask to visit him. Ethan advised against Jubilee mentioning she was his sister, because she might then be considered an accomplice.

As fate would have it, Loretta Clemens was working at the Mercy General Hospital visitor's desk, and she was a friend of Olivia's. Ethan figured that to be in their favor and approached the desk with a big smile.

"Hey, there, Missus Clemens," he said. "Mighty fine day, ain't it?"

She eyed him suspiciously. "Ethan Allen, what are you doing way over on this side of town?"

"I'm watching out for her." He shook a thumb toward Jubilee. "She's here to see the guy what got shot."

"Shot?" Loretta repeated. "She's a friend of Sid Klaussner?"

"No, the other guy."

Loretta raised an eyebrow. "What business has a kid got visiting a criminal?"

"He ain't really no criminal," Ethan said. "He's a friend of Jubie's brother, so she figured it would be neighborly to stop by and ask how he's feeling."

"Does your grandma know you're here?"

"I can't say exactly, but I sorta think she does."

"Yeah, well, I sort of think she doesn't," Loretta said emphatically. "Now you kids get out of here and haul your butt back to the other side of town where you belong. Nobody's seeing nobody, especially not that criminal."

Until now Jubilee had kept quiet as Ethan told her to do, but as they turned to leave she gave Loretta a black look and said, "He's not a criminal!"

"That's for the law to decide, missy," Loretta answered.

Ethan whispered something in Jubilee's ear, and they turned as if on their way out. It was too late; Loretta had already seen the glint in his eye.

"Ethan Allen, I hope you're not thinking you'll sneak upstairs, because there's a policeman standing guard and he'll shoot your butt off the minute you step foot on that floor."

"I wasn't thinking no such thing," he answered and kept walking.

"Does that mean we ain't doing it?" Jubilee said in a too-loud whisper.

"Yeah," Ethan answered, "it means we ain't doing it."

Before Ethan and Jubilee were back across Mercer Street, Loretta had telephoned Olivia and reported the incident.

OLIVIA

When the telephone rang, I suspected it was going to be trouble. I rather thought it would be Missus Brown telling me Ethan had skipped school or, worse yet, brought Jubilee in with him. It wasn't. It was Loretta over at the hospital.

Loretta's a bit of a gossip and I knew she was itching to learn more about Jubilee, so when she started hinting around I played dumb. When she came right out and asked who the girl was and why the kids were chasing after that criminal, I opened the apartment door and pushed my own doorbell. I've got to go, I told Loretta, somebody's at the door. It may not have been the most honorable thing to do, but telling Loretta anything is the same as putting it on a billboard in the center of town.

At least Loretta didn't let the kids in, which is something to be thankful for.

I've come to the conclusion that Paul is either in the hospital or running from the law. There simply is no other explanation for why he'd leave Jubilee and not bother coming back. I can't for the life of me understand a boy who would carry a Bible around if he was planning to rob a store. Maybe he wasn't planning it; maybe he just got to the point where he had no other alternative. If a person gets desperate enough, they'll do most anything. Right now I'm feeling pretty desperate myself.

I'm fearful that without her brother's help, I'm never going to find Jubilee's aunt. If I could just talk to the boy I know he'd have the decency to give me Anita's address. Even a criminal would do that for their baby sister. But if Paul is the one in the hospital and I show up asking to talk to him, somebody will put two and two together and realize I've got Jubilee. Once that occurs the authorities will scoop that child up and ship her off to an orphanage. I'm just not willing to let that happen.

Funny, I never thought I'd be the one taking in orphans and telling lies so they could stay safe. If Francine Burnam could see me now, she'd most likely laugh her panties off. Even I'm laughing...that is, when I'm not worrying.

Thank the Lord I've got friends willing to help. Fred McGinty said his niece works at the hospital, and he's going to ask if she can get him to talk with Paul. George Walther is also going to help. He's got a part-time job cleaning up at the police station, just the offices not the prison part. George said he'll keep his eyes and ears open, but if I know George he'll most likely do a bit of pilfering through the waste baskets before he empties them.

If neither of these things work out, there's one more person I can call on. Of course, it's been a while and I'm not sure Jack Mahoney will even remember me.

In the Wee Hours

When Paul's eyes fluttered open, the room was darkened. He saw little more than a blur of sights and sounds, none of them familiar. In the distance there were lights and people—ghostly figures that moved slowly and without sound. Strange whooshes of air sounded in his ear. The feel of it was close, too close. He listened for a moment. More sounds: whirring, beeping. Green lights bouncing and jumping. Smells: harsh bitter smells, like the lye used on wash day. Paul tried to call out for his mother, but there was only a raspy whisper in a voice that was not his.

Every instinct said run, but when Paul slid his hand toward the edge of the bed there were bars. Bars? Where was the narrow bunk he slept on? What was this place? His heart began to beat faster. He felt something thick and suffocating in his throat, something tied around his neck, tubes in his arms. Fear turned to panic and his heart started banging against his chest. No words came, but his entire being screamed, *Let me out!*

Nancy Polenski was on duty at the nurse's station. So far it had been a quiet night, and she was glad. For eight straight nights she'd worked the eleven-to-seven shift, and she was weary of it. Although there was less work to do—no bathing, few medications, and only an occasional doctor passing through—the boredom made the hours seem twice as long. Tonight she'd come prepared. Nancy was on page 76 of

Peyton Place when she heard Paul's monitor start beeping fast and loud.

"Holy Toledo!" she gasped and went running into his room.

Paul's eyes were wild with fear, blinking, blinking, blinking. His head swiveled right, left, right. Beads of perspiration rose up and rolled from his forehead onto his cheeks. He blinked again and again; each time the blinking seemed more frantic.

Nancy took his hand and tried to calm him. "It's okay," she said, sounding like the mother of a frightened child. "It's okay. You're in the hospital. There was an accident. But you're going to be fine." She switched on the room light. "See, nothing here to hurt you." Nancy put her fingers to his forehead and soothed his brow.

Paul grappled for the tube in his throat.

"No, no," Nancy said. "You've got to leave that in. It's a tracheostomy tube. It's there to help you breathe."

Paul's arm fell back onto the bed as he looked up with a thousand questions in his eyes. His lips mouthed a single word. "Why?"

"Why" wasn't a question Nancy could answer. There was never an explanation of why—why one man lived, another died. Only God knew why.

"Doctor Brewster is on duty tonight. He'll be here in a few minutes," she said. Her voice was soft and even. Paul heard the sound of his mother speaking. Everything will be all right, she was saying. Everything will be all right.

The patrolman standing guard picked up the phone and called the station house. "The kid's regained consciousness. The nurse is in there right now."

Ed Cunningham was working the station house desk and after witnessing the ugliness of the crowd at Klaussner's store, he did not want to be even slightly involved in this particular case.

"Talk to Gomez," he said and patched the call through to the number Gomez had left on the desk.

Hector Gomez was the detective assigned to the case. He'd gotten the promotion two weeks earlier and was champing at the bit to make a mark. So far it had been nothing but routine investigations—car thefts, kids running amok, break-and-enters. Then Wednesday morning there was a robbery with a near-fatal shooting at Klaussner's. This, Gomez believed, was going to be his big break.

Before leaving the station house Gomez said to call him the moment the kid regained consciousness. He wasn't wild about the thought of a middle-of-the-night call but couldn't afford to take chances. Last year Mahoney, a know-it-all detective from the Northampton precinct, pushed him into believing there was no real crime in the Doyle case, and he'd regretted it ever since. That, Gomez knew, was why it took so long for him to make detective. Open-ended shootings didn't warrant a promotion. Luckily this case had no loopholes. Everything was there; all he had to do was wrap it up and hand it over to the district attorney.

When the telephone rang at three o'clock, Gomez said, "I'm on it." He reached for his pants in the darkness of an unlit bedroom, then grabbed a crumpled shirt with the smell of yesterday. Less than ten minutes later the garage door rumbled up. He backed the car out and headed for the hospital.

Doctor Brewster was standing at the nurse's station when Gomez arrived. "How's he doing?" the detective asked and gave a nod toward Paul's room.

Brewster answered with a *who knows* shrug.

"Is he awake? Talking?"

"He's regained consciousness, if that's what you're asking."

"So am I going to be able to talk to him?"

"Not now. He's heavily sedated."

"When?"

"Two, three days, maybe."

"Maybe?"

"I'm not going to let you question him now," Brewster said flatly. "And even if I did the boy wouldn't be able to tell you anything. He's too disoriented. He doesn't understand where he is or why he's here."

"Brain damage?" Gomez asked.

Doctor Brewster shook his head. "The bullet fractured his skull but didn't penetrate, so there's no injury to the brain."

"Then what's the problem?"

"My guess is shock. He's thrown a protective wall up to keep from remembering what happened, but it's also preventing him from remembering other things."

"Did you get anything? His name? Where he's from?"

The doctor shook his head again. "No, and for now I don't think you're going to."

"This shock thing," Gomez said, "how long does it last?"

"We have no way of knowing. Shock is the brain's way of shutting down to let the body heal. Sometimes as the body starts to heal, a person's memory returns. Other times, well..." Brewster gave another *who knows* shrug and turned away.

When the doctor left Hector Gomez walked to the vending machine down the hall and returned with two coffees. He handed one to Nancy. "You look like you could use this."

"Thanks." She slipped a marker in front of page 77 and closed her book.

For the next two hours they sipped lukewarm coffee and chatted.

Hector, who had a way of getting information through what seemed to be a casual conversation, learned that Sid Klaussner was still in a medically-induced coma. "Too bad. Sid's a damn nice guy, doesn't deserve this."

"Nobody does," Nancy commiserated.

Once he found out that Sid had been unable to speak, let alone provide details of the robbery, he moved on to asking about Paul. "So, the kid is still a John Doe?'"

"Yeah." Nancy nodded. "A real shame. Doesn't even know his name."

Gomez was determined to move up in the ranks—this year detective, next year maybe lieutenant.

"The shame is, these punk kids think they can get away with it," he said. When he saw the grimace on Nancy's face, he softened his stance. "But you've still gotta feel sorry for them. You gotta wonder what drives them to something like this."

"We never know," Nancy said sadly. "We just never know."

On the way out, Gomez stopped to talk with the patrolman standing guard outside John Doe's room. "Has anybody been to see him?"

The patrolman shook his head.

Hector peered through the plate glass window in John Doe's room. "Damn," he grumbled. "Nobody's reported him missing, nobody's been here to see him. What kind of nut-ball family does this kid come from? You sure nobody's been here?"

He got the same answer. *Sooner or later,* he thought. *Sooner or later somebody would show up, and when they did...*

Name or no name, Gomez had already decided this one was going to be a conviction. He drove home imagining the gold bar that would one day be pinned to his chest.

On Saturday morning when Loretta reported for work, the hospital gossip line was filled with chatter about how the Klaussner's gunman had regained consciousness. Before Loretta was fully seated behind the visitor's desk, she'd dialed Olivia's number.

"I understand the boy is awake," she said in a deliciously whispery voice. "The police suspect he's an out-of-towner, but he won't tell them his name or where he's from!"

Although Olivia was shaken to the core at hearing such news, she said, "Well, I'm certain that's none of my business."

"Oh, I think it is," Loretta replied slyly. "Ethan Allen and that little girl were here yesterday, and they were looking to get in and see the boy."

"Yes, you told me that yesterday," Olivia said. "But I fail to see how—"

"Those kids know something," Loretta taunted. "I *know* they know something!"

"Oh, Loretta," Olivia said, "you know how kids are. They were just looking for adventure. Ethan Allen has been watching that *Dragnet* show on television, and I think it's influencing—"

"Don't give me that malarkey, those kids know something!"

"Well, if they do, it's news to me." Although Olivia cringed at giving an answer so borderline close to a lie, it was, in actuality, true. If she knew who the family was and where the boy was headed, she would deliver Jubilee Jones to the mysterious Aunt Anita and be done with the whole affair.

"Harrumph," Loretta snorted. "If that's your answer, then so be it. I've got other sources for finding what I want to know!" She paused a moment, then added, "Including the name of that girl Ethan's been running with!" She slammed down the telephone without bothering to say goodbye.

For the first time in more than a year, Olivia's heart began fluttering again. In an effort to calm herself she took three different cookbooks from the kitchen shelf and searched them page by page, but there was not a single recipe for okra soup. Time had not dulled the memory of those days following Charlie's death. It was Canasta's okra soup that had restored her will to live. The soup had magical powers, it enabled a person to look inside themselves and find a cure for the heartaches of life.

Olivia searched long and hard but there simply was no recipe for the life altering soup. Left with no other resource, she retrieved the card she'd hidden in the bottom of her jewelry box months earlier and dialed the number printed in the lower right hand corner.

Reaching Out

The telephone rang once and a voice answered, "Detective Griffin."

"Oh," Olivia said, "I was looking for Jack Mahoney."

"He's off today. Maybe I can help you."

"I don't think so," Olivia replied. "It's about Aunt Anita—"

"Gotcha, a family matter. Jack's at home; give him a call there."

Without correcting the impression that Aunt Anita was Jack's aunt, Olivia replied, "I don't have his number handy, do you..." She made note of the numbers he rattled off.

This time the telephone rang five times before a childish voice answered, "Hello."

"Good morning," she said. "This is Olivia Doyle, and I'd like to speak with Jack Mahoney."

"Big Jack or little Jack?"

"Um, big Jack, I think."

Without any further conversation there was the clunk of a dropped telephone and the voice yelled, "Hey, Dad, it's for you."

Olivia didn't count the number of heartbeats she waited but she easily could have, because each thump banged against her chest like the gong of a clock. It wasn't long before she started wondering if the mention of her name was enough to make Jack Mahoney reluctant to answer the call. On three different occasions, she came close to hanging up but didn't. Finally the familiar voice said, "Mahoney."

"Good morning, Mister Mahoney," she said. "This is Olivia Doyle, Ethan Allen's grandmother."

"Is something wrong?"

"With Ethan Allen? Oh, no, not at all."

"Good," Mahoney replied. "That's good." He waited to give her time to say something more, but all he got was a lengthy silence. "So," he said cautiously, "to what do I owe the pleasure of this call?"

Olivia had planned to start the conversation by inquiring about Mahoney's family; from there she would ask about the healing of Sam Cobb's knee, then segue into a few comments about the coming summer. Once the pleasantries were over, she could address the issue of Jubilee's missing aunt. But that plan was lost when Jack asked the point-blank question. Olivia's courage failed her and she stammered, "I just wanted to say hello and once again thank you for all you did for Ethan Allen," then hung up without asking what she'd called to ask.

"Strange," Jack murmured as he replaced the receiver in the cradle.

After the call Jack went back to the porch he'd been painting, but thoughts of Olivia's call picked at his mind. He knew unexplained silences were not simply a lack of words. Silences often covered a secret. What secret could Olivia Doyle be harboring, he wondered. There were no loose ends in the Doyle case, at least none he knew of...unless he'd missed something. A small detail he'd overlooked? A threat that still lingered?

He rolled through the case in his mind. Horrible as the murders were, the facts confirmed every detail of the story. Scooter Cobb was dead. Sam Cobb had retired from the police force a broken man, a man who, despite the number of friends he had, never once stopped by the station to say goodbye. Who else could pose a threat to Ethan Allen, he wondered. Who else, and why? By eleven thirty a number of questions pushed against Mahoney's brain, so he left the porch half-painted and went down to the station house.

Dan Griffin was sitting at the desk. "Your aunt get hold of you?"

"My aunt?"

"Aunt, cousin, something like that. Can't recall the name but she telephoned here this morning, and I gave her your home number."

"Oh, yeah," Mahoney said, "I spoke with her." *Why would Olivia Doyle pretend to be my aunt?* Something wasn't right.

"Aunt Anita," Griffin said "That was it; some problem with Aunt Anita."

"Anita huh?" Mahoney prided himself on remembering the details of a case. Small details; that's what made the difference in nailing the guilty guy and exonerating the innocent one. *There was no Anita involved in the Doyle case. Unless...*

Five minutes later he was in the storage room digging through a carton of closed case files. *Da...De...Dod...Dol...Dur*

The Doyle file was missing.

A double murder produced reams of paper, hundreds of pages of investigative reports, interviews, lab tests, blood analysis, fingerprints. How could a file of that size disappear?

Mahoney turned to the storeroom manager. "Hey, Charlie, anybody sign out the Doyle file from that double murder last year?"

"Nope, nothing's out right now."

"Nothing, huh?" Mahoney went back to his desk. A troubled feeling had already settled in his stomach. He'd taken longer than he should have to tag Scooter Cobb as a suspect in Benjamin Doyle's murder. Maybe he'd also missed something else. Maybe friendship blinded him to other involvements. It was never easy turning against a fellow officer, and given his fondness for Emma he'd been reluctant to see the truth of the Cobbs, even when it was staring him in the face. If he'd been blinded then, was he being blind now? Was there a chance Scooter Cobb's death didn't end the story?

If there was nothing more to hide, why was the Doyle file missing? Something wasn't right. After eighteen years on the force, Mahoney knew there was seldom a smoking gun. The truth hid behind small, everyday details that were right there in plain sight. The Doyle murders had been an especially troubling case, one that bothered Jack to the point where he kept a slim folder of notes in the locked drawer of his desk. He unlocked the drawer and pulled the folder out. No mention of an Anita. He dialed Olivia Doyle's number.

When Olivia picked up the receiver a familiar voice said, "Missus Doyle, this is Detective Mahoney."

Thinking this time she'd start the conversation the way she originally intended, Olivia answered, "How delightful to hear from you, Detective. The family's well, I hope."

"Everyone is fine." Without giving Olivia a chance to ask about Sam Cobb's knee, he said, "Why don't you just go ahead and tell me what's wrong?"

"Wrong?" Olivia tried to sound casual, not like a person whose stomach was turned inside out from a serious case of nerves. "Why on earth would you—"

"Who's Aunt Anita?"

Olivia hesitated a moment, then said, "Well, it's a long story." She started at the beginning, told of the robbery at Klaussner's, and how Ethan Allen brought seven-year-old Jubilee Jones home with him that evening.

"At first I thought the child was lost, that maybe she'd wandered off and forgotten where she was to meet her brother. Then Ethan told me she'd been sitting right where the brother had left her."

"And the brother didn't come back?" Mahoney asked.

"That's right," Olivia replied. "According to what Ethan Allen said her brother went into Klaussner's, and that was the last she saw of him."

"Are you saying the girl's brother was involved in the robbery?"

"I don't know for certain, but I have my suspicions. I suppose it's possible her brother was, but I know for certain she had nothing to do with it. Jubilee honestly believes her brother went into the store looking for a job."

"What about the parents?"

"Deceased. I think the kids came here expecting to live with their aunt."

"Do you have the aunt's name or address?"

"Regretfully no." Olivia's answer was tentative at best. "I think Anita was related to the mother, which would make her maiden name Walker. But she could have been a sister-in-law, not sister, and in that case her maiden name would be Jones."

"This aunt, is she married?"

"No idea," Olivia said.

"What's the brother's name?"

"Paul. Paul Jones."

"Any chance he has the aunt's name and address?"

"I can't say." Olivia went on to tell him the boy could be in the hospital, or he could be the escapee who disappeared. After explaining the belongings in Jubilee's travel bag she asked, "Don't you find it rather hard to believe a boy who'd value that sort of memorabilia over more material things would be involved in crime?"

"You never know," Mahoney answered. "You just never know."

Olivia went on to tell the few facts she knew. Anita lived in Norfolk twenty years ago. Seven years ago she'd mailed five letters from Wyattsville, and in her younger days Anita and her sister, Ruth, had lived somewhere close to a bay.

When there was nothing more to tell, Olivia said, "Detective Mahoney, I've trusted you with the fact that Jubilee is staying with me, but I'm hoping you'll not tell anyone else."

Mahoney chuckled. "Well, I'm not going to report it, but if the child has a family she really should be with them."

"I know," Olivia said, "and that's what I'm hoping for. But until we find them..." She left the alternative unspoken.

"For now that's okay. But—"

Before he could say something about calling the authorities, Olivia said, "Right now Jubilee has no one. She sees Ethan Allen as a replacement for her brother, and I know this is only a temporary solution, but ..."

Mahoney pictured his own daughter who had turned seven a few months earlier. She had two siblings, a mother, a father, grandparents, but what if there was no one? He pushed aside the thought and said, "I'd like to help, Missus Doyle, but this case is not in my jurisdiction. What you really should do is call the authorities in Wyattsville and—"

"Chesapeake Bay," Olivia said. "That's where Ruth and Anita grew up. They swam in the bay when they were younger, so she's obviously from your area." Olivia told him of her telephone conversation with Frances Margaret Jones. Although the woman had never mentioned Chesapeake Bay it seemed a logical enough guess since a good part of the bay lapped at the edges of Virginia's eastern shore.

"Chesapeake Bay?" Mahoney repeated dubiously. "Well, I guess in that case I could check around, see what I come up with. But I still think you should—"

Not wanting to hear the same advice several others had already given, Olivia thanked him and hung up the telephone before he had a chance to mention the child welfare department.

Jack Mahoney

Okay, you and I both know the Chesapeake Bay isn't exactly an area for beach swimming, so this isn't really a case I can justify taking on—officially, that is. But after dragging my feet on the Cobb arrest, I figure I owe Olivia Doyle.

The woman is a bit odd at times, but she's someone with good intentions and I don't doubt she's got the kid's best interest at heart. I'll buy that she honestly believes the girl is telling the truth about her brother looking for a job. But I've come across some pretty convincing liars in my day, and it wouldn't be the first time one kid lied to cover up for the other.

I'll give this Frances Margaret Jones a call and see if she knows anything more than she's saying. On Monday I can take a run over to Wyattsville and check on the kid in the hospital. We're talking about a few hours maybe. I've got no problem with that.

This job forces you to be cynical and focus on the facts, but when something is out of sync my gut starts arguing with reason. Right now I've got a serious case of indigestion. It's telling me kids who cart around family pictures, a Bible, and a baby sister aren't the type to be robbing stores.

It doesn't stand to reason—but then I've been wrong before.

The Long Weekend

After Loretta called on Saturday, Olivia immediately grounded both Ethan Allen and Jubilee.

"Neither of you are to step foot out of this house," she said, "and there are absolutely no exceptions."

"What if Dog gets loose and I've got to go chase him?" Ethan asked. "What if—"

Before he could grab onto another outrageous thought, she repeated, "No exceptions!"

Olivia had a growing fear grumbling through her stomach and was not in the mood for discussing the fine points of their punishment. Not only was finding Anita proving to be far more difficult than she'd originally thought, but Jim Turner had for the third time called a special meeting of the Rules Committee to discuss the disruption a child brought to the building. At the latest meeting Jim insisted he'd seen Ethan Allen riding his bicycle across the lobby, a stunt which he believed would ultimately be the ruination of Wyattsville Arms. When a heated argument broke out, Fred McGinty told Jim that being president of the association wasn't the same as being God and that he should stop making a mountain out of a molehill. When the other members of the committee applauded, the meeting ended.

Fred assumed the complaint was forgotten, but Olivia knew better. Jim Turner was a man who didn't forget. If he got wind of a second child being in the apartment, there would be an eviction notice shoved under her door within hours. It was a necessity that she keep both kids out of sight until she could locate Anita Walker-Jones or Missus whatever her married name might be.

Ethan Allen had barely finished his breakfast when he began wheedling to go outside. It was Saturday morning, and chances were good his friends already had a basketball game going.

"You need anything from the store?" he asked.

"No, I don't," Olivia answered. "And I've already said you're staying in today."

"But errands ain't the same as—"

"No."

It continued all morning. Ethan had seventy-six arguments for going out and not a single reason for staying inside. First he complained checkers were boring. Then they couldn't do the one thousand piece puzzle because some of the pieces were missing. When Olivia suggested a game of cards, he looked up with a grimace.

"I ain't interested in playing Old Maid," he said emphatically.

He went on to say he wasn't one bit interested in straightening the mess in his room or watching television shows meant for little kids.

"What about Jubilee?" Olivia asked. "Maybe she wants to see those shows."

"She ain't interested either," Ethan answered.

"Let her decide for herself," Olivia said. She turned to Jubilee and asked, "Don't you want to see the Saturday Cartoon Carnival?"

For a moment it looked as though Jubilee was going to nod yes, but then she looked over at Ethan Allen and defiantly shook her head in exactly the same way he'd done. "Unh-unh," she echoed. "Cartoons is for babies."

Ethan Allen gave a proud grin.

Now defeated on two fronts, Olivia handed over the poker chips and a deck of cards. When they settled at the family room table, she whispered in Jubilee's ear, "Please don't tell your Aunt Anita I allowed you to play poker." She turned and started to walk away, but Jubilee's answer trailed after her.

"I don't think Aunt Anita gives a damn," she said.

Olivia turned back in her tracks.

"Jubilee! Who taught you to say such a thing?" she demanded. She knew the answer when Ethan Allen slinked down in his chair and started looking smaller. After an obviously overdue reminder of her rules about cussing, Ethan Allen settled into playing cards and gave up trying to gain his freedom.

Although the child's answer had shocked Olivia, she walked away with an odd feeling of gladness. She could see how Jubilee had indeed latched onto Ethan Allen as a substitute for her brother. Apparently it didn't matter whether a person was seven or seventy, when you lose someone you love you cling to any life raft floating by. Right now Ethan Allen was her life raft. For now it was a workable solution. Finding Anita would change things. It would give Jubilee a new life of loving and being loved.

Having one child to care for had been more challenging than Olivia ever thought she could handle, and this sample of having two was proving nearly impossible. She couldn't imagine why young couples rushed to add a second, third, fourth, and sometimes fifth child to the family tree.

Weary of thinking such weighty thoughts, Olivia brewed herself a cup of cinnamon tea and sat at the kitchen table. Although she tried to concentrate, map out the possible ways a person could be found, the slightest sound threw her off track. The children laughing, a horn beeping, the rustle of trees—they were all saying something, but Olivia didn't know what. She was lost in thought when the doorbell bonged.

Certain it could only mean trouble, Olivia shushed the kids and did not answer the door.

"Open up!" Clara yelled.

"Thank heaven it's only you," Olivia said and swung the door open.

"*Only* me?" Clara repeated. "What kind of a greeting is that?" She bristled her way past Ethan Allen who was telling Jubilee he'd raise her five and call.

"Do you know what those kids are doing?" Clara frowned.

Olivia rolled her eyes and nodded. "Playing poker." Without any further explanation, she headed back to the kitchen.

Clara followed along and plopped down on a chair. "I suppose you heard?"

"Loretta called first thing this morning. She said the boy in the hospital has refused to talk. He won't even give them his name."

"Yeah, well, Loretta ain't got all the facts," Clara sneered. "I just came from Fred's, and he was on the phone with his niece. She was there and knows what happened!" Before Clara could get to what she was trying to tell, the doorbell started bonging again. Not just once but several times with no pause between one gong and the next.

When the door opened Fred McGinty rushed in looking as if he were about to explode. "We've got problems! Last night Linda was at the hospital—pediatrics not intensive care—but after I asked her to check on the kid, she stopped by ICU and found out he's regained consciousness."

"But that's not the problem," Clara added.

Olivia's eyebrows shot up. "What is?"

"The boy can't remember anything," Fred said. "Nothing. Not even his name."

Olivia gasped. "Dear God!"

"Worse yet," Fred continued, "Sid Klaussner is still in a coma!"

Olivia gave a second gasp, and Clara nodded knowingly.

"Detective Gomez was there last night trying to talk to the kid." Fred lowered his voice and continued in a gravelly whisper. "Gomez said if Sid don't make it, they're gonna charge that kid with murder."

"Oh dear," Olivia replied. "What if the boy is Paul and what Jubilee says is true?"

"That's a problem," Fred said. "Right now he don't even know his own name, so how's he gonna tell what happened?"

In a terrified voice Olivia said, "Without him, how are we going to find Anita?"

"And," Clara added, "if he isn't Paul, then where's Jubilee's brother?"

Olivia's cinnamon tea suddenly became far too inadequate for the situation. She set a pot of coffee on to brew and added a small strip of okra. Although Canasta swore there was nothing magical about okra, Olivia simply couldn't lose the feeling of contentment that came from knowing it was there.

Olivia filled three cups, and they sat around the table trying to create a plan that would enable them to find out what they needed to know without giving away what little they knew about Jubilee and her brother. George Walther joined them a short while later. The only thing he had to report was that the scuttlebutt around the station house indicated they'd gotten a good set of fingerprints from where one of the assailants had banged open the cash register.

"But they haven't gotten an identity yet," George said sadly.

"If the fingerprints belong to that kid in the hospital, he's had it," Fred said, "whether or not he remembers what happened."

"There seems to be no good answer," Olivia said sadly.

Clara slapped her hand down on the table. "I ain't for giving up! We had a bigger problem with Ethan Allen and found a way to fix it."

"Yeah," Fred agreed. "Ethan's situation was a lot worse. We found a way to stop that crazy-ass murderer after him. If we could do that, we can for sure handle this."

"In case you don't remember," Olivia said, "we weren't the ones who stopped Scooter Cobb; it was Ethan Allen."

"Oh, right," Clara mumbled and gulped down a large swallow of okra-flavored coffee.

Fred glared at Clara with a look that indicated she should've kept her mouth shut. "What about that policeman friend of yours?" he asked Olivia.

"Jack Mahoney?" she replied. "I called and asked if he'd help us."

"Well?" Clara grumped, "what did he say?"

"At first he said finding Anita was out of his jurisdiction."

"So he's not gonna help?" Fred asked.

"No, he's agreed to look into it." Olivia gave a mischievous smile. "But I had to tell a little white lie to get him to do it."

"Little white lie?" Clara repeated.

"Yes." Olivia nodded. "I told him I was pretty sure Anita came from over that way, because she and her sister used to go swimming in Chesapeake Bay."

Clara doubled over laughing. "And you think he believed you?"

"Why wouldn't he?"

"Nobody swims in that part of Chesapeake Bay. It's good for fishing but too rocky and deep for swimming."

"Oh." Olivia's face fell, and her shoulders dropped into a downward slump.

When there was nothing more to be said, Fred and George left. Clara stayed and shared the remainder of the okra coffee. Once Olivia had drained the last of it, her heart felt emptier than the pot. Thinking that another homeless child had been dropped on her doorstep, she gave a long soulful sigh and said, "Where's hope when I need it?"

"It's probably right where you left it," Clara replied.

"Right where I left it?"

"Unh-huh." Clara nodded. "Hope don't leave. People just forget it's there."

Olivia leaned into Clara's words.

"A while back you went around hoping for this, that, and the other thing. 'I hope I find happiness,' you'd say, 'I hope I find love.' Then Ethan Allen showed up and you said, 'I hope I can find this boy a home.' After that you got to loving him and said, 'I hope I can keep this boy safe.'"

Olivia smiled at the truth of Clara's words.

"Hope didn't leave." Clara drained the last of her coffee. "You just ran out of excuses for using it."

"That's not true," Olivia argued. "I still hope for certain things."

"No, you don't," Clara said. "You just say you're hoping for something. Saying, 'I hope it don't rain' ain't really hoping; it's wishful thinking." Clara pushed back from the table. "Think about it. When's the last time you really and truly used your whole heart to hope for something?"

Olivia sat there for a long minute thinking, and she had to admit Clara was right. All this time she thought she was hoping for different things—a birthday cake, a telephone call, a new dress—but the truth was they were small things, and she'd done little more than sprinkle a bit of hope over them the way you'd sprinkle salt on a potato. When she cored into herself she had to admit the last time she'd used every last drop of hope she could muster up was when she hoped Detective Mahoney would believe she was the one who shot Scooter Cobb.

"You're right." She smiled at Clara. "I haven't been using all my hope." She reached across the table and clasped her hand over Clara's. "You're a life raft."

"Life raft?" Clara repeated quizzically. "I may have put on a few pounds, but—"

Olivia laughed. "No, you're my life raft, the thing that keeps me afloat when I start to believe this time I'm going under."

"Well, good," Clara said. "Now stay afloat, because little Jubilee Jones is gonna need a whole lot of hoping if we're to find her aunt."

"Jones!" Olivia slapped her hand to her head. "Why didn't I see this before?"

She bolted from the chair and into the family room where Ethan Allen and Jubilee were now watching television. Ignoring the fact that the girl was as fair as a white rose and Canasta as black as a piece of ebony, she asked, "Jubilee, is it possible that you know a woman named Canasta Jones?"

Jubilee looked up and shrugged. "I don't think I know no Canasta, but I suppose it's possible."

Convinced the similarity of names was a sure sign, Olivia's hope took flight and fluttered its wings in a way that made her heart race. Suddenly she knew they would find Anita, and Jubilee Jones would have her forever home.

But of course Olivia was always prone to over-exaggerated expectations.

Olivia

I know you're thinking it's a preposterous idea, Jubilee being connected to Canasta, especially given the difference in age and race, but it's not as preposterous as you might think. Bloodlines aren't the only thing tying people together. Look at Ethan Allen and me.

The thinking part of my head understands they can't possibly be blood relatives, but the feeling part of my heart knows it's no coincidence. Jubilee and Canasta both being Joneses is exactly the same as finding spare change in my pocket. It's a sure sign that everything is going to work out just the way God intended. A person shouldn't rationalize their blessings; you just accept them for what they are and be glad you've got them.

For a while I was worried sick we'd never find Jubilee's aunt and I'd have to turn the poor girl over to the child welfare people. Now I feel totally different. I know for certain we'll not only find Anita, but that she'll love Jubilee just as much as I do Ethan Allen.

Paul, unfortunately, I'm not so certain about. I've searched my soul trying to decide whether or not I think the boy could do such a thing, but it's impossible to come up with an answer. One part of me argues that if he's the boy shot in an attempted robbery, he must be guilty. But once that answer is settled in my brain, my heart reminds me he's Jubilee's brother. He's a boy born of the same parents, a boy who cared enough to try to make a home for his baby sister. I know the decision of guilty or not isn't mine to make, but if I knew one way or the other maybe I could prepare Jubilee for what lies ahead.

Times like this I look back on Charlie's death and realize how foolish such thinking is. We can plan ahead until we're blue in the face, but regardless of what we do events will happen as they will. The truth is we don't have a bean of say in the matter.

Following A Trail of Breadcrumbs

Monday morning Jack Mahoney checked in at the station house. It was a quiet day with little more than a handful of paperwork that needed to be done. "I've got some personal stuff to take care of," he told Griffin, then took off.

His first stop was the county clerk's office. The gal at the front desk was talking on the telephone and making no move to end the conversation.

"You gotta be kidding," she said into the phone. She looked up but continued talking. "Well, if I was her, I would have given him the boot."

Mahoney flashed his badge and said, "Archives?"

She waggled her finger toward a long hallway, put her hand over the mouthpiece, and whispered, "Third door on the right."

Mahoney nodded and disappeared down the hall. Olivia Doyle hadn't given him much to go on; actually it was more like nothing. No hard facts, just lots of maybes mixed in with a few possibilities. What he needed was one fact—one spot that he could point to and say Anita Walker-Jones was here. From that single spot he could move backward or forward through her life and chances were good he'd find her. But until he located that spot, Anita Walker-Jones didn't exist.

For nearly three hours Mahoney went from one records division to the next. School Registrations, Property Records, Voter Registration— one by one they produced nothing. The clerks were pleasant enough; they smiled and sympathized, but mostly they said the recordkeeping thirty-plus years ago wasn't what it should have been. Shortly after one o'clock Jack left the building with exactly what he'd come in with: nothing. After a quick stop at Hamburger Heaven, he returned to the station and tried calling Frances Margaret Jones.

On the fourth ring, a man answered.

"Good afternoon," Mahoney said. "I'd like to speak with Frances Margaret Jones."

"Yeah, I bet you would."

"Excuse me?"

"You're the one she's been running around with, ain't ya?"

"I'm Detective Mahoney from the Northampton County Police Department."

"Don't give me that load of crap! Frances is a married woman! She's got no business—"

Mahoney was momentarily taken aback. "This isn't a personal call. "I'm trying to find a woman who—"

"Take that trash elsewhere," the man snarled. "Frances ain't for sale no more. She's locked in the bedroom and ain't coming out 'till she's sworn to behave." With that the man slammed the phone down.

Griffin, who was sitting across the desk and could hear the shouting, said, "Sounds like you've been sticking your finger in somebody else's pie."

Mahoney rolled his eyes. "Funny, real funny."

"So who's your telephone friend?"

"My guess is he's her husband." Mahoney chuckled. "I was just following up a lead."

"On what?"

"Favor for a friend," Mahoney said. "Remember the Doyle case?"

"Everybody remembers that one."

"Well, the kid's grandma asked me to help her find somebody called Anita Walker or maybe Jones."

"Oh, so that's Aunt Anita." Griffin laughed. "And Frances, who ain't for sale anymore, she knows this Anita?"

Mahoney shrugged. "It's worth checking." From the Northampton Station, it took about three hours to get to Wyattsville. "Feel like taking a ferry ride?"

Griffin grinned and grabbed his jacket.

Frances Margaret's husband had started drinking early that morning, and by the time they arrived he was in a worse than ugly mood. When Griffin and Mahoney rang the bell the door banged open like a hurricane coming through. The man standing in the open door was wearing polka dot boxer shorts and a tee shirt soaked through with sweat.

"What the hell do you want?" he screamed.

"Take it easy, buddy," Griffin said and flashed his badge. "We're just looking to ask a few questions."

Mister Boxer Shorts narrowed his eyes. "If this is about Fran—"

"It's not about Frances Margaret," Mahoney cut in. "But we think she might have some information that will help find the person we're looking for."

"Margaret? She say her name was Frances Margaret? Margaret my ass!" A spray of spittle flew from the man's mouth and landed on his chin. "Myrtle; she's a Myrtle!" He swiped the back of his hand across his chin and finished, "A low-life-tramp-with-no-morals Myrtle!"

Griffin grinned. "I know what you mean, buddy," he said. "I used to be married to one just like her."

Boxer Shorts gave a sorrowful nod. "Hell, ain't it?"

"Sure is," Griffin replied. "If you want I could have a talk with her, maybe explain how carrying on this way could get her in trouble with the law."

"She ain't listening to me; what makes you think she'll listen to you?"

"She'll listen." Griffin made it sound like a threat rather than a promise.

"I guess it's worth a try," Boxer Shorts said. He stepped back, motioned them in, then said he'd get Myrtle.

Once Boxer Shorts was beyond hearing range, Mahoney turned to Griffin. "Where'd you get that story?"

"It just came to me," Griffin said and grinned again. "Anyway, I figured he's never gonna meet Sarah, so what's the harm?"

They heard footsteps in the hall and stopped talking. The woman who Boxer Shorts led into the room was as angry and puffed up as a wet hen.

"I'm Frances Margaret," she said. "What do you want?"

Boxer Shorts flared up. "You ain't a Margaret! You was Francine Myrtle when I married you, and you're still Francine Myrtle!"

"Blockhead!" she yelled back. "Forty-seven times I told you I changed it. You ain't never gonna learn, are you?"

Before things could get any worse, Griffin pulled Boxer Shorts aside and gave Mahoney room to talk to Frances-whoever-she was.

"I believe you spoke with Missus Doyle last week," he began.

"You mean Olivia? Yeah, I talked to her. She said something about a reunion party for telephone company people."

"You ain't going to no party!" Boxer Shorts yelled from across the room.

"Try and stop me!" she yelled back.

"Can we step outside for a moment?" Mahoney asked.

She nodded and followed him out the door.

Standing on the front stoop, Mahoney said, "I'm looking for a woman named Anita Walker or possibly Jones. I understand you know someone who's related."

"Knew," Frances-whatever corrected. "Not know. I knew Bartholomew Jones and his missus twenty years ago. They used to rent the upstairs flat in my sister's house."

"Where was that?"

"Norfolk. But, like I told you, that was twenty years ago. I ain't spoken to Bertha for more than ten, and it was way before we quit talking."

"Bertha's your sister?"

Frances gave a disgusted nod. "Yeah, I guess you could call her that."

"This Bartholomew. Was his wife's name Anita?"

Frances laughed. "Shoot, no. Bartholomew's missus was Ruthie. She was a sweetie, but this other one that used to come visit, she had a temper on her, woo-whee!"

"The one who came to visit, was her name Anita?"

"I'm thinking it was but can't swear to it."

"You think Bertha might know?"

"You're asking me what's in Bertha's head?" Frances gave cynical snort. "If I knew what was in that woman's head, I'd of quit talking to her long before I did. She's pure ugly, so I gotta guess there ain't nothing but ugly in her head!"

Seeing that this was going nowhere, Mahoney asked, "Can you give me an address or telephone number where I can get hold of Bertha?"

"Men!" Frances muttered and rolled her eyes. "Didn't you hear me say I ain't talked to her in ten years? I ain't even got a guess as to where she is now."

"Can you give me the last address you had for her?"

"I suppose," Frances said and pulled a piece of wadded paper from her pocket. "Here. If you talk to Bertha, tell her I said holding grudges ain't gonna do nobody no good."

Mahoney thanked her, then called Griffin and said it was time to get going.

It was nearly six o'clock in the morning when Hector Gomez got home from the hospital. For three hours he'd stood there chatting with Nancy, waiting for her to drop some little tidbit she'd gotten from the kid but got nothing. She'd gone in and out of his room a half-dozen times and each time Hector waited, thinking she'd come back with a name. Nothing. Now he had a serious case of indigestion from all the coffee he'd consumed and needed a cold glass of milk. He pulled the car into the garage and came through the kitchen door.

Hector knew it was going to be a bad day when he opened the refrigerator door and saw an empty shelf where the milk was supposed to be.

"Gloria!" he screamed. "Where's the damn milk?" Although he phrased it as a question, he knew the answer.

"We're all out!" his wife hollered back. She snapped on the hairdryer so any further conversation was impossible.

Hector Gomez was a man who needed seven hours sleep. Six hours at a minimum. He'd gotten two, and it was already wearing on him. He eyed the clock. Ten minutes past six—plenty of time for a short nap. A half-hour maybe. A quick shower, and he'd be ready to go by seven. Hector stretched out on the sofa and closed his eyes.

The next thing he knew the clock was striking twelve. He sat up in a panic.

"Damn!" he shouted and hurtled himself off the sofa. His right knee came down hard on the wrought iron coffee table, and before he could scramble to his feet an egg-sized lump swelled up on his leg.

When Gomez walked into the station house, he thought he was smack in the middle of the worst day a man can have. Then he spotted Detective

Mahoney across the room.

"What the hell?"

If there was one thing Hector Gomez didn't need, it was a smart-mouth detective from Northampton sticking his nose in on a sure thing. If it hadn't been for Mahoney, he would have had a conviction on the Doyle case. To this day, he believed one of them guilty of murder—either the grandmother or the kid—but once Mahoney got involved it became a bleeding heart issue.

"Not this time," Hector grumbled as he crossed the room.

When he stopped at the Wyattsville station Mahoney planned to ask about the kid involved in the Klaussner shooting. He didn't feel there was a solid connection between the kid and the missing aunt, but there was enough to warrant a few questions. He barely had a foot through the door when he saw a pissed-off Gomez coming toward him. Remembering the outcome of the Doyle case, Mahoney knew this was going to be a confrontational situation unless he did something. He stuck his hand out

"Hey, Gomez, how's it going?"

Hector eyed him suspiciously. "Okay, I guess. And you?"

"Real good." Mahoney nodded. "Real good."

In no mood for small talk, Hector asked, "So what brings you over here?"

"Search for a missing person. Run-of-the-mill stuff, nothing exciting."

"You're not working the Klaussner robbery?"

"Nah, that's one you're gonna have to handle on your own."

Still suspicious, Gomez asked, "This missing person you're looking for wouldn't be a teenage boy, would it?"

"Nope. A woman, probably mid-forties."

Gomez breathed a sigh of relief. There was a sense of satisfaction in knowing he'd bested Mahoney on this one, and Hector couldn't help but brag. "I've got the lead on the Klaussner job. Right now it's attempted murder, but if Klaussner dies—"

"So you got the guy?"

"We got one, but it looks like it was a team. Klaussner shot one; the other one got away." Gomez hesitated for a moment then added, "We're running the prints now, so we'll get him."

"Sounds like you've got this pretty well wrapped up."

"Yeah," Gomez boasted. He was going to add something about not needing Mahoney's help but was interrupted by Officer Cunningham.

"Hey, Gomez," Cunningham called out, "the ID on those prints you've been waiting for is on your desk."

When Gomez turned and walked back toward his desk, Mahoney trailed along. He knew men like Gomez had a hungry ego, one that needed to be fed. "Impressive work," he said. "Us Northampton boys could learn a few things from you."

Gomez smiled. "Yeah, you could." He was tempted to remind Mahoney of the erroneous assumptions made on the Doyle case, but given this newfound-respect for his work Hector decided to let that dog stay dead.

With Mahoney looking over his shoulder, Gomez picked up the lab report. They had a positive match. The prints belonged to a small-time crook out of Pittsburgh. "Hurt McAdams, armed robbery," Gomez said. "Spent seven years in Camp Hill, released five days ago."

"Is this the guy Klaussner shot?"

Gomez shook his head. "No ID on that one yet. The kid is faking amnesia, but once he knows we've got his partner he'll open up."

"Impressive," Mahoney repeated.

"Just good detective work." Gomez gave a grin of satisfaction. When he turned to pull on his jacket he didn't notice Mahoney eyeballing the open file on his desk.

Miami Beach

Minutes after Hurt McAdams stepped off the bus wearing his leather jacket, a river of sweat rolled down his face and his shirt became plastered to his skin. He stuck his hand in the jacket pocket and rubbed his fingers across the cool metal of the gun. Knowing it was there made him feel good; it was comforting.

Inside the Union Street Terminal, Hurt pushed through the crowd until he found a telephone booth. He pulled the phone book from the rack and began searching. "McAdams, McAdams," he mumbled as he traced his finger down the listings. Plenty of McAdams, but not one George. Hurt slammed the book shut. Daddy George was here, Hurt could feel it in his bones. He was here but didn't want to be found.

Hurt pushed back through the crowd and into the street. The sun was hot, so hot he knew that if he stood there long enough it would burn a hole in his head. Miami was a city, and he'd expected it would be more like...well, like Pittsburgh. It wasn't. In Pittsburgh the buildings were grey, the streets grey, even the sky was grey most of the time. He could blend in, get lost, go unnoticed. Here people looked at him strangely. Everything was a glary white and pink, colors so bright it gave him a headache. He tried lifting his eyes, but the sky above wasn't the sky he knew. It was a garish blue with a sun so fierce he had to look away. He ducked into a drugstore and approached the clerk.

"You got sunglasses?" he asked.

"Sure," she said and waggled a finger toward the far side of the store. "There's a whole rack, right behind the suntan lotion."

Without bothering to thank her, Hurt turned and walked in that direction. He picked the darkest pair he could find and returned to the counter.

"Dollar-forty-nine," the clerk said.

Hurt pulled two dollar bills from his pocket and laid them on the counter.

The girl punched $1.49 into the register. "New in town?"

Hurt didn't answer. Her words seemed little more than buzzing in his ear. He had one thought and one thought only: find Daddy George.

When the clerk handed Hurt his change, she smiled. "Ain't that jacket kinda hot?" she asked laughingly.

Hurt slipped the change into his pocket, then looked at her with an icy cold glare. *Stupid girl*, he thought. *A stupid girl doesn't deserve to live.* He felt for the gun, then turned and walked out of the store. He should have stolen the sunglasses; that's what he should have done. *You steal something, you don't have to talk to stupid girls.* He had no time now; maybe later.

Hurt stood outside the drugstore with sweat rolling down his face and splatting onto his jacket. He tried to think of where Daddy George might hide, but everything here was different; strange and unfamiliar. Where were the row-house neighborhoods? Where were the dark gin mills? He turned and walked south on Second Street. On the corner of Flagler he passed a newsstand and a headline grabbed hold of him.

THUNDERBAY WINS AGAIN AT TROPICAL PARK

Hurt looked at the front page photo of a racehorse and smiled. The track. For more years than he could remember, Daddy George took money that should have put food on the table and played the ponies. He'd skip work, spend the day at Heidelberg Raceway, then come home rip-roaring drunk and in the foul mood that came from never winning.

Hurt plunked down a dime and bought the paper, then asked for directions to Tropical Park Racetrack.

"Union Terminal," the news dealer replied. "They got a bus that goes direct."

Hurt gave a nod and turned back in the direction he'd come from.

When Hurt stepped off the bus at Tropical Park, he caught the smell of his father—the stink of cigars and sweat mingled with meanness. Then he heard the sounds, the all-too familiar sounds of angry words with hard Ks and an intolerance that slammed against his ears and rumbled through his head with a roar.

He paid his entrance fee and entered the track.

Inside there was a crush of people moving, shifting from one place to another. Hurt grabbed a program and moved through with the crowd. Twice someone shoved him in the back, and he slid his hand inside the jacket pocket just to feel the gun. As long as it was there, he'd be okay. A gun was bigger than Daddy George.

A gun was more powerful too.

Daddy George could beat a boy into submission, but a gun could put an end to it.

Hurt's eyes were open as he moved with the surge of people, but behind those wide open eyes he was picturing his daddy with a blown-out hole in the middle of his chest—a hole where a heart never was.

As Hurt walked, he shifted his eyes—right, left, forward, right again. Too many people. Faces crowded together, and arms reached across one another. "Gimme two on the Daily Double," someone yelled. Then another voice echoed the same command. "Five across the board," a voice called out—a woman, not Daddy George.

A swirl of confusion began to circle Hurt. Too many people; too many sounds. It was impossible to pick out even one person in the pressed together mass of flesh. How would he ever find Daddy George?

Hurt opened the program and found his answer.

King George V, in the fifth race.

Turner's Turn

When Mahoney left the station house, Griffin was waiting in the car.

"Well," Griffin said, "how'd it go?"

"Hard to say." Mahoney shrugged. "I got the feeling Gomez didn't want me poking around the Klaussner thing, but I'm not sure why."

"You ask about the kid they caught?"

Mahoney shook his head. "No. I'm thinking there might be more to this than we know. Let's stop by the Doyle place first and see what she's got to say."

It was close to one-thirty when they pulled up in front of the Wyattsville Arms. After the Sam Cobb incident, Mahoney knew Olivia Doyle would be wary of any tag-along partner, especially one the size of a grizzly.

"Hang back," he told Griffin. "Give me ten minutes or so to explain you're an okay guy, then you can come up."

"I'm an okay guy?" Griffin laughed. He was a big man with a big laugh that at times had the sound of thunder.

Mahoney climbed out of the car and walked into the building. Nothing had changed—at least nothing he could put his finger on—yet a strange sense of foreboding had settled into his stomach. *It's that damn Gomez,* he thought. Then he rang Olivia Doyle's doorbell.

Olivia was half-expecting it to be Jim Turner. She'd had four different friends call and report that he was going door to door asking if anyone had seen kids running through the building. To be on the safe side, she'd told Ethan Allen to use the back stairs for coming and going to school and leave his bicycle in the back lobby mud room. She also kept Jubilee hidden inside the apartment. When the doorbell sounded, she figured for sure it was Jim Turner waving another copy of the building rules in her face or, worse yet, an eviction notice. Olivia shooed Jubilee into Ethan's bedroom and closed the door.

"Not a sound," she whispered, "and no matter what you hear, do not come out of the room until I say it's all right to do so."

When she looked through the peephole and saw Detective Mahoney's face, Olivia was pleasantly surprised. After her lie about Anita swimming in Chesapeake Bay, she'd pretty much given up on eliciting his help.

"Come in," she said in an extremely gracious voice.

Olivia thought she'd first sweeten things up with a plate of homemade cookies and fresh coffee, but Mahoney said not to bother and they settled on the sofa. "If you don't mind," he said, "my partner and I would like to run through—"

Olivia's mouth fell open. "Partner? I hadn't counted on..."

"I realize that you had a bad experience last time, but Sam Griffin is—"

"Sam!"

"This isn't Sam Cobb." Mahoney tried to use a soothing tone, but with every word he spoke the alarm in Olivia's face became more apparent. Finally he fell back on the tactic he'd seen Griffin use.

"Sam Griffin is godfather to all three of my children," he said. "I've known him for almost thirty years. He loves kids, got five of his own. Every year he plays Santa Claus at the church festival."

Olivia's right eye was still twitching and the look of wariness remained on her face, but at least she was now listening.

Mahoney went on to detail any number of kind deeds Sam Griffin had done, and by the time the doorbell bonged a second time Olivia had settled into a low level of tolerance—not acceptance, merely tolerance.

Expecting the large red-haired man Mahoney had described, Olivia opened the door without her customary check through the peephole. Sharp-nosed Jim Turner stood there with a bound copy of the building bylaws tucked under his arm.

"I've had numerous complaints!" he said and angrily tromped into the apartment. "Rumor has it you're harboring any number of children here." As Turner spoke his head swiveled back and forth looking for a clue, some indication that what he suspected was true.

"I am not harboring any number of children!" Olivia snapped. Since "any number" did not mean one small girl, she was certain it could not be considered a lie.

The exchange went on for a minute or two and then Detective Mahoney, who'd been listening, stood and walked toward Turner. "Is there a problem here?"

"There most certainly is," Turner answered. "We have rules in this building, and I've had numerous complaints about—"

"Numerous complaint, huh?"

"So many I've lost count!"

"If they're legitimate complaints, we can do something about it." Mahoney fingered his chin pensively. "Of course, it means that you and all the complainants will have to appear in court. You'll need to have a lawyer, witnesses to swear to the legitimacy of complaint, and evidence—"

"What the...what are you, some kind of shyster lawyer?"

Mahoney pulled out his badge. "No, I'm an officer of the law."

"This isn't a police matter!"

"Oh, but it is," Mahoney replied. "Missus Doyle called to report a case of harassment." He turned to Olivia. "Is this the fellow you were talking about?"

Olivia smiled and gave a half-nod, not a yes or no, merely a maybe.

"That's preposterous," Turner sputtered. "I'm not harassing anybody!"

"It looks like you are," Mahoney said. "You came here uninvited, stuck your nose in Missus Doyle's face, and tried to intimidate her. That's considered harassment."

"This has gone entirely too far," Turner said. He began edging his way back to the door.

"I agree." Mahoney turned to Olivia. "Missus Doyle, if this fellow agrees to stay clear of you, would you be willing to drop the complaint?"

Olivia nodded.

"Okay then." Mahoney looked at Turner. "And, sir, if Missus Doyle is willing to drop the complaint, will you stop pestering her?"

Turner nodded. Before anything else could be said, he pulled open the door and scooted out with such speed that he ran smack into Griffin who was reaching for the doorbell. Turner looked up at the bearded face towering over him. "Sorry," he said and kept going.

Seeing Jim Turner dash off as he did, Olivia felt a weight had been lifted from her chest. Moving past the fact that Griffin was another policeman named Sam, she invited him in with a smile.

Mahoney took the lead in the conversation. "I understand your predicament, and we're going to do everything we can to find the child's missing aunt."

Griffin nodded.

"But there's a lot of open-ended questions," he said. "So, if you don't mind, can we go back over the girl's connection to the Klaussner robbery?"

The thought of linking Jubilee to such an event rumbled through Olivia's head and sat uncomfortably against her brain. Suddenly she felt telling all might not be the best thing. She hadn't counted on a partner, nor had she counted on a full-scale investigation. The thought of detectives scouring through the child's history and turning over rocks best left undisturbed made her nerves twinge and tighten.

"Jubilee has no actual connection to the robbery," Olivia answered. "Our only problem is locating her aunt."

Mahoney gave her a questioning look. "But when we spoke on the phone, didn't you say she might be related to the boy who was shot?"

"Perhaps I did, but I was only echoing the supposition Ethan Allen made." Olivia was now certain she had said too much and added, "You know how imaginative children can be."

"That's true," Mahoney said.

"It sure is," Griffin added. "I've got three of my own and they're always—"

"Three?" Olivia eyed him suspiciously. "I thought you had five?"

Mahoney winced, and Griffin caught on immediately. "I do, but the two older ones are from my wife's first marriage, so I can't really take credit for them."

Olivia looked a bit doubtful but continued. She explained that Jubilee's parents were deceased and the girl had come to Wyattsville looking for her aunt. After disappearing into the bedroom and returning, she handed Detective Mahoney one of the letters postmarked Wyattsville. In telling the story Olivia simply eliminated the missing brother who might or might not have been involved in the Klaussner shooting.

"So this girl was alone when Ethan Allen met her?"

Olivia nodded.

"And she's seven years old?" Griffin said.

Olivia gave a second nod.

"Seven, huh? That's awfully young to be traveling alone. How'd she get here?"

Feeling a bit bottled-up, Olivia simply shrugged. "I can't say. My primary concern is in helping her find her aunt."

"Maybe we ought to talk to the girl and Ethan Allen both," Griffin suggested. "Let them tell us exactly how this meet-up happened."

Olivia glared at Griffin as if he'd gone stark, raving mad. "Absolutely not. The child has been through enough already."

Mahoney walked over and put his hand on Olivia's arm. "I know you're trying to protect the girl, but hiding from the truth never helps."

Perhaps it was the sincerity in his voice, or perhaps she saw the light of truth in his eyes again. Regardless of what caused it, Olivia's resolve started to crumble. With a quivering voice that edged close to tears, she said, "Expecting a child to accept that her brother is guilty of shooting a man is asking too much."

"Maybe he's not guilty," Mahoney answered. "We're not trying to prove anybody did anything; we're just looking for the truth."

Truth. The word landed softly on Olivia's ear. Truth was okay. It was not always pretty or sweet, but it was okay. "Promise me you won't turn her over to the authorities," Olivia said. "Promise me that much."

"Okay," Mahoney answered. "I give you my word." He hesitated a moment then said, "But please realize, there may come a time when you're the one who has to do it."

"Me?" Olivia gasped. "Why me?"

"Because it might be the right thing to do."

The thought of a child like Jubilee having no one to love her was almost unthinkable, so Olivia pushed it to the back of her mind and finally agreed to let Mahoney question the children. "Just you," she said, turning her back to Griffin. "No one else."

"We'd be more likely to get at the truth if one of us talks to Ethan Allen and the other talks to the girl," Mahoney argued, but Olivia stood firm on her decision and told him to come back at three-thirty when Ethan Allen got home from school.

As they left the building Griffin nodded knowingly to Mahoney. "Right," Mahoney answered. They parked the car in front of the building and sat there waiting to catch Ethan Allen on his way home from school.

Twenty minutes later Mahoney spotted the boy coming down the street. He stepped out and called to him. After a few minutes of chit-chat about Dog and whether Cal Ripkin could carry the Senators to a winning season, Mahoney said, "This girl you brought home, how'd that come about?"

"Does Grandma Olivia know you're here?" Ethan asked suspiciously.

"She sure does. She's the one who said it'd be okay to talk with you."

With the look of doubt spreading across his face, Ethan said, "Grandma wants me to tell you about that?"

"Honest. I was up there a few minutes ago, and she said 'When Ethan gets home from school you can ask him.'"

"I don't know." Ethan shook his head. "That don't sound like Grandma Olivia."

"You think I'd lie?"

"I suppose not," Ethan answered, but the expression on his face argued the point.

Trying to move back to the questions he had in mind, Mahoney said, "About this girl you brought home. She was just sitting on the bench across from Klaussner's on the day of the shooting?"

"You're sure Grandma Olivia said I'm supposed to talk about this?"

Mahoney nodded.

"I ain't looking to get Jubie in trouble."

"Nobody's in trouble. I'm just trying to get the facts."

Ethan shrugged as if he still had some doubt. "I'd feel a lot better about this if we was to check with Grandma first."

"Okay," Mahoney relented, "let's go upstairs. That way I can talk with Jubilee also."

"Who told you her name was Jubilee?" Ethan asked suspiciously.

"Your grandmother," Mahoney answered, and the boy smiled.

When they arrived at the apartment, Clara and Fred McGinty were sitting on the sofa. Clara had a notepad and pencil in her lap, and McGinty had a camera.

"I have witnesses," Olivia warned, "and as I said earlier I will not allow you to badger or scare Jubilee. Right now she has no family, and I feel it's my responsibility to see to her well-being until we locate her aunt."

"Agreed." Detective Mahoney nodded.

Olivia disappeared into the bedroom and came back with the girl. After introducing her to the detective, she sat Jubilee between Clara and McGinty and told Ethan Allen to squeeze in alongside. Olivia sat in her silk chair, which left only the club chair on the far side of the seating arrangement for Mahoney.

He knew it would have been better if he could have sat alongside the girl, close up. He could tell when a person was lying, but across the room could be iffy. Mahoney began with cordialities meant to put the girl at ease.

"That's a very pretty dress you're wearing."

"I got seven more," Jubilee answered, "and I got panties with—" She stopped when she saw Olivia frown and shake her head. That had been the plan. Jubilee was to watch Olivia—a nod meant it was okay to answer, a shake of the head indicated she shouldn't answer. So far, so good.

The first few questions were about the missing aunt, and Olivia nodded for each one. When Mahoney got to the part where he asked how she came to be sitting on the bench, she forgot to look at Olivia first and blurted out, "Paul told me to wait there."

Olivia's head was going back and forth like a tennis ball when Mahoney then asked if Paul was her brother. Jubilee saw Olivia's head shake, turned to her, and asked, "Why ain't I supposed to say Paul's my brother?"

Rolling her eyes wearily, Olivia was pushed into saying, "Of course you can say Paul's your brother. You should always tell the truth."

"Oh, okay." Jubilee stopped looking at Olivia's nods and shakes and answered the rest of the questions. When Detective Mahoney asked if it was a customary thing for Paul to leave her alone that way, Jubie narrowed her eyes and said, "He don't never leave me alone!"

"Why do you think he left you alone this time?"

"He had to do a job so we'd have money."

"Were those Paul's exact words? Did he say he had to do a job?"

"Yes!" she answered angrily. "He saw the sign!"

"What did the sign say?"

"It said working was for a lot of money." Jubilee's eyes began to fill with tears. "If you find Paul, tell him not to do working. I don't want a sleeping room and good food."

Ethan Allen spoke up. "If you're figuring Jubie was in on that robbery, you're figuring wrong. She didn't have nothing to do with it."

Mahoney asked several more questions. By then Olivia had given up trying to steer the conversation one way or the other, so Jubilee told the story pretty much as it happened. As he sat and listened it seemed the girl grew smaller, more vulnerable with each word. Even from clear across the room, he could see she spoke the truth—but he had yet to find out the brother's intentions.

By the time Mahoney stood to leave, Clara had scribbled five pages of notes and Fred had used up the entire roll of film. Ignoring both of them Mahoney walked over, knelt down in front of the girl, and lifted her hand into his.

"Jubilee," he said, "I'm going to do everything possible to find your brother and your Aunt Anita."

Before he left the building, Mahoney knew he had no choice but to keep the promise he'd made to Jubilee Jones. Unfortunately, it probably meant tangling with Hector Gomez again.

Olivia Doyle

I should have realized Jubilee is too young to be devious, and Detective Mahoney is too smart to be fooled. I can't be angry with the child, because all she did was tell the truth. I've always believed the truth can't hurt you, but times like this I find myself doubtful.

If Jubilee's brother was involved in the shooting, I'm hoping he's the one who got away. Seeing a person you love go to prison would shatter the heart of a grownup; I can't begin to imagine what it would do to a tiny little thing like Jubilee. I think it would be better for her to believe Paul ran off and is safe somewhere else than to know he's locked up behind bars for shooting a man. I pray before any of this comes to pass Mister Mahoney will find this Aunt Anita so Jubilee can be with her. If a child has someone to love them, a family to call their own, hardships are easier to bear. If not easier, at least they've got a caring shoulder to cry on.

I suppose every nickel has its shiny side, and the shiny side of this one is getting rid of Jim Turner. Unfortunately, there's also a second side, and right now it's warning me that people like Jim don't give up. They make you think they have, but if you could see inside their head you'd discover they're just thinking of another way to come at you.

I'd like to believe I can stop worrying he'll come knocking on my door again, but the sorry truth is that I'd better start worrying about finding Anita so Jubilee will be living with her when Jim finally comes up with something else.

Verdict Before Trial

As soon as Mahoney settled himself in the car, Griffin asked how it had gone. Mahoney shrugged and didn't answer for several minutes.

"After thinking about this," he finally said, "I believe we've got to get involved."

"It's not in our jurisdiction," Griffin warned. "We've got no authority."

"I know."

"The kid got to you, didn't she?"

"Yeah." Mahoney nodded. "But as I said before, there's a lot going on here."

Griffin turned onto the highway and headed for the ferry. Tomorrow was another day.

That evening Jack Mahoney took his wife and all three kids out for ice cream. After that they stopped down at the dock to do a bit of fishing.

"You're being awfully patient with the children this evening," Christine said. "Did you have an especially good day or something?"

"On the contrary," Jack answered and left it at that.

After the rest of the family had gone to bed, Jack sat on the front porch pushing back and forth in an old rocking chair that had been there when they bought the house. In his mind he lined up his three children with scrubbed clean faces and shiny bright smiles, but before he could save the image a fourth child stepped into the picture: Jubilee Jones, a sad-eyed little girl who seemed as purposeful and determined as Olivia Doyle. No matter how many times he pushed her aside, she kept coming back. If he pictured his children reading a book or playing a game Jubilee was there on the sideline, not playing, but watching with melancholy blue eyes.

At twelve-thirty he tiptoed upstairs to check on the children. In the shadows of a darkened bedroom he thought he saw Jubilee sleeping between Sara and Jessica, but when he moved closer to look it was only Jessica's brown teddy bear.

Jack got very little sleep that night, and by morning he had reached a decision. He was at the precinct waiting when Captain Rogers arrived.

"Got a minute?" Mahoney asked and followed Rogers into his office. Before the captain had time to set his coffee down on the desk, Jack launched into the argument he had spent the night thinking through.

"I know this is a little out of our jurisdiction, but I have reason to believe the missing woman is from this area."

"A little out of jurisdiction?" the captain repeated. "It's not even in the same county!"

"I know, but given the extenuating circumstances—"

"Hannigan is out sick and Peters is on vacation, so I'm already short two men."

When it began to look like he was about to get a flat no, Mahoney played his ace. "I think this case might be related to the Doyle murders."

"The Doyle murders?"

Mahoney nodded. "The Doyle file is missing from archives."

"Hmm. Nobody signed it out?"

"Nope," Mahoney answered. "Doesn't that strike you as strange?"

It was bad enough to have one of their own involved in something like the Doyle murder cover-up. It was even worse to think there might be something else to come. "Okay," the captain said, "you can go. But until you get something more, work it alone." He agreed to make a few phone calls so Mahoney would be granted access to whatever the Wyattsville Station had.

"This better not be a crapshoot," he grumbled as Jack was leaving.

It was ten-thirty when Mahoney arrived at the Wyattsville station house.

Luckily Gomez was nowhere in sight, so he got to talk to Pete Morgan.

"Captain Rogers called," Morgan said. "Thought your missing person might be tied into the Klaussner shooting. How so?"

"It's possible this woman I'm looking for is the aunt of the kid who got shot." Mahoney deliberately made no mention of Jubilee Jones.

"You know the kid's name?"

"Not yet, but I'm hoping to talk to him today."

"Lots of luck on that. Gomez has been working this for five days. Yesterday he talked to the kid and got nothing." Morgan lifted a folder from the desk and handed it to Mahoney. "This is all we've got right now. Take a look."

Mahoney took the folder and lowered himself into the available chair. In all it was only nine pages. It detailed the pitiful life of a small-time crook named Hurt McAdams. Mom left when he was twelve, father a racetrack junkie with ties to several bookies, the kid bounced out of school, spent seven years in a correctional institution. Plenty of disturbances; no visitors.

Mahoney shook his head sadly. "Guy like this never had a chance."

"We've got an APB out," Morgan said, "but my bet is he's long gone."

"What about the kid in hospital? Any prints tie him to scene?"

"No prints, but Klaussner put a bullet in him."

"Ballistics indicate the bullet came from Klaussner's gun?"

Morgan nodded. "Gomez said this one is a slam dunk. The kid's guilty, period."

"Klaussner identified him?"

"No such luck. Klaussner's still in a coma."

"Any witnesses?"

"Neighborhood woman, Martha Tillinger. Apparently she was in the back of the store and hid behind some cereal boxes when the shooting started."

"So she identified the boy?"

"She didn't see the shooter, just heard the shots."

Mahoney began rubbing the back of his hand across his chin, the way he did when something was troubling him. "Any chance the kid was a bystander?"

Morgan chortled. "Not according to Gomez."

Mahoney's next stop was Mercy General Hospital. During the drive he ran through the details of the case. A ballistics match pointed to the kid being guilty; a witness who hadn't heard the voices was a zero. The prints on the register tagged Hurt McAdams as the guy who grabbed the cash, but was he working alone or working with the kid? There were too many questions and too few answers. Mahoney kept wondering if the kid was with Hurt or simply standing in the line of fire. But the most troubling question, the one that pushed him to pursue answers, was the identity of the kid in the hospital.

If he was Jubilee's brother that might tip the scales in his favor, not necessarily showing innocence but making him less likely to team up with someone like Hurt McAdams. The kid wasn't in the system, which meant he had no priors. Hurt was from Pittsburgh. Jubilee Jones was from Coal Fork, West Virginia, a place so far out in the boonies you had to know it was there to find it. So where was the thread that connected McAdams to this kid? Too many loose ends—way too many.

When he arrived at the hospital, Mahoney found Gomez had already been there and gone. "I think he's coming back later," the duty nurse said. Mahoney saw this as an opportunity. Captain Rogers, true to his word, had called ahead so there was no problem getting in to talk with the boy.

Mahoney showed his badge, spoke briefly with the officer at the door, then entered the room. A kid with the body of a man and the face of a teenager lay in the bed, his head raised slightly and his eyes staring up at a water-stained ceiling. The television flickered, yet he seemed unaware it was there. The boy was no longer on a respirator, but the bandage on his throat was evidence that he had been.

"Good morning," Mahoney said.

No response. Nothing.

Mahoney continued. He asked the kind of nebulous questions that answered nothing. "Do you know where you are?" "Do you remember being shot?" "Do you remember walking into Klaussner's Grocery Store?" Not one of these questions generated even a flicker of the boy's eyelid. He looked neither right nor left, just continued staring at the faded brown stain that said some time in the near or distant past water had seeped through there.

Once he'd run through the gamut, Mahoney asked the question he had come to ask.

"Paul, do you think Jubilee is still sitting on the bench waiting for you?"

The boy did not respond, turn his head, or speak, but his eyes grew wide and flickered nervously. His heart began racing, and the neon heart monitor flew past 160. It climbed to 190, then jumped to 210. Mahoney saw the reaction and continued. "Your sister needs your help," he said, but before he could go any further a nurse came running into the room.

"What going on here?" she asked.

"Routine questions," Mahoney answered. He reached across the bed and gave the boy's leg a comforting pat. "Rest easy, son," he said. "I'll stop back later."

As Mahoney stood in the hallway waiting for a down elevator, Gomez stepped out of one on its way up. His displeasure was obvious.

"What are you doing here? I thought you weren't in on the Klaussner case."

"I'm not, actually. I just thought there was a chance the kid you had might be related to my missing person."

"Yeah, I bet," Gomez sneered. "So what'd you find out?"

"Like the file indicated, the kid's non-responsive." A down arrow flashed green, and Mahoney stepped into the elevator. As the doors were closing he glanced back and thought he saw a look of malice on Gomez's face.

With his face turning redder by the second, Gomez rumbled down the hospital corridor, pushed through the intensive care department doors, and headed for the boy's room. The duty nurse stopped him before he was halfway across the floor.

"Not now," she said. "He's had enough for a while. His heartbeat's still over two hundred."

"That last detective who was here," Gomez said, "what'd he find out?"

"Ask him," she answered and turned off in a huff.

"Damn," Gomez grumbled.

Hector Gomez

Did you ever get a thorn caught under your skin? It hurts like hell, but you can't get it out. That's what Mahoney is to me: a thorn under my skin. He shouldn't even be here. He belongs in Northampton. So why is he sticking his nose in where it don't belong? Why is he looking to screw up another case for me?

If not for his meddling, I'd have made detective last June instead of waiting another ten months. Mahoney's why the Doyle case went south. I could've had the kid for the shooting, but then he shows up with this do-gooder attitude and makes me look bad. Justice don't give a crap about how old a person is; guilty is guilty. And that kid was guilty. I could feel it in my bones.

You know what I think? I think Mahoney's got it in for me. Don't ask why, 'cause I don't know. Maybe 'cause I'm younger or better looking. Who knows? I really don't care what his reason is. This much I can tell you, he ain't getting away with it again.

Klaussner put a bullet in the punk's head to keep him from robbing the store, and that's all the proof I need. This kid is guilty, no question.

If Mahoney thinks I'm gonna roll over on this one, he's got another think coming.

Jubilee's Choice

When Mahoney left the hospital he was all but certain the boy lying in the hospital bed was Jubilee's brother. There were no new facts, no spoken word, not even a nod, but the glimmer of recognition was there. Some relationships were so close that the bond of love bypassed locked doors, ignored time, and paid no attention to circumstance.

He thought back to the day his own dad died. It was June twenty-first, seventeen years ago. Jack was new on the force and working days. That morning as he stood in front of the mirror shaving he felt it: a wrenching pain in his chest. It came sharp and sudden, hammered him for a minute, then passed. Jack gave a sigh of relief and got dressed, but even though the pain was gone the bitterness of acid indigestion continued all day. He gulped down two rolls of Tums, but nothing helped. At four o'clock he got the call: seven-thirty that morning the man he loved and respected more than any other human on earth had suffered a massive heart attack. For the remainder of the day it had been touch and go, then at three-thirty-seven Jack's dad passed away.

Seventeen years had gone by, but the acid indigestion was still with him. Sometimes he could go for weeks, months even, without a trace of it. But when something was not right there it was, back again. It was a warning sign, a red flag, a smack in the head that said, "Listen up, this is important!" Mahoney stopped at the drug store, bought a roll of Tums, then drove to the Wyattsville Arms apartment building, uncertain of whether what he had to say was going to be perceived as good news or bad.

Ethan Allen was already home from school, and he was the one who answered the bell. "Hey, Mister Mahoney," he said and yanked the door open. "You here for more questioning?"

"Perhaps," Mahoney answered, then asked if he could have a moment alone with Olivia.

Ethan screamed, "Grandma!" and moments later, Olivia came from the kitchen drying her hands on a dish towel. She knew by the look on Mahoney's face he had something.

Turning to Ethan Allen she said, "You and Jubilee scoot on out of here. Go work on that puzzle you've been doing."

"There's pieces missing," Ethan answered and stayed put.

"Then go do your homework."

Ethan gave a disgusted sigh. "I guess we'll work on the stupid puzzle." He turned and motioned for Jubilee to go with him.

Jubilee, who had begun to tag after Ethan like a shadow, didn't move. Instead she narrowed her eyes and looked at Mahoney suspiciously. "You gonna ask me more questions about Paul?"

"Maybe later," Mahoney answered.

"Scoot," Olivia repeated. She led Mahoney into the kitchen and closed the door. He settled into a chair, and after she'd poured two cups of coffee she sat across from him. "Have you found Anita?"

"Not yet," Mahoney answered, "but I'm pretty sure I've found Jubilee's brother." He went on to tell of the hospital visit and how the mention of Jubilee's name brought a glimmer of recognition. "Right now he seems to have very little memory of anything, but I believe seeing his sister could change that."

Olivia gasped. "Absolutely not. The child has been through enough. If he is her brother and doesn't recognize her..."

"I know it's chancy, but I think the kid will respond."

Olivia shook her head. "There's got to be another way to find Anita. If Jubilee had some real family to care for her, she might be better able to handle her brother going to jail."

"Whoa there," Mahoney said. "First off, you're jumping to conclusions. I'm not even sure the boy was involved in this. And secondly—"

"Not involved? But you said—"

"No, I never said I think he's guilty. Gomez is heading up the investigation and he thinks the kid is guilty, but—"

"Sargent Gomez? The one with the bushy black mustache?"

Mahoney nodded. "But he's not Sargent Gomez anymore, he's Detective Gomez."

"Oh, dear." Olivia remembered Hector Gomez all too well and wasn't eager to have another encounter with him. "We have simply got to find Anita."

"Yeah, well," Mahoney said with a sigh, "right now I'm coming up with a lot of dead ends. Your F.M. Jones gave me a lead on a woman in Norfolk who years back rented an apartment to Bartholomew Jones and his wife. Supposedly there was a woman named Anita who visited frequently, but I've gotta say this is thin at best; more than likely going nowhere."

"You never know," Olivia said hopefully.

For several minutes they sat there saying nothing. Mahoney stirred his coffee three times even though there was not a drop of cream or sugar mixed in. Olivia fussed with folding and refolding her napkin. After a long while she asked, "Do you honestly think there's a chance Paul's not involved?"

"Possibly," Mahoney answered. "But we won't know anything until we hear Paul's version of the incident. That's not going to happen until he remembers who he is."

"What about Mister Klaussner? What does he say?"

"Unfortunately, Sid is in a medically-induced coma. And the prognosis is iffy." The last of Mahoney's words hung in the air weighted with an ominous unspoken question mark.

Olivia thought back to the beginning of their conversation. "Earlier on you started to say secondly. What was that secondly?"

Mahoney rubbed the back of his hand across his chin pensively. "I was gonna say if Paul does get his memory back, maybe he can also tell us where to find the aunt."

Olivia nodded knowingly.

The coffee was gone, and the cups had grown cold before she spoke again. "I don't believe in forcing a child to needlessly face the terrible truth of reality, but neither do I want to make a decision that could change her life. I know Jubilee is only seven, but she's sensible enough. I think we should explain this to her and ask how she feels."

"That's a wise decision," Mahoney said. "A very wise decision."

After going through what would or wouldn't be said, Olivia called Jubilee into the kitchen. Ethan Allen was right behind her.

"You don't really need to be here," Olivia told him.

"Yeah, I do," he said. "I promised to stay by her." Before he sat, Ethan scooted his chair to where it was bumping up against Jubilee's. Once everyone was settled, Jack Mahoney began to speak. His words were wrapped in a softness only parents are capable of.

"Jubilee, I know you love your brother, and he loves you too. When Paul told you to wait for him I'm sure he had every intention of coming back, but sometimes things happen and we can't do what we've promised."

As he spoke, an odd sense of knowing settled on Jubilee's face. There was no frown, no smile, just an empty look of resignation. Before Mahoney finished the speech he was working through, she asked point blank, "Did you find my brother?"

"Yes, Jubilee, I think I did."

"Did he say he's not coming back to get me?"

"No, he didn't."

"Then he'll be back," she answered flatly. A thin shell of resolve crusted over the outside of who she was. Inside there were a million broken pieces, fragments of things taken from her life—a mother, a father, a brother, a place to call home, friends, familiar roads, a garden—the shell kept all those things from spilling out like handfuls of Cheerios.

"What makes you so sure?" Mahoney asked.

"Because he *promised*."

Mahoney saw the certainty in her face. She trusted Paul would be true to his word. There was no maybe or extenuating circumstance, it would happen. She believed in someone bigger than herself. Someone for whom even the impossible was possible. This tiny little girl had a faith that most grownups prayed for.

With a heavy heart Mahoney said, "Sometimes bad things happen and no matter how much you love someone, you can't keep the promise you made."

The look on Jubilee's face was one of wariness. "What kind of bad things?"

Mahoney explained how Paul had been hurt in an accident and was now in the hospital. As Olivia had insisted, there was no mention of the robbery. He said, "Your brother doesn't remember anything, not even you. He's sad and scared, but he might start remembering if he could see you."

"He'll remember," Jubilee answered. "I know he will." Coming from her mouth the words had a ring of surety, but if you looked closely you could see the tears welling in her eyes.

Ethan Allen

Jubie is scared. Not scared like when you scream on a roller coaster. Scared like when you have a bad dream and can't get woke up. People ain't really scared on a roller coaster, they just scream 'cause it's fun-scared and they know it's gonna end soon. Jubie don't know if her being alone is ever gonna end.

I can tell when she's most scared, 'cause she curls up like a snail and sticks her thumb in her mouth. When Jubie does that, I say, Let's play poker, and let her win a few hands. It makes her happy, and she forgets feel happy; I know 'cause when I play with Grandma I win most every time. But it's not 'cause she lets me; Grandma's just not real good at poker.

Yesterday I asked Grandma if maybe Jubie could live here with us and she rolled her eyes like it was the most dumb-ass thing she ever heard. "No, she can't," Grandma said. "She has a family and needs to be with them."

I was gonna remind Grandma that right now she ain't got nobody and it ain't looking none too promising, but she'd already said to get on outta there and quit bothering her.

After Detective Mahoney told Jubie Paul didn't remember nothing, she got curled up and didn't even wanna talk about playing. "Don'tcha get it?" she said. "If Paul don't remember me, I got nobody!"

You got me, I said, and I meant it. If Grandma ain't gonna do something to help Jubie, I'm gonna do it myself. I ain't too sure of what it'll be, but I'll think of something.

Leastwise, I hope I will.

According to Bertha

When Mahoney left the Doyle apartment he called Captain Rogers, reported his finding, and tried to get clearance for bringing Jubilee Jones to the hospital.

"I'm okay with you working the case," Rogers said, "so long as it doesn't turn into a pissing match between you and Gomez. Work with him, or step back."

Mahoney agreed to share what he had with Gomez, but as he hung up the telephone he muttered, "When I've got time."

He turned the car around and headed toward Norfolk and the address Frances Margaret Jones had written on a scrap of paper.

Bertha Kaminski was no longer at that address. A frazzled mother carrying a baby who wouldn't stop crying answered the door. "We bought the house a year ago," she said. "They didn't leave a forwarding address."

"Do you know if they were staying in town?"

She shifted the crying baby to her other shoulder. "No idea," she said and pushed the door shut using her foot.

Mahoney's next stop was the post office.

After going through two different clerks, he was able to speak to the shift supervisor who dug through the files and came up with a change of address for Benjamin Kaminski.

"You're lucky we still got it," she said. "Generally we only keep these six months." She wrote the address on a note paper and handed it Mahoney.

He looked at the address, a bad section of Norfolk on the far side of town. Before heading over, he checked the telephone listings—nothing. He got back into the car and started toward the side of town where people seldom went unless they had to.

The address was a tenement building with a whiskey bottle leaning against the rail and cement steps broken on both sides. The windows of the ground floor apartment were covered with different-colored bed sheets, too dirty to see through. He climbed the steps and entered the vestibule. Several broken mailboxes hung halfway open.

Apartment 5A was tagged B. Kaminski. Could be Bertha, could be Benjamin, or could be both. Mahoney started up the dark narrow staircase.

When he rapped on the door a male voice called back, "Whaddya want?"

"I'm looking for Bertha Kaminski," Mahoney answered.

The voice yelled, "Hey, Butterball, it's for you."

For a long minute there was nothing more; then heavy footsteps thumped across the floor and the door swung open.

The woman looked nothing like Frances Margaret or Myrtle, as the case might be. She was round and nearly as wide as she was tall. "Yeah?" she said looking square into his face.

"Bertha Kaminski?"

She nodded.

"You owned the house on Kilmer Street in Norfolk?"

"If this is about the basement flooding, I don't want to hear it. We sold that house as is, and we told them—"

"It's not about the basement," Mahoney said. "When you lived there, did you rent an upstairs flat to a couple by the name of Bartholomew and Ruth Jones?"

"Good Lord, that was twenty years ago. I don't see how they could have a complaint after all this time."

"There is no complaint. They're both deceased."

"Lord have mercy," Bertha murmured. "Young folks like that dying already." She gave a weary shake of her head.

"Do you remember a woman named Anita visiting them? Anita Walker or maybe Jones?"

"Shoot, yeah, I remember Anita. You don't forget one like her."

"Is her last name Walker or Jones?"

"Was. It was Walker, but it ain't no more."

This was the first solid lead Mahoney had and he jumped on it. "When did she change her name?"

"Sixteen, maybe seventeen years back, when she married Freddie Meyers." She gave a sorrowful shrug. "Poor Freddie. If Ben would've known how she was gonna treat Freddie, he would've never matched them up."

"Ben, he's your husband?"

"Sort of," Bertha answered. "We never really got around to the official marrying part."

"Oh." Mahoney gave a nod, unsure of whether to say "sorry," "good," or nothing. He opted for nothing and moved on. "You got an address for this Freddie Meyers?"

Bertha turned her head and screamed, "Hey, Ben, you got Freddie's address?"

"Not the new one," Ben hollered back.

Bertha turned to Mahoney. "Ben said—"

"I heard him."

"It's someplace out on the Eastern Shore," she said. "Franklin, Federal. something sounds like that."

"Fairlawn Bay?"

"Yeah, I think that's it."

"Thanks." Mahoney turned to leave.

Before he'd taken a step, Bertha said, "But if you're looking for Anita, finding Freddie ain't gonna do you no good."

"Oh?"

"They got divorced five, maybe six, years ago."

"Did Anita go back to using her maiden name, or did she stay Meyers?"

"No idea."

"So you didn't keep up with her? Get her new address?"

"Hell, no. That woman ain't one you wanna be friends with." She went on to itemize Anita's multitude of shortcomings, which included that she was lazy as sin, mean-tempered, and cheap to a fault. "Don't never ask her to pick you up a quart of milk from the store," Bertha said, "'cause she'd charge you double!"

It was close to five when Mahoney thanked Bertha for her help and returned to the car. The hour gave him justification for not stopping by the Wyattsville station. Tomorrow he'd report his findings to Gomez. Tomorrow, after he finished taking Jubilee to see her brother. Better that way, he figured. Less intimidating. Gomez had been hammering the boy with questions for three days, and it stood to reason that by now the boy had built up a wall of resistance. If it was just him and Jubilee, Paul would be more likely to respond. In the meantime he could look into finding Freddie Meyers.

He turned onto the causeway and headed back to the ferry.

Mahoney had planned to have a quick dinner, then head back to the station house and see if he could find anything on a Freddie Meyers, but when he arrived home the dining room table was set for seven. "Hurry and get changed," Christine said. "Lynn and Henry will be here in fifteen minutes."

"Lynn and Henry Ontiveros? On a Tuesday?"

"Yes," Christine answered. "She gave me an absolutely wonderful recipe for baked chicken but it serves eight, so I invited them over to share."

"Can't it wait? I've got something I wanted to take care of down at—"

Christine turned and looked at him with a sad-eyed expression. "I've already invited them."

Of course, dinner turned into an evening of conversation and then expanded itself again when Christine insisted that Lynn show Jack the pictures of their vacation. It was near eleven when they ended the evening.

All through dinner Mahoney thought about Olivia's words. "If Jubilee only had someone—real family, someone to love her." His children had so much, and that little girl had so little. The more he thought the slower he ate. Twice Christine glanced at the food still on his plate and asked if perhaps he didn't care for the chicken. "No, no," Jack answered. "It's good, very good."

The truth was his mind simply wasn't on food. He was thinking of the possible ways he could track down Anita. Although one side of his brain chastised him for not being down at the station searching for Freddie

Meyers, the other side counted up the blessings of being here with friends and family. He tried to imagine one of his girls in the same dilemma, but it was impossible. It could never happen. Even if something were to happen to him and Christine, the kids had their grandparents, aunts, and uncles. They were loved.

Jubilee Jones had one person, a brother who quite possibly wouldn't even recognize her. And an aunt she had never laid eyes on; an aunt who was proving herself impossible to find. He had to find Freddie Meyers. He'd know where Anita was. He had to know.

When Jack Mahoney climbed into bed that night, his heart was far heavier than his eyelids. He couldn't rid himself of the image of Jubilee Jones standing in a giant circle of aloneness. On the far edge there were crowds of people, but no one reached out. The pain she felt was visible; it was a jagged scar that ripped across her face and ran toward her heart. As Jack tossed and turned, a second image came into view—the memory of Ethan Allen scooting his chair closer to Jubilee's.

Ethan Allen was a boy who understood loneliness. He'd been there himself. He'd reached out and a stranger—a woman who never wanted children—answered the plea. Now he was ready to do the same for Jubilee. "I promise I'll stick by you," he'd said.

One small boy who understood loneliness was ready to step up to the plate to do what no one else seemed willing to do: stick by Jubilee Jones.

She'd turned to him and he'd answered.

I promise I'll stick by you.

The Road to Remembering

Mahoney left his house long before dawn and was knocking on Olivia's apartment door at six-fifteen. He had hoped to search out Freddie Meyers and have some good news to report, but now it would have to wait. He needed to get Jubilee in and out of the hospital before Gomez got there. If there was any chance of the boy opening up, it wouldn't be with an antagonistic cop hovering over him ready to pounce. It was a good plan, and it might have worked—if not for Ethan Allen.

Olivia had anticipated that just she and Detective Mahoney would accompany Jubilee on the trip to the hospital, but Ethan Allen thought differently. Last night she'd told him they were going to leave early, and Clara would come and wake him when it was time for school.

"Tell her not to bother," he'd answered, saying that he didn't plan on going to school. "I done promised Jubie I'd stick by her, and I'm gonna do it."

"You can stick by her all you want when we get back from the hospital, but tomorrow morning you're going to school." As far as Olivia was concerned that was the end of the discussion.

Not so with Ethan Allen. He'd stayed awake for most of the night so he'd be ready when they started to leave. When Jubilee sat down at the breakfast table he was right beside her.

"Go back to bed," Olivia told him. "There's no need for you to be up this early."

"Yes, there is," he answered. "I promised Jubie I'd stick by her, and that's what I'm gonna do."

"Not this morning. Paul's more likely to remember Jubilee if she's alone."

"I gotta be there in case he don't remember."

"No," Olivia said flatly. "Now shoo on out of here, and let me fix breakfast."

"If you ain't gonna let me come with you in the car, I'll take my bike and be following right behind."

Slowly losing patience, Olivia said he was going to lose his allowance for a full month if he didn't listen. "You've already missed two days of school this term, and I was none too happy with that D on your last report card."

Words flew back and forth, and the argument continued until Jubilee spoke up. "I'm scared, Miss Olivia," she said. "Please let Ethan come with me."

With those few words, she reached in and took hold of Olivia's heart. The child's fear was painfully real, close to the surface like sunburned skin blistering and ready to pull away in torn bits and pieces.

"Well," Olivia relented, "I suppose if he promises to catch up on his homework and get better grades..."She hadn't quite finished the sentence when Ethan grinned and said, "Thanks, Grandma."

On the drive to the hospital Olivia sat in the front seat alongside Mahoney, and the two kids sat in the back. As they pulled onto Monroe Street, Mahoney checked them in the rearview mirror. Ethan Allen was squeezed close to Jubilee on the right side of the seat. It was a sharp contrast to his son and youngest daughter who, when there was an occasion to ride together, sat on opposite ends of the seat, as far away from each other as possible, acting as if one had poison ivy and the other was wary of catching it.

In this moment of relative calm, he tried to warn the child. "Jubilee, you know your brother's been very sick, right?"

"Yes."

"Do you know what happened before Paul came to the hospital?"

"He got shot."

"Being shot has caused him to not remember things, so he might not recognize you."

"I know."

"That doesn't mean Paul doesn't love you."

"I know, Ethan already told me," she said sadly. Although you would think it impossible for the boy to be any closer, he leaned his head over and whispered something in her ear.

Mahoney watched them through the review mirror. "If Paul doesn't recognize you, are you going to get upset and cry?"

Instead of answering Jubilee turned and looked at Ethan Allen. He shook his head, then whispered in her ear a second time. She listened then said, "I'm not gonna cry. I'm gonna be patient and wait for him to get better."

After answering, she turned back to Ethan Allen. He nodded and smiled.

They arrived at the hospital at seven-ten and went directly to the intensive care unit. The night supervisor, Leslie Storey, was still on duty. She eyed the foursome and said, "Only two of you can be in the room at one time."

"No problem," Olivia answered. "We can wait outside." She nabbed Ethan Allen's arm and wrested him to her side.

"Hey, I was gonna—"

Before Ethan could finish his thought Olivia said, "I know what you were *gonna* do, but forget about it. You're staying here with me."

Mahoney took Jubilee by the hand and walked into room 412.

Paul was lying partway up. Even though his hair was gone and his head swaddled in bandages, Jubilee recognized him the moment she came through the door. She darted across the room, flung her arms around him, and began chattering about how much she'd missed him. "You should have come back," she scolded. "I was there a long time, and I got scared, and then this boy—"

Paul eventually turned his head so that he was face to face with her.

"Where's Mama?" he asked.

Jubilee stopped talking and loosened her vise-like grip on him. "Why you asking me about Mama? Mama got buried a long time ago."

"Mama's dead?"

"Cut it out, Paul, that ain't funny!"

Mahoney squatted down beside her. "Jubilee," he whispered, "I don't think Paul's trying to be funny. I think he's trying to remember, but he's only got bits and pieces and your mama's death might be a piece that's missing."

Jubilee turned and looked at Mahoney curiously. "Does he have the piece of who I am?"

"I don't know. Why don't you go ahead and ask him?"

"Ask Paul if he knows me?"

Mahoney nodded, then stood and moved back several feet.

Jubilee couldn't find the courage to ask that question right away, so she began with others, others that would lead up to what she really wanted to know.

"Do you remember Daddy got killed in the mine?"

Paul lowered his chin, said nothing, and shook his head.

Jubilee turned back to Mahoney. "He don't remember Mama and Daddy died."

Mahoney put his index finger to his mouth, shushed her, then with a nod and a slight movement of his right hand indicated she should continue.

When there was nothing more for Jubilee to hang on to, she finally asked, "Do you know who I am?"

Paul cringed as if he'd felt a sudden pain, then he looked at her and gave a very slight nod. "Jubie?"

"You remember!" she shouted and lunged at him again.

Paul's face still wore a look of confusion. "You're big?"

"I ain't no bigger than I was," she said. "It's just Miss Olivia bought me these fancy dresses, and they make me look growed."

Mahoney began to realize what was happening. Paul was remembering, but the present was gone. He remembered only the past.

"Paul, do you know what year this is?"

For a few moments it seemed as though he was thinking; then Paul shook his head.

"Do you remember taking the bus to Wyattsville?"

Thinking. Thinking. Finally another head shake.

Question followed question, and as he continued to nod or shake his head at things not remembered tears began sliding down Jubilee's cheeks. Paul noticed. He stretched his arm out and curled her into it.

Mahoney listened as Jubilee reminded Paul how they'd walked down off the mountain and taken the Greyhound bus to Wyattsville. She explained how he'd told her to wait on the bench while he went inside to do a job.

At that point Mahoney interrupted. "Jubilee, did Paul say he was going to do a job or get a job?"

Jubie stretched her mouth into a straight line then crooked it to the right. "I'm not real sure on that," she said, then turned to Paul and asked, "You remember which?"

He gave an apologetic shrug and shook his head.

Jubilee went on to remind Paul of the year their mama died and the awful time when the man from the mine came to tell them that Bartholomew had been killed in accident.

"Don't you remember any of this stuff?" she asked.

Her brother responded with a lowered chin and a sad shake of his head. Once in a while some event or name would cause a flicker of memory to light his eyes, but for the most part those years were a blank. There were no memories to look back on, no sign of who he had been or what he had done.

Shortly after nine, Hector Gomez walked into the room. "What the hell do you call this?" he asked angrily. Before he could say anything more Mahoney pulled him out the door, leaving Jubilee alone with her brother. When Olivia turned to see what Mahoney was doing, Ethan scooted past them and into the room.

"This is the boy," Jubilee said. "Ethan Allen. He's the one what found me."

Paul gave a half-smile and a nod. "Thanks," he said. It was a single word rich with the sound of sincerity.

Ethan returned the smile, then went on to say how Jubie was settling in real good and could stay as long as she'd a mind to. "Seeing as how she's none too anxious to go live with your Aunt Anita, maybe you ought to tell Detective Mahoney to not bother with looking anymore."

"Aunt Anita?" Paul repeated, and the look of puzzlement returned to his face.

Gomez sputtered and stammered as Mahoney filled him in on what he'd learned.

"You couldn't call me?" he argued. "It's my case, but you come up with something big and don't bother with even a phone call? One minute, that's what it would have taken. One minute!"

"As I said, I didn't know it would turn out to be anything."

"Yeah, I bet."

"It's true. My missing person case being tied to the Klaussner shooting is a fluke. I was checking out a lead on the girl's aunt and ended up here." Mahoney went on to explain that as it turned out the John Doe was Paul Jones, Jubilee's brother.

"They're two kids from West Virginia. Both parents are dead so they came to Wyattsville looking for an aunt, somebody they could possibly live with."

"That's what the kid told you?"

"No, he didn't tell me anything. He doesn't remember any of it."

"That is such a load of—"

"No, it isn't," Mahoney said. "The morning of the Klaussner shooting, those two kids were fresh off the bus. I doubt the boy had any intent of committing crime; he was just looking for their aunt."

"Believe what you want to believe, but back off and let me get this case to the DA."

"Why the DA?" Mahoney questioned. "Don't you think there's a good possibility the kid is innocent?"

A cannon firing next to Gomez's ear would have gotten less reaction.

"You've got to be kidding! First you screw me over on the Doyle case, now this? No way!"

"This isn't about you or me," Mahoney said. "It's about determining guilt or innocence."

"Don't give me that crap. This is about you wanting another hero button to pin on your chest. Well, this time you're not getting it! The kid had Klaussner's bullet in his head, and as far as I'm concerned that's proof enough!"

Gomez turned and stomped into Paul's room. He gave Jubilee and Ethan a menacing look and said, "Scram, visiting hours are over."

Jubilee lingered a minute, promised she'd be back, then followed Ethan out of the room.

Before they left the intensive care unit, Mahoney informed the nursing supervisor John Doe now had a name. It was Paul Jones.

When the foursome turned and left the ICU, no one notice the angry-faced woman watching from afar. With her husband still in a coma Carmella Klaussner had for the past week sat silently by Sid's side, praying perhaps, but also gathering up her anger and hatred toward the boy who had caused this to happen. When she heard the raised voices of Gomez and Mahoney, she stepped out of the room and listened. As she watched Mahoney's back disappearing down the corridor, her resentment came to a full boil.

"He won't get away with this," she muttered, then went in search of Detective Gomez.

Jack Mahoney

A cardinal rule in this business is never get emotionally involved, but dammit I am. How can I not be? I look at that little girl and think that, but for the grace of God, it could be one of my kids. I can't do anything about her parents dying, but I can sure as hell do something about helping her brother.

If I turn my head and look the other way, that kid is going to be railroaded. Gomez isn't interested in justice. He's interested in making a name for himself. Yeah, there's a chance the kid is guilty, but I'm just not convinced. I watched the boy reach out for his sister, and you can see the love there. If you love somebody you don't put them in harm's way.

Say Gomez is right, and the kid did plan to rob the store. Then he wouldn't have parked his sister right across the street. At the bus station maybe, but not across the street. And how did a kid from a coal mining town get hooked up with a street thug like McAdams? Too many missing pieces. I keep asking myself, why now and why here? None of it makes sense.

Gomez claims because Paul was shot with Klaussner's gun, he's guilty. With no eye witnesses, that could be enough to pin it on him. At least Gomez has something. All I've got is a gut feeling the boy is innocent. The shit-kicker is that with no memory, he can't even tell us what happened. And the same thing can happen with Klaussner. It's not uncommon for trauma victims to blot out the memory of something terrible. When Mack Wilson got hit by lightning, he was in a coma for nearly a month. When he finally came out of it, he remembered reading the newspaper that morning but couldn't remember stepping foot outside of the house. Trauma, that's why.

The whole thing stinks, but I'm not letting it go. Somewhere there's got to be something, some little piece of evidence that's been overlooked, something that will prove Paul Jones just happened to be in the wrong place at the wrong time.

I know it's not in my jurisdiction and I know I may catch hell for getting involved, but at least I'll be able to look myself in the eye tomorrow morning when I'm shaving.

The Sign

Although Olivia had not entered Paul's room, she'd stood on the other side of the plate glass window close enough to hear most everything. She'd also heard Mahoney's conversation with Gomez, and it was troubling to say the least. There was a growing list of "what ifs" bouncing around in her head. What if Paul goes to jail, what if he never remembers what happened, what if they can't find Anita, what if there's no other family, what if Jubilee has no one, what if... The list seemed endless. After they'd crossed Monroe Street, she turned to Mahoney and asked, "What happens now?" All of her "what ifs" boiled down to that single question.

Mahoney kept his eyes straight ahead and his expression unreadable. He gave an audible sigh and said, "I guess we keep looking for Anita, and I try to find something that will prove Paul didn't do it."

"Do what?" Jubilee asked.

Ethan Allen answered before anyone else had the chance. "Shoot Mister Klaussner.".

Jubilee yanked her hand loose from Ethan's and turned to him with an angry glare. "Paul didn't shoot nobody! That's killing, and the Bible says no killing."

"I ain't saying he did," Ethan countered. "I'm just telling you what that detective was saying."

"Well, I ain't interested in hearing it!" Jubilee folded her arms across her chest and scooted to the far edge of the seat looking mad as a bullfrog.

Mahoney glanced into the rearview mirror and saw her expression. It was genuine. There was no pretense, no sneakiness, no covering over. "Jubilee, has Paul ever been in trouble before? Has he maybe stole something, or –"

Mahoney didn't have a chance to finish what he was asking because Jubilee came back with a loud, "No, no, no, no, no! Stop asking me if Paul does bad stuff, 'cause he don't!"

"That's pretty much what I was thinking," Mahoney answered. After that the only sound heard inside the car was the din of traffic, and once they turned off of Monroe even that ceased.

Aware that Gomez was most likely still at the hospital, Mahoney drove to the Wyattsville stationhouse after he dropped off Olivia and the kids.

"I'd like to take another look at the Klaussner shooting file," Mahoney told Pete Morgan.

Morgan handed him a file folder that was only marginally thicker than it had been last time. "Anything new on this?"

"If there is Gomez is keeping it to himself. That's all I've got."

One by one Mahoney leafed through the pages. A background of Hurt McAdams, the statement from Martha Tillinger, the ballistics reports saying the bullet in Paul's head came from Klaussner's Browning, and another report saying the three bullets that tore through Sid Klaussner's chest and abdomen came from an unregistered 45 caliber handgun. The prints on the cash register were those of Hurt McAdams. Prints on the door handle came from the John Doe shot by Klaussner.

Mahoney set aside the reports and continued looking through the crime scene photos. There were several showing the area in back of the counter and outlining the spot where Klaussner had fallen after he was shot. There were also several showing the area in front of the counter and three outlining where Paul had fallen. The third picture had been taken from a further away spot, and it included areas not shown in the first two.

Mahoney studied the shot carefully. Everything was the same except that on the far edge of this picture, he suddenly saw what looked to be a piece of paper lying a few feet from where Paul had fallen. Probably nothing, but worth checking.

"Have you still got the keys to Klaussner's store?" he asked Monroe.

Monroe reached into the desk drawer and pulled out a ring of keys. "Be sure to get these back, or Gomez will have a shit-fit."

"Yeah, I know," Mahoney answered. He pocketed the keys, then turned and left.

By the time Mahoney reached the store it was early afternoon, and people were coming and going along the street. He parked his car directly in front of the bench Jubilee had supposedly been sitting on and climbed out. He pulled a Polaroid camera and a pair of white cotton gloves from the trunk, then crossed the street, stepped through the Caution tape, and unlocked the door.

With the windows still boarded over, there was only enough light to find his way across the room but not much more. Mahoney made his way to the light panel and flipped the switch. At first there was only an eerie blue flicker; then brightness flooded the room. Everything was as it had been the morning of the shooting. Chalk marks where the bodies had fallen, a cigarette display swept to the floor, several cans of green beans rolled to the far side of where they'd been stacked, and there, partway under the counter, the piece of paper. Mahoney took a Polaroid shot; then with a gloved hand he lifted one corner. It appeared to be a sign, but for what?

He eased the paper from beneath the counter and flipped it over. "Help Wanted" it read. "Stock Boy -- $30 week." Based on where he had found the sign, it seemed likely that Paul had been holding it in his hand when he was shot. Mahoney photographed the sign, then returned it to its original position.

After spending almost an hour in the store Mahoney switched off the light and left. As he relocked the door, footsteps came up behind him.

"Saw the light on and thought I'd check," the man said. "I'm Ernie, barber shop next door." He stuck out his hand.

After the handshake, Mahoney asked, "Were you here on the day of the robbery?"

"Yeah, I was," Ernie answered. "Awful, ain't it? You just never think in a town like Wyattsville..."

The only witness report in the file was that of Martha Tillinger, but Mahoney took a chance and asked, "Did you see or hear anything?"

"Sure did," Ernie answered. "Ken Spence was here for a shave that morning. Since he lost sight in his right eye he don't trust himself with a razor, so he comes in same time every Wednesday and Saturday. I was lathering him up when I saw the young one come from across the street and head into Sid's place. I was shaving Ken when the second one came by."

"They didn't go in together?"

"Not when they passed here, but after that who knows?" Ernie shrugged.

"How long was it from the time the first man went in and when you saw the second one go by?"

"A minute maybe."

"Did the two men come from the same direction?" Mahoney asked.

"Can't say. I know the boy came from across the street, but I didn't see the second one 'til he passed by here."

"What happened after that?"

"I heard the gunshots. Three or four of them, so close together I can't say for sure how many there were."

"Anything else?"

"A minute or so later the second guy hightailed it past here and disappeared."

Mahoney asked if he had seen the girl sitting on the bench across the street or noticed anything else unusual the morning of the robbery, but Ernie shook his head and said he couldn't tell much else because he wasn't facing that direction.

As Mahoney climbed back into the car and headed for the ferry, he again thought, *Too many questions.* Jubilee said her brother went into the store. Could it be that he wasn't there to "do" a job, but to get a job? To a seven-year-old kid the two things most likely sounded the same, so did she say one and mean the other? And which one was the truth? If Paul had by some chance partnered with Hurt McAdams, then why did they come into the store separately? Where was the gun that shot Klaussner? As the questions accumulated, it seemed as though each new thought muddied the water a bit more. It was like trying to put together a jigsaw puzzle with half the pieces missing.

Mahoney's earlier indigestion kicked into high gear, and halfway to the ferry he had to stop and buy another roll of Tums.

Once Mahoney was back at the Wyattsville station, he began a search for Freddie Meyers. He started with Property Records and then moved on to Voter Registration. Neither search produced any results. His next move was going to be a telephone directory search, which was none too reliable because people not looking to be found used fictitious names or had no listing. There were nine directories that covered the stretch of land considered the Eastern Shore. Two of the areas were across the state line in Maryland, and five were in Virginia. Mahoney went through the first three and found nothing. In the Watertown County directory, he found a listing for F.W. Meyers in Exeter.

It was on the same road as the Doyle farm had been.

"Impossible," Mahoney mumbled. "What are the odds of…"

He dialed the number and let it ring seventeen times before finally hanging up. It was just about dinnertime. Maybe Freddie Meyers, if this was Freddie Meyers, didn't bother to answer a ringing phone if his mouth was full of food. Mahoney sat for a moment and thought. He dialed a second number.

"Hello," a youthful voice said.

"Hi, Jack," Mahoney replied. "Is Mommy there?"

"Hi, Dad." A whisper of disappointment was threaded through young Jack's words. "Yeah, she's here. Mom made spaghetti tonight. Are you coming home soon?"

"In a while," Mahoney answered. "Let me talk to Mommy."

"Mom!" Jack screamed. "Daddy's on the phone!"

"I'll be there in a minute," she called back. "Ask if he's on his way home."

"Mom said are you on your way home?" Jack repeated.

"Not yet," Mahoney answered.

A disgruntled grunt was the only answer. Mahoney heard the sound of the receiver clunk against the table and waited. A few minutes later Christine's voice came on the line.

"What now?"

"I've got to take a run out to Exeter, so don't hold dinner."

There was a space of silence, the kind of silence that meant Christine was angry. "I spent the whole day making a pot of that homemade spaghetti sauce you like. With meatballs."

"I appreciate that, but this is something I've got to take care of."

"Can't it wait until tomorrow morning?"

"Afraid not," Mahoney answered. After several more apologies and a promise to take everyone for ice cream when he got home, he hung up. He scribbled the listing address on a note paper and started out to Exeter.

The town of Exeter was not really a town but a stretch of back roads that twisted and turned with not a single house visible from the next one. Mahoney took the same turn he'd taken when he'd gone out for the Doyle murders. He drove for nearly a half mile and did not see even one house until he came to the long drive leading past the field in front of the Doyle house. Standing at the end of the driveway was a mailbox with the number painted on the side: 1722.

"Damn," Mahoney said. Apparently F.W. Meyers lived in the house where Susanna and Benjamin Doyle were murdered. He turned down the drive and continued to the house.

The front window had been replaced, but other than that there was no visible change in the appearance of the place. It still had the look of a house in need of repair. The lights were on, and strains of Gogi Grant wailing "The Wayward Wind" came from inside. Someone was obviously living there. Mahoney stepped to the door and rang the bell. Nothing; no sound. It was still broken. He knocked on the door. No answer.

After knocking several times and getting no answer, he banged his fist against the door and shouted, "Hey, there, anybody home?"

The music clicked off, and moments later a small, paper-thin man opened the door. "Sorry," he said, "couldn't hear, what with the music."

"I figured," Mahoney answered.

F. W. Meyers was indeed Freddie Meyers, and, yes, he had moved here from Norfolk. Freddie explained how he'd bought the Doyle place at an auction. "Paid the past due taxes and the house was mine. 'Course, the place needs a bit of fixing up, and the farmland's nothing but a weed patch, but in time..."

Freddie Meyers was as pleasant a man as Mahoney could hope to meet, until he heard the mention of his ex-wife's name.

"I've got no more money," he snapped, "so if that's what this is about you're wasting your time."

"It's not about money," Mahoney assured him. "I'm just looking to find Anita."

"Why would anybody want to find Anita?" His words had the sound of an ex-husband filled with bad memories.

"I've got a little girl with no place go, and I think she's Anita's niece. Her parents were Bartholomew and Ruth Jones."

Freddie nodded his head sadly. "Yeah, Ruthie was Anita's sister, but they haven't talked for maybe six or seven years."

"Unfortunately, Ruth died several years ago."

Freddie winced. "Damn. She was the one who deserved to live. What about Bartholomew?"

"He's gone too."

"The mine got him, didn't it?" Not leaving room for an answer, Freddie continued. "That's one thing Anita was right about. She was always harping on Ruthie about that life being unfit for man or beast. Anita used to write Ruthie letters saying she ought to leave Bartholomew and come live with us. She thought if Ruthie left, Bartholomew would see the error of his ways and move back to Norfolk." He hesitated a moment, then added, "That was the better side of Anita."

"Then she ought to be pretty pleased to learn she's got a niece who'd like to come and live with her."

Freddie crumpled his face into a giant question mark. "It all depends."

"Depends on what?" Mahoney asked.

Freddie shrugged. "If I could've figured that out, we'd still be living together."

When Mahoney asked for Anita's address, Freddie wrote it on a piece of paper and handed it to him. "When you talk to Anita, you might mention that if she and the girl want to come out here to live I'd be willing to consider it."

"I'll do that," Mahoney answered and turned to leave. Before he got to the door, Freddie asked about Ruthie's boy. Mahoney had hoped to avoid that issue, but now he had no choice.

"He was involved in a shooting, and he's now in the hospital."

"Paul? Ruthie's boy? Involved in a shooting?"

Mahoney nodded.

"Damn," Freddie repeated. "I'd of never figured Ruthie's boy for such a thing." He stood there shaking his head sadly as Mahoney scooted out the door.

When Mahoney finally arrived home it was almost ten o'clock, the kids had gone to bed disappointed at not having another ice cream outing, Christine was barely speaking to him, and the plate of spaghetti sitting on the kitchen counter had turned a cold greyish pink. On top of all that he spent another sleepless night—tossing, turning, rolling the still-unanswered questions over and over in his mind. He worried about a dozen different things but didn't realize Carmella Klaussner was the one thing he should have been worrying about.

JUBILEE

I'm still feeling mad inside, even though Ethan Allen done said nobody means nothin' by those mean things. He claims they was just guessing at what the truth might be.

Paul never did nothin' bad to nobody, and I'll fight anybody what says he did! I know girls ain't supposed to fight, but I figure folks ain't supposed to tell lies neither. If they can tell lies, then there ain't nothin' wrong with me fighting.

I'm gonna go see Paul more times, and I'm gonna keep reminding him all the things what happened. Soon as he starts remembering stuff, I'm gonna remind him about how we're gonna get us a nice place to live and not bother about finding Mama's sister. If I thought Aunt Anita was nice like Ethan's grandma, I might feel a bit different but I can't say for sure I would.

I like Miss Olivia a lot. She's real nice to me. Yesterday when me and Ethan was asking for more cookies he called her Grandma, and 'cause I forgot she just belongs to Ethan and not me I called her Grandma too. She laughed real loud and said she wasn't actually Ethan's blood kin grandma, but they'd agreed it was a good name to call her and if it was good enough for Ethan to use, then I could go ahead and use it too.

I was real happy until she added, "For now."

I guess Paul's right. Good things don't always last forever.

Front Page

After Carmella Klaussner overheard the conversation between Mahoney and Gomez, she began to sizzle inside. For more than a week she'd sat beside Sid's bed, watched a machine force breath in and out of his almost-lifeless body, and counted heartbeats as the neon green monitor light zigzagged up and down.

Even when her arthritic hip was inflamed and painful, Carmella fell to her knees and prayed. "Please, God," she said, "spare my Sid." Every time there was an involuntary muscle twitch, she'd jump to her feet believing Sid was now going to open his eyes and speak. Each time she'd been wrong, and her dashed hopes brought more heartache.

Carmella had cried enough tears to fill an ocean, but she'd also cursed the evildoers who caused this turn of events. For the first three days Carmella's prayers asked only that Sid be healed. On the fourth day she added a second prayer asking for vengeance on those responsible.

"Curse them," she'd prayed. "Strike them down as you would Satan!"

Two doors down from Sid's room, Paul had opened his eyes. He had spoken and today he had family come to visit. "How can this be?" Carmella asked God. "How can it be that a sinner is healed, and a saintly man lingers on death's doorstep?"

Not long afterward, she'd overheard the heated conversation that took place outside the boy's room. The thought of someone even suggesting the boy might be innocent was like a razor slicing through Carmella's heart. "Are you not listening, God?" she raged. "Do you not care about justice?" After nearly an hour of arguing with her soul, Carmella

Klaussner decided that it was on her shoulders to see justice was done.

Gomez was still in Paul's room questioning the boy about things he had no memory of. "Where did you first meet Hurt McAdams?" he'd ask, but the look in Paul's eyes was nothing more than one of confusion.

When he heard a rap on the door, Gomez turned. It was Carmella Klaussner. "May I speak with you for a moment?"

Gomez gave Paul a menacing look and snarled, "Don't think this is over. I'll be back." He walked outside to where Carmella was waiting.

"Is it true?" Carmella asked. "Can that other man get this boy off scot free?"

Gomez gave a disgusted shrug. "Yeah, I guess it could happen."

"You know he's guilty! How can you let a man go free when he's guilty?"

"It's not me," Gomez said defensively. "It's Mahoney. He's the one."

"Why do you let him get away with it? Don't you care?"

"Of course I care," Gomez said. "I care, but sometimes caring ain't enough. You need proof positive."

"My Sid shot him!" Carmella's bottom lip quivered as she spoke. The anger she was holding back was almost too much to bear. "Sid's a God-fearing man. He would never shoot another human being if he didn't have good reason!"

"I know that, and you know that," Gomez replied, "but try telling the rest of the world."

At that point Gomez walked away and left Carmella stewing in her own rage. "That's exactly what I will do!" she grumbled. Already a plan was forming in her mind.

Carmella returned to Sid's room, and for almost three hours she sat beside his bed. Only now she wasn't listening to the whoosh of the machine pushing air into Sid's lungs, nor was she watching the green bleeps traveling across the monitor screen. Now Carmella was thinking of how to get the revenge she wanted. It was four-thirty when she picked up the phone and dialed Lucinda's number.

"I need a favor," Carmella said.

"For you, sweetie, anything," Lucinda answered.

Carmella explained that it wasn't just for her, it was for her dear, sweet Sid. She went on to remind Lucinda how Sid supported the school baseball team, hand-delivered groceries when anyone was sick, and gave generously to the church. Then she launched into the unfairness of the man who shot Sid getting off scot free. "Is that a fitting tribute for a man like Sid?" she sobbed.

"But," Lucinda stuttered, "what can I do about that?"

Carmella's sobbing stopped. "Not you. Mike."

"Mike?"

"Yes," Carmella answered. "If Mike were to run a story about how someone is trying to circle around justice, I think public opinion would turn against that detective and he'd have to do the job he's supposed to do. As the editor of the paper, he has an obligation to let folks know what's happening."

"You could be right."

"I absolutely am. Remember when Mike wrote about that butcher over on Elm weighing meat with his thumb on the scale?"

"Seven or eight years back, wasn't it?"

"Yes," Carmella answered. "But people remember. Now everyone insists on getting a pound–and-a-half of sausage for every pound they buy."

"That's true," Lucinda agreed.

By the time Carmella finished pouring out her version of a crooked cop getting a hoodlum off scot free, Lucinda was nearly in tears. She promised that Mike would do something to right this travesty of justice, or he'd be cooking his own dinner for a month.

On Friday morning the headline in the *Wyattsville Daily* read, "SHOOTER TO GO FREE?" Mike felt putting the accusation in the form of a question would serve the purpose, but an angry Lucinda disagreed. Numerous times he'd explained how making an unsubstantiated statement could be cause for libel, but his wife turned a deaf ear and suggested a week of sleeping on the sofa might change his mind.

When Mahoney arrived at the hospital that morning, he was greeted by squinty-eyed looks of suspicion. It was not until he saw the newspaper on the nurses' station countertop that he understood why. The bold headline was all but impossible to miss, and the story went on to describe how the suspect was shot by Sid Klaussner, the store owner. After detailing a myriad of good deeds attributable to Klaussner, the article reported that according to a reliable source the suspect in custody had not yet been charged with the shooting. Mike had added a closing paragraph.

"Certain sources indicate that despite the preponderancy of evidence, it is questionable as to whether the suspect will in fact be set free. We have to ask you, Detective Mahoney, is this justice?" Twice the article had mentioned his name, and it had also questioned why a detective from Northampton would be involved in a Wyattsville case.

Mahoney cringed. "Damn." He walked into Paul's room. The boy remembered nothing more than he'd said yesterday. Mahoney questioned him about whether he might have seen a "Help Wanted" sign and gone into the store to ask about a job.

"Is any of it even a little bit familiar?" he said.

Paul's expression was an absolute blank. None of the suggestions generated a smile, a frown, or even a blink.

After almost twenty minutes Mahoney knew nothing more than he did when he walked into the room, and given the article in today's paper there was sure to be a greater push than ever for prosecution. So far the evidence was all circumstantial. The truth was out there, but only three people saw what happened that morning in Klaussner's Grocery. Hurt McAdams was missing and Sid Klaussner was still in a coma, which left only Paul.

Paul knew what happened, but the image of it was hidden in the darkest corner of his mind, a place where ugly, mean, and hurtful things could be forgotten and left to die a death of anonymity. Normally that was a good thing; this time it wasn't. The road to redemption ran smack through that black hole, and Mahoney had to uncover whatever was there.

He thought back to yesterday. Seeing Jubilee had jogged the boy's memory; not all of it, but some. Questions went without answers, but Paul had responded to visual stimulation. Things he could see, touch, and feel brought back memories.

Mahoney left the hospital and headed for Olivia's apartment.

Before she had the door fully open, Mahoney started asking about the things Olivia had found in Jubilee's travel bag. He followed her into the living room, then said, "Mind if I take a look at them?"

Olivia pulled the tattered bag from the closet and set it atop the coffee table. "This is everything," she said. "There were a few pieces of underwear but no other clothes or…"

Mahoney ignored the words as he pulled the miner's hat from the bag, then the pictures, and a child's story book. These were all personal treasures, things that had little or no value to anyone but the boy who had carried them with him when he left home. For a few moments Mahoney stood there leafing through the worn pages of what was obviously a family Bible. Then he said, "If it's okay with you, I'd like to take Jubilee and this bag back to the hospital."

"I don't know," Olivia said. "Seeing her brother in such a state is awfully hard on Jubilee, and she was there just yesterday."

"I think Jubilee and the things in this bag might help us unlock Paul's memory," Mahoney answered. "Unless he can tell us what actually happened in that store…" The rest of the sentence trailed off, too unthinkable to consider.

When Olivia suggested they wait a bit for Ethan Allen to return from school, Mahoney said it would be better for him and Jubilee to go alone. "I'm trying to do this as quietly as possible." He made no mention of the newspaper article. When Olivia appeared reluctant, he added, "Let's ask Jubilee if she wants to go."

Since they both knew what the child's answer would be, Olivia went ahead and nodded her consent.

On the drive back to the hospital, Mahoney explained that he was hopeful the things Paul had packed in the bag would jog his memory of leaving home.

"Oh, they will," Jubilee said confidently.

Mahoney smiled and said nothing. He knew children Jubilee's age had a faith that was all too soon outgrown. They believed in princesses, fairy tales, and happily-ever-after endings. Even when there was no bread for the table, they believed Santa would show up simply because it was Christmas Eve. Times like this Mahoney wished he could slide back into such a faith instead of struggling with the reality of a situation.

When they arrived back at the hospital, a uniformed policeman stood at the door of Paul's room. For three days there had been no one. Now he was back.

"What's up?" Mahoney asked. "I thought they'd called off the guard dogs."

"Things change." The patrolman gave a chagrined shrug.

Paul was alert and sitting straight up. The large bandage that had swaddled his head was now gone, replaced by a smaller one held in place with strips of adhesive. He looked considerably better than he had earlier in the day, with one singular exception.

Paul was now handcuffed to the bed.

"What the..." Mahoney stormed out the door and headed for the nurses' station.

Jubilee stayed behind and stood beside her brother. At first she made no mention of the handcuffs and spoke only about how they were going to help Paul remember.

"Mister Mahoney got good intentions," she whispered. "You can say the truth and he don't get mad, even if you say stuff what ain't like he's thinking."

"Say the truth about what?" Paul looked at Jubilee quizzically.

She went through the same things she'd told him yesterday. Mama died. Daddy was killed in the mine. They were gonna find a new place to live. Only after she'd gone through all of those things did she mention the handcuffs.

"How come you got chained to the bed?" she asked.

"They said I shot somebody," Paul answered.

Jubie frowned. "You ain't never shot nobody."

Paul's eyes began to water. "They say I did. So maybe I did."

"That's a lie! A big, fat, dirty lie!" The screech of her voice was so loud it brought both Mahoney and the guard running into the room.

"What's wrong?" Mahoney asked.

"Paul's lying!" Jubilee's voice trembled as she spoke. "He's saying he maybe shot—"

Mahoney grabbed the girl's arm with a firm grip and gave her a look that quickly silenced her. "I don't think that's what Paul intended—"

"Maybe not," the guard dog said, "but sometimes the truth slips out."

When Jubilee went back to reminding Paul of all the things he should be remembering, Guard Dog slipped out of the room. Moments later Mahoney spied him talking on the telephone and turned to Paul.

"Son, I'm trying to see justice done, but justice isn't always quick to see the truth of things. I'd suggest you hold back on saying you maybe shot Sid Klaussner until we've got something more to go on."

Jubilee gave Mahoney a hard glare. "I told you—"

"I know, I know," Mahoney mimicked her words. "He didn't shoot nobody."

Jubilee gave a satisfied nod and turned back to her brother. "Remember when—"

Mahoney interrupted. "Let's try something else," he said and lifted the bag they'd brought onto the chair. He reached in, pulled out the Bible, and handed it to Paul. "Remember this?"

Paul held the book in his hands and leafed through the pages, studying the names. After the Bible, he was handed the photographs one by one. He smiled and touched his finger to the faces of those he loved. Mahoney knew when a look of anguish settled on his face he was remembering the passage of years and the death of his parents.

The last thing Mahoney took from the bag was the miner's hat with "Jones" printed across the back in black letters.

Paul took the hat in his hands and held it as though it were something precious. He brushed his thumb across the rough edge and said nothing. Moments later a tear dropped from his eye.

"You remember your daddy wearing this hat, don't you?"

Paul pulled his gaze away from the hat and gave a sad nod.

"Do you remember the last time you saw him wearing it?"

Paul took on the pained look of trying to remember, then the left side of his face crumpled into a grimace. "Yes."

"That was the day he died, wasn't it?"

Paul nodded. "I thought Daddy was just late coming home, but then Mister Brumann came and told us there'd been an accident..." Paul's voice trailed off, and a flow of tears began.

"I'm sorry, son," Mahoney said. "I know this is painful."

Jubilee looked up at Mahoney. "Then why you doing it?"

"Because, like you, I don't think Paul was involved in the robbery—"

"I ain't just thinking," Jubilee said. "I know for sure."

"Fair enough," Mahoney conceded. "We know for sure Paul wasn't involved. But the only way we can prove it is for him to tell us what actually happened that day, and in order to tell us he's got to remember."

"Oh. Okay." Jubilee stepped back and allowed Mahoney to continue.

Bit by bit the memories began to surface: the house, the school, the garden, teaching Jubilee to read and count numbers. All of those things came back, but after their days on the mountain, there was nothing. Paul had no recollection of the bus ride, Aunt Anita, or the reason why they'd come to Wyattsville.

"Try harder," Jubilee urged. "Remember the big bus? What about the place with turnaround stools? The lady gave me a free biscuit and told where to get sleeping rooms, you remember that?"

Although Paul was still shaking his head side to side, Mahoney's eyebrow shot up. "The biscuit place? Was that after you got off the bus here in Wyattsville?"

"Unh-huh." Jubilee nodded.

"If I took you back to the place, you think you'd remember it?"

She gave another sad-eyed nod. "Yeah, but it ain't me what's gotta remember."

Mahoney smiled. "That's true, but maybe what you remember can fill in some of the holes to help Paul remember."

A few minutes later they left the room. Mahoney stopped at the nurses' station, scribbled a telephone number, and handed the piece of paper to Barbara Walsh, the head nurse. "Don't forget," he said.

"I won't." She nodded.

Mahoney took Jubilee by the hand, and they left the hospital. The slightest trace of a smile was visible under his mask of determination.

The Bread Basket Café

Mahoney's original intention had been to go directly to the bus station and try to retrace Paul's steps, but Jubilee insisted on first stopping at the apartment.

"Grandma Olivia's a worrier," she explained, "and I ain't supposed to go nowhere 'less she says okay."

"You call her Grandma Olivia?"

"That's her name, even if you ain't blood kin."

"Who said?"

"Ethan Allen."

Mahoney laughed and shook his head. "Figures."

Once Mahoney told Olivia of his plan, she insisted on coming along to see to Jubilee's welfare.

"Don't worry," she said, "I'll sit quietly in the car, and you'll never even notice I'm there."

"I'm gonna have to go too," Ethan Allen said, "'cause I promised Jubie—"

"...that you'd stick by her," Mahoney said, finishing the thought.

Although he knew the likelihood of Olivia going unnoticed was improbable, Mahoney agreed because he'd seen the way Jubilee clung to Ethan Allen. If she was in doubt about one thing or another, she'd look his way and wait for a nod or a shake of his head.

"Okay," he said, looking over at Ethan Allen, "but we're going to let

Jubilee be the one to decide what she remembers and what she doesn't, right?"

Ethan Allen gave a sheepish nod.

Within a mile of the Greyhound Bus Station, there were five coffee shops. Two were on the north side of station, but Main Street was to the south. Mahoney pulled up in front of the station and turned to Jubilee. "You remember which way you and Paul walked?"

She hesitated a moment then pointed toward the front of the car, which was north.

Mahoney pulled out, circled the block, and parked on the back side of the station, facing the opposite direction. "Which way now?"

Jubilee craned her neck looked around and shrugged. "This ain't where we was."

Three times Mahoney circled the block and parked in different places, and all three times he got the same answer. While the back side of the station remained unfamiliar, Jubilee was consistent in pointing north from the front of the station.

Mahoney was feeling good when they pulled up to Millie's Luncheonette. "Does this look familiar?"

Jubilee scrunched her face and shook her head. "Unh-unh."

"Not even a little bit?"

She shook her head again.

"Let's go inside and take a look."

"This ain't the place, but we can look if you want."

As it turned out there were no stools at all, just square tables with straight-backed chairs. They moved on to the Happy Burger, but that fared no better.

"This ain't the place," Jubilee said. Her answer was absolute, no shred of doubt.

They got back in the car and headed south. Mahoney drove past the bus station and parked in front of the Bread Basket Café. "Does this look familiar?"

"Unh-huh." A smile spread across Jubilee's face.

When she jumped out of the car Ethan Allen was right beside her and before Olivia could tell him not to go, he was through the door.

"See, Ethan." Jubilee climbed on the first stool and started swiveling herself around. "It's like I said."

Mahoney followed them. He stood behind Jubilee and put a halt to her spinning. "Is this where you and Paul had breakfast?"

She nodded. "I got two biscuits."

"Is that the woman Paul spoke with?" Mahoney pointed to a short stocky woman standing at the register.

Jubilee shook her head. "That ain't her."

Mahoney asked if Jubilee could describe the woman who waited on them that day, but the best she could do was, "Real pretty." He looked around, and the only other person he saw was a skinny man stooped over and clearing dirty dishes from a back booth. Mahoney rose from the stool and walked over to the register to ask about other employees, but before he could do so Jubilee squealed, "That's her!"

She pointed toward the kitchen and the blonde who came through the door carrying three dinner plate specials. She gave a bright smile and waved to the waitress. "Hey, there," Jubilee called out. "Remember me?"

The blonde looked over. "Be with you in a minute, sweetie," she called back. Connie set the plates she'd been carrying in front of the three elderly gents at the far end of the counter and walked up to where Jubilee was sitting. "With all that hollering, you must be wanting another biscuit real bad." She laughed.

"I don't want no biscuit," Jubilee answered. "I'm just looking for you to say me and Paul was here." Before Connie had time to answer, Jubilee launched into the story of how a man said Paul shot somebody when he didn't shoot nobody.

Mahoney reached over and clamped his hand onto the girl's arm. "Hold on, Jubilee," he said. "Before you start telling your side of the story, let's hear what Connie has to say."

"Maybe it'd be good if Jubie gave her a bit of reminding first," Ethan Allen said. He was going to mention how folks can possibly forget something important, but the look Mahoney gave him put an end to his saying anything.

Mahoney started with the simplest question. "Do you remember Jubilee being in here on Wednesday, March sixth?"

"I remember her being in here, but the date? Hmm…" She turned and called out to the stocky woman at the register. "Hey, Martha, you remember when you had that dentist appointment?"

"Wednesday 'afore last."

Connie turned to Mahoney. "That's when this little sweetie was here. I know 'cause I was all alone that day and worked my butt off."

"Was she with anyone?"

"Yeah, a boy. Not this one." She gave a nod toward Ethan Allen. "A bigger kid, seventeen, maybe eighteen. Her brother, or maybe her daddy, I ain't too sure on that."

"You recall what the time was?"

"Seven, maybe a bit after. It was before the rush, I'm sure of that."

"How long were they here?"

"Half-hour or so. The boy was in the back a good part of the time."

Mahoney glanced toward the rear of the store—two phone booths and a shelf with three telephone directories hanging from it. "He make a phone call?"

Connie shook her head. "Don't think so. He was looking in the phone books. Trying to find an aunt, I believe. I doubt he found her, 'cause before they left he asked about a place to stay."

"You suggest any place special?"

"Missus Willoughby's," Connie said. "It's clean and cheap."

"Did the boy ask for cheap?"

"No, but I knew. You work here long enough and you can tell when a body's looking at the prices and figuring how much they can afford to eat." Connie gave a saddened sigh. "Kids like them manage to get along on next to nothing."

This discussion of money piqued Mahoney's interest. "Did the boy order anything?"

"Just coffee for him, but for the little one he got milk and a biscuit. I give her an extra biscuit on the house, but him nothing. Giving somebody who's down on their luck a handout just makes them feel poorer," Connie said. "I know 'cause I've been there."

Mahoney turned to Ethan Allen and Jubilee and asked if they'd like something. They both nodded yes. He ordered Pepsi and a bag of chips. She listened to his order, then said she'd have a Pepsi also along with another of those good-tasting biscuits.

While the kids ate, he continued asking questions. Did the boy meet anyone here? Did he talk to anyone? Did he seem nervous, edgy? The answers Connie gave substantiated Mahoney's suspicion that the boy had no plans beyond those of watching over his sister and finding a place to stay. Before they left Connie recounted most everything that had transpired, including her directions to the Willoughby house.

When they returned to the car, Olivia turned to Mahoney. "Well?"

He smiled. "It's all good," he answered and slid his key into the ignition. Once they'd turned onto Rosemont Street he explained. "Given the timeline the waitress indicated, I think Paul just happened to be in the wrong place at the wrong time. He didn't meet anyone at the restaurant, and he didn't have enough time to strike up a new acquaintance before the robbery took place."

"Is it enough to prove he's innocent?" Olivia asked.

"Probably not, but it's enough to generate serious doubt." Mahoney glanced in the rearview mirror at Jubilee; he could see she was listening. Addressing the comment to Olivia, he said, "Don't mention the S-H-O-O-T-I-N-G"

"I can spell," Jubilee said, "and I know those letters spell shouting!"

Ethan Allen looked up from the Superman comic he'd been reading. "I ain't shouting."

"Well, see it stays that way," Olivia said. Then she turned around and chuckled.

After Mahoney dropped Olivia and the kids at the apartment building he turned the car around and headed for Harrison, a town thirty-eight miles west of Wyattsville. It was almost five o'clock, and he was hoping to catch Anita Walker Meyers, or whatever name she was now using, on her way home from work. If she worked. Mahoney found himself wondering if he'd find a woman with red lipstick and high heels or an ex-housewife who flip-flopped her way to the door in a gingham duster.

After a week of searching, he was oddly intrigued by the thought of actually meeting the elusive Anita. She seemed to be a woman everyone remembered but no one knew. Hopefully she was a woman who loved kids, because she was about to get two of them.

Mahoney had thought of going there early this morning but waited because he was uncertain of what to say about Paul. Paint the wrong picture, and the boy would look like a low life or a criminal. In either case, it was a brand that would stay with him. Unfortunately human nature was such that when people whiffed the scent of scandal they closed their heart and snapped a padlock on it, lest they also be caught up in the horror.

Now that Connie had brushed away the last crumbs of suspicion, things could be seen in a more positive light. Now it was nothing more than an unfortunate accident. He could say Paul had been shot but was recovering nicely, making no mention of how the boy had been suspect in a robbery. It was much better that way. In a week, two at the most, he would be out of the hospital and he'd need a place to stay. After all he'd gone through, Paul certainly didn't need a cloud of ugly suspicions hanging over his head.

Without knowing when it started, Mahoney found himself whistling when he pulled into the parking space a few doors down from Anita's building.

The Alcove

Mahoney rang the doorbell labeled Walker and waited. Several minutes passed; then he rang it again. He'd been waiting almost ten minutes when a stooped woman hobbled into the vestibule.

"Most of them doorbells don't work," she said. "You gotta bang on the apartment door." She slid a key into the locked entrance door and nodded for Mahoney to follow.

"Who you looking for?" she asked.

"Anita Walker."

"Three-ten, two flights up. But she most likely ain't there."

"Oh? You know where she is?"

"Probably Ocean City," the woman answered. "Anita and that man she claims to be her husband go there most every weekend."

"Husband? A skinny man, short, narrow-faced?"

"Him, skinny? You got to be kidding. He's wide as a trailer truck."

"Oh?" Freddie Meyers had said nothing about Anita being remarried so Mahoney asked, "This fellow she's married to—"

The woman cut in with a cynical guffaw. "I never said they was married. He moved in one day, and she started calling him her hubby-dubby. Does that sound married to you?"

After fifteen minutes of talking with the woman who lived in the next-door apartment, Mahoney learned Anita would most likely not be back until Monday. Nonetheless he trudged up the two flights of stairs and pounded on the apartment door.

"I told you she wasn't there," the woman repeated, then disappeared into her own apartment. Mahoney pulled a card from his wallet and wrote a note on the back asking Anita to call when she returned home.

By then it was seven o'clock on Friday evening, and the probability was that Gomez was also gone for the day. Mahoney called Olivia and told her that it was unlikely anything more would happen until Monday. He didn't mention finding Anita. Before saying anything he wanted to make certain the woman he'd been tracking was actually Jubilee's aunt.

It was close to eight when Mahoney pulled his car onto the ferry destined for the Eastern Shore of Virginia. He planned to make a quick stop at the Northampton Stationhouse, then head home for the weekend. By now Christine was already more than a little bit peeved about the number of dinners he'd missed this week, but he'd make it up over the weekend. Hopefully.

Since Jim Turner had stepped back from dogging Olivia's every move, she relaxed her restrictions on Ethan Allen and Jubilee.

"You can use the elevator to come and go," she said, "but there is to be no running, shouting, or playing in the hallways. Is that understood?"

Ethan Allen, glad to have the curfew lifted, nodded agreeably. "If Jubie had a bike," he wheedled, "we could ride across to the park and not be bothering anybody."

"Well, she doesn't have one," Olivia replied and left it at that.

Shortly before noon on Saturday Seth Porter rang the doorbell, and when Olivia answered he was standing there with a green bicycle shined up and ready to go.

"Emily rode this when she was a teenager," he explained. "It might be a bit big for Jubilee, but I was thinking that maybe she could use it while she's here."

"Did Ethan Allen ask you to—"

Seth shook his head no before Olivia could finish, but the sheepish grin on his face told another story.

As soon as they'd gobbled down a quick lunch, Ethan Allen and Jubilee left for the park. Olivia stood at the window and watched as they pedaled away, Ethan in the lead and Jubilee following behind like the tail of a kite. He was fond of Jubilee; it was obvious in the things Ethan said and did. Without Olivia knowing when it happened, he had somehow stepped into the role of being Jubilee's big brother. This new position made him seem taller, more grown up, more responsible. He was wearing a look of pride that Olivia had never before seen on his face.

Aglow with the warmth of a new observation, she picked up the telephone and dialed Clara's number. "I need help," Olivia said and explained her plan. The second call was to Seth Porter; she also asked for his help and told him the same thing she'd told Clara.

Before Ethan Allen and Jubilee returned from the park, the alcove Olivia used for a sewing room had been converted into a tiny bedroom. Sara Perkins had donated the rollaway bed she used for sleepover guests, and while Olivia covered the walls with bubble gum pink paint Clara drove over to Greenblum's Home Store and returned with sheets, a pink comforter, and a tiny lamp. The small chest of drawers from Olivia's bedroom was now in the alcove, and the sewing machine it replaced was in the bedroom. The easy chair that once occupied the alcove was in Seth Porter's storage bin in the basement.

Although Seth had been agreeable enough about moving the chair, he reminded Olivia that the girl was only here on a *temporary* basis. "Don't go getting attached," he said, "else you'll be in for a load of heartbreak."

"I'm not," Olivia assured him, but in the back of her mind there was a troublesome tick warning that she already was.

When Mahoney arrived back at the Northampton Stationhouse, he expected the place to be near empty, a few duty officers on hand perhaps, but not Captain Rogers. He was wrong.

Rogers was sitting behind his desk and looking none too happy. He spotted Mahoney walking in and called out to him.

"I'd like a word," he said, but the truth was he wanted way more than a word.

"What's going on with this Wyattsville case?" Rogers asked, the agitation in his voice apparent.

"I've located Jubilee's aunt," Mahoney said, "but she's away for the weekend. I'm figuring to talk to her on Monday."

"I'm not talking about the girl." The captain moved to within inches of Mahoney's nose. "I'm talking about the kid involved in the Klaussner shooting!"

"I just happened to get lucky and—"

"Lucky? You didn't get lucky, what you did was piss off the entire Wyattsville department. I got three calls today, and they want you off the case."

A look of defeat swept across Mahoney's face. "Off the case?"

"Yeah, off the case. That means keep away from the Wyattsville stationhouse and have no further involvement with the kid."

"Before you make that call," Mahoney said, "I think there's something you ought to know." He lowered himself into the chair opposite the captain's desk and began the story. It started with how the Doyle case had unfolded and went on to tell how the then-Sargent Gomez was ticked off by losing the chance for a conviction. "He's got a grudge going, and the bottom line is that he's going to railroad this kid to prove a point."

Rogers shook his head doubtfully.

Mahoney explained how the sister's story had been confirmed by the waitress, and the timeline left no room for an unplanned meet-up with Hurt McAdams.

"Then why did Klaussner shoot the kid?" Rogers asked.

Mahoney grimaced; he had theory, nothing but theory. "I believe it was a stray bullet intended for McAdams."

Captain Rogers leaned back in his chair. "Damn. This puts me in a tough spot."

"It puts Paul Jones in an even tougher one," Mahoney replied.

After nearly an hour of back-and-forth discussion the captain agreed Mahoney could continue to investigate, but he had to stay clear of the Wyattsville stationhouse.

"And," he added, "I don't want you anywhere near Detective Gomez."

It was nine-thirty when Mahoney left the Northampton stationhouse, and by then he'd decided to take the weekend off. He'd spend some time mending bridges at home and let the Wyattsville boys cool down a bit before he went back. With Anita gone until Monday, nothing much would happen until then anyway.

OLIVIA

There's a lot of merit in what Seth Porter says. I am opening the door for heartache to come crawling through, but now it's too late to do anything about it.

Looking back, I can see the truth; I made a place in my heart for Jubilee the night I saw her tiny little shoe with a piece of cardboard covering up the hole. She had the look of a stray kitten that comes mewing at your door asking for nothing more than a bit of kindness and some warm milk. If you can turn your back on a child like that, you've lost your worth as a human being.

The good Lord is probably laughing up his sleeve by now, and He sure enough has cause for doing it. After all those years I spent running away from marriage just because I couldn't bear the thought of children hanging to my coat-tail, now here I am wanting a second one who's not even mine to want.

It's not just me; Ethan Allen's also taken Jubilee to his heart. I know he's wishing she could become a part of our family. He doesn't come right out and say it 'cause that's not his way, but I see the things he does, the way he watches out for her. Yesterday they came in from playing, hungry as bears and wanting a snack. Of course they both wanted chips. I looked in the cupboard, and there was just one packet left. Given the way Ethan loves his chips, I figured he'd be first to grab for it but he didn't. He gave it to Jubilee and took a bag of pretzels for himself.

Mister Mahoney has yet to find that Anita, and in my mind it's just as well. Any aunt who doesn't know her niece is wandering around with no place to go doesn't deserve to have the child. Maybe Anita feels the way I used to, and if that's the case I'm going to say right up front that Jubilee's welcome to stay here and live with us.

Once I do that, the probability is I'll have to find someplace else to live.

Jim Turner's calmed down for now, but me bringing another child into the building is not something the Rules Committee is likely to overlook.

When Monday Comes

As far as Detective Mahoney was concerned, the weekend passed uneventfully. On Saturday afternoon he took the kids fishing; then in the evening, he and Christine had dinner at Mario's. Over a bottle of red wine, he promised to be more conscientious about getting home in time for dinner.

"I should hope so," she answered. Before she got to the part where she'd list all the dinners he'd missed, Jack switched to saying how the blue of her dress made her eyes twinkle. Christine smiled, and the evening moved on with no further discussion of missed dinners.

Sunday was sunny and warm so Mahoney finished painting the porch he'd started over a week ago, then settled into an easy chair with a book he'd been wanting to read. Before he finished the first chapter he began thinking of a way to help Paul Jones.

On Monday morning he crafted a "Help Wanted" sign exactly like the one he'd seen at Klaussner's store; then he drove back to the Bread Basket Café and took Polaroid pictures of both the inside and outside. He even took one shot of Connie holding a plate with a biscuit on it. Although Paul had trouble answering questions, he responded well to visual images. Mahoney hoped these things would bring back the memory of that ill-fated Wednesday.

It was almost noon when Mahoney headed over to the hospital, totally unprepared for what he found.

The bed Paul had been shackled to was empty. The officer at the door, gone.

A sick feeling settled in Mahoney's chest, and his heart started beating faster. On Friday he'd given Barbara Walsh a card with his home telephone number; she was supposed to call if anything happened. He looked around. No Barbara.

Mahoney stopped the first nurse passing by and asked, "Where's Paul Jones, the kid who was in this room?"

"I dunno." She shrugged. "I been off for a week."

After fifteen minutes of searching for Barbara Walsh, Mahoney learned she'd come down with the flu on Saturday and was expected to be out for the remainder of the week.

"One-hundred-and-two fever," Maureen explained.

"Damn," Mahoney said.

"Is there a problem?"

Mahoney explained he was looking for Paul Jones, the boy who'd been in room 412. "Has he been transferred to another ward?"

"No, he was discharged yesterday."

"Discharged? How could you let him—"

"I didn't do anything. Doctor Brewster decided the kid was well enough to leave and released him."

Mahoney began growing hot under the collar. "Who picked him up? Signed him out? Did you just let the kid walk out of here with no place to go?"

"Don't use that tone with me!" Maureen snapped back. "Detective Gomez signed the kid out. They took him out of here in handcuffs, so he's probably on his way to jail."

"Barbara was supposed to call me if anything happened—"

"Barbara wasn't here!" Maureen turned and walked off in a huff.

Although Captain Rogers had expressly instructed him to stay away from the Wyattsville stationhouse, Mahoney got back in his car and sped across town. He bypassed the front desk and went looking for Hector Gomez. He found him in the coffee room.

"We've got to talk!" Mahoney said.

"There's nothing to talk about," Gomez replied with a smug smile.

Mahoney pulled out a chair and sat opposite him. "Yes, there is."

Weighing his words carefully, he continued. "Paul's profile, his movements on the day he arrived in Wyattsville, the fact that he had his sister with him, everything points to him being nothing more than a kid in the wrong place at the wrong time."

"The store owner shot him," Gomez argued. "Sid Klaussner wouldn't shoot someone for simply being there."

"It could've been a stray shot."

"Not likely." Gomez took a bite of his sandwich and began chewing.

"Hear me out," Mahoney said. He went on to detail the things he'd found. "I believe the kid came in there looking for a job. When I went out to the store, there was a Help Wanted sign on the floor over by the counter. I think Paul was holding that sign when he was shot. Check it out. My bet is you'll find his prints on the sign. That alone is enough to raise a question of doubt." He ended by showing Gomez the duplicate sign he'd made and the Polaroids. "The boy responds better to visuals. Give it a try; maybe you'll get his side of the story."

Gomez took another bite and chewed, slowly and deliberately.

Mahoney sat and waited.

After he'd finished what was left of the sandwich, Gomez said, "You must think I'm some kind of fool. This isn't about the kid; it's about you wanting to play hero."

Without the backing of Captain Rogers, Mahoney knew there was only one way to right the wrong and he took it.

"Nope," he said. "You're wrong. I've been pulled off the case." He handed the sign and pictures to Gomez. "This time you're gonna have to be the hero and find out the truth. From here on in, it's your ballgame."

As he watched Mahoney disappear down the hall, Gomez mumbled, "What the hell was that about?" On the way back to his desk, he dropped the pictures and sign into the trash can.

Mahoney left the Wyattsville stationhouse with discouragement weighing heavy on his heart. This was a part of the job he hated; all too often it made him wonder if he shouldn't have listened to his father and become an engineer. Engineers had dinner with their family every night. They seldom worked weekends and never carried a burden of guilt for something they could do nothing about. He heaved a regretful sigh, shifted the car into gear, and pulled away from the curb.

Moments after the Wyattsville stationhouse disappeared from sight, he began thinking about what he could do. The most obvious answer was to find a home for Jubilee, because if Gomez didn't change his viewpoint Paul was not going to be around to look after her. Mahoney knew such a change was none too likely. Men like Hector Gomez were born with a shell around their heart, a shell solid as cement and with about the same amount of flexibility.

He pulled the roll of antacids from his pocket, popped two in his mouth, and headed toward Anita Walker's apartment. Hopefully she was home.

Mahoney rang the bell for the third time before an answer came through the intercom.

"Go away, I'm trying to sleep."

"Is this Anita Walker?" Mahoney asked.

"Yeah."

"Detective Mahoney from the Northampton precinct," he replied. "I'd like a word with you."

"If Freddie sent you, I ain't interested!"

"This isn't about Freddie, it's about your niece."

"Lord God, what now?"

"If you'll buzz me in, I'll come up and explain."

"I doubt there's anything about those hillbillies I want to hear."

Mahoney, who by then was weary of this day, said, "Either you let me in, or I'll come back with a warrant."

"All right, all right," Anita answered. Moments later a shrill buzz sounded.

When he rapped on the door of apartment 310, a frowsy-looking redhead answered. "What?" she said impatiently.

"Can we go inside?"

"I'd rather we didn't; the place is a mess right now."

"That's okay," Mahoney answered and eased past her into the apartment.

Once he was inside she asked, "You want coffee?"

"No, thanks."

"Well, I gotta have some. I'm no good 'till I've had at least two cups." She poured a cup for herself, then sat at the kitchen table facing Mahoney. "Now what's this urgent bit of news you've got?"

"It's about your sister, Ruth. Were you aware she'd passed away?"

"Yeah. It was five years ago."

"So you knew she had two children?

Anita nodded. "Unfortunately."

Ignoring the comment, Mahoney moved on. "Apparently their father had been caring for the children, but about three weeks ago he also passed on. Paul, the older of the two, has been caring for his sister until recently. However, he's no longer able to…"

Up until this point Anita had been fairly disinterested, but suddenly the muscles in her face turned hard as stone.

"…which leaves your niece with no one to care for her."

"What do you mean he's no longer able take care of her?"

"The boy is only sixteen," Mahoney said, avoiding any mention of the fact that he was also locked up in the Wyattsville City Jail.

Anita immediately launched into a story of how it would be impossible for her to take in two kids because her apartment was way too small. "It's just two bedrooms, and that second one's the size of a closet."

"It's just the girl," Mahoney said. "Paul's got a place to stay for now."

Anita didn't waver from her original position. "Even one child is way too much for me to handle. Surely there's someone else—"

"No one who's family. As far as we can tell, Bartholomew has no living relatives."

"What about friends? Neighbors?"

"Even if one of those people was willing to take Jubilee, they couldn't. Unless it's a family member, an orphaned child has to be turned over to the children's welfare department."

"Jubilee, huh? Cute name."

"You didn't know your niece's name?" Mahoney said.

She shook her head, "Unh-unh. Ruth and I had quit speaking by that time." A look of regret settled on Anita's face. "When somebody ain't willing to take care of themselves, you can't tear your heart out worrying. The only thing you can do is close that door and pretend they already died."

Mahoney sensed a level of sadness that might have been soft and pliable at one time, but through the years had turned rock hard. "It may be too late to mend fences with your sister," he said, "but it's not too late to do the right thing by her daughter."

"You can't ever go back; only a fool tries to do it."

"You wouldn't be going back, you'd be starting over."

"I don't think—"

"Jubilee's a sweet child; I think you'd love her."

Anita shook her head sadly. She had a faraway look in her eyes, one that Mahoney found impossible to read. They spoke for more than an hour, but she didn't budge an inch.

"If I wanted kids, I would have had them years ago," she said. "It's too late to start now."

Before he left, Mahoney suggested Anita sleep on the idea.

"With something this important, you don't want to make a decision you'll regret forever," he said.

She rose from the table and dumped the remainder of her coffee down the drain. "I'll think about it, but I seriously doubt I'll change my mind."

As Mahoney left the building he reached into his pocket and pulled out the last of his antacid chews. He also doubted Anita would change her mind.

Ethan's Gift

When Mahoney left Anita's apartment he couldn't stop wondering what angry words had torn the two sisters apart. Anita's bitterness was so thick you could almost see it seeping from her skin. Surely, he thought, there was some way to reach inside and find the heart that had long ago stopped caring. Maybe if Anita met Jubilee—saw the child, heard the lilt of her laugh, and felt the touch of a tiny hand in hers. Even as he considered the possibilities, a nagging voice in the back of his mind kept asking, *Is that what's best for Jubilee?*

Mahoney knew he was far too involved in this case. It was no longer a situation where he was trying to locate a missing aunt. He had segued into trying to piece together broken lives. He needed to stop, take a breath, and think things through.

He'd planned to visit Olivia and tell her of his conversation with Anita, but once he did that—once it was an established fact that Jubilee's aunt was unwilling to lay claim to her—Jubilee would be put into the system. It was what it was. Through no fault of those who ran it, the child welfare system was without a heart. When a child was freefalling through life the system was the safety net, a paper-thin layer of protection that prevented them from splatting against a concrete bottom. It provided a home, food to eat, and a place to sleep. Period. Once in a while a kid got lucky and ended up with a family who cared. But that wasn't an everyday occurrence; it happened once in a while. A very long while.

Mahoney didn't need to close his eyes to see Jubilee's face. It was right there. For a fleeting moment she was visible in the rearview mirror. He thought back to the image of a bewildered Paul stretching his arm to curl his sister inside. She was not an unwanted child; she was loved.

In that instant Mahoney knew he was not ready to give up. Right now the situation seemed impossible, but he would find a way. He had to. At the end of the block, he made a U-turn and headed for the ferry.

Tomorrow he might have to be the bearer of such bad news, but tonight he would simply be a father. He would spend time with his own children and hold them to his heart with a prayer of thanksgiving.

Almost a full two hours before he normally arrived home, Jack Mahoney walked through the front door of his house and called out, "Honey, I'm home."

There was no answer.

"Christine?"

Still no answer.

He walked through the house, a house that was usually filled with noise and laughter—so much noise, in fact, that he often wished for just such a silence. But today, on a day when he was hungry to hear the laughter, to be smack in the middle of all the noise, there was nothing.

He snapped on the television and dropped down on the sofa. Images moved across the screen and spoke words, but what those words were he couldn't say. Jack Mahoney's thoughts were elsewhere. He looked at the clock. Five-forty. He would have thought Christine would be starting dinner by now. Peeling vegetables, setting the table, fussing about the kitchen, doing whatever it was she did to make the nightly dinner seem such a momentous event.

He stood, walked into the backyard, and looked around. There were no kids anywhere. Not next door, not two houses over. Even the troublesome twins who lived cattycorner were missing.

Mahoney shook his head. *How sad,* he thought. *All these nice yards and no kids playing in them.* He returned to his spot in front of the flickering television, then sat and watched the minutes tick by.

It was five minutes before seven when Christine and the kids burst through the door in an explosion of laughter. She looked over at Jack. "What's wrong?"

"Nothing's wrong."

"But you never come home this early."

"I've been home for over an hour-and -a -half."

"Oh, my gosh," Christine said. "Why didn't you tell me you were going to—"

"I hadn't planned on it," he answered and left it at that. There was no reason to start explaining something that was almost unexplainable anyway.

Jack followed Christine into the kitchen and listened as she and all three kids spoke at the same time. "It was so much fun," Jack Junior said. "I got to ride on the Ferris wheel."

"I wasn't tall enough," Chrissie pouted. "I had to go on baby rides."

"Oh, I wish you had been with us," Christine said. "The whole neighborhood was there, even the twins."

Only after several minutes of listening to the fun they'd had at the Saint Vincent's festival did Jack remember Christine mentioning it weeks earlier. At the time it was something he was too busy to care about, but today he found himself wishing he'd been there.

After dinner Jack dried the dishes, played checkers with his son, and once again told the story of Sleepy Hollow to all three children. He would have thought the girls might ask for something sweeter—Cinderella or perhaps Sleeping Beauty, but no. On the all-too-infrequent occasions when he was home to tell a story, they repeatedly asked to hear about the headless horseman.

That evening after the children were tucked in their beds, he and Christine sat in the backyard and talked.

"When did we get so busy that we stopped doing this?" he asked.

"We didn't," Christine answered. "You did."

It was a full minute before Jack answered. "That will change," he said, and he meant it.

That night while his family slept, Mahoney tossed and turned. By the time sunrise crawled across the horizon, he had decided that first he would tell Olivia of the conversation he'd had with Anita and then he'd speak with Anita again. There had to be a chink in her armor. Everybody had one. It was up to him to find it.

When Olivia answered the door, she was tearful and red-eyed. "Shhh," she warned Mahoney. "Jubilee doesn't know yet, so don't mention a word."

Mahoney, a bit taken aback, cautiously asked, "Don't mention what?"

"About Paul."

Although he wondered how Olivia could have known about Paul, Mahoney followed behind as she tugged him through the living room, past where the kids were playing, and into her bedroom. Once inside Olivia closed the door, then pulled a newspaper from beneath the mattress.

"How could you let this happen?" she said and handed him the newspaper.

The headline read, "SHOOTING SUSPECT CHARGED!" Below the boldfaced headline was Paul's mug shot. He had the expression of a deer standing nose to nose with a hunter's rifle. The small bandage was still taped to the right side of his head.

"I had nothing to do with this," Mahoney sputtered. "It came as a surprise to me also." He explained how he'd learned of it yesterday when he visited the hospital. "I've since gone to see Gomez and given him everything I had. Hopefully he'll do something with it."

"Doesn't he have to—"

"Sometimes there's a grey area between evidence and opinion."

"But those things you found out, aren't they evidence?"

"All circumstantial. They point to the fact that Paul might have been an innocent bystander, but they *prove* nothing."

He looked for a more positive note on which to end the conversation, but there was none. When the words stopped and there was little but silence, the sound of Jubilee's laughter pierced the air. It was followed by Ethan Allen's voice, "Aw, nuts," he complained. "You got another straight."

Mahoney's eyebrows went up. "Are they playing—"

Olivia finished the thought. "Poker."

"Poker?"

"I know." She gave a shrug of resignation. "I used to think it was something kids shouldn't be doing, but then I listened with my heart." She explained how Ethan Allen could win a poker game even if he was blindfolded. "He's letting her win. It's his way of making her happy."

They stood and talked for several minutes, about nothing and everything. Mahoney searched for a way to say what he'd come to say, to tell her about his conversation with Anita. As it turned out, he didn't have to broach the subject. Olivia did it for him.

"Anything new on Anita?" she asked. Her words were casual, a throwaway question that hopefully would not be answered.

"Actually, yes," Mahoney said. "I met with her yesterday."

His answer caused Olivia's heart to skip several beats, and she immediately regretted asking the question. Ten days ago she would have welcomed such news, but not now.

"It's not good news." Mahoney spoke like a man apologetic for what he had to say. "There was apparently bad blood between Anita and her sister, so she wants nothing to do with either of the kids."

Olivia's lips curled. "Well, then, Jubilee is welcome to stay here."

"Here?" The shock in Mahoney's voice was apparent.

She nodded. "It's the most sensible solution. You see how well the children get along, and I've already fixed up a little nook where she can—"

"Olivia, stop right there. I can't leave Jubilee with you. If she's not with family, she has to be turned over to the child welfare department. It's the law."

"Nonsense," Olivia argued. "This is exactly the same situation we had with Ethan Allen, and there was no law that said I couldn't keep him."

"It isn't the same. Ethan Allen was related to you."

"Not really," Olivia said. "I'd never even heard of the boy before he showed up here. I was almost a total stranger."

"His grandfather was your husband, so there was a legal relationship."

"Well, that just doesn't make sense. If Anita doesn't want the child and I'm willing to take her..."

Although Mahoney could easily sympathize with the situation as it now stood, he had a responsibility to abide by what the law mandated. There might be a certain amount of give and take, but it only stretched so far. Move beyond that point, and something would snap.

They spent close to twenty minutes going back and forth, arguing the fine points of what could or could not be considered a legal relationship. In the end, Olivia had to accept that she had no ground to stand on.

"I've given Anita a few days to rethink what she wants to do," Mahoney said. "Until then Jubilee can stay here."

A few days seemed like such a small amount of time. They'd already had thirteen days together, and now there were just a few more. *How sad,* Olivia thought. She counted the hours Ethan Allen would have to spend with Jubilee—how many more poker games he'd let her win, how many peanut butter sandwiches... Then she caught something that shed a new light on the situation.

"I thought my bringing Jubilee with me might change Anita's way of thinking," Mahoney said. "The girl is her sister's child, so she's got to feel something."

Olivia's face brightened. She knew she'd found the opportunity she'd been looking for. "That's a wonderful idea," she replied.

The Awakening

On Wednesday morning Carmella Klaussner did exactly as she had been doing for the past two weeks. She climbed out of bed, went down on her knees, and prayed. "Please, God, save my Sidney. Make today the day he opens his eyes."

Those were the same words she repeated every morning, but each day she added something, an extra pledge or promise that might entice God to answer her prayer.

"Return my Sidney to me," she said, "and from this day forth I'll care for the orphans and provide shelter for the homeless."

Carmella offered those pledges with an open heart and paid no heed to the fact that Wyattsville had no orphans, no homeless, and no soup kitchen in need of food. The Saint Peter's Thrift Shop was the only thing Wyattsville had to offer when it came to charitable organizations.

It was on the sixth day that Carmella had begun adding an extra request to each and every prayer. It was the same every time. Once she'd pleaded for Sidney's life and vowed to do good deeds she added, "And, Father, in the name of all that's righteous and merciful, punish those who did this to my Sidney." On several occasions she detailed the punishment she deemed most appropriate. At times when she was feeling benevolent, the punishment was simply living with the guilt of their sins, but when she was angriest it was death.

Three days earlier Carmella watched the detectives take the boy from the hospital in handcuffs and felt God was at long last answering her prayers. But that was three days ago, and since then nothing else had changed. The respirator still whooshed air in and out of Sidney's lungs, the monitors continued to count his heartbeats. Yet Sidney's eyes remained closed.

On Monday when the *Wyattsville Daily* announced Paul's arrest, Carmella bought two copies of the newspaper. She kept one copy at home to serve as a reminder of answered prayers. The second copy she took to the hospital so when Sidney awoke she could prove to him justice had been served.

But two weeks of hoping and praying had taken its toll on Carmella, and she felt weary as a woman who'd given birth to quintuplets. When the alarm buzzed at six-thirty Wednesday morning, she simply could not pull herself from the bed. Carmella silenced the alarm and buried the clock in the bottom drawer of the nightstand.

When Sidney Klaussner's eyes fluttered open, he was alone in the room. Groggy and dazed, he tried to remember when he had fallen asleep. Then he heard the machines and felt the weight of tape against his forearm. Slowly he began to realize this was not home. He was not lying in his own comfortable bed. He was lying on something that moved. He could feel the pressure of swells rising and falling beneath him. He tried to call out, and only an indistinguishable grunt came from his lips. Fear grabbed Sidney by the throat, and when he lifted his hand to his face he felt the tube. That's when his heart began pounding against his chest, hammering to be free of whatever prison this was.

Barbara Walsh was on duty Wednesday morning, and when Sidney's heart monitor beeped its warning she went flying into his room.

"Good Lord, you're awake!"

Within minutes Sidney's room was crowded with nurses and doctors.

In the frenzy of explaining to Sidney that he'd been shot and was now in the hospital, no one thought to telephone Carmella.

Twenty minutes after he opened his eyes, Carmella pushed the entrance button for the ICU ward and spotted a number of nurses coming and going from Sidney's room.

"Oh, my God!" she screamed and took off running. Circling around an orderly she'd never before met, Carmella pushed her way into the room. Before she could squeeze past the crowd of nurses hovering over the bed, she realized the respirator was no longer whooshing.

"Sidneeeeeey!" she screamed and fell to the floor in a dead faint.

When she came to, Carmella was sitting in the chair on the far side of Sidney's room and Barbara Walsh was holding a cool cloth to her head.

"You fainted," Barbara explained. "Nothing's wrong. It was simply the stress of all you've been through and the shock of..." Her words droned on, but Carmella heard nothing else. She was looking at Sidney and trying to believe that what she was seeing was not another dream but the actual answer to all her prayers.

Sidney was sitting up and the tracheostomy tube that had been taped to his face was gone. He was neither smiling nor frowning but had a look of confusion stretched the full width of his face. Carmella waved Barbara off, then rose and wobbled across the room to stand beside the bed.

"Oh, Sidney," she said, "you have no idea how worried I've been."

"Worried?" he repeated quizzically.

She nodded. "I thought you might never wake up. I thought—"

Still not fully comprehending the situation, Sidney said, "I was asleep."

Carmella leaned over and allowed the full weight of her bosom to settle on his chest. For several minutes she remained in that position, her body blending with his, her finger tracing the edge of his face, her lips whispering how terrified she'd been at the thought of losing him. When a spasm grabbed hold of her lower back, she stood and lifted his hand into hers.

One by one she kissed his fingertips; then she held his hand to her chest and placed it in a spot where he could feel her heartbeat. "I love you, Sidney," she said. "Love you more than life itself. If you were to die, I'd surely follow you to the grave."

Sidney wrinkled his brow and asked, "How long was I asleep?"

"Asleep? You weren't asleep, you were in a coma."

"Coma?"

"Yes. After they removed the bullets—"

"What bullets?"

"You were shot. Don't you remember?"

Her question went without an answer, and with each new revelation Sidney appeared more and more confused.

Carmella began at the beginning. She talked of how it had been a perfectly normal Wednesday morning; they'd had breakfast together and he'd gone off to open the store.

"An hour later," she said, "I got a call saying you'd been shot." She told him of the horror she'd felt as the ambulance sped crosstown toward the hospital. "I didn't know if you'd live or die."

Sidney gave a slight smile. "I'm too ornery to die," he said. "Seems you'd know that."

As she continued to tell the story, bits and pieces became familiar to Sidney. Not the whole picture, just tiny snippets. He remembered Martha Tillinger walking into the store and asking where the cake mixes were but little beyond that.

Before Carmella got to the part about Sidney shooting one of the would-be robbers, Barbara Walsh, who'd been in and out of the room numerous times, pulled her aside and suggested she switch to another subject. "When a person's been through such a trauma, it's not a good thing to keep reminding them of it."

Carmella, who wanted nothing more than her husband's return to health, did as suggested. She began talking about how she couldn't wait for Sidney to come home.

"We'll take a vacation," she said. "Maybe drive through the Blue Ridge Mountains, or maybe spend a few weeks in Ocean City. Agnes Shapiro went there and she said it's wonderful. Lots to do..."

As the minutes of the day ticked by, Carmella rambled on. She spoke of vacations, planting spring flowers, Crystal Otto's new baby, and dozens of other things. From time to time Sidney smiled, but most of the time he just listened, his face expressionless. When he dozed off, Carmella kept watch over him. She waited for each rise and fall of his chest, to make certain his breath was steady and even. Long after the final visitor's bell had chimed, Carmella was still sitting beside Sidney.

The Final Shot

Tom Wilson was the newest detective on the Pittsburgh police force. He was full of energy and enthusiasm, and after spending five years as a beat cop he knew what life on the street was like. He didn't just know what it was like; he was determined to make it better. While Charlie, his partner and a twenty-year veteran on the squad, was ready to write off Butch Wheeler's murder as something that was justified anyway, Tom was not. He spent two weeks gathering evidence, pulling together the ballistic reports, and talking to everyone who'd ever known Butch. When the finger of guilt pointed to Hurt McAdams, Tom began interviewing everyone who had ever known Hurt, including the elderly Kubick who lived next door to the house where Hurt grew up.

"Sure I seen him," Kubick said. "He came looking for his daddy."

"How long ago?" Tom asked.

"A week, two maybe."

Kubick explained that George McAdams had moved off to some place in Florida, but by now he had no notion of where that someplace might be.

"You tell that to Hurt?" Tom asked.

Kubick nodded.

Tom's next visit was to the Camp Hill Correctional Institute. After that Tom knew his hunch was right. There was no longer any question about it. Hurt McAdams was the one who put a bullet in Butch Wheeler's head.

That evening an All-Points Bulletin went out. It said Hurt McAdams was armed and dangerous. The bulletin said McAdams was most likely seeking shelter in Florida with his father. The whereabouts of the father were unknown.

When the bulletin arrived in Miami Beach, it sat buried beneath a stack of others. Killers, kidnappers, and wife-beaters, all supposedly headed south.

For five days straight Hurt had gone to the Tropical Park Racetrack looking for his daddy, and for five days he'd returned to the sparsely-furnished room disappointed. During those five days, he'd not showered or changed his clothes. At night he removed the sticky leather jacket and draped it across the back of the straight chair beside the bed. Before he hung the jacket, he removed his gun from the pocket and held it in his hands throughout the night. That gun was the one thing Hurt trusted. It was the one thing that could right the wrongs he'd suffered.

On the sixth day Hurt climbed out of bed and pulled on his jacket. His eyes were burning and his throat felt parched. In the room there was no food, no drink, and no glass to drink from. Two days earlier he'd gone on a rampage when thoughts of his daddy banged into his head. He'd paced the floor and screamed obscenities until there was nothing more to say. That's when he hurled the bathroom glass against the wall and smashed it into smithereens. While Hurt was at the racetrack someone had swept away the broken glass, but they'd not bothered to replace it.

"Cheap dump," Hurt growled as he stumbled to the bathroom, turned on the faucet, and cupped his hands. He scooped the flow of water to his mouth, and as he drank it dribbled down his face and onto the leather jacket. When Hurt caught sight of the dark stain, he found a new level of angry. It rose up and raged inside of him. He cursed the fate of ever being born, then pounded his boot against the pipe below the sink until it burst open and began flooding the room. With water pouring from the broken pipe, he turned and walked out the door.

He didn't need that room. He didn't need a place to stay. He didn't need shit. Today he was going to find his daddy. He'd do what he came to do, then move on. Before the day was over he'd be gone from Miami.

When Hurt stepped out onto the street the heat of the day was already crusted over the concrete. Before he had gone two blocks he was drenched in perspiration and thirstier than ever. He stopped at an orange juice stand and ordered a Coca-Cola.

"No Coke," the boy at the window said. "Just juice."

Hurt shot his fist through the window, knocked the boy to the floor, then walked off.

Continuing his trek toward the station where he would take a bus to the racetrack, Hurt walked three blocks, then stopped in an air-conditioned coffee shop and again ordered a Coca-Cola.

The pretty blond waitress smiled. "Coming right up."

Hurt hated friendly. He hated people who went around smiling at one another for no apparent reason. "Phony bullshit," he grumbled. When she sat the Coke in front of him, Hurt downed it without taking a breath, then stood and walked out.

"Hey, mister," the waitress called. "You forgot to pay."

Hurt kept walking and didn't bother to glance back.

When the early bus left for Tropical Park Raceway, Hurt was on it. He was first off the bus and first in line to purchase a ticket. When he entered the racetrack, there were only a handful of early-comers wandering about. He walked past the hot dog stand and circled around to where most of the betting windows were. Once he thought he saw George, but when he came closer he could see the man was an Oriental and looked nothing like his daddy.

Hurt rubbed his eyes. The brightness of the ever-constant sun made them burn and ache. It was a pain that drilled holes through his vision and ricocheted around the inside of his head. He had to find George today. He had to find George and leave this scorching hell.

Once Hurt had circled through the park he returned to a spot close to the entrance, a spot where he could watch the people who came through the gate. A spot where he was sure to see George.

He waited. And watched.

As he stood and watched the faces pass, Hurt counted up every angry word that had ever been spoken. He thought back to the sting of George's hand across his face and the shame of being dragged down the street by the scruff of his neck. The hatred swelled in his chest and pushed up into his throat.

Sweat trickled down Hurt's forehead and dropped into his eyes.

More people pushed through the gate. They came at him so quickly Hurt couldn't catch all the faces. He thought he saw his daddy's beard, then a corner of his ear, an eyebrow, a thick neck, an angry voice, but a complete picture of George never surfaced. Today was the day. Hurt knew it; he felt it in every twinge of muscle. Today was the day he would find his daddy.

All afternoon Hurt stood there with the sun baking him and the taste of bitterness stuck to his teeth. Then shortly after the sixth race had been called and scattered groups of people had begun to leave the track, he spotted his daddy. Not the face, but the back of him. He saw the belligerent swagger he had come to hate and a swatch of long grey hair hanging from the back of a baseball cap. Hurt wiped the sweat from his right eye, then pulled the gun from his pocket and stretched his arm toward the back of a daddy he'd spent a lifetime hating.

A woman shrieked, "He's got a gun!"

Gun...gun...gun. The word echoed through the crowd and people began running, dropping behind trash cans, lying flat with their faces to the ground and their hands covering their heads.

Hurt lost sight of his daddy for a moment; then he spotted him running toward the ticket booth. Everything was moving. It was fuzzy. Hot. Spinning. The sting of sweat and sun blinded him. He no longer saw the people around him. He no longer heard the screams. It was just his daddy, his daddy coming at him with a raised fist.

He blinked back the red sun, squeezed the trigger, and fired. He couldn't know the man he thought to be his daddy was actually an elderly woman, a woman with arthritis in her knee and a limp that caused her to swagger.

Hurt did not hear the call to drop his gun, nor did he see the officer. The two shots came in rapid succession; Hurt's went wild, flew over the heads of people scrambling to get away, and lodged itself in the roof of a lemonade stand. The second shot fired at almost the same moment tore into Hurt's chest. Before he felt the pain he fell backward and crashed against the concrete.

"Get back! Get back!" the officer screamed. In three long strides he closed the gap and leaned over the shooter.

"Why'd you do that, Daddy?" Hurt moaned. "Why, Daddy? Why"

Those were the last words Hurt ever spoke. He was gone before the ambulance even arrived.

Two days later Hurt was identified through his fingerprints, but it was another week before Detective Kurtzman was looking through the pile of APBs and came across the one on Hurt McAdams.

"I'll be damned," he said. "This is the shooter from the racetrack."

That afternoon Tom Wilson received a message saying his APB suspect was now in the Miami morgue.

Three weeks passed, and no one claimed Hurt McAdams' body so he was eventually given a number and buried in the Florida state cemetery.

Visiting Anita

Mahoney waited until Friday before he called Olivia and asked to pick up Jubilee for a visit with the elusive aunt. "I think once Anita meets her," he explained, "she'll feel differently about having the child."

That was exactly what Olivia was hoping wouldn't happen. Once her days with Jubilee were numbered she wanted to stretch them out, make them into more than they were and shove the inevitable into the distant future. Unfortunately, that wasn't the way it was destined to be. After losing Charlie as she had, Olivia knew that closing your eyes to reality didn't make it disappear. Whether or not you looked it square in the face it was there, waiting to rip loose the comfort you thought you had. After several minutes of trying to persuade Mahoney that Monday, Tuesday, or even some time next fall would be better, she gave in.

"You can come by about three-thirty," she said. "Ethan Allen will be home from school by then."

"It's got to be earlier. Anita goes away most weekends. I don't want to chance that she'll leave early and we'll miss her."

"Ethan doesn't get home from school until after three."

"That's okay," Mahoney said. "I think it's better for Jubilee to go alone."

"Alone?" Olivia gasped. The thought of sending a seven-year-old child off to face the unknown was horrifying. She said so and argued the point for a full five minutes. Weary of listening, Mahoney finally agreed that Olivia could come if she was willing to wait in the car while he took Jubilee inside to meet Anita. The time was set for one o'clock.

While the children were eating breakfast, Olivia sat across from them at the kitchen table. She tried to picture Anita, but the image was always contorted: angry eyes, a sharp nose, a mouth set straight and rigid. Try as she might, she could not conjure up the picture of a plump rosy-cheeked aunt who would hug Jubilee to her generous bosom. With a long face and heavy heart she finally said, "Jubilee, that phone call was from Detective Mahoney. He's going to take you to visit your Aunt Anita today."

"Paul too?" Jubilee asked warily.

"No." Olivia let her gaze drift to the salt shaker sitting at the end of the table. It was an insignificant thing, like a dish towel or a can of beans, just something that enabled her to avoid looking directly into the child's eyes. "Paul can't come this time."

"Why not?"

Believing the truth of Paul's situation would be too painful for a child to hear, Olivia mumbled something about the probability that he might not be well enough.

Tears welled in Jubilee's eyes. "I don't wanna go without Paul. I'm afraid."

Trying to sound convincing, Olivia told her, "There's nothing to be afraid of. Anita's your aunt. She'll love you because you're family."

"No, she won't!" Jubilee's face folded into a grimace. Then a stream of tears started rolling down her face. "I don't wanna go. Please don't make me, please."

"Grandma, you ain't really gonna *make* her go, are you?" Ethan Allen argued.

"I'm not the one making her," Olivia replied defensively. "Detective Mahoney said it's his duty to uphold the law."

Ethan scrunched his eyebrows together in a dubious frown. "What kind of law says a kid's gotta talk to somebody she don't even know?" His words had the sound of challenge packaged inside a wrapper of doubt.

Olivia explained that only a family member could claim ownership of a child without parents, but when it came time to describe the alternative words failed her. She stuttered and stammered over an explanation that said nothing. By then Jubilee was sobbing hysterically, and Ethan Allen had an angry look of defiance stretched across his face.

Before her words cleared the air, Ethan Allen snapped, "That's a stupid law! Just 'cause a kid's got no mama or daddy, they've got no say over where they live?"

Were it not such a sorrowful situation Olivia would have pointed out that it wasn't all that different from the circumstance he'd been in, but since he was already upset and ready to pounce on anything she let it pass.

"Let's not worry about this until it actually happens," she said. "I've got a feeling that time will set things straight."

"I don't wanna live with Aunt Anita!" Jubilee wailed.

Olivia gave a long heartfelt sigh. "That might be what you think right now, Jubilee, but try to be patient. Let's just wait and see what God has in mind."

"I know what He's got in mind," Ethan argued. "He don't want Jubie to go nowhere, He wants her to stay here!"

"You're sure of that?" Olivia shook her head with a sense of weariness, then turned, picked up the breakfast dishes, and set them in the sink. "This extra-special knowledge of yours, is that something you've come by recently?"

"You know what I mean," Ethan grumbled.

Still sobbing, Jubilee again wailed, "I don't wanna live with Aunt Anita!"

If not for fear that emotional children could inadvertently throw a monkey wrench into a person's plans without realizing what they'd done, Olivia might have told them what she was thinking. But given the mood of the moment, she decided it was better if they didn't know. This was something she had to feel her way around. It was only the start of a plan; the remainder she'd figure out as she went along.

Pretending to be coerced into allowing it, Olivia finally agreed to let Ethan skip school and go with them. "But bear in mind," she said, "you will have to wait in the car with me."

A less-knowing person might not have noticed how Olivia's words were not laced with rigidity, nor was she wearing the stern look that generally accompanied such a command. Ethan Allen noticed.

As she turned and left the kitchen, she heard him tell Jubilee, "Don't worry. I'll be sticking right by you."

When Mahoney arrived at twelve-thirty, he was greeted by a red-eyed girl and an angry-faced boy. Before he had both feet inside the apartment, Ethan Allen announced, "Grandma said I'm going with you."

"I think it's better if you don't," Mahoney answered. Before he could say anything more, Jubilee began wailing again. It wasn't something easily ignored, because along with the shuddering sobs came a high-pitched keening that scraped across his ears like nails on a chalkboard.

"Enough," he finally said. "Ethan can come with you, but he has to wait in the car."

It took almost twenty minutes for Olivia to calm everyone down. First she had to change Jubilee's dress because she'd wiped her nose on the one she was wearing. Then there was the challenge of finding the left shoe Ethan was missing. Once everyone was put together, they climbed into Mahoney's car and started out.

Mahoney drove, Olivia sat in the front passenger seat, and the two kids squeezed together on the left side of the back seat. From the corner of her eye, Olivia watched them whispering back and forth. It was precisely what she expected. The trip took thirty-five minutes, and as Mahoney drove Olivia made note of each turn off and street sign. She also noted the town limits sign for Harrison. When Mahoney pulled up in front of Anita's building, Olivia had already fixed the route for returning in her mind.

Mahoney climbed out of the car and opened the back door. He extended his hand and smiled, "Come on, Jubilee. It's time to meet your Aunt Anita."

"No," she answered and slid closer to Ethan. "I don't wanna go." She latched onto Ethan's arm.

"Now, Jubilee," Mahoney cajoled, "we've already talked about this. Your Aunt Anita is anxious to meet you."

A flood of tears started again. "I don't wanna live with Aunt Anita." Her tight grip on Ethan's arm made her knuckles turn white.

"You don't have to live here if you don't want to. This is just a visit."

"I don't wanna visit."

"Do you want your aunt to feel bad because you won't even come to visit her?"

Jubilee shook her head but held tight to Ethan's arm.

"I promised her you'd come visit." Mahoney again reached for Jubilee, but she scooted toward the center of the seat. Ethan moved with her. The truth was that Mahoney had made no such promise. In fact, Anita didn't know they were coming. Had he informed her ahead of time, chances were she'd be long gone.

"Please," he begged, "just a short visit. Fifteen minutes, Then we'll all go out for ice cream."

"I don't want ice cream," Jubilee answered. "I want Paul to come with me."

At the mention of Paul's name, Olivia gave Mahoney an apprehensive shake of the head and signaled that Paul's circumstances were not something to be spoken of.

He nodded and said only that Jubilee's brother couldn't come right now. "Maybe next time," he suggested, figuring he'd cross that bridge when he came to it.

Ethan Allen, who had positioned himself between Jubilee and the open car door, had said nothing until now. "Since Paul ain't here," he suggested, "how about I go with Jubie?"

Jubilee nodded.

Mahoney frowned. "I don't think that's—"

Before Mahoney could finish the thought, Jubilee said, "I ain't going 'less Ethan comes."

After he'd given six different explanations for why Ethan coming along was not a good idea and suffered through another round of Jubilee's tearful hysteria, Mahoney agreed.

"You can come to keep her company, but you are not to get involved in the conversation with her aunt. Understood?"

Ethan nodded, and the three of them started toward the building.

They rang the bell several times before Anita answered. "What?" she said in heavy voice.

"Detective Mahoney," he answered.

"I thought we already talked," Anita said. "You gonna keep bothering me?"

"This is the last time. I've got something for you."

"Yeah, I bet."

The buzzer sounded, and they entered the building. After

practically pushing Jubilee up the stairs, Mahoney rapped on Anita's door.

When the door swung open, Anita took one look at the kids and gasped. There were no words, just the stunned look of a woman who had seen the dead. With a nod of her head, she motioned them inside.

Mahoney led the way but said nothing. He knew this moment had to carry its own weight. Words could not smooth the pathway. Anita had to feel the family connection. Although he was not a church-going man, Mahoney knew that whatever happened from this moment on was up to God. Nothing he could say or do would change things.

Although it seemed like a length of time had passed, it was less than a minute before Anita bent down and wrapped her arms around Jubilee.

"You look just like your mama," she said soulfully.

Jubilee said nothing and stood rigid as a board.

When she let go of Jubilee, she turned to Ethan. Making no move to hug him she gave a sad shake of her head and said, "You're awful small for your age and don't look one bit like your mama or daddy, do you, Paul?"

"I ain't small, and I ain't Paul," Ethan replied.

"Well, who—"

Before Anita finished her question, Mahoney explained Ethan was the grandson of the woman Jubilee had been staying with. "Jubilee was feeling a bit shy, which is why Ethan came with her," he said.

"Oh." Anita gave a sigh that reeked of relief. "So, it's just the girl you want me to take?"

"For now," Mahoney nodded.

"For now? You know I ain't exactly in a position of—"

Mahoney cut in before she got to the point of saying something Jubilee shouldn't hear. "I'll bet you're anxious to know more about this pretty little niece of yours, aren't you?"

Anita turned her attention back to Jubilee and began talking about how as a girl Ruth had looked exactly the same. "Do you sing?" she asked. "Your mama had the most beautiful singing voice."

Without waiting for answers to her questions, Anita opened a floodgate of memories about their childhood and the years they'd shared in Norfolk. "I was with your mama the day she met your daddy," she said sadly. "That's a day that ain't easy to forget."

When Olivia watched the trio disappear into the building, a fear of the unknown began to pick at her heart. While earlier she had imagined Anita as a stern-faced, uncaring woman, a different picture now emerged. Anita became rounder, her mouth softer and upturned in a smile. As she waited she could see the new Anita clasping Jubilee to her chest and showering her with kisses. She could hear the woman's voice cooing about how she had been frantic with worry over her sister's missing children.

Anita most probably already had a room set up for Jubilee, a little girl's room with frilly pink curtains and a fancy new doll waiting for its owner. All Olivia had to offer was an alcove, with a not-fancy folding bed and a way-too-small chest of drawers. As she waited each second seemed to stretch itself into a minute, and the minutes had the feeling of hours. Fear settled into her heart, and when Olivia could no longer hold herself back from following them inside she climbed out of the car.

Inside the lobby Olivia scanned the mailboxes. Walker, Anita: Apartment 310. As fate would have it, Missus Lyndhurst from 308 was on her way out of the building at that time, and as the inner lobby door began to close behind the woman Olivia reached out and snagged hold of the handle. She hadn't exactly planned to go upstairs. In fact she hadn't finalized any type of plan, but here it was presenting itself. Olivia stepped inside and started up the stairs.

As she lifted her hand to knock, Olivia heard Anita's voice. She hesitated and listened. The words were not clear enough to distinguish what was being said, but the tone was soft and sentimental. Her arm felt as though it weighed ten thousand pounds as she lifted it and knocked.

"Now what?" Anita grumbled and slid back into the person she'd been before memory took hold of her.

Although Olivia hadn't heard the words, she heard the change in tone. Quickly rummaging through her handbag, she pulled out a flowered hankie. When the door pulled open she flounced the hankie in the air and walked in saying, "Ethan Allen! You went off without a hankie in your pocket, and I just know—"

"I got a hankie," Ethan replied.

"Oh. Well, then, I supposed I needn't have bothered." Olivia tucked the hankie back into her purse and introduced herself to Anita. "Sorry to barge in like this, but you know how kids are. You've got to watch them every minute."

"Every minute?" Anita replied.

"Yes, indeed. Turn your back for a few minutes, and they're off and into trouble."

"Sounds like a lot of work." A washboard of ridges appeared on Anita's forehead. Mahoney cringed.

"You can't begin to imagine!" Olivia continued. "Once Ethan Allen came to live with me, my life truly did change." Although she could reason that saying such a thing wasn't a lie, Olivia deliberately held back from saying it had changed for the better.

She had barely finished speaking when Mahoney suggested it was time to leave. "We've interrupted Anita's day enough," he said and began hustling Olivia out the door.

"It's no bother," Anita mumbled weakly, but by then both Ethan Allen and Jubilee were scrambling down the stairs.

"I'll be back in touch," Mahoney said and followed them out.

"Yeah," Anita said, "I hope so."

After the door was closed, Anita was once again alone with the life she had created for herself. The memory of years spent with Ruth by her side settled in like an illness she'd been fighting, and the ache spread throughout her body. She felt the loneliness in her fingertips and down to her smallest toes. Jubilee looked so much like Ruth that the sight of her was like tiny little knives tearing away bits of hardened skin, exposing the soft underside, the side that felt pain, heartache, and a forever sense of loss.

Anita sat at the table and cried. She allowed her head to drop into her arms and sobbed a tearful prayer that Ruth could somehow forgive her. "I should never have written those things," she said. "Now it's too late."

The suitcase Anita had packed remained at the foot of her bed for the entire weekend. And after she ran out of cigarettes, she didn't bother going out for more. On Friday evening when she was supposed to meet Henry Miller in Ocean City, she was instead stretched across her bed sobbing so loudly the upstairs neighbor began banging on the radiator pipe.

"Hush up that noise!" he'd yelled, but Anita continued to sob.

Henry Miller waited at the Ocean Breeze bar all evening. For the first two hours he sipped on a tall Tom Collins, but once he figured Anita wasn't coming he switched over to martinis. It was nearly eleven when he walked out of the bar with a giggly blonde hanging on his arm and gave up any thoughts of calling Anita.

Olivia

I should never have gotten out of the car. If I'd have left well enough alone, I wouldn't be remembering the way Anita looked at Jubilee. Nobody has to tell me how she feels about the child; I saw it in her eyes. If she said once she said twenty-three times how much Jubilee looks exactly like Ruth did at that age. I don't think there's any question about the woman wanting Jubilee to come live with her, but looking at the messiness of that apartment and the melancholy in Anita's eyes I can't help but wonder if that's what's best for Jubilee.

It isn't good for a child to carry the weight of someone else's regret. Only God knows what happened between those sisters but it must have been pretty ugly, because Anita has sorrow written all over her face. Jubilee doesn't need that poking her in the eye; she'll have plenty of her own sadness when she learns the truth about Paul being in jail.

I don't see any alternative other than to call Anita and explain the situation. I'll say how Ethan Allen has become like a brother to Jubilee and how he's the one who can ease the pain of her not having Paul to count on. I'll suggest she claim Jubilee, but let her stay here with us. It isn't like I'm asking Anita to give up the child. She'd be welcome to come for a visit anytime she had a mind to.

Okay, I'm a bit cramped for space, but with two kids the Rules Committee is going to ask me to leave anyway. When that happens, I'll look for a larger place. Yes, I hate the thought of losing my apartment, but it's nowhere near as tragic as poor little Jubilee losing her entire family.

There are times when God gives you a load to carry, and it's a lot heavier than what you had in mind. When that happens the only thing you can do is pick up the load and get moving. You've got to trust He knows just how much you're capable of carrying.

Jubilee's Discovery

Olivia had first imagined Anita as an uncaring woman, someone with hard edges and unyielding opinions. She'd then switched over to thinking she might be a loving aunt, someone Jubilee could turn to in time of need. But after spending a short time looking into the woman's face, Olivia had come to understand Anita was neither of those people. She was simply a woman weighed down with regret. The weariness was visible in her face, in the way her eyes were colored with sadness and her voice hollow with echoes of loneliness.

It had been a sleepless night for Olivia. She'd tossed and turned, thinking through every scenario the conversation with Anita might take. She'd wondered if the woman might welcome such a simple solution or fly off the handle and demand that Jubilee be returned to her immediately. It was a chance Olivia had to take.

With every bit of thought focused on what she would say to Anita, Olivia failed to notice the way Ethan Allen and Jubilee whispered back and forth. At the breakfast table she'd casually asked, "What are you kids going to do today?"

"Maybe ride our bikes over to the playground," Ethan answered. He make a point of including the word *maybe* and didn't look up as he sawed a bite-sized square of waffle into three tiny pieces.

Jubilee said nothing but began picking at a loose thread on the placemat. After a few seconds she glanced sideways at Ethan and, seeing his head tucked down, returned to picking at the thread.

When Olivia disappeared into the bedroom to call Anita, the two kids scooted out the door, climbed on their bikes, and headed toward Monroe Street. It wasn't often that Ethan so flagrantly defied Olivia's rules, but in this case he had no alternative. Jubilee had pleaded with an urgency that made it impossible to say no.

"We can't stay long," he'd warned. "If we're not back by lunchtime, Grandma's gonna know something's up and she's likely to come looking for us."

"A few minutes," Jubilee promised. "I just wanna tell Paul about Aunt Anita."

At Monroe Street they paused for the light, and as soon as it turned green they continued to the hospital.

Loretta was on duty that day, and she was none too happy to see Ethan Allen and his sidekick sneaking toward the hallway elevators. "Hold up there!" she called out and scurried across the lobby. Seconds before the elevator door opened, she nabbed Ethan Allen by the back of his shirt and didn't let go.

"You let go of him!" Jubilee screamed and gave her a kick in the shin.

The sharp edge of Jubilee's Mary Jane shoe caused a bump to rise up, and Loretta momentarily loosened her grip. With a strong tug Ethan Allen pulled free, but before he got two steps away Loretta screeched, "Security!"

It seemed the officer came from out of nowhere, a burly policeman who towered over the two kids. "These monsters," Loretta stammered, "were trying to sneak in again."

"Again?"

"Yes, *again*. They've done it before. The boy's been in trouble any number of times, and the girl's related to that shooter who was in ICU."

"Is that true, son?" the officer asked.

Ethan shrugged. "It ain't how she says."

"Oh?" The officer raised an eyebrow. "So what's your side of the story?"

"We wasn't sneaking nowhere. We come to visit Jubilee's brother."

"Liar!" Loretta huffed.

"Enough!" The officer shot Loretta a warning glare, then turned back to Ethan. "So, who is this brother you're here to visit?"

Jubilee spoke up. "Paul Jones."

"See?" Loretta snapped. "Crime obviously runs in that family!"

"Let them tell the story," the officer warned. He turned back to the kids. "Are you aware Paul Jones is no longer here at the hospital?"

"Not here?"

A tear was already overflowing Jubilee's left eye. "Where is he?"

Before the officer had time to answer Loretta said, "Hauled off to jail where he belongs!"

"Missus Clemens!" the officer growled. "Go back to your desk, and leave this to me!"

By then Jubilee was bawling so loudly the folks back in Campbell's Creek most likely heard her.

When the telephone rang at eleven-fifteen, Olivia thought it might be Anita calling back with a decision. Their conversation had gone reasonably well, and while Anita hadn't agreed to anything she did concede that having full responsibility for a child might be a bit overwhelming for a woman in her position.

"I'm divorced," she'd said sadly. "Husbandless. Freddie was a good man but I constantly picked at him, blamed him for my own shortcomings. I suppose it's because after I lost Ruth…" The remainder of what Anita wanted to say never came. Olivia waited for nearly a minute thinking she might go on, but the only thing she added was a long heavy sigh. The weight of that sigh ricocheted through the telephone wire and spun Olivia back to the days when she too had been alone. The days after Charlie's death, the days when no friends knocked at the door or delivered casseroles. Those days were long and lonely. They were something she would not wish on anyone, let alone this poor unfortunate woman who was Jubilee's blood relative.

Before hanging up the telephone Olivia suggested Anita come for dinner sometime soon. She didn't specify when but left the invitation open-ended.

When Olivia picked up the receiver for the second time she was prepared to say Sunday. "Come for dinner on Sunday," is what she was going to suggest, but the caller wasn't Anita. It was Loretta Clemens.

Loretta's voice was almost gleeful. "I don't suppose you know where that ill-mannered grandson of yours is right now, do you?"

Right off Olivia suspected Loretta knew something and was itching to tell. "At the moment, I suspect he's at the playground," she said warily.

"Ha! A lot you know! He's nowhere near the playground.

He's here at the hospital with that little ragamuffin he's befriended."

During the past two days Olivia had come to know the sound of Jubilee's wail, and she recognized it in the background. "Oh, my God! Is Ethan Allen okay? What's wrong with Jubilee?"

"Nothing that a little discipline won't fix," Loretta replied smugly.

"Loretta, if you've done something to those children—"

"I've done nothing. They did it to themselves."

"Did what?" Olivia demanded.

"Got themselves arrested. George has them in custody right now."

Loretta was winding up for a lecture on how such behavior didn't surprise her one little bit, but before she could say anything Olivia slammed the phone down.

Without wasting a second Olivia called the Mercy General Hospital admissions desk.

"Linda Foust," the voice said. "How can I help you?"

"Linda, it's Olivia. I don't know what Loretta has done, but she just called and said George has Ethan Allen and Jubilee in custody."

"Who's Jubilee?"

"Ethan's friend." Olivia hesitated for a second, realizing the child was so much more than her words had said. "Actually," she qualified, "Jubilee is more like Ethan's sister. She's a child I feel responsible for."

After hearing Olivia's explanation, Linda hung up the phone and paged George.

"Yeah, I'm with the kids," he said. "They apparently didn't know the boy was arrested, and the kid sister's taking it pretty hard."

Moments later Linda was downstairs in the lobby. She knelt and hugged Jubilee to her chest. "There, there, now," she said giving the words a soft and gentle tone. Pulling a dry hankie from her pocket, she wiped Jubilee's eyes and nose.

When Olivia got to the hospital she left the car in front of the main entrance and stormed through the glass door. Loretta spotted her coming and stepped from behind the visitor's desk to stand in the center of the lobby, her arms defiantly folded across her chest.

"You're not allowed to park there!" she said.

Not bothering to answer, Olivia slammed her shoulder into Loretta's and kept going. Before she rounded the corner she saw George and Linda with the children.

Linda raised her arm and waved.

Olivia crossed the lobby in a few long strides, then bent and hugged Jubilee.

"I'm so sorry you had to find out this way," she said. "But it's not the final word. There are still things that can be done. This is just a bump in the road, and I'm going to help you get past it."

Jubilee stopped sniveling for a moment and looked into Olivia's face. "Me?" she said. "It ain't me what needs help, it's Paul."

Projecting a confidence more manufactured than real, Olivia replied, "We're going to get Paul the help he needs. I promise."

She stood, thanked Linda and George for taking care of the children, then left with both kids. Other than a glance that sent icicles down his spine, she'd not said one word to Ethan Allen. Marching past the visitor's desk like a mama duck with two ducklings following behind, Olivia did not give Loretta so much as a nod. When they neared the exit, Ethan Allen, who was last in line, turned and gave Loretta a smug grin.

Leaving the bicycles behind, Olivia loaded the kids into the car and started home. They were well past Monroe Street when she finally spoke to Ethan Allen.

"I hold you responsible for this," she said. "You're older and you know better. You know you're not allowed to go past Monroe Street."

For what might have been the first time in as long as she'd known him, Ethan Allen didn't defend himself. He didn't argue back or say a word, just hung his head and stared down at his feet.

"I'll have Mister Porter pick up your bicycles later," Olivia continued, "but you'll not be using them for a month. And there's no television—"

Before Olivia could list all the punishments she had in mind, a small voice came from the back seat. "It ain't Ethan's fault," Jubilee said. "I'm the one what ought to be punished."

"You?"

In the rearview mirror Olivia saw the girl nod.

"Why?" she asked.

"I wanted to tell Paul about Aunt Anita."

"Tell him what?"

Jubilee shrugged and sat silently for several minutes; then she spoke in a voice smaller than before. "I don't wanna live with her. I wanna live with Paul."

At that point there was little Olivia could say. Her thoughts were jumbled, and words impossible to find. She'd been wrong in thinking Ethan could replace Paul. He was nothing more than a Band-Aid on a boil that could burst open with the slightest bit of pressure. Olivia wished she could promise the child that everything would be okay, that she wouldn't have to live with Anita, that Paul would be exonerated, that he'd come back to her—but the sorry truth was she could promise none of those things. With a heavy heart Olivia made the only promise she could.

"We will get help for Paul," she said. "I swear we will."

The words still hung in the air when Olivia realized it was the second time she'd made such a promise. Now it had become a commitment.

Plea for Help

Once they arrived home Olivia set aside thoughts of punishment and began concentrating on what she could do to fulfill the promise she'd made. Her first call was to Clara, whose only answer was that she'd just made a tray of chocolate cupcakes and would bring some over.

"Cupcakes?" Olivia asked. "What good will that do?"

Clara said a certain amount of sugar was sure to stimulate brain activity, then five minutes later she came barreling through the door.

Although Olivia insisted she was in no mood for snacking, the plate was near empty when Clara declared there was only one person who could do something to help.

"You've got to call Jack Mahoney again," she said.

"I can't. I'm certain he's still pretty annoyed with me because I barged into Anita's apartment when he told me to wait in the car."

"Pshaw," Clara huffed. "He wouldn't stay mad over a little thing like that."

"I also said a bunch of things about how difficult it was to have the responsibility of raising a child."

"Oh." Clara reached for the last cupcake. "How insistent were you on that?"

"Pretty insistent. I thought if I could discourage her…"

They discussed the possibility of a fundraiser to pay for a lawyer but nixed it because there was not enough time. One by one they went through the list of people they knew or their friends knew, but not one was in a position to help. Finally, when there was nothing but crumbs left on the plate, Clara said, "You've got to call Mahoney."

Olivia spent the next half-hour rehearsing what she was going to say. She'd start with an apology, then explain how it had simply been her jangled nerves that pushed her into talking and acting as she had. Once he'd forgiven her, she'd tell of Jubilee's heartache and say how much the girl needed her brother. After she'd won him over to her way of thinking, she'd address the issue of getting help for Paul.

Luckily she'd kept his home number, because on a Saturday it was unlikely he'd be at the stationhouse. She dialed the number and waited. It rang five times; then a woman answered.

Not expecting this, Olivia blurted, "Is Mister Mahoney there?"

"He's outside," Christine answered. "Who's calling?"

"Olivia Doyle. It's an emergency."

"Hold on."

As she waited Olivia heard the woman, who was obviously Mahoney's wife, holler for him to hurry in, there was some kind of emergency. "It's that Missus Doyle," she'd said.

There was the clunk of the receiver being lifted from the table; then Mahoney spoke. "What's the emergency?"

Although Olivia thought she was prepared, the words jumped out of her mouth in random fashion, with each thought not giving the previous statement time to settle.

"You've got to help," she pleaded frantically. "Jubilee knows about her brother, and the poor child is hysterical. Somebody's got to do something!" Her plea continued for almost a minute before she began to wind down.

"What brought this on?" Mahoney finally asked.

Olivia explained the hospital incident and moaned, "I've promised Jubilee that you'll do something to help. I gave the child my word."

"I don't know what I can do," he replied. "My hands are tied. Captain Rogers took me off this case. There's nothing—"

Olivia started all over again. "There's always something," she said "A way to prove..."

Finally, when Mahoney was weary of listening to her, he agreed to call Detective Gomez and speak to him. "He's in charge of the case," Mahoney said, "but I'm warning you, he's none too sympathetic to Paul's situation."

"Oh, dear," Olivia murmured.

When he hung up the telephone Mahoney went back to pruning the azaleas, but the urgency of Olivia's voice stayed with him. Less than an hour later he changed into a pair of slacks and drove to the stationhouse.

Captain Rogers sat at a desk piled high with papers. "What are you doing here today?"

Mahoney shrugged. "This Wyattsville thing is still bothering me. I need to take one last look at it."

Rogers shook his head. "I'm thinking all you're gonna do is stir up a can of worms and make more enemies."

"A few questions, that's it. A few questions, then I'm out of their hair."

"Go on," Rogers grumbled. He dismissed Mahoney with a quick wave of his hand.

Mahoney's next move was to call Gomez.

Hector Gomez was feeling none too good about the case as it was. When the story in the *Wyattsville Daily* suggested the department had gone soft on Klaussner's shooter, the captain came down hard on Gomez.

"Sloppy work," he'd said, and any accolades Gomez expected were out the window.

After that, Gomez had no tolerance for Carmella Klaussner and her busybody attitude. If he had any say in it, he'd let the boy go free just to spite Carmella. But of course that wasn't possible. If she sniffed even the slightest hint of leniency, she'd have her newspaper buddy all over it. Sick of working a case that had brought him nothing but grief and aggravation, Hector Gomez moved on to working a Friday night break-and-enter that was proving far less troublesome. When he lifted the receiver and heard Mahoney's voice, he was tempted to hang up.

"Hold on," Mahoney said. "Let me ask a few questions; then you'll be rid of me."

"Yeah, sure."

Without waiting for an actual go-ahead, Mahoney started asking if Gomez had checked out the lead that Paul Jones was in Klaussner's store applying for a job.

"No," Gomez answered flatly. "And I'm not about to either. I've already had my ass handed to me once, so I ain't looking to do it again."

"But, if there's a chance the boy's innocent—"

"Innocence or guilt have nothing to do with it. This is about revenge!"

"Revenge? Why would you—"

"Not me, stupid! Carmella Klaussner!"

"The store owner's wife?"

"Yeah. She's sure the kid's the shooter and wants him punished."

"Even so, how does she figure into—"

"Connections! She's got somebody at the newspaper."

"But—"

"But nothing," Gomez snapped. "She threatened it last time, and look what happened. I'm not messing with her again. If you do anything, it's on your head."

Mahoney hung up the telephone and checked his watch. It was three-forty. He'd promised Christine he'd be home in time for dinner. If he left now he could make it to the hospital and back before seven. Close enough. He called home, to say he might be a few minutes late, but when there was no answer, he just left.

When he pulled out of the parking lot, he was certain Carmella Klaussner would be at the hospital. She was almost always there. Day after day she arrived early in the morning and stayed until long after the other visitors had gone home. She sat next to her comatose husband and seldom left his side.

Mahoney knew he'd find her there. What he didn't know was that three days earlier Sidney Klaussner had opened his eyes and began to remember.

The Telling Story

Carmella Klaussner saw Mahoney when he stepped off the elevator. She'd seen him coming and going, visiting the shooter, consoling the kid, doing everything he could to set a guilty man free. "What now?" she wondered aloud.

Leaving Sidney to finish the pudding on his tray, Carmella rose, stepped outside the door, and confronted Mahoney before he got to the room.

"What do you want?" she said, her words clipped and short.

"I have a few questions I'd like to—"

"You have some nerve!" Carmella shouted. "Why, I wouldn't give you the right time of day, let alone answer any questions!"

"It's just that—"

"Just nothing! I know what you're trying to do. You're one of those bleeding hearts. You want me to feel sorry for the kid, but I don't. He deserves whatever he gets!"

"What if he's innocent?"

"Innocent?" Carmella's voice grew so loud it ricocheted off the walls and bounced back as an echo. "He's not innocent. My Sidney shot him! Sidney is a God-fearing man, never in million years would shoot someone unless—"

Mahoney interrupted. "What if Sidney was aiming at someone else, and the kid just got in the way?"

Carmella's face turned as red as the inside of an overripe watermelon. "Get out of here!" she screamed. "Get out, and don't come back. There ought to be a law protecting people from the likes of you!" Before Mahoney could get another word in, she whirled on her heel, stormed back into Sidney's room, and closed the door behind her. By then Carmella's heart was thumping with such force you could see her chest rising and falling.

Mahoney watched as she walked away. The light in Sidney's room was on, and through the plate glass window he saw it. Sidney Klaussner was sitting up in the bed. Maybe Sidney had the answers; maybe not. It would depend on how much he remembered. With Carmella on the rampage, it would be impossible to try to question him right now, but if Mahoney waited...

Luckily Barbara Walsh was on duty. After letting Mahoney down last time, she owed him. He walked over to the nurses' station and started up a conversation.

Sidney Klaussner had been married to Carmella for more than thirty years. He knew her moods as well as he knew the roundness of her body and the timbre of her laugh. She was a kind woman, a patient woman, a woman who didn't anger easily—a woman whose behavior was uncharacteristic of what he'd seen outside his hospital room. He waited until she sat down and let go of a deep sigh; then he asked, "Who was that?"

Still tight lipped and red-faced, Carmella answered, "That detective from Northampton."

"Northampton?" Sidney repeated curiously. "What did he want?"

Caught up in a burst of anger and forgetting she'd been told not to keep reminding Sidney of his experience, she answered, "He wants to get the kid who shot you off scot free. Can you imagine? The nerve—"

"What kid who shot me?"

"The robbery at the store. Remember?"

"Yeah, I remember the robbery. But I don't remember any kid."

"He was one of the robbers—tall, lanky, sixteen or seventeen years old."

"One of the robbers?"

Carmella nodded. "You shot this one, but the other one got away."

Since they'd already started talking about it, Carmella saw no harm in showing Sidney the newspaper. She reached down and pulled her copy of the *Wyattsville Daily* from the lower shelf of the bedside table. "This is the kid," she said, thrusting the paper in front of him.

Sidney lifted the paper and stared at the picture below the headline.

"That detective was trying to get him off," Carmella said, "so I spoke to Lucinda. She agreed such a thing wasn't right and got Mike to do the story."

Sidney looked up with a furrowed brow. "This isn't the guy who shot me."

"He's the shooter's accomplice and every bit as guilty."

Sidney let the newspaper fall into his lap and placed his hands over his eyes. Behind his darkened eyelids he saw the day as it had happened. He saw the boy in the picture, not with a large white bandage taped to the side of his head, but with a full crop of dark unruly hair. Sidney's mind flooded with memories. Before this he had only vague shadows of the shooter, but now he saw him clearly. He was older—not old but older than the boy. He walked with long strides and an angry stance. Without saying a word, he'd pulled a gun from his pocket and raised his arm to fire. The boy lunged. The gunman fired.

Sidney saw that split second. It was a moment frozen in time, a moment waiting to be rediscovered. But after that there was nothing. No image of either bullet hitting its mark, no image of falling, nothing but a big void of black nothingness. Tears came to Sidney's eyes and he began to sob.

"Dear God," he moaned. After several minutes had passed, he lifted his head and looked at Carmella.

"That kid saved my life," he said.

Carmella shook her head vigorously. "No. It's impossible. You shot him. The police said it was your bullet. You wouldn't shoot an innocent—"

Barely able to speak because of the sorrow rising from his chest, Sidney held up his hand and motioned for Carmella to stop talking. "I wasn't trying to shoot him," he said, squeezing the words out. "I was aiming at the gunman."

Carmella's face twisted itself into a mask of fear. "But how…?"

Sidney couldn't answer.

Jumping up so fast you'd think she'd been zapped by lightning, Carmella dashed out of the room and ran toward the nurse's station screaming, "Wait, wait, there's been a mistake!"

"A mistake?" Barbara Walsh and Mahoney replied simultaneously.

Now almost out of breath, Carmella nodded. "The boy didn't do it."

Taken aback, Mahoney said, "I don't understand—"

"Don't understand? What is there to not understand?" Carmella's words came like the rapid fire of a machine gun, landing on top of each other and not leaving a millimeter of space in between. "The boy is innocent. He's not the one. He saved my Sidney's life!"

"Sidney said that?"

"Yes." Carmella grabbed hold of Mahoney's arm and tugged him toward the room. "Come ask him yourself!"

For the better part of an hour Mahoney sat and listened. Sidney sobbed, and Carmella sobbed with him. The memories were painful. They caused his hands to tremble and his heart to pound hard against his chest, but Sidney had to remember. He had to know. The locked vault of memories opened slowly, and he began to recall the bits and pieces of that day. In looking back he began to see even the smallest things: the key in his hand, unlocking the door, switching on the lights, Martha Tillinger asking for a cake mix. A few minutes later, a boy came in, a tall skinny boy carrying the "Help Wanted" sign he'd plucked from the window. Sidney recalled the overalls the boy was wearing, clean but frayed at the bottom.

"I'm ready for working," the boy had said with a grin.

Before there was any further discussion, the bell above the door jingled and a second man walked in. The boy stepped to the side of the counter and said, "I can wait."

"We'd been having a warm spell," Sidney recalled, "and it struck me why that man would be wearing a heavy leather jacket on such a hot day." He went on to tell how the man came at him, not looking left or right but with dark hooded eyes fixed straight ahead.

"There was early morning sun, and for a second, maybe less than a second, I saw the glimmer of it on the metal thing he was pulling from his pocket. That's when I grabbed the Browning I keep under the counter."

The encounter had come and gone in less than a minute, but in Sidney's memory it stretched itself to an expanse where he could stop and look at each frame of action, each tiny movement. He could see the shooter's boots, smell the anger he wore. He could detail every move the boy made—how his head swiveled, his arm shot out, and he slammed his shoulder into the shooter. The shooter had taken dead aim, but he was off balance when he fired. Sidney clenched his fist and once again felt the pressure of his finger pulling back on the trigger of the Browning. He closed his eyes and listened; then he heard it. A noise roared through his head, two shots so close together they had the sound of one.

Three times Sidney told the story, and each time he recalled another small piece of the puzzle—the time, the amount of money in the register, even the brand of cake mix Martha Tillinger had been looking for.

Once Sidney had told all there was to tell, Mahoney stepped out to the nurse's station and telephoned the Wyattsville stationhouse. He asked to speak to Gomez.

"Not here," the voice said. "Can someone else help you?"

"Afraid not." Mahoney explained that he was a detective with the Northampton Precinct and asked for Gomez's home number.

"It's probably better to wait 'til Monday," the voice said. "Gomez is none too fond of you Northampton boys."

"Will do," Mahoney said and hung up. He then grabbed the Wyattsville directory and started calling the Gomezs. Although the directory listing was for a Maria Gomez, Hector answered the third number he called.

"I've got something for you," Mahoney said.

"Who's this?" Hector replied.

"Jack Mahoney, Northampton."

"What the hell—"

"Look, I'm doing you a favor here," Mahoney said. Then he went on to explain what he'd just heard. "I'm off the case, so this's a chance for you to step in and grab the glory."

"How do I know this ain't another one of your hot shot deals?" Hector asked.

"You don't," Mahoney answered. "But I'm at the hospital right now, and it's seven o'clock. I'll sit on it until eight-thirty. If you're not here by then, I'm going to turn it in to Captain Rogers." He hung up the telephone.

Mahoney's next call was to Christine. "I'm going to be later than I thought," he said and promised to make it up to her.

Minutes later he called Olivia Doyle.

The Carmella Encounter

When the telephone rang Olivia didn't answer it. She glanced up at the clock. Seven-fifteen; it was probably Clara. If not Clara, then Seth, or perhaps Jeanine. *I'll call back in a few minutes,* she thought and slid a tray of cookies into the oven. While the cookies baked she washed the dishes, tidied the kitchen, and leafed through the latest issue of "Ladies Home Journal." It was nearly a half-hour later when she remembered about the call.

Olivia hurried to the telephone, expecting to hear Clara's voice. Instead it was Detective Mahoney.

He was short and to the point.

"Missus Doyle, this is Jack Mahoney," he said. "I'm at the hospital and wanted to let you know your suspicion was right. We've confirmed that Paul Jones was *not* involved in the robbery."

"Oh my goodness," Olivia gasped, but before she could say anything more, Mahoney said he couldn't talk now and would explain it all later.

That was it. He'd given no details saying how such information came to light, just that it was what it was. But Olivia noticed how Jack Mahoney's voice sounded a lot happier than it had in their earlier conversations.

Olivia hurried into the living room. "You were right about your brother," she told Jubilee. "Detective Mahoney called and said they know Paul was not involved in that robbery."

A smile such as Olivia had never before seen lit up the girl's face. "Can we go see Paul now?"

"Yes, I believe we can," Olivia answered happily.

While Ethan went in search of the shoes he'd been wearing, Olivia called Clara to share the news. "It seems a small miracle that the children will finally be reunited."

"Thank heaven!" Clara replied. Then she went on to say how all along she'd suspected Jubilee's brother couldn't possibly be involved in something so scandalous. "Family upbringing shows through, and I'm betting the brother is a fine young fellow."

By then it was after eight and rapidly approaching what should have been the children's bedtime. Instead of telling them to go brush their teeth and get their pajamas on, Olivia loaded both kids into the car and started for the hospital. Mahoney had only mentioned that he was there. He'd said nothing about Paul, but Olivia's listening was love-impaired and she heard what she wanted to hear.

Once Sidney regained consciousness, Carmella Klaussner's heart swelled to five times its normal size and overflowed with the joy of living. For the past three days she'd walked around so deliriously happy she found it impossible not to smile. She held on to that smile from the time she opened her eyes in the morning until she closed them at night. When Carmella crawled into bed, her face ached from all that smiling but she didn't care. She once again had her Sidney.

Until today nothing in the entire world could have taken Carmella's smile. But in mere moments everything changed. Now a sliver of regret stabbed her skin like a steel splinter. She thought back on the phone call she'd made. She remembered the words she'd said. They were cold, heartless. She hadn't waited for justice to take its course. She'd demanded it right then and there. The boy who had saved Sidney's life was in jail, and she was to blame. After three days of thanking the Lord for returning her Sidney, Carmella fell to her knees and began praying for forgiveness.

Just as she uttered her last "Amen," she lifted her eyes and saw the boy's sister coming down the hallway. Certain it could only be divine providence, Carmella jumped up and ran from the room. Without any explanation, she squatted and hugged Jubilee to her chest. "You poor child," she moaned. "I have wronged you and your family terribly."

Olivia and Ethan Allen exchanged looks of confusion.

"Do we know you?" Olivia asked.

Carmella stood. "Maybe not, but I'm the one responsible for your boy being in jail."

"I'm not in jail," Ethan Allen said, "Paul is."

"And it's entirely my fault," Carmella acknowledged. She explained that she was Sidney's wife. "I was beside myself with grief over Sidney, and I wanted your boy to suffer the way I was suffering."

Olivia noticed how the woman continued to refer to Paul as "her boy."

"I was wrong," Carmella said. "I see that now, and I'm going to make things right. I'll make certain your boy goes free. In fact, I'll do it right now," Carmella added. "I'll march myself into that police station and demand they let your boy go free!"

After several minutes of listening, Olivia began to put the pieces together. "So, you're saying it was you who put that story in the newspaper?"

"Yes, and I'm ashamed to admit it." Carmella's shoulders drooped. She stood hunched over with a penitent gaze focused on the floor. "According to Sidney, your boy came into the store looking for a job and had nothing whatsoever to do with what happened. He got in the way of that bullet because he tried to stop the robber." After she'd finished her story, Carmella grabbed Jubilee's hand and tugged her toward Sidney's room. Olivia and Ethan Allen followed along.

Mahoney stood to the side of the room. Gomez was next to Sidney, asking questions and scribbling notations of what was said.

"The boy came in asking for a job," Sidney said.

Gomez wrote "asking for job."

"Then what?" he asked.

"The man in the leather jacket came in maybe a minute later."

Mahoney's eyes were fixed on Sidney, so at first he didn't notice Olivia standing behind Carmella. When he finally caught sight of her, he asked, "What are you doing here?"

"You called and Jubilee was anxious to see her brother."

"Paul's not here," Mahoney said. "He's still in holding."

In an unexpected burst of generosity, Gomez said, "I can fix that." He gave a sheepish smile. "Now that I've got Mister Klaussner's testimony, there's no longer a reason to hold the kid."

"Blessed be the Lord," Carmella murmured. "Your boy will be at home with you tonight!"

Jubilee's grin stretched ear to ear. "Tonight?"

"I guess so," Gomez nodded. "I'm gonna need an hour or so to wrap up the paperwork. Then he can go." The grumpy face Hector Gomez usually wore was gone; he'd returned to thinking about the possibility of a promotion.

Without looking inside her head, a person could tell Jubilee was celebrating the thought of being with her brother again.

Happy as Olivia was for Jubilee, she couldn't help thinking about how Carmella kept calling Paul "her" boy. The lower part of her face was curled into a smile, but her forehead was creased with worry lines. Where , would she put another child? And what would the Rules Committee have to say about it? Olivia could already picture a steamy spiral of smoke coming from Jim Turner's ears. While there had been a remote chance of her remaining in the building once she'd taken Jubilee in, with three children such a thought was beyond thinkable.

Gomez finished questioning Sidney Klaussner, then left with a smile on his face and a fistful of notes in his pocket. Mahoney followed him out a few minutes later. It was already nine-thirty. On the way out of the hospital, Jack stopped in the gift shop and bought Christine a bouquet of yellow daisies and baby's breath. He'd hoped to get roses, but this was the last remaining bouquet and the florist had closed hours earlier.

Olivia stayed behind because Carmella latched onto her hand and said, "Please don't go, Sidney just loves talking to the children."

It was apparent that Jubilee and Ethan Allen were enjoying it also, because they were both locked into listening to Sidney's account of the robbery.

"I knew that man was ill-intentioned when I saw the look on his face," Sidney said. "Then a speck of sunlight flashed against the gun he was pulling from his pocket, so I reached down and grabbed the Browning."

"Was you scared?" Ethan Allen asked.

"Sure I was, but being scared don't count for much when you're facing up to a hell-bent crazy person with a gun."

"And Paul punched the crazy man?" Jubilee added.

"More like shoved him," Sidney said; then he continued with the story.

While the children listened wide-eyed to Sidney, Carmella kept a tight hold on Olivia's hand. "I can never begin to make up for the heartache I've caused you and your boy, but rest assured, I will spend the rest of my days trying."

"Well, I don't really think that's necessary."

"I insist. Surely there's something I can do? Some way to help? Some way to atone?"

"Well, I suppose if you really want to, you could make a contribution to the Bicycle Ball. It's an event the Wyattsville Arms hosts every August."

Olivia told how the ball got started the summer Ethan Allen came to live with her. "We use the proceeds to buy bicycles for needy children."

A sparkling glimmer suddenly appeared in Carmella's eyes. "Oh, we'd be thrilled to help. We won't just contribute. We can serve on the decorating committee, provide food, and, of course, attend the ball."

Sidney, who was none too fond of lace-napkin teas or dances, glanced over. "What if I'm not up to dancing yet?"

"Don't worry," Carmella assured him. "You will be."

By the time Olivia and the kids left to pick up Paul at the Wyattsville stationhouse, Carmella could see herself becoming Olivia's best friend and Sidney a benefactor to the children.

She sat beside Sidney and smiled. It was apparent that the Lord had not only forgiven her but also shown her how she was to atone for such rash judgment.

The Homecoming

It was ten-thirty when Olivia walked out of the Wyattsville stationhouse with all three children. Paul was taller than she'd expected and, compared to Jubilee or Ethan Allen, a lot quieter. Jubilee had climbed atop Paul's shoulders and sat there so comfortably, so snuggled close, it made Olivia think the girl had done this same thing for much of her short life. Even with the added weight on his shoulders Paul stood tall and straight. As he walked side by side with Ethan Allen, the two boys talked.

Olivia slowed her step so she could watch the trio. They walked as a family, close together, words passing from one to the other. At first it seemed as though an aura surrounded them, but when Olivia looked more closely she could see it was more than an aura. It was a love so palpable it generated the feeling of warmth, of contentment, of quiet family nights and wordless devotion.

They crossed the parking lot and climbed into the car, Paul and Jubilee in the back seat, Ethan Allen up front next to Olivia. For a short while Jubilee talked about the things she'd done and the people she'd met, but before they crossed Monroe Street her words slowed and her head dropped sleepily onto Paul's chest. He lifted his arm and wrapped it around her shoulders. Without opening her eyes, she snuggled into him the way one might bury their head in a feather pillow.

Olivia watched in the rearview mirror and felt a stirring in her heart.

The arrival of Ethan Allen had changed her life. He had awakened in her a love greater than any she'd ever known, but with that love had come responsibilities, worry, and, at times, even fear. Everything had a price. The price of not loving was an empty and cold existence. It meant a lifetime of wordless evenings and nights where the chill of loneliness rattled through your bones. The price of loving was beyond measure. Olivia thought back on the night she lost Charlie, a night so horrible she could not even find a comparison. She wanted to tell herself that going forward no heartache could ever be as great as that one, but she knew better.

Ethan Allen was young, Jubilee even younger. If disaster befell one of them it, Olivia knew it would shatter her heart. Worrying over, caring for, and protecting one child was difficult enough; could she possibly do it for three? Stretched out in front of her, it seemed a Herculean task, a job too big for even the mightiest, and yet it was slowly settling into her mind.

She'd given thought to letting the boy go his own way. He seemed big, strong, and capable of taking care of himself. But that was outside. Inside he was simply a boy, a sixteen year old teenager. Too young to know the hardships life could thrust upon his shoulders. Perhaps if he had been surly or outspoken she may have found justification for not caring.

But he was none of those things. He was softspoken, gentle, and genuinely likeable. Jubilee obviously adored him, and Ethan Allen was giving him the type of admiration usually reserved for baseball players.

While Olivia would have welcomed the alternative, the truth was that watching them together was like seeing the missing piece of a jigsaw puzzle slide into place. It completed the picture. She knew that whatever hardships lay in front of her, she could never separate the children.

When they arrived back at the Wyattsville Arms, Paul lifted his sister and carried her to the apartment. After Olivia turned back the covers, he gently laid her in the bed. She rustled around a bit but never woke.

Even though the hour was late, Olivia sat the boys at the kitchen table and served up tall glasses of milk and a plate piled high with the cookies she'd baked earlier. After Paul had eaten his fifth cookie, he lowered his eyes and said, "Hope you don't mind me eatin' up all these cookies—"

Before he finished, Olivia said, "Not at all Paul, go right ahead. There's plenty more where those came from."

"I know it ain't none too polite to make a pig of myself but, Missus Doyle, these is the best cookies I ever tasted."

"Well, then," Olivia said with a smile, "I'll have to get busy and make another tray of them." She poured each of the boys a second glass of milk, then turned to the sink and began washing the cookie tray she'd left earlier. Although her back was to the boys, she listened to their conversation.

"How come you call Grandma 'Missus Doyle'?" Ethan Allen asked.

Paul awkwardly stumbled over his answer. "I been taught using a body's proper name shows respect."

"Yeah, but Grandma's family. You ain't supposed to call family same as other folks."

After more than a year of correcting Ethan's grammar, Olivia did it without thinking. "You're *not* supposed to call family."

Thinking the words were meant for him, Paul answered, "I'm not."

Olivia laughed. "I didn't mean you, Paul. Actually, I'd be real pleased if you'd call me Grandma, just as Ethan Allen and Jubilee do."

"Really?" Paul answered.

"Yes, really."

It was nearing midnight when they finally started off to bed. Olivia offered Paul her room, but he refused it. "I'll be just fine here," he said and stretched out on a sofa that was a foot shorter than his lanky body, his head propped up on the arm at one end and his feet dangling over the other end.

"That doesn't look any too comfortable," Olivia said, but by then Paul's eyes were already closing. Seconds later he was sound asleep.

As she was pulling a blanket over Paul, Olivia noticed the peaceful look on his face. It suddenly seemed so obvious. He was a boy with no shame attached to him, a boy with a squeaky-clean conscience. Chances were that in all his years he had never even uttered an obscenity. How, she wondered, could they have suspected such a boy would commit a crime?

Olivia snapped off the light, went into her own room, and closed the door. It had been a long day, and she welcomed the thought of sleep. Tomorrow would dawn with a whole new set of problems, but tonight she would sleep. She slid a cotton nightgown over her head and climbed into bed.

After plumping the pillow as she always did, Olivia lowered her head onto it expecting to drift off in seconds. But for some odd reason the nightgown itched in places where it had never itched before. After fifteen minutes of moving one way and then the other, she decided it was the sewn-in label rubbing against her back. That was easy enough to fix. She got out of bed, pulled out the sewing basket, removed the label stitch by stitch, and then climbed back into bed.

Although the nightgown was now without a label, sleep was still impossible to come by. Olivia's pillow had somehow developed a lump that poked her in the neck no matter which way she turned. She sat up and flipped the pillow on the opposite side. No better. She exchanged it for the one that was originally Charlie's. Still no good; that one was way too firm.

"Hard as a rock," she grumbled and switched them back again. After seven plumps and two more flips, the lump disappeared and Olivia curled into the pillow.

She wanted to sleep. She wanted to not think about moving, not think about leaving her friends, not think about the responsibility of three children, but such a thing was impossible. When she closed her eyes she saw the three of them standing at the top of a faraway mountain.

"Grandma," they called with their arms stretched out. Olivia looked up and saw a black sky with an angry wind ripping pieces of the mountain loose.

"Come down from there!" she screamed. "Come down right now, before you get hurt."

Instead of running from the danger, the children remained where they were, again calling her name. She heard the reedy sound of Jubilee's voice, the husky sound of a boy not yet a man, and underneath those was the familiar cry of Ethan Allen. A bolt of lightning shot across the sky and slammed into the side of the mountain. The ground shook, and several large chunks of stone tumbled down.

The children huddled together as edges of the mountain top began to crumble. Olivia started toward them running as fast as she could, but the faster she ran the steeper the mountain became. Her legs grew weak and her lungs gasped for air.

"You'll never make it," a voice thundered, and a roar of laughter rolled across her ears.

Olivia turned and looked around. It was an old man, dressed head to toe in dark grey. "You'll never make it," he repeated and sounded another uproarious roll of laughter.

"I have to!" Olivia cried and started to run again.

"Run, run, run!" the voice cackled and pointed a bony finger at the face of the mountain.

Olivia looked up and saw what she hadn't seen earlier. Carved into the mountain were the names and faces of suitors she'd walked away from. In the center of the mountain was an empty black hole. It was the lonely years, the years when she'd been afraid to trust, the years when she'd been afraid to love. "Nooooooooooo!" Olivia screamed and bolted up.

It took several seconds for her to realize she was sitting in her own bed. For several minutes her heart continued to race. She looked at her own fears and recognized them for what they were. Stones that had littered her pathway. Obstacles that had held her back from loving.

"Never again," she vowed. "Never again."

It was several hours before Olivia could again find sleep, and when she finally did silver threads of daylight had begun to crease the night sky. By then she had reached a decision. It was the only decision her heart would allow her to make.

Olivia

I'd like to tell you I'm not frightened, but the truth is I'm scared to death. It's been almost two years, and I can still remember the ache of loneliness I felt after Charlie died. I came back here expecting to pick up the life I had before we got married. But such a thing is not possible. It never is. Life has only one direction and that's forward. If you don't move with it, you might as well go ahead and jump into the grave.

It's hard to imagine that Olivia Westerly Doyle, a woman who avoided marriage because she couldn't bear the thought of children, should one day end up responsible for three of them. I guess God looks past what you claim to want and gives you what you need.

Having Ethan Allen has brought me a great deal of joy, more than I ever dreamed possible. But having Ethan didn't mean I had to move away from my friends. If you don't think friends are important, just try doing without them. If it wasn't for Clara and the others, I'd still be walking around this apartment like a dead person.

There's a spot in my heart that wants to tell Anita, These kids belong to you, go ahead and take them. That would be an easy out. It's an answer that satisfies my selfish soul but puts those two sweet children in a place that a blind man could see wouldn't be good for them. I watched the way Anita looked at Jubilee, and it wasn't something you'd expect from a loving aunt. If she feels that way about Jubilee, I can't imagine how she'd react to having Paul as well. When I come face to face with the reality of measuring my own happiness up against their well-being, it's a pitiful comparison.

I know the responsibility I'm taking on, but I've still got a good chunk of Charlie's insurance money and if I'm prudent about spending, we'll be okay. At least I think we'll be okay. As for the part about leaving my friends, I'm not ready to think about that right now. I'll do what I've got to do, and once it's done then I can think about wallowing in my own sorrow.

Future Plans

The next morning as Olivia and the three children sat at the breakfast table, she told them of her plan.

"I'm pretty sure your Aunt Anita will agree to having you live with me," she explained. "So once I get her okay, I'll start looking for a larger place."

"That's real generous, Missus Doyle," Paul said, "but I wasn't really counting on living with Aunt Anita. I figure—"

Jubilee interrupted with a giggle. "You're supposed to call her Grandma!"

Paul began again. "Okay, Missus Grandma—"

"Just Grandma," Olivia cut in. "No missus."

"Okay, Grandma. What I was trying to tell you is that I can care for Jubilee on my own. I'll be getting a job and—"

"A full-time job?" Olivia exclaimed. "What about school?"

"I don't figure on going back to school."

"If he ain't going," Ethan Allen said, "I ain't going either."

Olivia grimaced. "There's to be no more talk about not attending school. It is not a matter for discussion, and that's that!" She turned to Paul and asked, "Have you already graduated high school?"

He shook his head sheepishly. "I fell behind and missed a few years."

"Then there's no question about it," Olivia declared. "You've got to go back to school, because without an education—"

"I appreciate your kindness, but I've got responsibilities."

She looked at the newcomer; he had the stature of a man but the face of a boy. At a time when lads his age were swinging at a baseball and chasing after pretty girls, Paul was stepping up to the plate ready to be both mother and father to Jubilee. It was unfair. It was something that should never be asked of a child. "Ah, yes, responsibilities," Olivia murmured.

"I made a promise to Mama and Daddy—"

Olivia cut in. "I made a promise too. I promised Charlie I'd care for Ethan Allen."

Paul nodded. "Then you can understand why I've gotta do this."

Olivia said nothing for a few moments; she waited to let thoughts settle in and sprout new ideas. Finally she spoke. "I think there's a way we can both fulfill our responsibilities if you're willing to listen."

Paul looked across and gave a slight nod.

"My taking care of Ethan Allen and your taking care of your sister means making sure they're happy, right?"

Paul nodded again.

"Well, as you can see, they're pretty happy being together, so I'm thinking that if you're willing to stay, they could both keep right on being happy. And I'd be happy to have you to help out with some chores Ethan Allen's not capable of doing."

Olivia knew there was nothing Ethan was incapable of doing, but she had to find a way of making Paul feel necessary. The boy had his daddy's pride, and it was something that stood in the way of anything that remotely resembled charity.

Paul furrowed his brow. "I'm not so sure—"

Before he could give voice to an objection, Olivia suggested they give it a try and see how things worked out.

After a fair bit of back and forth, Paul finally agreed. "Just for a while," he said and suggested Olivia might want to remain in her apartment since he was none too sure they'd be there on a permanent basis.

"I'm fine with sleeping on the sofa," he added.

"We're going to be here for a few weeks anyway," Olivia explained, knowing she'd need time to find a place. Then there'd be all that packing and moving. She could already imagine the farewell parties and the unabashed tears that would flow. Not from Jim Turner maybe, but certainly by many of the other residents and Olivia herself.

After breakfast she handed Paul a five-dollar bill and asked if he would take the kids to the park and get lunch at the coffee shop on Williams Street. "I've a lot to do," she said, "and it would be a big help if the kids were out of my hair."

Olivia put on the pretense of this being something the children couldn't do on their own, but in truth they'd been doing almost the exact same thing since the day after Jubilee arrived. When they left she stood at the window and watched. Ethan Allen and Jubilee rode their bikes, and Paul trotted alongside them. Even in the bright sunlight she could see the same aura she'd seen last night, and she was certain she'd made the right decision.

After the dishes had been cleared from the table, washed, and set in the drainer, Olivia made two telephone calls. The first was to Clara and the second to Seth Porter. What she had to say wasn't something you shared with friends over a twist of telephone wire, so she invited them both to come for a cup of coffee.

Right off Clara was suspicious of a special invitation to do something she did every day anyway. "Something's wrong, isn't it?"

"Not really wrong, just different."

"I knew it!" Seconds after she hung up the telephone, Clara was at the door.

Seth Porter followed along a heartbeat later.

Olivia led them to the kitchen and poured three cups of coffee. As they sat at the table, she told them of the decision she'd made.

"It's not that I want to leave here," she said. "It's that I have no other choice. These children have no one else. Caring for them is something I have to do."

She told of her meeting with Anita and how the woman had seen the girl as an unwelcome stranger. Her voice faltered and cracked twice as she spoke about the way Jubilee cried and begged not to be sent to live with Aunt Anita.

"Yes, it will break my heart to leave here," Olivia said, "but it's what I have to do." As Olivia spoke the final words she nervously stirred a third spoonful of sugar into her coffee then looked up. Clara had tears streaming down her face, and Seth Porter had the ghastly pall of a man on the verge of death.

"There's got to be another way," Clara sobbed.

"If there was, I'd jump at it," Olivia replied. "But Jim Turner doesn't even like Ethan Allen being in the building, so there's no way he'd allow me to bring in two more kids."

Seth Porter pulled off his cap and scratched his mostly bald head. After several moments he suggested that perhaps they could change the building bylaws.

Olivia's face brightened for a moment, then fell. "It has to be approved unanimously."

"Oh, right." Seth then suggested that Paul could live with him.

"Jim's not going to want him living with you any more than he wants him living with me," Olivia said. "He just doesn't want any more kids in the building. He's already said it was a mistake to allow Ethan Allen to stay."

They sat there for nearly two hours suggesting first one thing then the other until finally there was nothing more to suggest.

"For the time being," Olivia said, "let's keep this quiet." She explained that she hadn't yet received Anita's approval of her keeping the children and still had to find another place to live.

That afternoon Olivia cleared her things out of the bedroom she'd shared with Charlie and moved them into Ethan Allen's room. The silver tray with a jar of cream and the crystal perfume bottle Charlie had given her was moved to the desk Ethan used for homework. The picture of her and Charlie on their honeymoon moved to Ethan's nightstand. Three times Olivia started to cry, and three times she brushed back the tears and moved on. There would be time enough to cry in the future; right now she had work to do. From beneath Ethan's bed she dug out an assortment of dirty clothes, poker chips, and a baseball mitt. The dirty clothes went into the laundry basket, and the remainder was moved into her room. She cleared her desk and set Ethan's school books atop it.

As she hung Ethan's pants, shirts, and sweaters in her closet, it became painfully apparent that Paul had nothing to call his own. No clothes, no bicycle, no baseball mitt.

They would go shopping. She would start to build a life for this boy as she had built a life for Ethan Allen.

When the kids arrived home, the space that had once been hers had been converted into a room that would be shared by the two boys. For however long they stayed in the apartment, no one would sleep on the sofa.

Unlike Ethan Allen, Paul asked for nothing and ate whatever was set in front of him. As Olivia scooped food onto their dinner plates, she turned to him and said, "String beans?"

"Yes, ma'am," he answered.

It was the same for the potatoes, the sliced pork, and raisin bread. No matter what was offered he accepted it graciously and never asked for seconds.

"I want you to feel at home," Olivia said, "so feel free to say if there's something you don't like."

"Thank you, ma'am," he answered and continued as he had before.

"You really like those string beans?" Ethan Allen asked suspiciously.

Paul nodded a smile.

Ethan, who had fought tooth and nail against any vegetable on his plate, gave a shrug of doubt, then told Olivia he'd be willing to try a few. "Not a whole lot; three, maybe four."

Olivia smiled. Having Paul was going to be a good thing.

After dinner Ethan Allen and Jubilee plopped down in front of the television, and Paul stayed to dry the dishes as Olivia washed. They settled into an easy conversation where he told her about his life in West Virginia. He told how his mama died with the fever and his daddy was killed in the coal mine.

"Daddy made me promise never to be a coal miner," he said, "and that's why me and Jubilee came looking for Aunt Anita."

"Well, I guess that will be an easy enough promise to keep," Olivia said with a laugh, "because there's no coal mine in Wyattsville." After that she asked about Aunt Anita—had he ever met her, had his mother ever spoken of her, did he know what she was like, were there more letters?

All of her questions came back with a simple no. The answers, however ugly they might be, had gone to the grave with Ruth. Two sisters knew the truth of what had happened. One of them was dead and the other unlikely to tell.

Olivia moved on and spoke about going shopping for clothes. "You're going to need everyday clothes, something to wear to church and for school..." By the time the dishes were put away, she'd decided he also needed a bicycle. Tomorrow they would go shopping. Looking for a new apartment would have to wait a few more days.

Once Paul had joined the others watching television, Olivia closed the kitchen door and picked up the telephone. She dialed the number and waited. After five rings, Anita answered.

"Who's this?" she asked, no hello, no greeting.

"Good evening," Olivia said in the nicest imaginable voice. "This is Olivia Doyle. I spoke with you last week about the possibility of having Jubilee live with us."

"Yeah, I remember," Anita answered. "I'm still thinking it over. I ain't made up my mind yet."

"I understand," Olivia said, "but there's something more I thought you should know. Jubilee's brother is now with her, so he'll also need a home."

There was a long silence on the other end of the line.

Olivia waited for an answer, but none came. "Did you hear what I said?"

"Yeah, I heard," Anita finally answered. "Are you saying if I take one of those kids, I've got to take them both?"

"That would seem to be the best answer. After all, separating children who have gone through such trauma in their life would not be advantageous."

"Not advantageous to who?"

"Why, to the children, of course."

"What about me? You saw the size of the apartment I've got."

Olivia knew that Anita was a woman standing on the sharp point of a needle—one wrong word and she could topple over, and if that happened there was no telling what she would do.

"Yes, I have seen your apartment," she answered. "I can certainly see what you mean."

"I'm not saying I don't want the kids," Anita clarified. "What I'm saying is that I need some time to think this thing over."

"Fair enough," Olivia replied. "I can keep the children with me until you've decided." She started to say that it was far better than shipping them off to some foster home but cut the words short before they escaped into the air. A statement such as that might awaken the familial ties in Anita's heart and cause her to feel compelled to protect her sister's children.

Olivia breathed a sigh of relief and hung up the telephone.

Unfortunately she still didn't know whether she'd be moving.

Clara

Every once in a while you hear a person say how it's better to give than receive, and I can tell you it's the honest-to-God truth. When Olivia Doyle came here, she was a shattered woman. Someone who'd wasted away to nothing more than a stretch of skin filled with the bones of what used to be. If ever a person needed a friend, it was Olivia.

I gave her that friendship. She didn't take it willingly, but I forced it on her. When she said she was too busy to come to a party, I refused to take no for an answer. When she claimed she was too sorrowful to come to a club meeting, I said Poppycock *and dragged her out the door. Taking care of Olivia gave me way more joy than she could ever know. It made me feel almost as happy as I was when my sweet Henry was still alive.*

Giving Olivia my friendship didn't cost me anything, but she's willing to give up a life she loves to take care of those kids. I'm thinking I can't let her do it.

There's always another way to skin a cat, but the problem is Olivia's not a woman to ask for help. Whatever needs to be done to keep her from making this mistake is gonna have to move ahead without her.

I'm gonna talk to Seth Porter. Ten to one he's got some thoughts on how to get the building bylaws changed.

No kids, no dogs—that's not living; that's just a bunch of old folks waiting to die. It's time we put some life back into this old building.

No Children Allowed

On Monday Olivia began to scan the *Wyattsville Daily* looking for an apartment. There were four listings close by, but all four specified, "No kids, no pets." Those words were in bold face type. She moved on to the listing for houses. There was a three-bedroom ranch and two four-bedroom colonials, all of which were beyond her price range.

"Oh, dear," Olivia said and ran her finger down the column of listings again. This time she spotted a tiny ad, just two lines, no bold face type. "For rent" it read. "4 bedrooms, 1 bath, large yard, doghouse."

She dialed the number listed and waited. After five rings a young man answered.

"This is Olivia Doyle," she said and I'm calling about the apartment. Would you be willing to rent to someone with a dog and—"

"The landlord's not here right now," he interrupted. "Call back later."

Olivia hung up the receiver wishing she had given her telephone number and left off the part about a dog. Renting to someone with children might not be the owner's first choice, but since the ad didn't specify no children there was a possibility. Instead of redialing the number in the ad, Olivia called Seth Porter.

"Can you come down for a minute?" she asked. "I need you to make a phone call."

When Seth arrived, she explained the situation and asked him to call and leave her telephone number for a call back.

"You'll have to leave a message but don't say your name and don't mention kids or a dog," she instructed.

Looking a bit puzzled, Seth asked, "So what am I supposed to say?"

"Say you're interested in the apartment and give my telephone number."

Olivia dialed the number and handed the receiver to Seth. Again, the young man answered after the fifth ring. Seth said, "I'm interested in the apartment; have the landlord call me back." He rattled off Olivia's telephone number.

Seth hung up and looked at Olivia with that same puzzled expression. "I don't get it. If they don't want kids, what difference is my calling gonna make?"

"I'll go see the place, then worry about whether or not they'll take kids." She left it at that, figuring once the owners met her three lovely children they could hardly say no. She'd already decided when they went to look at the house she'd bring the children but not Dog. Definitely not Dog.

After Seth was gone, Olivia sat down to wait for the phone call. For three hours she sat in the chair next to the phone, watching the clock tick minutes off slowly. Very slowly. In time she grew restless and began to pace across the living room, far enough to stretch her legs, but always within hearing range of the telephone. When the afternoon passed with no call, she reasoned the owner most likely worked and would call in the evening. But at twenty minutes past eleven she crawled into bed, and there had been no telephone call.

Sleeping in Ethan's room did not come easy to Olivia. The narrow bed felt lonely, like part of who she was had suddenly gone missing. *It's only for a while,* she told herself, but still she remained wide-eyed and sleepless for most of the night.

It was close to two o'clock when she snapped on the light and picked up the bedside picture of Charlie smiling down at her. "I wish you were here," she said. "You'd know what to do." She continued the conversation for almost an hour, telling Charlie of the things that troubled her and somehow knowing he listened to every word. By the time she set the picture back on the nightstand and snapped off the light, a strange new peace had settled inside her heart.

Olivia was still asleep when the telephone rang at seven-thirty. Ethan Allen answered it.

"You called about the apartment?" a woman said.

"I didn't call about no apartment," Ethan answered.

"Somebody did. This is the call back number they left."

"It must've been Grandma." Ethan clunked the receiver on the counter and yelled, "Grandma, you got a phone call!"

Olivia's eyes popped open. But by the time she'd pulled on her bathrobe and gotten to the telephone, the caller had hung up. Minutes later the phone rang a second time. Olivia grabbed the receiver. "Good morning," she said with the sweetness of sugar coating the words.

Avoiding any mention of children and a dog, Olivia made an appointment to see the apartment on Wednesday afternoon. Her plan was to take three well-groomed and well-mannered children with her and hope for the best. But first she had to get Paul some clothes. Well-groomed meant he had to wear something other than the plaid shirt and overalls he now had.

Olivia spent most of the day shopping for Paul's clothes. She started in the young men's Department of Kline's and had him try on shirts, pants, and sweaters, none of which fit properly. The boy was built like a sapling—tall but not yet filled out. Pants that fit at the waist were inches too short, and the long-enough ones bagged at the waist. Without purchasing a single item, they moved on to Wellerman's Menswear but fared no better. After they'd visited five different stores, Olivia spied a young man built much like Paul. She tapped him on the shoulder and asked where he bought his clothes.

"They're mostly custom made," he answered, "but I got these pants at Smart Shoppe."

Smart Shoppe was at the far end of town and considered quite pricey, but that was their next stop. They left there with two pair of trousers, a pair of blue jeans, and five cotton shirts. After lunch at Woolworth's and a stop at the shoe store, they started home late in the afternoon. By then Olivia had decided the bicycle would have to wait for another day and another pension check.

On Wednesday morning Olivia roused all three children early. She fed them breakfast, then sent them off to get dressed.

"We're going to look at a new apartment," she said, "and you all need to look your very best."

The address was on the far side of town—seventeen miles from the Wyattsville Arms. The trip dragged, and with every mile Olivia's heart grew heavier. Three times she started to turn around and go home, but when such urges came upon her she forced herself to remember that this was something she had to do.

Olivia had expected it might be an apartment building or a garden apartment complex with shaded walkways running between buildings. Instead it was a two-story house. A house with an almost brown lawn and a look of sadness hanging over it.

"This don't look so good," Ethan Allen said.

"It's probably a lot nicer on the inside," Olivia replied. "And, besides, it has a backyard and a doghouse."

"Dog ain't gonna be happy sleeping in no doghouse," Ethan grumbled.

Olivia eyed the house again. "You three wait here. I'll go check it out, and if it's a place we'd be interested in I'll come back and get you." She stepped out of the car and started up the walkway.

The kids watched as she pushed the doorbell, then disappeared inside the house. Olivia was gone for nearly fifteen minutes, and returned to the car with her mouth in a pout. "Not the sort of place we want to live," she grunted. With no further explanation, she pulled out and headed for home.

They had just stepped off the elevator when Olivia heard the telephone ringing. She hurriedly pulled the key from her purse, unlocked the door, dashed across the living room, and grabbed the phone.

"Good afternoon," the woman said. "Is this Missus Doyle?"

Olivia thought it might be Anita but didn't recognize the caller's voice. "Yes, it is," she replied cautiously.

"This is Carmella Klaussner."

"Carmella?"

"Yes. We met at the hospital. You remember, my husband Sidney's the one who was shot in the same holdup as your boy."

"Of course I remember," Olivia answered, "but the Bicycle Ball isn't until October. We don't have tickets yet—"

Carmella laughed. "I'm not calling about the Bicycle Ball. I'm calling to tell you the good news; Sidney was released from the hospital yesterday."

"That certainly is good news," Olivia replied, wondering why Carmella chose to call her about it.

"Sidney is anxious to reopen the store," Carmella said, "but before he does so we'd like to have a chance to talk to you and your boy."

"Oh, I don't know." Olivia gave a weary sigh. "Paul will be returning to school in September, and I don't think he should be taking on a full-time job."

Carmella gave a big hearty laugh. "All the more reason we need to talk. Sidney has something special for the boy."

"Something special?"

"Yes, but I'm not going to spoil the surprise. I know Sidney wants to be the one to tell Paul about it. "

Carmella's voice had the sound of happiness jangling through the words, so Olivia had to assume it was something good. She asked if Carmella and Sidney would like to come to dinner the next evening.

"That sounds wonderful," Carmella said and hung up without giving the slightest hint about Sidney's surprise.

The day had brought both good and bad, but in the end there had been no resolution to anything. Olivia served an early dinner, then just after seven o'clock settled down to call Clara. She had a million mixed thoughts troubling her and needed to talk.

Olivia dialed the number and waited. She listened to a dozen or more rings, then finally hung up. Odd that Clara had not stopped by; odder still that she was not at home at an hour when she'd generally be watching the news. Olivia waited a half-hour and called again; still no answer. She tried another five times and got nothing more than a ring in her ear. At nine o'clock she decided that if she didn't reach Clara by nine-thirty, she would go in search of her. Olivia could already feel an ache in her bones, an ache that meant something was not as it should be.

At nine-twenty Olivia shrugged on her sweater and was ready to walk out the door when Clara knocked.

"Where on earth have you been?" Every word had worry attached to it.

Clara, winded as if she'd run a marathon, answered, "I had a bunch of errands to do."

"Errands? In the middle of the night?"

"It's not even nine-thirty."

Olivia looked at her watch: nine-twenty-five. "It seems much later." Shepherding Clara into the kitchen, she brewed a pot of chamomile tea. "It'll calm our nerves."

"I'm not nervous," Clara replied. "Just tired."

"From what?" Olivia asked. Again she got that vague say-nothing answer, so she moved on to tell of her day. "We went to look at an apartment but it was way on the other side of town, and—"

Clara's mouth dropped open. "You didn't take it, did you?"

"I didn't have the chance. The ad said doghouse and yard, but to be on the safe side I asked if having a dog was okay. 'Sure,' this guy says, 'I got no problem with dogs.' So then I ask about the schools. All of a sudden he starts looking at me like I've got two heads. 'Schools?' he says, 'why you wanna know about schools?' I thought it was pretty obvious, but I answer and tell him, 'I've got three children.'"

"And?"

"He starts yelling about how he can't stand kids. 'Dogs is okay,' he says, 'but no kids!'"

"Good," Clara said. "I'm glad you didn't take the place. It's too far away, and, besides, you're rushing things. You don't even know if Anita is going to let you keep those kids."

"I think it's pretty safe to say she doesn't want them."

"Wait until you know for sure."

The conversation went back and forth with Olivia insisting that it was better to be prepared for the inevitable and Clara insisting that the inevitable wasn't always inevitable. When that subject was worn threadbare, they moved to a discussion of Carmella's phone call.

"I've invited them to dinner tomorrow," Olivia said. "From the way Carmella was talking, I think Mister Klaussner has some sort of reward for Paul."

"So you're going to be busy tomorrow evening, right?"

When Olivia answered yes, Clara sat there with a strange curl pulling at the corners of her lips.

Dinner Guests

In the wee hours of the morning, when a chorus of snores was all a person could hear in the hallways of Wyattsville Arms, Olivia found sleep impossible to come by. When she tried to conjure up the image of something pleasant—taking the children to the zoo, a day at the beach, a picnic in the park—it quickly became a flashback to the dreary house she'd visited. If a place such as that didn't allow children, what, she wondered, could she expect?

By morning Olivia had come to the conclusion that this dinner party might be the last one she'd have in this apartment, so she vowed to make it special. Once the children had gone off to play, she polished the silver, shined her very best crystal glasses, and took out the package of Irish linen napkins she'd been saving for a special occasion.

When the doorbell rang at six o'clock, all three children were dressed as if they were going to church and Olivia was wearing a green dress the exact shade of her eyes. Before the door was fully open, Carmella held out a huge bouquet of peonies. "For you."

"Oh, my goodness," Olivia gushed, "I've never seen anything so beautiful."

With a smile stretched clear across his face, Sidney stood there balancing a stack of giftwrapped boxes. "We've also got a few things for the kids."

"A few things?" Olivia exclaimed. "Why, it looks like Christmas!"

Sidney gave big, hearty chuckle, the kind of laugh that could make a person feel happy even if they had no idea what he was laughing about.

Once they were seated in the living room, Olivia went in search of a vase large enough for the flowers. She pulled three vases from the kitchen cupboard, but not one was large enough. Surely one of her friends had a good-sized vase. Dialing one number after the other, Olivia first called Clara, then Agnes Shapiro, and finally Jen Hemmings. Not one of them was at home, which was not only annoying but also odd. Stuck with no other alternative Olivia put half of the flowers in one vase and the remainder in the other, then carried the two vases into the living room. By then the floor was covered with shredded bits of wrapping paper.

"Grandma, look at this!" Ethan Allen held up a Dick Tracy Junior Detective Kit. "It's got a decoder ring!"

"I got a present too." Jubilee cuddled a Betsy-Wetsy doll that drank and wet its diaper, something that apparently pleased her no end.

Paul, far more reserved than the other two, was wearing a baseball cap from the College of William and Mary.

"There's more to come," Sidney said. In a little less than two weeks he'd gone from a nearly-dead man to a man so filled with life it almost burst out of him. In fact, Sidney's happiness was so contagious that before two minutes had passed by Olivia was laughing like a woman with not a care in the world.

In addition to the gifts the children had already opened, there were comic books, paper dolls, and a book on the history of America for Paul.

"All this," Olivia said. "You really shouldn't have. There's no need—"

"Of course there's no need." Sidney chuckled. "But not having to do something is what makes doing it fun."

"You're going to spoil the children." Olivia's mouth curled into a smile that began to resemble Sidney's.

He laughed even harder.

"There's no way we could ever really make amends for all we put your family through," Carmella said softly. "But we were hoping this would be a start."

Olivia assured them no harm was done, and now that Paul was free to go about life they were looking toward the future. She mentioned nothing about the need for a larger apartment. When the oven timer buzzed, she announced dinner was ready and led everyone to the table. Sidney sat next to Paul. Carmella sat alongside Jubilee.

"I'm glad you like those paper dolls," Carmella said. "I had ones just like them when I was a girl, and they were my favorite." Carmella went on to tell how she created a world of flat paper furniture and voices for each of the paper people. Jubilee eyes glistened as she latched on to every word.

"Would you show me how to make flat furniture?"

"I sure will," Carmella answered. Then she hugged the child to her chest. "As long as your grandma doesn't think I'm making a pest out of myself coming here."

"Grandma don't mind at all." Jubilee looked for confirmation from Olivia, but by then Olivia had bustled to the kitchen to get the casserole.

When she sat the oversized dish on the table she announced, "This is my favorite chicken noodle casserole. I hope you like it." That's when she noticed the apprehensive look on Carmella's face.

"Is something wrong?"

"Well," Carmella said, "Sidney doesn't really like chicken."

Sidney cut in with a loud chuckle. "I used to not like chicken," he said and scooped a double-size portion onto his plate. He then turned and scooped a like amount onto Paul's plate. "Eat up, son. You're a growing boy!"

When Olivia looked across at the two of them, she could swear Paul's grin was starting to resemble Sidney's.

Olivia had doubled the recipe so she'd be sure to have enough, but when the conversation slowed and everyone stopped eating not a morsel of chicken noodle casserole was left in the dish. Sidney had not only polished off that first large helping, he'd gone back for seconds. Olivia smiled proudly as she cleared the dishes from the table.

"I'll start coffee and get dessert," she said and disappeared into the kitchen.

With a number of conversations going back and forth and laughter rolling out with the words, Olivia did not hear the knock on the door.

Ethan Allen did.

He scooted from his chair and opened the door. Anita was standing there, looking ragged and red-eyed. "Uh oh," he muttered, then yelled, "Grandma, you better get out here!"

The alarm in Ethan's voice sent Olivia scurrying from the kitchen.

Still wiping her hands on a dish towel, she crossed over to the open door. Upon seeing Anita's face she turned to Ethan. "Where on earth are you manners?" she asked. She then turned back to Anita. "I apologize for my grandson's manners. Please come in."

Anita followed Olivia into the living room. When she glanced across and saw the people crowded around the table, she gave a rather pitiful sigh. "I'm sorry if I've come at a bad time but there's something I've got to get off my chest, and it can't wait any longer."

Olivia grew nervous as to what Anita might have to say. If she was ready to let go of the kids, she'd be smiling. It would be a burden lifted from her shoulders, two less things to tie her down and keep her from the life she was living. Olivia's thoughts flashed back to the memory of Jubilee crying because she didn't want to live with Aunt Anita.

Not ready to hear Anita had decided to reclaim the children, Olivia sputtered something about how decisions should never be made on an empty stomach. "We were just about to have cake and coffee. Please join us."

Anita glanced at the crowd warily. "I don't know. What I've got to say is a rather personal."

Sidney stood and walked over to Anita. "We're almost family," he said and clamped a well-intentioned arm around her shoulder. "So come on over here and get yourself a piece of cake." He looped his arm through Anita's and pulled her to the table.

Although she allowed herself to be moved along, Anita did not look happy. She had the pained expression of a woman with kidney stones.

Anita sat and Olivia introduced her by name, saying only that she was the children's aunt. Olivia said nothing about the fact that she was also their only living relative.

Sidney, having positioned Anita on the other side of himself, turned to her, "Sidney Klaussner, the lucky dog who's still alive because of your nephew." Motioning toward Carmella, he added, "And this here's my wife, Carmella."

"Pleased," Anita said and gave a slight nod.

At that point Olivia stood and said she was going to get the coffee. Halfway to the kitchen she heard Carmella's voice saying how she envied Anita for being able to spend time with such wonderful children.

"Spend what time?" Anita replied. "I haven't spent day one with these kids!"

Olivia turned around and headed back to the table. "Coffee is still brewing," she said and sat back down. In an effort to change the subject, she turned to Anita and said, "I hope you like chocolate cake."

"Chocolate's fine," Anita answered.

"Why would you not spend time with these children?" Carmella asked accusingly. "They're wonderful children, some of the nicest I've ever met!"

"There's good reason for me not seeing the children," Anita said coldly.

"There can be no reason," Carmella argued. "Children grow up so quickly, you've got to grab every precious moment you can with them. Shame on you, ignoring these kids!"

Olivia wanted to reach across and stuff a napkin in Carmella's mouth to shut her up, but doing it would have only increased the tension bouncing back and forth across the table. With her eyes fixed on Carmella, she said, "I have some wonderful oatmeal raisin cookies if you'd prefer not to have chocolate cake."

"Chocolate's fine," Carmella replied, then went back to Anita. "Looks like you'd be thanking the Lord for these three wonderful kids instead of making excuses for—"

"Wait a minute," Anita interrupted. "First off, I ain't even related to that one!" She pointed a finger at Ethan.

He grinned and nodded. "She ain't. I ain't even blood related to Grandma, but she took me in anyway."

A look of confusion spread rapidly across Carmella's face, and a lead weight had suddenly settled in Olivia's stomach.

Carmella looked at Olivia. "But aren't you grandmother to all three?"

"Not exactly," Olivia said. She explained that Ethan Allen was related to her late husband, and she was simply caring for the other two children because they didn't have anyone else.

"But they do have someone else!" Carmella argued. "They have an aunt who is right here at this table. You yourself said she was their aunt!"

"So I did," Olivia said. "So I did."

The Meeting

Jim Turner banged his gavel against the podium for the third time, and he did it with such ferocity that the chattering crowd stilled. It was the largest turnout the building association had ever seen. Every resident was in attendance, with the lone exception of Olivia Doyle. Olivia was missing because no one had told her of the meeting; in fact, they went out of their way to keep her from knowing of it.

The crowd began filtering in at five-thirty, and by six o'clock the room was filled with residents standing shoulder to shoulder and pressed against the back wall.

Jim Turner had already sensed a wave of rebellion wafting through the room, and he was determined to squash it right from the start. "This meeting will come to order!" he shouted. "Or there will be no meeting!"

"That's what you think!" a voice in the rear of the room yelled back.

"Quiet!" Turner angrily slammed his gavel down again. "The bylaws of this building specifically state that all association meetings will be chaired by the president and conducted in an orderly fashion!"

"We're sick of your bylaws!" Cathy Contino shouted.

"Quiet!"

"We've been quiet long enough!" Seth Porter yelled. "It's high time we said something!"

"Yeah," a chorus of voices echoed. "We been quiet long enough!"

Anticipating just such a reaction, Clara smiled. She'd carried a wooden milk crate to the meeting and while an angry undertone still circled the room, she stepped onto the crate and gave a loud two-finger whistle.

The murmuring stopped and everyone turned to look at Clara who now stood a head taller than anyone else in the room. Trying to give her message an air of propriety she said, "I would like to make a motion that we impeach Jim Turner."

Before she could say anything else, Fred Wiskowski yelled, "I say we just kick his ass out of office!"

Cindy Hamilton leaned over and whispered in Fred's ear, "That's what impeach means."

"Well, then, they ought to come right out and say it."

Clara gave another whistle. "Having bylaws means we're regulated. It means we've got no choice in what we do! Is that what we want?"

A chorus of voices yelled, "Hell, no!"

"You're out of order!" Turner yelled and banged the gavel so hard the head flew off and went rolling across the floor.

Everybody applauded the broken gavel.

After three bounces, the gavel rolled to a stop in front of Linda Foust. She picked it up and dropped it into the waste basket.

There was another round of applause.

Without the gavel Jim Turner was helpless. Several times he tried yelling "Quiet!" but when his throat began to close up, there was little more he could do. He finally said, "I relinquish the floor to Clara Bowman," and sat down.

It was a good ten minutes before the wolf whistles and cheering subsided and the room grew silent enough for Clara to speak.

"We've become a bunch of old fuddy duddies," she said. "We've closed our minds to new ideas and look down our noses at anyone who dares to bring a bit of fun and laughter to this building. I say it's time to change that!"

Several "Woohoo's" came from the back of the room, followed by another round of applause.

Clara continued. "It was against the bylaws when Ethan Allen came to live here, but we all agreed he was a welcome addition."

Turner gave a sideways glance of disagreement.

"Okay," Clara amended, "we almost all agreed." She looked at Beth Lillis. "Beth, when your arthritis was acting up, who did your errands?"

"Ethan Allen." Beth smiled.

"Tom," Clara said, pointing her finger, "who carted all that stuff to the storage bin when you had your apartment painted?"

He nodded. "Ethan Allen."

Clara then called on Frank Casper, Wayne Dolby, Barbara Harris, and Jeanine Elizalde. Every one of them had the same kind of story. Ethan Allen had helped out, he'd run errands, fetched medications, carried laundry up from the basement.

"Has the child ever done one thing that makes this building a less lovely place to live?"

A murmur of no's floated through the room.

"Well," Eloise Fromm said, "he does from time to time push all the buttons in the elevator and keep riding up and down."

When a crowd of angry faces glared at her, Eloise added, "But that's certainly not much to complain about."

"Let's face it," Clara said, "these bylaws are outdated, obsolete, of no use whatsoever."

Several heads nodded as she spoke.

"All they do is tell us what we can't do. Those bylaws say we can't bring grocery carts through the front lobby, we can't paint our door a different color, we can't do this, and we can't do that. The bylaws even tell us we can't park anywhere but in our assigned spots—"

"Yeah," Agnes Shapiro shouted, "and Jim Turner took the best spot himself!"

Turner stood up. "I have that parking spot because I'm the president of the association!"

"Well, we can change that!" Seth Porter yelled. He then insisted they have an immediate vote to impeach Jim Turner.

Clara, who by now had pretty much taken over the meeting, said, "All in favor of removing Jim Turner as the association president, raise your hand."

There were two or three on the far side of the room who stood without moving, but most everyone else raised their hand. A few people raised two hands. When Clara did a count, the number of hands exceeded the number of residents, so she gave another whistle and declared the motion had passed unanimously.

"Wait a minute," Turner said. "That wasn't unanimous."

"Shut up and sit down!" Fred Wiskowski yelled. "You been kicked out!"

"I say we make Clara president," Barb Harris suggested.

Several cheers echoed throughout the room.

Turner stood up again. "This is not proper procedure!" Before he could finish explaining how people had to be nominated first, a chorus of boos forced him to sit back down.

"Anybody got any other suggestions?"

"Maybe Seth Porter?" a voice said.

Clara looked over. "What about it Seth? You wanna be president?"

Seth shook his head. "Nope. Too busy."

"Anybody else?" Clara asked.

When there were no further suggestions, a show of hands went up and Clara declared herself president. "My first act as president is to abolish the bylaws."

There was a round of applause along with a number of folks making comments like "Good!" and "About time!"

When Clara asked if there were any objections to doing away with the bylaws altogether, three hands went up: Jim Turner, Eloise Fromm, and a man from the ninth floor who nobody knew by name. Clara shot an angry glare at Eloise.

"What is your problem?" she asked. Eloise's hand went down as did the hand of the man from the ninth floor. Only Jim Turner's hand was still raised.

"We cannot have a building without bylaws," he said emphatically. "It's against the law."

"There's no such law!" Jack Schumann yelled.

"Jack ought to know." Clara nodded. "He used to be a lawyer!"

Turner's hand remained up. Fred Wiskowski, an ex-wrestler and a man with shoulders as wide as a doorway, inched his way through the crowd. When he got to where Turner was standing, Fred leaned in and whispered something in Turner's ear. There was a moment of hesitation; then Turner lowered his hand and sat down. That was the last objection he made for the remainder of the evening.

By ten o'clock the meeting was over, and most everyone went home happy.

A number of things had been decided. There was no longer a set of bylaws that residents had to adhere to. The building would be open to all residents, including children, young adults, dogs, cats, and any domesticated animal other than pigs. Everyone agreed pet pigs were not a good idea. They also decided that residents would no longer have to put in quarters to use the community laundry machines, nor would they be required in park in assigned spots.

Clara Bowman, they declared, was by far the best president they'd ever had.

Finding Family

Once Carmella got started on why Anita had not taken responsibility for the children, she refused to let go. "Here you are, turning your back on these sweet things, when you ought to be gathering them to your bosom!"

Anita's bottom lip began quivering.

Olivia nervously twisted her beautiful linen napkin into a knot and then plopped it on top of the butter dish. "Perhaps we should change the subject," she said.

Paying no attention whatsoever to the comment, Carmella continued. "Why, if these kids were related to me, I'd be praising God with every breath I draw!"

"It isn't that I don't care about the kids," Anita said. "I do, but there's extenuating circumstances." Her eyes narrowed, and her voice sounded brittle as a dried twig.

Sidney turned to Anita. "I apologize for Carmella's actions. She gets very emotional when it comes to children."

"And rightfully so!" Carmella answered. "All my life I've prayed for a child. A boy, a girl, that didn't matter. All I wanted was a child to care for, a child to love!" She turned back to Anita. "Now here you have two wonderful children and care nothing for them."

Anita stood up so quickly that her chair toppled backward. "I don't have to listen to you tell me what I care about! It so happens I do love these kids, love them the same way I loved my sister!"

Sidney rose from his chair and wrapped his arm around Anita's shoulders. "Now, now," he said and squeezed her arm. "We're all friends, family almost, so let's put an end to this conversation and have some of that delicious chocolate cake Olivia's been talking about."

"Yes," Olivia agreed fervently, "that's a good idea." Before she could rise from her seat, Anita grabbed hold of the conversation.

"I haven't seen these kids because that's the way Ruth wanted it!"

Jubilee's mouth dropped open, and Paul's eyes shifted from Anita to Carmella then back again to Anita. Neither of the children spoke. Even Ethan Allen had nothing to say, which was somewhat unusual.

"Your sister didn't want you to see the children?" Carmella asked, her voice now softer, the words without undertones of accusation or anger.

Anita nodded, her eyes filled with tears. When she spoke it was in a small, fragile voice.

"It wasn't Ruth's fault," she said. "She was doing what she thought best for the children."

"Why?" Carmella asked. "Why would your sister do such a cruel thing?"

"Because she knew what it was like to live with me." Anita heaved a great sigh, one that came from the depth of her soul, one that carried years of sadness and regret.

No one else spoke. For a long moment there was only silence, a silence that was deafening and painful as it shadowed the table.

Anita twisted her hands together and looked down at them. Without raising her eyes she began to speak again. "Ruth was only nine when it started. I was twelve. At first it seemed like just the ordinary ups and downs of life; then it got worse. I'd have days when the world seemed black as a tar pit, and other days when for no reason at all I'd be crazy happy."

Everyone's eyes focused on Anita. Sidney reached across and covered her hands with his. That's when she lifted her eyes and looked at Carmella.

"I was seventeen when they finally diagnosed me with a schizophrenic disorder."

Carmella gave an audible gasp. "You poor thing. Isn't there some medication, something that—"

"Yes." Anita nodded. "And I take it most of the time. But it makes me feel like I'm wearing heavy boots. The off-and-on times of happiness I had are gone."

Paul was the one to speak. "Is that why Mama never brought us to see you?"

"Actually," Anita said, "she did bring you to Norfolk for a visit. You were just a tiny baby, and Ruth was so proud of you. I was having one of my good times, so I grabbed you up and started dancing across the room. At first it was harmless enough, but then it got crazy, frenzied almost. I threw my hands up into the air and let go of you. Ruth screamed like someone had stuck a knife in her heart. She scooped you off the floor, and when you finally stopped crying she said coming to see me had been a mistake. That same afternoon she took the train back home to West Virginia."

"But wasn't it just an accident?"

Anita shook her head. "No, that's the way I get. Sometimes I'll be mean enough to kill a person, and five minutes later I'll be crazy happy. Ruth knew what it was like to live with me. That's why she never wanted you kids to suffer what she'd gone through."

Jubilee climbed out of her chair and ran to Olivia. "I don't want to live with Aunt Anita," she sobbed.

"You won't have to," Anita eyes looked like a river of sadness as the tears streamed down her cheeks. "That's what I came here to tell Miss Olivia."

Up until now Olivia had thought it would be just the opposite and she smiled. "I'd be more than happy to take care of the children for you."

"In this little bitty apartment?" Carmella gasped.

"For a while," Olivia answered. "I've started looking for another place. Unfortunately, this building just isn't—"

Before she could finish, Sidney asked, "What's wrong with this building?"

"Nothing is wrong with it," Olivia replied. "It's a wonderful place to live." A thread of nostalgia and sadness crept into her words.

"But this apartment isn't large enough for three children," Carmella added.

"No, it isn't," Olivia said. "That's why I'm looking for a larger place, an apartment with three, maybe four..." she sniffed back the sadness creeping into her words, "bedrooms."

"An apartment?" Carmella said. "Why, an apartment is no place for children. They need to be in a house, with their own bedrooms, friends, a yard to play in..."

Feeling the need to defend Olivia's position, Ethan Allen said, "It so happens I like it here. Me and Grandma's real happy."

"Maybe so, but children need friends—"

"I got plenty of friends. I got friends what chipped in to buy me a brand new bicycle!"

"But your grandmother—"

"Grandma got plenty of friends too. She got so many friends they said I was allowed, even if no dogs and kids ain't supposed to be here!"

Carmella, now engaging in a conversation with Ethan Allen, smiled. "Well, then why do you and your grandma want to move away?"

"We don't! Grandma's willing to do it 'cause she cares about kids."

Carmella nodded. "I can see that." She turned and looked Olivia square in the face. "What if there was another way?"

"Another way?"

"Yes." Carmella reached across and took Olivia's hand in hers. "You have a life here, but the apartment is too small for three children. Sidney and I have a big house with rooms closed off because there's no one to occupy them. It's a house that needs to have children running through the halls, laughing and playing."

"Wait a minute," Anita said. "I'm not giving Ruth's children to some stranger! I was okay with letting them stay here with Olivia because she's shown she cares about them, but you?" Anita shook her head doubtfully.

Carmella looked at Anita. "I'm not asking you to give us the children. They're your niece and nephew, and that will never change. I'm just asking if maybe you'd consider letting them live with us for a while." She went on to explain how Paul had saved Sidney's life and how that was a debt she could never repay.

Sidney, who'd been rather quiet during the exchange, spoke up. "Carmella's right. Our house is sadly lacking in the sound of children, and the worst of it is that Carmella's got a heart full of love to give." He paused for a moment, then reached inside his jacket, pulled out an envelope, and handed it to Paul. Paul pulled the letter from the envelope and unfolded it. The letterhead bore the same crest as the baseball cap he'd been given. He looked at the letter and silently let the words settle in his head. After a long while he looked up with tears in his eyes. "Is this for real?"

Sidney nodded. "Yes. When you are ready for college, the College of William and Mary has a fully-paid scholarship waiting for you."

A smile bigger than any Jubilee had ever seen spread across Paul's face, but then it grew sheepish. "I haven't yet graduated high school."

"That's okay," Sidney said. "We'll see that you do." He pushed back his chair far enough that he could address both Olivia and Anita at the same time. "I know it's asking a lot, but having the kids live with us would mean the world to me and Carmella."

A swirl of emotions raced through Olivia's heart, some pushing her toward such a solution and some pulling her back. She looked across and gave Anita a helpless shrug.

Before anyone had the chance to make a decision Carmella said, "The doors to our house would be flung open! You'd be welcome to come anytime. You could come to visit the children and stay for a day or a week or a month! Every Sunday we could have dinner together, all of us!" She lifted her arms and opened them in a sweeping motion that encompassed all those at the table. "We'd be a family!"

Judging by the open smile on her face, it would be almost impossible for anyone to believe she had anything but the purest of motives.

It was Olivia who finally spoke, and when she did it was with weighted words addressed to Anita.

"I know we both love the children, but I think Carmella and Sidney also have the capacity to do so. If it's okay with you, I think we should let Paul and Jubilee decide what would be best for them."

Anita gave a solemn nod.

Olivia turned to Paul. "You've taken care of your sister for a number of years and shouldered more responsibility than any lad your age should have to. But we're going to ask you to make one more decision, and whatever you decide is what we'll do."

Jubilee let go of Olivia's arm and ran around the table to where Paul was sitting. She leaned in and whispered in his ear. After almost two minutes of listening to what she was planting in his head, Paul laughed and pulled her into an affectionate hug.

He whispered something back, and she gave an eager nod.

"Well," he said, "I guess we've made a decision."

And It Came To Pass...

At eleven o'clock that evening, there was a soft knock at Olivia's door. The children were already in bed, and she was in the bathroom brushing her teeth. At first it seemed something she'd simply imagined hearing, but then it came again. When it happened the third time, Olivia rinsed her mouth and hurried to the door. Knowing that only people with a great sense of urgency came to the door at this time of night, her heart was racing when she loosened the latch and pulled open the door.

Clara stood there with a grin so wide that it took Olivia a moment to recognize her.

"It's after eleven!" Olivia gasped. "Is there some kind of emergency?"

"Not really," Clara answered, "but I've got news so good it couldn't wait until morning."

"Oh?" Olivia pulled back the door and Clara trotted in.

She bypassed the living room and headed for the kitchen. "Got any coffee?"

"Coffee? It's eleven o'clock at night!"

"Don't I know it," Clara answered. Then she went on to say she was far too wound up to go to sleep, so there was no harm in enjoying a good cup of coffee.

As Olivia set the pot to brew, she asked what could be so important that it drove Clara to come calling at this unearthly hour.

"It's about the building rules committee—"

"Well, they needn't have bothered," Olivia huffed. "Paul and Jubilee won't be staying with me anyway."

"That's just it." Clara's face was bright as a neon streetlight. "They don't have to go. They can stay as long as they want. They can live here!"

Olivia turned with a look of surprise. "How…what?"

"We had an association meeting tonight," Clara said. "I wish you could have been there."

She continued, telling Olivia how Jim Turner had been ousted as president and she had taken his place. As the words tumbled out, she went on to say that there were no longer rules as to who could or could not live there.

"Even pets are okay," Clara added, "but not pigs."

Olivia sat and listened to the words coming from Clara's mouth but could scarcely believe her ears. "Are you saying it's okay for kids to live here in the building?"

"Yes." Clara nodded. "Jackie Lane said she's going out tomorrow to buy a dog, maybe even two. It seems she's been wanting a dog for some time. Already has the name picked out."

Olivia gave a soft chuckle. "I'm glad to hear all this, but Paul and Jubilee are leaving on Saturday."

"Oh, no!"

"It's nothing to be sad about. It was actually the best possible solution." She told Clara about the dinner, Anita's arrival, and Paul's ultimate decision.

"I suppose that is the best solution," Clara said, "but I'll miss having Jubilee around."

"So will I," Olivia replied, but there was no trace of sadness on her face.

On Saturday morning Paul and Jubilee dressed in their finest clothes, and although Ethan Allen insisted there was no need for him to be gussied up he was wearing his Sunday best pants and shirt when they left the apartment. Olivia set the two shopping bags of clothes they'd accumulated during the past weeks in the trunk of the car along with the weathered tote Paul had carried off the mountain.

Olivia slid behind the wheel; then she looked in the rearview mirror.

"Everybody ready?"

Paul and Jubilee both nodded. Ethan Allen grumbled, "I suppose."

She pulled out of the lot and headed for the highway. Remembering the road to Anita's was easy enough. She'd observed every landmark on the day she came with Detective Mahoney. Olivia made a mental note to send Jack Mahoney a thank you note. Without him she would never have found Anita, and Paul could well be sitting behind bars instead of stepping into a new life.

When Olivia arrived at the building, Anita was standing on the front stoop. She hurried down the stairs and climbed into the front seat of the car.

"This is an exciting day, isn't it?" Olivia said.

Anita smiled and nodded.

When they finally arrived at the Klaussners' house, a bouquet of balloons was tied to the railing of the front porch. The house was everything Carmella had said. It had a look of happiness that stood two stories tall, three in the area where peaks rose above the tree tops.

"Where's my room?" Jubilee asked excitedly.

"Just be patient," Paul said. "It's not polite to go asking for stuff the minute you walk through the door."

"I have a feeling Carmella won't mind her asking for anything," Olivia said, laughing.

Anita gave a wink and a nod of agreement.

When Carmella heard the car door slam, she came running from the house with an oversized apron flapping in the breeze. "Oh!" she squealed. "I'm so glad to see you." She gave Paul a warm hug, then swallowed Jubilee into the folds of her arms.

Sidney was right behind her and grinning like a man filled with the joy of life. He took Paul by the arm. "Come on in." Side by side he walked with the boy, leaning close as he spoke. "I was wondering if maybe you'd be interested in learning the business. I'm still holding that job open for you."

"I'd be more'n happy to do the work," Paul answered, "but with all you've done for us, Mister Klaussner, I can't take no thirty dollars a week."

Sidney gave a big roaring laugh. "You're not taking anything from me. You're taking it from the business. And since you'll one day most likely own the place, it's like taking the money from your right pocket and putting it in your left."

He gave another chuckle and slapped Paul on the back so gregariously you'd think they'd been friends forever. "Now about this calling me Mister Klaussner..." Sidney suggested Paul call him Uncle Sid and Carmella, Aunt Carmi. "How's that sound?"

"It sounds real good," Paul answered.

Before they sat down to dinner, Carmella took Anita, Olivia, Paul, and Jubilee on a tour of the house. Ethan Allen stayed behind because he was once again questioning Sidney on the facts of the robbery. As they started up the stairs toward the bedrooms, Olivia heard Sidney laugh again.

"I swear, keep this up, Ethan Allen, and someday you're gonna make a darn fine lawyer."

Years later Olivia would remember those words and smile. She'd wonder if Sidney Klaussner was the person who set Ethan Allen down on the pathway that would change countless lives.

Of course all of that is in the distant future. Today there is only laughter, happiness, and a table laden with more food than Jubilee Jones had ever seen before.

Acknowledgments

For I know the plans I have for you declares The Lord...
Plans to prosper you and not to harm you,
plans to give you hope and a future...
Jeremiah 29-11

Writing a novel is never easy; writing a novel that explores the truth of people offers an even greater challenge and I could not have done it alone. Every day I thank Our Heavenly Father for blessing me with the talent to do this and for providing the daily inspiration that motivates me to write stories about the good and bad of life. I hope you'll forgive me when my characters use profanity; it's part of who they are. Without exposure to the darker aspects of humankind, there is no barometer by which to measure the goodness, generosity and love we have all been gifted with.

I want to thank the people who have contributed to this book. I am extremely grateful to Naomi Blackburn for her guidance on storyline and manuscript evaluation. She is an amazing talent with a sharp eye for quickly identifying the flaws in a character or storyline. I also want to thank my Editor Ekta Garg, a genius in her own right. Ekta rights my wrongs without ever losing sight of the character's Southern voice. A special thank you goes to Coral Russell for the million and one things she does to keep the promotion schedule running smoothly. Coral is not only my Literary Assistant, she is my right arm and I would be lost without her.

A very special thank you goes to all the Gals at my BFF Clubhouse, a fan club that is more about friendship than you might think possible. I have been extremely blessed in knowing each of these gals. They are avid readers, astute listeners, caring friends and an unending source of inspiration. The ladies in this group are so supportive and special that I find myself sprinkling their names throughout many of my books.
Lastly, I thank Dick, who absolutely hates when I refer to him as Richard. He is my husband, my life partner, my business partner and my reason for living. He listens when I need someone to listen, and offers sage advice when I tend toward irrational. I am truly blessed in working with, living with and loving such a husband.

From the Author

If you enjoyed reading this book, please post a review at your favorite on-line retailer and share your thoughts with other readers.

I'd love to hear from you. If you visit my website and sign up to receive my monthly newsletter, as a special thank you, you'll receive an e-book copy of "Stories" – A behind the scenes look at the inspiration behind each novel.

To sign up for the newsletter, visit:
http://betteleecrosby.com

The Books in the Wyattsville series include:

SPARE CHANGE
Book One in the Wyattsville Series

JUBILEE'S JOURNEY
Book Two in the Wyattsville Series

PASSING THROUGH PERFECT
Book Three in the Wyattsville Series

THE REGRETS OF CYRUS DODD
Book Four in the Wyattsville Series

BEYOND THE CAROUSEL
Book Five in the Wyattsville Series

Also by the Author

THE MEMORY HOUSE SERIES

Memory House

The Loft

What the Heart Remembers

Baby Girl

Silver Threads

THE SERENDIPITY SERIES

The Twelfth Child

Previously Loved Treasures

STAND ALONE STORIES

Cracks in the Sidewalk

What Matters Most

Wishing for Wonderful

Blueberry Hill, A Sister's Story

About the Author

AWARD-WINNING NOVELIST BETTE LEE CROSBY brings the wit and wisdom of her Southern Mama to works of fiction—the result is a delightful blend of humor, mystery and romance.

"Storytelling is in my blood," Crosby laughingly admits, "My mom was not a writer, but she was a captivating storyteller, so I find myself using bits and pieces of her voice in most everything I write."

Crosby's work was first recognized in 2006 when she received The National League of American Pen Women Award for a then unpublished manuscript. Since then, she has gone on to win numerous other awards, including The Reviewer's Choice Award, The Reader's Favorite Gold Medal, FPA President's Book Award Gold Medal and The Royal Palm Literary Award.

To learn more about Bette Lee Crosby, explore her other work, or read a sample from any of her books, visit her blog at:

http://betteleecrosby.com

Book Club Discussion Questions

1. The story starts in a coal mining community. When you think of coal mining what sorts of things do you picture?

2. Do you think Bartholomew gave up too soon looking for work outside of the coal mine? Why or why not?

3. If you were Ruth would you have stuck by Bartholomew or would you have asked family for more help?

4. Paul makes some decisions in the beginning about what to take when they left. What three things would you take if you had to leave your home and could never go back?

5. Do you think Paul made the right decision to leave Jubilee on the park bench? Why or why not?

6. Olivia steps in to take care of a complete stranger. How important do you think Ethan was in convincing Olivia to help Jubilee?

7. Sharing someone's problems takes courage. In Olivia's position would you have stepped in the same way? Why or why not?

8. If you've read Spare Change, how has Ethan Allen changed from then to Jubilee's Journey?

9. If you've read Spare Change, how has Olivia changed from then to Jubilee's Journey?

10. What is your favorite quote or saying from Jubilee's Journey?

11. Do you feel Detective Gomez was justified in judging Paul in the beginning? Why or why not?

12. Do you feel Hurt's path was inevitable? Was there anything that could have happened differently that would have changed the course of his life?

13. Everyone feels protective of Jubilee, why do you think that is? What part of Jubilee's character makes people want to help her?

14. What does Olivia do when she feels stressed? What do you do when you feel stressed and want to relax or calm down?

15. How does Olivia draw Mahoney in to help her find Jubilee's family?

16. Were you surprised by Anita's reaction when she learned about her sister's children? Why or why not?

17. Olivia and Anita both have people that enter and change their lives. How has a new person who has entered your life changed you?

18. Carmella wants to find out who shot her husband. Do you feel her methods were justified? Why or why not? Who finally sets the record straight on what happened to Paul?

19. At the end several people step forward to help Paul and Jubilee. Do you agree with how things turned out? If not, what would you have done differently?